BUNNYDOGS

The worm was Papa-sized. It was five meters long, nearly two meters thick at the shoulders. Its eyes were shuttered against the dust.

And then I saw—

There were bunnydogs riding on top of the beast. The largest was perched on the brain-bump, and steering it with chirps and tugs and slaps. He was a chubby fellow—he looked and acted like a fat little bus driver. There were three other bunnydogs riding farther back on the worm. They looked like tourists. All they needed were cameras. If they hadn't been riding a two-thousand-kilo eating machine, they would have been cute.

The worm flowed to a stop and faced us. It blinked—*sput phwut*—and warbled a soft sound. "Trllp?" then it shuttered its eyes again. It looked like it was dozing.

I looked at Duke. I'd never seen a worm do this before. He looked back at me and shrugged. But he kept his torch at the ready. "Jim . . ." he said. "What are we looking at?"

"I don't know."

Abruptly, the worm woke up. Its eyes popped open and stared directly at Duke. At the same instant, all the bunnydogs on its back yipped and leapt off. Were they commanding it? Or getting out of its way?

The worm said, "Chtorrllpp?"

It looked *questioningly* to Duke. It started to slide forward—

"No!"

The War Against
The Chtorr: Book Two

A DAY FOR
DAMNATION

DAVID GERROLD

BANTAM BOOKS
NEW YORK · TORONTO · LONDON · SYDNEY · AUCKLAND

A DAY FOR DAMNATION

*A Bantam Spectra Book / published by arrangement with
the author*

PRINTING HISTORY

Timescape/Pocket edition published 1985

Revised Bantam edition / March 1989

ISBN 0-553-27765-0

Published simultaneously in the United States and Canada

---

*Bantam Books are published by Bantam Books, a division of Bantam Doubleday Dell
Publishing Group, Inc. Its trademark, consisting of the words "Bantam Books" and
the portrayal of a rooster, is Registered in U.S. Patent and Trademark Office and in
other countries. Marca Registrada. Bantam Books, 666 Fifth Avenue, New York,
New York 10103.*

PRINTED IN THE UNITED STATES OF AMERICA

O   0 9 8 7 6 5 4 3 2

for Anne McCaffrey, Gigi, Todd, and Alec,
with love

THANK YOU:

Dennis Ahrens
Seth Breidbart
Jack Cohen
Richard Curtis
Diane Duane
Richard Fontana
Bill Glass
Harvey and Johanna Glass
David Hartwell
Robert and Ginny Heinlein
Don Hetsko
Karen Malcor
Susie Miller
Jerry Pournelle
Michael St. Laurent
Rich Sternbach
Tom Swale
Linda Wright
Chelsea Quinn Yarbro
Howard Zimmerman

Chtorr (ktôr), *n*. 1. The planet Chtorr, presumed to exist within 30 light-years of Earth. 2. The star system in which the planet occurs; possibly a red giant star, presently unidentified. 3. The ruling species of the planet Chtorr; generic. 4. In formal usage, either one or many members of the ruling species of the planet Chtorr; a Chtorr, the Chtorr. (See **Chtor-ran**) 5. The glottal chirruping cry of a Chtorr.

Chtor-ran (ktôr´in), *adj*. 1. Of or relating to either the planet or the star system, Chtorr. 2. Native to Chtorr. *n*. 1. Any creature native to Chtorr. 2. In common usage, a member of the primary species, the (presumed) intelligent life form of Chtorr. (*pl*.**Chtor-rans**)

—The Random House Dictionary
of the English Language,
Century 21 Edition, unabridged.

Q: What's the Chtorran word for idealist?
A: Lunch.

1

Crazy Time

"Never trust a tall dwarf. He's lying about something."

—SOLOMON SHORT

The chopper looked like a boxcar with wings, only larger. It squatted in the middle of the pasture like a pregnant sow. Its twin rotors stropped the air in great slow whirls. I could see the tall grass flattening even from here.

I turned away from the window and said to Duke, "Where the hell did *that* come from?"

Duke didn't even look up from his terminal. He just grinned and said, "Pakistan." He didn't even stop typing.

"Right," I said. There wasn't any Pakistan any more, hadn't been a Pakistan for over ten years. I turned back to the window. The huge machine was a demonic presence. It glowered with malevolence. And I'd thought the worms were nasty to look at. This machine had jet engines large enough to park a car in. Its stubby wings looked like a wrestler's shoulders.

"You mean it was built for the Pakistan conflict?" I asked.

"Nope. It was built last year," corrected Duke. "But it was *designed* after Pakistan. Wait one minute—" He finished what he was doing at the terminal, hit the last key with a flourish, and looked up at me. "Remember the treaty?"

"Sure. We couldn't build any new weapons."

"Right," he said. He stood up and slid his chair in. He turned around and began picking up pages as they slid quietly, one after the other, out of the printer. He added, "We couldn't even replace old weapons. But the treaty didn't say anything about research or development, did it?"

3

He picked up the last page, evened the stack of papers on a desk top, and joined me at the window. "Yep. That is one beautiful warship," he said.

"Impressive," I admitted.

"Here—initial these," he said, handing me the pages.

I sat down at a desk and began working my way through them. Duke watched over my shoulder, occasionally pointing to a place I missed. I said, "Yeah, but—where did it come from? Somebody still had to build it."

Duke said, "Are your clothes custom made?"

"Sure," I said, still initialing. "Aren't everybody's?"

"Uh-huh. You take it for granted now. A computer looks at you, measures you by sight, and appropriately proportions the patterns. Another computer controls a laser and cuts the cloth, and then a half dozen robots sew the pieces together. If the plant is on the premises, you can have a new suit in three hours maximum."

"So?" I signed the last page and handed the stack back to him.

He put the papers in an envelope, sealed it, signed it, and handed it back to me to sign. "So," he said, "if we can do it with a suit of clothes, why can't we do it with a car or a house . . . or a chopper? That's what we got out of Pakistan. We were forced to redesign our production technology." He nodded toward the window. "The factory that built that Huey was turning out buses before the plagues. And I'll bet you the designs and the implementation plans and the retooling procedures were kept in the same state of readiness as our Nuclear Deterrent Brigade for all those years—just in case they might someday be *needed*."

I signed the envelope and handed it back.

"Lieutenant," Duke said, grinning, "you should sit down and write a thank-you note to our friends in the Fourth World Alliance. Their so-called 'Victory of Righteousness' twelve years ago made it possible for the United States to be the best-prepared nation on this planet for responding to the Chtorran infestation."

"I'm not sure they'd see it that way," I remarked.

"Probably not," he agreed. "There's a tendency toward paranoia in the Fourth World." He tossed the envelope into the safe and shut the door.

"All right," he said, suddenly serious. "The paperwork is done." He glanced at his watch. "We've got ten minutes. Sit down and clear." He pulled two chairs into position, facing each other. I took one and he took the other. He took a moment to rub his face with both hands, then he looked at me as if I were the only person left on the planet. The rest of the world, the rest of the day, all of it ceased to exist. Taking care of the soul, Duke called it. Teams had gone out that hadn't and they hadn't come back.

Duke waited until he saw that I was ready to begin, then he asked simply, "How are you feeling?"

I looked inside. I wasn't certain.

"You don't have to hit the bull's-eye," Duke said. "You can sneak up on it. How are you feeling?" he asked again.

"Edgy," I admitted. "That chopper out there—it's intimidating. I mean, I just don't believe a thing that big can get off the ground."

"Mm-hm," said Duke. "That's very interesting, but tell me about James Edward McCarthy."

"I am," I said, feeling a little annoyed. I knew how to clear. You dump your mind of everything that might get in the way of the mission.

"There—" pointed Duke. "What was that?"

I saw what he meant. I couldn't hide it. "Impatience," I said. "And annoyance. I'm getting tired of all the changes in procedures. And frustrated . . . that it doesn't seem to make a difference."

"And . . .?" he prompted.

"And . . ." I admitted, ". . . sometimes I'm afraid of all the responsibility. Sometimes I just want to run away from it. And sometimes I want to kill everything in sight." I added, "Sometimes I think I'm going crazy."

Duke looked up sharply at that, but his phone beeped before he could speak. He pulled it off his belt, thumbed it to life, and snapped, "Five minutes." He put it down on the table and looked at me. "What do you mean?"

"Well . . . I'm not sure if it's even real or not . . ." I weaseled.

Duke glanced at his watch. "Come on, Jim—there's a chopper waiting for us. I need to know if you're going on it or not. What's this 'crazy' stuff about?"

"I've been having . . . episodes," I said.

"What kind of episodes?"

"Well, dreams. Sort of. I don't know if I should even be telling you this. Maybe I should plug into Dr. Davidson—"

"Yes, you should be telling me this!" Duke looked annoyed and impatient now. " 'Cause if you don't, I'm going without you." He started to rise.

I said quickly, "I've been . . . hearing things."

Duke sat back down.

"And," I continued, "—I've been remembering things. Mostly when I'm asleep or dozing. But it's things I've never heard or seen before. And—this one is the most confusing—you know how most people dream in pictures? Well, last night, I dreamed in sound. A symphony. It was cold and ghostly. It sounded like it was coming from another world, or another plane of existence. I thought I was dying. I woke up in a sweat, it scared me so."

Duke studied me like a father. His eyes were sharp. "Dreams, huh? That's what's been bothering you?"

I nodded.

He didn't say anything immediately. He looked away, out the window, then looked back at me. "I have dreams all the time," he admitted. "Nightmares, actually. I keep seeing all the faces of all the people—" He stopped in the middle of the sentence. He dropped his gaze and looked at his hands. His huge old battered hands. I wondered if I should say something. Abruptly he looked back up at me, and he was Duke again—and he'd left several volumes unsaid. "But I don't let it stop me. Jim, do you hear what I'm saying?"

"Uh-huh. It's just—"

"What?"

I was embarrassed to admit it. "It's just that I'm afraid of going out of control," I said. "It's almost like there are voices. . . . I think if I could make out what they're saying, I'd know the answer and everything would be all right. But I can never quite make it out. It feels like distant whispering." There. It was out. I waited for his reaction.

Duke looked troubled. He looked as if he couldn't find the answer he was looking for. He looked out the window at the chopper again. When he came back at me, his expression was unhappy.

"By all rights," he said, "I should ground you pending a medical exam. Except, I can't. I need you for this mission. That's the way this whole damn war is being run. There's not a one of us that doesn't deserve a couple of years of R and R. But we'll never see it. Instead, we'll just keep getting kicked from one crisis to the next and we'll have to take care of our sanity at the stoplights." He studied me sharply. "Do *you* think you're crazy?"

I shrugged. "I don't know. I certainly don't think I'm normal."

Abruptly, he grinned. "Now, *that's* normal! Nobody's normal on this planet, Jim. Everybody's crazy, remember?"

I nodded. "I know it. It's just that sometimes I think I'm even crazier than that."

"Right. And that's normal too. Jim, if you're aware of how crazy you are, you're not crazy. It's only when you start insisting that you're sane that we're going to lock you up."

"That's a very old joke, Duke." I quoted it for him: " 'Sanity— if you think you have it, you probably don't. If you're *sure* you have it, then for sure you don't.' I get the paradox. The only real proof you have of your sanity is that you take the time to worry about it. You know, you can go crazy thinking about that one too long."

"Jim," Duke said quietly. "Put all that aside for a moment. What are you here for? What's the job?"

"I'm here to kill worms. The job is to stop the Chtorran infestation of the Earth. By whatever means possible."

"Good," Duke said. "Now, let me ask you another question. Do you have to be sane or fit some standard of normality to do that job?"

I thought about it. I looked at the answer inside my head. Obviously not. "No," I said.

"Good. So you see, it doesn't matter if you're crazy or not. There's only one thing I need to know. Can I count on you today?"

Now it was my turn to grin. "Yes, you can count of me."

"Absolutely?"

"*Absolutely*." And I mean it.

"Good," he said. "Grab your kit and let's go."

I didn't move. There was one more thing. "Uh—"

"Something else?" He looked concerned.

"Um, not really. Just a question."

"Yes, what?"

"Um . . . Duke, who do *you* clear with?"

He looked startled. He turned away from me while he picked up his phone and his traveling kit. Then he turned back to me and said, "I check in with the boss from time to time." He jerked a thumb toward the ceiling—and beyond. "The man upstairs." And then he was out the door.

I followed him, shaking my head in wonderment. The universe was full of surprises.

Q: What's the Chtorran word for friend?
A: Lunch.

2

Derby

*"Television does not honor tradition.
Most of the time, it doesn't even
recognize it. Therefore, it can only
destroy."*

— SOLOMON SHORT

I was wrong.

A machine that big *could* get off the ground.

It lumbered through the air like a drunken cow, but it flew—and it carried enough troops and gear to overthrow a small government. We had three of the best-trained teams in the Special Forces—Duke and I had trained them ourselves—a complete scientific squad, and enough firepower to barbecue Texas. (Well, a large piece of Texas, anyway.)

I hoped we wouldn't need to use it.

I climbed into the back and sat down with the "enlisted men." Draftees, all of them. Except they weren't called draftees any more. The Universal Service Obligation had been rewritten—twice—by the New Military Congress of the United States. Four years of uniformed service. No exceptions. No deferments. No "needed skill" civilian classifications. And this means *you*. You were eligible on the day you turned sixteen. You had to be in uniform before your eighteenth birthday. Very simple.

To get into the Special Forces, though, you had to *ask*. In fact, you almost had to *demand* the opportunity. You couldn't end up in the Special Forces any more unless you *wanted* to be here.

And then you had to prove you could handle the job.

I didn't know how rigorous the training was—I'd fallen into the

Special Forces by accident, before the standards were tightened, and I'd been spending most of my career playing catch-up—but I could tell by looking at this team that it produced the result. I'd also heard that three-quarters of those who started the training dropped out before it was halfway over.

These were the survivors. The winners.

There wasn't one of them who looked old enough to vote. And two of the girls didn't even need brassieres yet. But they weren't kids. They were combat-hardened troops. That these soldiers still counted their ages in the teens was incidental; they were as dangerous a bunch as the United States Army could put together. And it showed on their faces. They all had that same coiled look behind their eyes.

They were passing a cigarette back and forth between them. When it came to me, I took a puff—not because I wanted one, but because I wanted to make sure it wasn't 'dusted,' before I passed it on. I didn't think any of my troops would be that stupid, but it had been known to happen—on other teams, not mine. The army had a technical term for officers who let their troops go into combat situations stoned; we called them *statistics*.

The team wasn't talking much, and I knew why. It was my presence. I wasn't much more than three years older than the oldest of them, but I was the Lieutenant and that made me "the old man." Besides, they were afraid of me. Rumor had it I'd once burned a man alive on a worm hunt.

I felt old, looking at them. A little wistful too. These kids would be the last ones on the planet for a long time who would be able to remember what a "normal" childhood was like.

They should have been in high school or their first year in college. They should have been putting up balloons in the gymnasium for some school dance, or worrying about their Global Ethics reports, or even just hanging out down at the mall.

They knew this was not the way the world was supposed to work. And this was definitely not the future they had planned on. But this was the way it had turned out; there was a job that had to be done and they were the ones who had to do it.

I respected their commitment.

"Sir?" That was Beckman, tall and gangly and dark. I remembered his family was from Guam. I glanced over toward him. "Are we gonna be back in time for *Derby*?" he asked.

I thought about it. We were headed into southern Wyoming. Two hours in the air each way. Four hours on the ground, maximum. *Derby* was on at 9:00 P.M.. T.J. had found out that

Stephanie was coming back from Hong Kong. Now, for sure, he had to locate the missing robot before Grant did. "Should be," I said. "If we're off the ground by six. No later." I glanced around at the others. "Can you guys target on that?"

They nodded agreement.

"Sure."

"Fine by me."

"Let's do it."

I gave them a grin. A trick I learned from Duke. Spend your smiles as if each one cost you a year off your life. Then your troops will bust their buns to earn them.

They looked so thrilled, I had to get up and go quickly forward—before I burst out laughing.

Duke glanced at me as I climbed up beside him. "They okay?"

"They're worried about the missing robot."

"Huh?"

"*Derby*. It's a TV program."

"Never touch the stuff myself," he said. "It interferes with my drinking." He checked his watch. He leaned forward and tapped the pilot's shoulder. "You can call Denver now. Tell them we've passed Go-NoGo Kappa. They can launch the follow-chopper." To me, Duke said, "You can start warming up the Jeeps now. I want to drop the hatch and roll as soon as we hit the dirt. I want this ship empty in thirty seconds."

"You got it," I said.

The target was nearly fifty klicks south of Wheatland.

It had been spotted, almost accidentally, by a Reclamation Scout. Fortunately, he knew what he was looking at. He called it in, then turned his Jeep north and drove like hell. He nearly made it, too.

A response team spotted the overturned Jeep from the air a day later. A drop squad pulled the Jeep's log-disk, and the video record confirmed the infestation site. Four worms. Three "children" and an "adult." The nest would have been burned or frozen within forty-eight hours—except this time, Denver had a *better* idea.

This time we were going to capture a whole Chtorran family *alive*.

Duke and I always got the *good* jobs.

Q: What do Chtorrans call humans who have sex with them?
A: Lunch.

3

The Nest

Armies aren't known for neatness.
—SOLOMON SHORT

We banged down onto the ground with a thump hard enough to rattle the teeth out of our skulls. Almost instantly, the rear door of the chopper blew open and the exit ramp popped out and down with a metal clang. It felt like the whole ship was coming apart at once. The lead Jeep was already bouncing down the ramp and onto the hard Wisconsin clay. The rollagons rumbled right down after it. And then the rest of the convoy.

The lead Jeep turned north immediately; its wheels stirred up the loose dirt on the ground and it left a thick cloud of dust in its wake. The dust tailed out quickly; the wind was strong today, not the best of conditions.

The other seven vehicles turned north also, forming a ragged diagonal line on the prairie. I was riding with Duke in the command vehicle, the largest of the rollagons. It looked like a landing barge with centipede legs and balloon tires, but it was steady and it was almost comfortable. In addition to our driver, we also had two auxiliary technicians and a drop squad. For the moment, it was their mission.

Duke and I were just cargo. Our job was to sit quietly and be delivered on-site.

We had a huge bank of tactical displays at our command. We could see our approach on a representational map, or as a color-coded radar scan of the surrounding terrain. We also had a dead-reckoning inertial guidance display and continuous confirmation by satellite Earthwatch. When we were two kilometers away, Duke halted the rollagon and sent the attack vehicles scurrying off to their positions for Go-NoGo Lambda, and I launched a skyball—an aerial drone—for one last look-see before we went in.

The image on the screen tilted and swooped dizzily as the skyball skidded and slid across the sky. It was having trouble navigating in the wind. After a moment, though, it figured out what it was doing and the image steadied into a long glide.

The nest came up on the screen suddenly. It was a squat brown dome with a bulging circular entrance.

"A textbook case," I said. "See the purple stuff around the outside?"

Duke grunted. "You can spare me the narration."

I nodded and tapped at the keyboard, bringing the drone lower. The image turned slowly as the skyball circled the nest. I punched for scanning. The image shifted colors then: blue for cold, red for hot, yellow for in-between. Most of the screen was orange. I had to turn down the range.

The corrected scan was mostly green and yellow. A faint orange track led to the dome. Or away from it. The track was at least an hour old.

I glanced at Duke; his expression was unreadable. "Scan the dome," he said.

We knew that the worms were hot when they were active. But we also knew that when they went torpid, which was usually during the hottest part of the day, their body temperatures could drop as much as thirty degrees. That was why the earliest mobile probes had failed to register their presence. The worms had been too cool.

We knew better now.

The worms went *deep* and they went *cold*. Men had died to find that out.

The skyball came in low and close now. The dome filled the screen. I punched in a sonic-scan overlay. There was something there, all right—a dark blue mass, mottled with quickly shifting colors. It was large and deep below the surface.

The screen said it massed four metric tons.

"That's a good-size family," said Duke. "Can we take 'em?"

I was wondering the same thing. "Denver says the gas is good. This is at the upper end of the range, but it's within the limit."

"How do you feel about it?"

"I say go."

"Good," said Duke. "So do I." He thumbed his mike. "All units. It's a go. I repeat, it's a *go*. Proceed to your final positions.

This is it." He leaned forward and rapped our driver. "Come on, let's move!" The big rollagon trundled forward, up a small ridge and then down the long slope on the opposite side.

I pulled the skyball up and directed it to circle the dome on a continual scan. If there was any change in heat level, it would sound an immediate alarm. We would have between ten and ninety seconds' warning, depending on the worms. I checked my earphones and mike. This was the most dangerous part of the mission. We were too vulnerable to ambush on the approach.

I had to read this dome quickly and say if it was safe to proceed. If not—if I thought it appropriate—I had the authority to abort the entire mission. This was the last Go-NoGo and I was the worm expert.

The troops liked to believe that I had some kind of uncanny "worm sense." I didn't, of course, and the rumor made me nervous. But they wanted to believe it—I was as close to a lucky charm as they had—so I didn't try to squelch the story.

And besides, I sort of halfway wished it were true. It would have made me feel a lot better about how little I really knew.

The rollagon bounced onto level ground then and I stood up in my seat to peer ahead. There was the dome. It looked deceptively small in person. Most of the nest was underground. We really didn't know how deep the worms would tunnel. We weren't willing to let a family establish itself long enough to find out.

I tapped the driver's shoulder. "This is close enough," I said. "It's spider time. I'll walk the rest of the way."

The rollagon slid to an uneven halt. I sat down again at my keyboard, and activated United States Military Spider ARAC-5714.

Beside me, I could hear Duke acknowledging each of the other vehicles as they slid into position around the dome. I didn't bother to look up. I knew that the teams were already dropping out of their vehicles, torches at the ready. We were eight tight little islands of death. Priority one: *survive*. Dead heroes do not win wars.

The green ready light came up. I slid the console back and pulled the spider control board up and into position. I slipped the goggles over my head, waited for my vision to clear, and slipped my hands into the control gloves.

There was the usual moment of discontinuity, and then I was *in* the spider. I was looking through its eyes, hearing through its ears, feeling through its hands. "Forward," I said, and the point of view moved down, out of the forward ramp of the rollagon, and toward the quiet-looking dome.

My point of view was closer to the ground than I was used to, and my eyes were farther apart, so everything looked smaller—and the perspective was deeper. I needed this walk to slip into my "spider-consciousness mode." I had to get into the *feeling* of it.

The military spiders were hasty adaptations of the industrial models. This one had a black metal body, eight skinny legs—each ending in a large black hoof—and an observation turret. The spider could function with half its legs disabled; any two of its legs could also function as arms. There was a waldo inside each hoof, complete with tactile sensors.

During the plagues, the spiders had been used extensively in situations where human beings could not—or would not—go themselves. The spiders had been very useful in hospitals. And in crematoriums. The spiders had gathered most of the dead.

"Slower," I commanded. We were approaching the entrance to the dome. "Scan. . . ."

The image before me shifted down the spectrum. The colors of objects changed, then changed again. Green and yellow again. Some orange, but very, very faint.

"Sonic scan. . . ." I said, and turned my attention into the dome. The large blue mass was clearer here. I could almost make out the shape of four huge worms. They were intertwined in a big spherical tumble, if I was reading the image correctly. And they were still cold.

"Well?" asked Duke at my shoulder.

"They're in the living room. It's a young nest; they haven't even had a chance to start branching tunnels."

"What color are they?" Duke sounded impatient.

"They're a *real* pretty shade of blue," I said. "It's go." I gave the command: "Forward."

We were committed now. There were no more Go-NoGo points.

The spider entered the dome.

Turn right, go up and around and enter the central chamber. Go to the center hole. Squat over the hole. Look down.

Nothing in the lower chamber?

Reset the image-processors. Look again.

The worms are huge. It's hard to see them as worms. Sometimes they look like a huge furry carpet.

All blue. All tumbled.

I wonder what it looks like when they wake up—but I'm not going to wait to find out.

Lower the nozzle.

And . . . give the command, "Gas."

There is a hissing noise.

The color of the worms goes darker—

I slipped my hands out of the gloves and pulled the goggles off my eyes. I looked to Duke. "Done," I said.

Duke grinned and clapped me on the shoulder. "Good job." He turned to the communications technician. "All right, bring the chopper down. We'll be ready to start loading in thirty minutes. Move the 'dozer unit into position and tell them to fix grapples and stand by for detox. Have everybody else move in to the primary perimeter."

The rollagon lurched forward again and Duke gave me a cheerful thumbs-up signal. He started to say something, but I didn't hear it. A second huge cargo chopper was just clattering in overhead. It sounded like a cosmic jackhammer—the one God uses for starting earthquakes.

This was the machine that would carry the worms back to Denver.

I wondered if it would be big enough.

Q: What do Chtorrans call a traffic jam?
A: Lunch.

Q: What do Chtorrans call an elevator?
A: Lunch.

Q: What do Chtorrans call New York?
A: Dinner.

4

"—fifteen steers a week."

"Artificial food is expensive. Nothing makes a steak as efficiently as a cow."
— SOLOMON SHORT

As soon as we pulled into position, I took a second reading on the mass of the worms. They were too big. I couldn't shake the feeling that I was making a mistake here. Perhaps I should have said no at the last Go-NoGo point.

I almost turned to Duke, then I stopped myself. I did this every time. As soon as it was too late, I started second-guessing. It didn't matter anymore what I thought. We were committed.

I took a second reading on the mass of the worms, recalculated the gas dosage according to Denver's mass-ratio equations, and detonated another pellet. I wondered if it should have been two. I'd rather kill the worms than have them wake up while we were loading them.

We gave the gas a full ten minutes. I took a final reading—the worms were the most wonderful shade of dark purple I'd ever seen—then brought the spider out.

Then we pulled the dome off its foundations. We anchored grapples in its base, attached two ropes to a Jeep, and backed up slowly. The hut ripped off like so much Styrofoam. The worms didn't build for strength. They didn't have to.

We had to do it twice; the dome shredded too easily. I felt like an intruder, a vandal. We had to pull it off in pieces. Then we had to rip off the top floor too.

That job was harder. We had to plant small charges in the floor to break it up. It was made out of the same material as the dome walls, but it was denser and had the strength of industrial Kevlar. It would have to be strong to hold the weight of a healthy worm family.

The worms built their nests by chewing up trees and spitting out foam. Apparently they could vary the mix enough to produce lightweight translucent walls and heavyweight hardwood floors all from the same basic ingredients. A neat trick.

When the lower half of the nest was finally revealed, there was a moment of . . . hesitation. The team, men and women alike, gathered in silence around the edge to stare down at the exposed worms.

They were huge. Just knowing they were huge from the readings on the screen was not the same as actually seeing them in the flesh. Even the smallest of them was a meter thick and three meters long. The "adult" was two meters high at its brain case and twice as long as the baby. I wished I'd given them that third pellet.

The worms were coiled around each other like lovers, head to tail, head to tail, in a circular formation. They were shadowed in the lower half of the nest, but even so their fur shone a brilliant red. It was almost alluring.

Duke came up beside me to look. His expression tightened, but he didn't speak.

"Looks like we interrupted a Chtorran orgy," I said.

Duke grunted.

"The baby's about three hundred kilos," I offered. "Papa bear is probably a thousand."

"At least," said Duke. He didn't like it, I could tell. He was too silent.

"Too big?" I asked.

"Too expensive," he grumbled. "You're looking at fifteen steers a week. That's a lot of hamburger." He clicked his tongue and turned away. "All right," he bawled, "let's get down in there and get to work." He pointed to a man with a headset. "Tell that chopper to drop the slings. Now!"

We had one bad moment with the loading.

We started with the baby. One squad dropped into the pit while the other two teams stood above them with flame-throwers, rocket-launchers, and incendiary bullets. The worm was too big to roll onto a sling—it had to be lifted so the canvas could be pulled beneath it.

The squad in the pit quickly slid a series of stainless-steel rods underneath the smallest worm to form a lattice of crossbars. These were then connected at their ends to two longer bars placed lengthwise against the worm. The baby was now lying on a ladder-shaped bed.

The chopper was already clattering into place overhead, whipping us with wind and noise. Its cables were already lowering. The team didn't try to grab the free-swinging ends. Instead they waited until the lines touched ground and there was enough slack. They grabbed the cables and ran to attach them to the ladder under the worm. Beckman gave a thumbs-up signal and the chopper began to raise the cables. They tightened visibly. The ladder shuddered and began to lift—

For a moment, the worm resisted—it was just a large limp bag of scarlet pudding—and then the connection with the other worms was broken and it pulled up into the air.

Immediately, every worm in the pit began to stir.

Papa worm grunted uneasily. The other two actually chirruped and rumbled. But the baby worm was the worst. It writhed as if in pain, and let loose a plaintive wail of anguish. It curled and looped like an earthworm cut in half. The ladder swung recklessly. The cables groaned—and then its eyes popped open. They were huge and black and round. They slid this way and that, unfocused and unseeing.

The team jumped backward, flattening themselves against the nearest wall.

"Hold your fire!" I was screaming. "Hold your fire, goddammit!" Somehow I made myself heard above the terror. "It's still unconscious! Those are automatic reactions!"

Indeed, the baby was already calming down again. Its eyes slid shut and it curled—tried to curl—into a swollen red ball, still hanging above the floor of the nest.

"Oh, Jesus—" gasped someone. "I don't need this—" He started scrambling out. The two men on either side of him looked uncertain—

Duke didn't give the team a chance to be scared. He jumped down into the pit with them and started snapping orders. "Come on—let's get that bastard onto the mat. Move it!" He grabbed the soldier who'd started to panic and pushed him straight at the worm. "You're riding up with it, Gomez. Thanks for volunteering." Gomez kept moving in the direction of Duke's shove. It was safer.

"Come on! Move that mat! Pull it under! Under—goddammit! *Under!* Good! All right—" Duke pointed up at the communications tech, still bellowing, and waving his arm like a semaphore.

"Down! Bring it down!" And then, back to the squad again, "All right! Let's get those bars out! Let's get those cables attached! Now! Goddammit! Now! Let's move!"

The pit squad moved like demons then, detaching the cables from the bars and reattaching them to the canvas faster than Duke could swear. They pulled the bars out from under the worm and backed quickly out of the way. The chopper lifted then—just a bit, to bring the edges of the canvas up—and the worm was strapped into its sling. Two of the bars were slid through the straps then to seal the worm into a steel and canvas cocoon, and four more cables were attached to the ends of these. This was for *its* protection as much as ours. We didn't want the creatures banging loose around the inside of the chopper. The worms would be kept strapped and hanging the whole trip.

"All right! Take it up!" Duke hollered and waved. The clatter of the chopper drowned his words and the wind whipped at his face. He didn't even watch; he was already turning to the next worm. "What are you slobs waiting for? Let's get those bars under—"

The other three worms were easier—but not much.

At least now we knew that when we separated them they'd react—but they wouldn't wake up. We could handle that. The team worked faster now.

The chopper hovered overhead, growling and rumbling, and we lifted the worms one by one into its massive cargo bay. The big creatures sagged ominously in the creaking slings.

It was a terrifying job.

The wind was rising and the chopper began to pitch and slide sideways in the air. I wondered if we were going to have to return without all four, but the pilot turned the ship into the wind and told us to keep going. Whoever she was, she was good.

Once—the worm in the sling was banged against the side of the nest; it moaned in its sleep, a dark purple rumble of despair. The pit squad turned and looked with wild expressions on their faces. The monster chirruped like a crying woman. The sound of it was *devastating*. Suddenly, this creature was an object of *pity*. Then the worm cleared the nest wall and rose swiftly into the air—and Duke was pointing and waving again.

Papa worm was last. As the big creature came rising up out of the ground, the afternoon sun struck highlights off its bright red fur. It shimmered with a thousand flickering colors—it looked like a heavenly pink aura. I couldn't help but marvel. It was the most beautiful color I'd ever seen. . . .

The creature lifted into the sky like a big pink blimp. I followed it all the way up. It disappeared into the belly of the chopper and the giant black doors of the machine slid shut with a *whump*.

Duke signaled the tech, the tech said something into his microphone, and the chopper whirred noisily off southward.

"All right," he said. "Let's go home and watch TV. Is T.J. going to tell Stephanie about the missing robot or not?"

Q: What do Chtorrans call Chicago?
A: Lunch.

Q: What do Chtorrans call Atlanta?
A: Lunch.

Q: What do Chtorrans call New Jersey?
A: Hardtack.

5

"You're right on schedule."

> *"Writing for television is a debilitating exercise. How can you inspire an audience to their best when every fourteen minutes someone interrupts to tell them that they're unfit to live with? The ultimate purpose of commercial television is to convince the viewer that he smells bad."*
>
> —SOLOMON SHORT

Stephanie stayed in Hong Kong for an emergency meeting with the Chinese ambassador, so T.J. didn't tell her about the robot. Grant found out who the baby's father *really* was, and confronted Karen with the lie. The robot remained missing.

Obviously, we made it back in time.

Toward the end of the show, an orderly came in and tapped Duke on the shoulder. He got up and left quietly. I noticed, but didn't follow. If Duke needed me, he'd let me know.

A few minutes later, the orderly came back and tapped me on the shoulder. "Duke wants to see you."

I thanked her and went up to the office. Duke looked unhappy. He was sitting at his terminal, staring glumly at the screen. His hands were hesitating above the keyboard.

"What's up?" I asked.

He didn't answer; he just punched up another display and studied it sourly.

I walked around behind him and looked over his shoulder. He was sorting through the list of targets for the mission we'd just completed.

"Those are the alternate targets, Duke. Are you planning another mission?"

He shook his head. "Just looking." He lifted his hands away from the keyboard and stopped. "I don't see what we could have done different. We made the best choice we could." He swiveled to look at me. "Or do you disagree?"

"No," I said. "We chose the right nest." I stood there before him, waiting.

He said, "What do you think about the Lake Hattie site? Would you recommend going in there?"

"You *are* planning another mission. What happened? Our worms died from the gas?"

"I wish," Duke said bitterly. He leaned back in his chair and folded his arms. "No. The gas wore off early. They woke up in the chopper. Thirty minutes short of Denver."

"Oh, no—" I felt weak, suddenly weak. I wanted to sit down. I had a sick feeling in my gut. Live worms aboard a chopper—?

"The chopper went down in the mountains," Duke said. "There were no survivors." He studied me for a moment, as if he knew what I was thinking. Then he swiveled to face the window and the dark night outside.

I wanted to say something, but I didn't know what. I felt like I'd been opened up with a machete and my guts were spilling out on the floor.

Duke said, "If it makes it any easier, they think it had something to do with the altitude."

"No," I said. "It doesn't make it any easier."

I went to the water cooler and filled a plastic cup. I wasn't thirsty, but it was something to do.

Behind me, Duke said, "There's a bottle of Scotch in the bottom drawer of the filing cabinet. Pour two."

I handed Duke his drink, found a chair, and sat down across from him.

"I should have followed my instincts," I said. "I looked at those worms and I wanted to detonate every pellet in the spider. I wish I had. Instead, I followed orders."

"That's right," said Duke. "Make it Denver's fault. To err is human—to blame the other guy is even more so. I'm glad to see you're taking it so well."

I ignored his comment. I was still putting the pieces back

together. I said slowly, ". . . I follow Denver's orders because I like to think they know what they're doing. But they don't—they really don't. And we both know that!" I was being careless, I knew it, but Duke didn't react or try to stop me, so I plunged on. I wanted to get it all said before I ran out of steam. "It's crazy, Duke. They're so insulated from the front lines of this war that all they've got left are their theories and speculations—and they're making policy based on those theories. When that filters down here, to our level, we have to make life-and-death decisions based on those policies and hope that it's appropriate! And sometimes it is! They get it right just often enough to keep us trusting them."

Duke said, "I've heard this all before, you know. None of it is original. Every lieutenant goes through it." He glanced at his watch. "You're right on schedule."

He was being flip about it, but he was right. Of course. Again. I felt embarrassed. I didn't know what to say. I was flustered.

I looked at my drink. I took a belt of it. "Duke—" My voice cracked. I was out of anger—I felt drained. I said, "Duke—I'm losing it. Really. It's *all* meaningless voices now. I mean, I don't know that I can follow *anyone's* orders any more. I mean, if nobody else knows what they're doing either, Duke, and *I'm* the guy who ends up being responsible, then I'm the guy who *really* has to be sure. And I know that I'm not. So I follow orders—not because it's the safest thing to do, but because I can't think of anything *better*! And that still doesn't work. People still die—and it's *still* my fault. I didn't even know that chopper crew! I didn't even know their names—"

"Wolfman. Wein."

"—whatever. They're still dead and it's my fault. No matter how you slice it, it still stinks!"

"And?" prompted Duke.

"And I don't like it!" I finished lamely. I wished it had been a little more *profound,* but at least this was the truth.

Duke had listened to my outpouring in silence; he had remained carefully blank the whole time. Now he looked up at me with a peculiar expression on his face. "I'll tell you something, Jim." He took a breath. "What you like is unimportant. I know you don't even like hearing that, but it's true. Whether you like it or not is ultimately irrelevant. This job still has to be done. And mistakes are always going to be made—again, like it or not."

He hesitated for a beat, as if considering his next sentence. He looked into his cup thoughtfully; his eyes were shaded. When he spoke again, his voice was lower. "I know it's frustrating. It's *always* frustrating. It's always going to *be* frustrating. You think I haven't been there? This is Pakistan all over again—only this time I know how deep the brown sauce is. You want to know what's really crazy? Almost all of our procedures are derived from a war that was *lost* twelve years ago. That's crazy. But—" he shrugged, "it always comes back to this. The job still has to be done."

"I don't know," I said. "I mean, I don't know if I can do this job any more." I didn't look at him when I said it.

"Jim, don't be stupid." Suddenly, there was a hint of metal in his voice. "Don't you think we've *all* gone through this? I have. Shorty did. It's part of the responsibility. You get to make mistakes. You can't help it. It's part of being human. Now, I'm going to tell you the other part. You don't get to use your mistakes as an excuse to quit."

"I'm sorry. I don't see it that way."

"Then you're missing the obvious. If we discharged every man or woman who ever made a mistake, we wouldn't have an officer left in the United States Army. Myself included."

"Yeah, but my mistakes kill people—"

"So do mine," he said quietly. His eyes were hard. "You think you have a monopoly on that one?"

I didn't answer. I'd already proven myself a fool. Why compound it?

Duke put his cup down on the desk next to him. "Listen, Jim. The truth is, a mistake is just one more opportunity to put in the correction. It's not a club to beat yourself with. It's just something to learn from. The only *real* failure is quitting. That's where you waste lives. Those pilots—Wein and Wolfman—they knew the risk. They were willing to take it"

"They trusted my judgment."

"So? So do I. So what?"

"But what if next time it's you—?"

Duke shrugged. "It could just as easily be you too, Jim. I have to trust you. You have to trust me. It's part of the job. So what? I mean, so what about it? Do you want to feel sorry for yourself, or do you want to get on with the job? You do want to kill worms, don't you?"

"Don't be silly."

"Well, then—this is where you learn to pick up the pieces and keep going. Consider it part of your training to be a captain. This is the part where you accept the responsibility for the decisions that *hurt*.

"But, it hurts—" I knew it was stupid even as I said it, but I said it anyway, "—and I don't know what to *do*."

"Nothing," he said. "There's nothing *to* do, Jim. Just hurt. Until you stop hurting. You don't even have to dramatize it. You can spare me the weeping and wailing. I've seen weeping and wailing. And better than yours."

Then he added quietly, "I know you're hurting, Jim. I'd worry about you if you weren't. What you need to know is that it's all right to hurt." His eyes were surprisingly compassionate.

I felt . . . grateful. But I was too embarrassed to meet his gaze. I said, "Thanks," and looked away quickly.

Duke added, "Is that it? Or is there anything else you want me to know?"

I shook my head. "I think that just about covers it." I finished my drink and wondered if I should get myself another. I deserved to get drunk tonight. Except I knew it really wouldn't help. This was something I was just going to have to work through by myself. One day at a time. Damn. I was getting too rational for my own good.

"All right," I sighed and slid my chair over to another terminal. "I guess I'd better start mapping another operation. At least we've proven we can get them out of the ground alive."

Duke said, "Hold it, Jim. I haven't given you the *bad* news yet."

I lifted my fingers from the keyboard and looked over at him. "It gets worse?"

He nodded. "We're being pulled out."

"The whole team?"

"No. Just you and I. There's a chopper on the way. It'll be here in an hour."

"Where are we going? Denver?"

"Oakland."

"Oakland?! What the hell is in Oakland?"

"The Gertrude Stein Memorial Plaque," Duke said. He levered himself to his feet. "Among other things. You've got an hour to pack. Be on the field at 23:30. We'll be briefed in the air."

I looked at the terminal display again. "But—" I said, hopelessly, "—I wanted to go to Lake Hattie!"

"If it's any consolation, Jim, so did I." He crumpled his cup and tossed it at the wastebasket as he left the room. The cup missed the basket and bounced into a corner.

I scooped it up and popped it in.

Damn.

Q: What do Chtorrans call San Francisco?
A: Quiche.

Q: What do Chtorrans call Oregon?
A: Natural food.

Q: What do Chtorrans call Southern California?
A: Granola. (It's all fruits, nuts and flakes.)

6

Tiny

"Don't be so proud. You are not an intelligence until after you pass the Turing test."

—SOLOMON SHORT

The chopper was an hour late, and it was another hour before we got off the ground. Then there was a spring storm over most of Utah, so the pilot chose to detour south. It would be daylight before we touched down in California.

And the only reading matter aboard was the briefing book. It was incomplete and took only twenty minutes to finish. It was all background, nothing about our assignment, and it didn't tell me anything I didn't already know. The infestations were spreading faster than our ability to burn them out.

There was one interesting footnote, however. Oakland had two worms now, but they didn't really know what to do with them because they didn't know how to interpret their behavior. The note said they needed a worm expert, someone who knew the creatures in their normal habitat.

I pointed out the word "normal" to Duke. He snorted too when he saw it.

"Not if I have anything to say about it." he added. He closed his eyes again and appeared to go back to sleep.

I envied him. I can't sleep on airplanes. I can doze, but I keep waking up suddenly. Any little noise, any little bump or bounce, any change in engine sound, and I'm instantly alert, wondering if everything is all right. I get off airplanes exhausted.

I stared out the window at the distant flashes of lightning. The storm was a nasty one. The cloud banks towered like the walls of a canyon—a gigantic one. The moonlight gave them an eerie blue sheen. Every few seconds, one or another of the towering masses would crackle and flare and light up the whole sky. Beautiful—and terrifying.

I wondered about the people below.

Did anyone still live there?

We were a planet of scattered survivors, all scrambling like mad to stay alive long enough to get the crops in. Somewhere between seventy and ninety percent—there was no way to know for sure—of the human race had died in the first three years. There was no way to know how many had been lost to the plagues and how many to associated disasters and aftereffects. I'd heard a rumor, unconfirmed, that the suicide rate was still climbing.

I wondered about that too. When you've lost everything and have nothing left to live for . . . I wondered how close I was—

It was a long flight.

Eventually the sun tinged the horizon behind us and we began dropping toward Oakland. I was on the wrong side of the ship to see San Francisco. I was disappointed in that—I wanted to see how bad it looked from the air. They said the city was still in pretty grim shape. I'd seen pictures, of course, but it wasn't the same. Besides, my dad had died in San Francisco—

Well, disappeared, anyway. . . .

There was a car waiting for us on the ground, but we were delayed by the inevitable decontamination baths—no telling what bugs were still floating around—and then had to wait again until our vaccinations could be updated.

It was another hour before we were in the Jeep and on our way south. We didn't have a driver—the car knew the way without one. There was the standard taped welcome on the screen, which Duke and I both ignored, and a thermos of tea and a box of breakfast rolls in the flashbox. The tea was already lukewarm; the rolls were stale.

The Jeep delivered us to the Special Forces officers' billet—formerly the downtown Oakland Holiday Inn. "Probably because they couldn't find worse," Duke explained. There were no humans on duty here, either—just a couple of terminals, a bell-cart, and a mindless robot, noisily polishing the lobby floor. We had to step around it to get to the desk.

The terminal beeped and clucked, checked our ID, issued us key-cards and wished us a nice stay. It also called us "Mr. and Mrs. Anderson."

Duke wasn't amused.

"It must have heard what you said," I pointed out. We were following the bell-cart down the hall. "You know, all these machines talk to each other. They compare notes."

Duke gave me a withering sideways glance. I shut up. One day I would learn: Duke did not appreciate whimsy. "Clean up quickly," he said.

"No sleep—?"

"You'll sleep in October. There's a war on, remember?"

Right.

A hot shower and a shave later—the second-best substitute for six hours sleep (the first being *eight* hours sleep)—Duke handed me hardcopy orders. "There's a colloquium at ten hundred about the worms. You're already cleared through. I want you to specifically see if anyone knows anything about nesting habits. They've already got the disks of yesterday's mission. Find out if they've seen them. I think we're seeing another shift in behavior. Oh, yeah—and be polite. The science boys are starting to chafe at the presence of the military."

"Right."

As interested as I was in the Chtorran ecology, I still would have preferred the sleep. With luck, I could sleep in the session—as long as they didn't put me in the front row.

The Oakland Control Section of the United States Ecological Agency was hidden behind a long range of rolling hills. The Jeep whined as it rolled up the winding slope. As it came over the top, I saw that most of the buildings below were hardened inflatables. They were large and roomy and blandly amorphous. A platoon of twenty shining robots was mowing the lawns around the buildings. Lawns! I didn't know whether to laugh at the extravagance or be annoyed at the waste of energy. But the grass was green and lush looking.

I showed my credentials to the gort at the entrance—it scanned them with an evil-looking eye; these machines weren't designed for friendliness—and then passed me through. I still hadn't seen another human being yet.

The Jeep headed toward the largest of the domes. It rolled right into the building and delivered me to a tall set of double-steel doors and an armed sergeant in a glass booth. The glass looked thick and the sergeant wore a grim expression.

The Jeep beeped. Something clicked. The red lights went on above the doors. Surveillance cameras swiveled to look at me—and so did other devices that weren't cameras.

Maybe this wasn't going to be as easy as I thought.

The sergeant looked up, saw I was an officer, and saluted perfunctorily. Then he directed me to approach the booth and stand on the white platforms in front of it.

After he finished scanning me, the sergeant let me take two steps forward to state my business. He studied his screen for a moment, nodded, and hit a button. The red lights went off, the surveillance cameras swiveled back into their housing—so did the other devices—and I relaxed. Somewhat.

The sergeant touched another button and the steel doors groaned and slid apart, revealing a bright-lit maze of doors, passageways, stairs, halls, catwalks, and elevators. There were conduits and pipes everywhere, all brightly colored and labeled with large stenciled letters and numbers. It looked like they'd forgotten the interior walls of the building.

I looked to the sergeant with what I hoped was a questioning expression.

The sergeant nodded—obviously he'd seen the expression before—and pointed to a door. He directed me down a long featureless corridor—follow the red stripe on the floor—and into an anteroom, through the double doors and—

A lady in a white coat looked up from her desk and greeted me with a frown. "You're—?"

"McCarthy, James Edward, Lieutenant, Special Forces."

She looked back at the terminal. "You're not on *my* list."

"I just arrived in Oakland two hours ago—"

"I'll have to double check this." She was already reaching for the phone. I said the magic words: "—and I'm in the Uncle Ira Group." She replaced the phone neatly on the hook. "Right."

She slid her chair back and stood up. I saw that she needed a cane to walk. "Follow me, please."

Through another set of double doors, and down another corridor—why bother with security, I wondered; just paint out all the stripes and nobody will be able to find anything—and into a small angular theater, already darkened. The seats were stacked in steep rows overlooking a curtained wall. A young-looking woman in a lab coat stood at the podium. I saw a lot of uniforms and lab coats and grim faces. I looked for a place in the rear of the room, Preferably a comfortable one.

"There's one down here, Lieutenant," the woman at the podium said. She looked familiar.

I threaded my way down toward the front row. Damn,

"Oh—it's McCarthy. I thought I recognized the Special Forces."

Now I knew her. I smiled back, weakly. Her name was Fletcher, but she'd once introduced herself to me as Lucrezia Borgia. I didn't know her first name. As I took my seat, she said, "Good to see you again, Lieutenant."

The man sitting in the next chair glanced at me curiously. I flushed with embarrassment.

"All right," said Dr. Fletcher. "Let's get back to work. Dr. Abbato at the Cairo Institute has raised an interesting question about the gastropedes—and their place in their own ecology—and that's opened up a very interesting and perhaps very fruitful line of research. I think you'll find today's demonstration very—" she allowed herself a smile, "—enlightening."

I propped my elbow on the chair arm and my chin on my knuckles, and tried to look awake.

Dr. Fletcher had close-cropped dark hair. She had high cheekbones and wore thin rimmed glasses—and she had a *professional* look, neither plain nor pretty. She looked competent. I guessed it was the crisp way she handled herself.

"Dr. Abbato has posed the question: What kind of ecology could produce creatures like the Chtorran worm? What is the home planet like? That's where he began.

"All right. These are *today's* answers:

"Heavier gravity, we know that. The musculature of Chtorran creatures, the strength of their shells and skeletons, the rigidity of Chtorran plant stems, and so on—all of that indicates that the home world is either larger or denser, or both.

"Um—" She interrupted herself, "just a little bit of background on the gravity thing. We're extrapolating this from adaptations previously observed of Earth plants and animals to Lunar gravity. We plugged in a modified Sternbach-Probert matrix to extrapolate Chtorran adaptations to Earth gravity and we think that gives us a pretty good approximation of the home world's mass. Allowing for statistical slippage, we're assuming that Chtorr has a minimum gravity of one-point-one Earth normal and a maximum of one-point-five. That latter figure is probably a little high, but we're allowing a larger than usual margin for error. That seems to be the normal procedure for anything Chtorran these days."

She bent back her notes. "Chtorr would have to have a thicker atmosphere, of course, but we have no way of really knowing its make-up. Chtorran plants and animals are extraordinarily good at extracting oxygen from this atmosphere, so we are allowing the assumption that the Chtorran air has somewhat less free oxygen.

"We do think that the Chtorran primary is a red star. Very old.

Perhaps very close to final collapse. Chtorran plants seem to prefer red light, the redder the better, and Chtorran eyes seem to work best in the red end of the spectrum.

"And finally, we think that the Chtorran ecology is at least a half-billion years older than ours. That means—if Chtorr evolved anything like Earth—that there were the equivalent of mammals, or even more advanced life forms, walking the surface of Chtorr when the best this planet had to offer was slime not even distinctive enough to make an interesting fossil. That means that the Chtorran ecology has at least a half-billion-year head start in the evolution race."

I tried to stifle a yawn. I knew all this.

Dr. Fletcher looked over at me. "We'll get to the good parts in a minute, Lieutenant. Try to stay awake until then, if you can."

I blushed embarrassedly and straightened in my seat.

Dr. Fletcher continued, "If the same processes of evolution have held true on Chtorr, then the planet should have evolved a particularly nasty and competitive food chain—and so far, that's exactly what we've seen.

"Using our own ecology as a model—the only ecology we have to base a model on—we know that the process of evolution is a process of continually adding links to the food chain. Reptiles evolved out of fish to eat fish—and then each other. Mammals evolved out of reptiles to eat reptiles *and* fish—and each other.

"What comes after mammals? And what comes after that? And after that? And whatever comes after that—presumably, that's what rules Chtorr. Whatever it is, it *has* to be at the top of its food chain.

"That was the *initial* hypothesis. I'll give you a minute to think about that. The implications are interesting. Dr. Abbato did his homework on this one."

Dr. Fletcher studied her notes for a moment, then looked back up with a smile. "The first one is that a sentient species has to be at the top of its food chain. It can't be otherwise. Think about it. New forms *always* arise to feed on the old. What else can they feed on? The high levels have to be predatory. And predators are the life forms most likely to develop intelligence. You're probably all familiar with Dr. Cohen's famous remark, 'Intelligence develops first in predators. After all, how much intelligence do you need to sneak up on a blade of grass?' "

There were polite chuckles. It was an old joke.

But Dr. Fletcher wasn't interested in laughs. She pushed on. "It's pretty clear that the higher level the predator, the higher its capacity for intelligence. Carrying that one step further, we think that sentience is most likely to develop in a top-level omnivore." Dr. Fletcher allowed herself an impish smile. "We recognize, of course, that we may be biased in that assumption, because we are the only proof of it we have.

"But, we think that is probably what we will find in the sentient Chtorran species . . . when we meet it. We expect that they will be nothing less than the most cunning and sophisticated predator of all Chtorran life forms. And, of course, that implies—given the half-billion-year evolutionary advantage of the Chtorr—that the primary perception that sentience can have of us, specifically our ecology, will be as *prey*. Food. Another kind of snack. At best lunch.

"In fact given that half-billion-year advantage, the rest of the Chtorran ecology can be expected to operate the same way. We are nothing more than fuel for them . . . and probably not even very efficient fuel, at least not as efficient as they're probably used to, which is probably why they need to burn so much of it—us. As a matter of fact, the Chtorran ecology has demonstrated a voraciousness that is nothing less than stunning. Of course, that also suggests that the Chtorran ecology has to generate a prodigious supply of life support to fuel its primary species.

"So, given all of that, we have been making the assumption—and so did Dr. Abbato—that the Chtorran species we've seen so far are just the advance guard of a much greater invasion still to come. The assumption is that whatever agency or sentience is responsible for the infestation depends on these creatures for life support, *and* that we are not going to see the arrival of the next level of infestation until such time as this life-support level is safely and solidly established. As a matter of fact, our whole war effort has been geared not toward eradication—because we don't yet have the resources or the knowledge necessary for that; perhaps someday—but toward destabilizing the interrelationships of the infestation. Finally, that brings us back to Dr. Abbato. And the questions he was left with.

"Dr. Abbato wondered, if all of these assumptions are indeed true, then what is the purpose of the gastropedes in the Chtorran food chain? What *function* do they serve?"

I wondered if she had an answer . . . and if we'd get to it today. I snuck a glance at my watch.

"This is one of those questions that seems very innocuous, until you get into it—then you find that it is actually a major paradigm-shifter. It's forcing us to rethink everything we know, so pay attention here. You too, Lieutenant."

She didn't miss a thing! No more front row seats.

"We've been assuming that the worms are at the top of the Chtorran food chain—that is, this particular subset of it. We've not yet found a worm predator. Considering the voraciousness of the worms, I'm not sure we want to see the next step. We still don't know how to cope with this one. But, if the worms actually are at the top of the food chain, then they would also have to be the sentient species . . . and so far there's no evidence of that. In fact, there's quite a bit of evidence to the contrary. So, we're pretty sure that the worm predator has not yet shown up or established itself. Which brings us back to Dr. Abbato's question. What *are* the worms?

"As a matter of fact, the worms seem to be something of an anomaly even in their own ecology. For instance, what do the worms feed on?"

They eat people, I answered; but I didn't say it aloud.

"We can't identify a prey species," Dr. Fletcher said. "Yes, we've seen the worms eating millipedes and other Chtorran life forms—that's to be expected—but for the most part, the worms have been feeding on the host planet ecology: Cattle, sheep, horses, dogs . . . and humans, unfortunately.

"We've analyzed the protein requirements of an average-sized worm and measured it against the amount of millipedes and other Chtorran life forms it would have to consume to generate that amount of protein, and the ratio is simply unworkable. The worms can't eat enough millipedes and shambler bushes and libbits to survive. These Chtorran life forms are simply not high enough on the chain to be the primary food source for the worms. The worms are not the predators for these Chtorran species, and these species are not the prey for the worms. If this is a food chain as we understand it, *then there are links missing from this food chain!*

"And that brings us to this very important question: If the worms are supposed to be predators, then where—or *what*—are the creatures they are suppose to prey on?

"Dr. Abbato has advanced a very interesting hypothesis—albeit an unpleasant one—that *we* are the intended prey."

Huh? I sat up straight.

Dr. Fletcher paused to allow the murmuring of her audience to die down. She looked out over the room. Abruptly she pointed at someone behind me. "Yes, you have a question."

I turned around in my seat to look. It was a tall man in an army uniform. A grim-looking colonel. He had a tight mouth. I wondered, do colonels get special training to master that expression? He asked, "Can you prove that?"

Dr. Fletcher nodded and rubbed the side of her neck thoughtfully. She looked as if she were debating whether to give the long answer or the short one. She glanced up at the rest of us. "The question is, how do we know that the purpose of the worms is to eat people? The answer is, because that's exactly what they're doing."

"That's not the kind of answer I was expecting," the colonel said.

Dr. Fletcher nodded in agreement. "I know it sounds flip," she said. "I'm sorry, but Dr. Kinsey summed up all animal behavior a long time ago: 'The only unnatural act is the one you can't do.' If the worms couldn't eat Terran life forms, they wouldn't."

I held my tongue—it made sense. Too much sense. The realization was a pain in the gut.

"Dr. Abbato has based a very interesting argument on this fact. He is postulating that this circumstance is *not* accidental. He is suggesting that the *real* purpose of the worms is a cleanup of the top level of the Terran ecology. The worms are *specifically* targeted to eat those humans who have survived the plagues."

My stomach felt like it was contracting into a pinhole. I almost missed what she said next.

"Dr. Abbato thinks that it is unlikely that the worms are food for the next step in the invasion. Anything that could eat a worm would have to be specialized for that purpose—so powerful—that it wouldn't need sentience. Given that thought, Dr. Abbato then had to ask, might not the worms themselves be the top-level sentience behind the invasion?"

I shook my head. I knew the answer to that one. No way. The worms were fearsome, yes. But builders of starships? Not hardly.

Dr. Fletcher continued. "Now, most of you already know that we have not seen any evidence to support that hypothesis, but Dr. Abbato wanted us to consider the possibility for a moment, so we could understand what follows next. Suppose, for just a moment, that most of the gastropedes that we are seeing are actually *wild* Chtorrans. What if these are feral individuals of a species capable of much greater intelligence than we've yet seen demonstrated anywhere? Now that much, we can already verify right here in Oakland. We're seeing a very wide range of behavior in the specimens we've captured live. Some of them are incredibly versatile, while comparable individuals have demonstrated so little intelligence that they seem retarded by comparison. So, we know that the worms are capable of great intelligence . . . even if we're not seeing it realized in the wild."

Feral Chtorrans? That was a new thought. I was wide awake now. My God—what would *sentient* worms be like?

"But," said Dr. Fletcher, in a strong cautioning tone, "the same caveat applies to worms as would apply to any species that might prey on them. The worms are *too* efficient as predators—too specialized. They don't need sentience. So, does that bring us back to where we started? No, not at all."

She paused for deliberate effect. The room was absolutely silent; nobody wanted to miss what she had to say next. "Dr. Abbato suggests that the worms may be a *partner* species, and that ultimately they will serve some kind of support function for the *real* invaders." She paused and looked carefully around the room. "Do you get it? *The worms are domestic animals*! Dr. Abbato guesses that they're the equivalent of sheep dogs; they function as guardians of the host species' property."

Urk. I squirmed uncomfortably in my seat. I didn't want to know this. My belly hurt.

"If this is so," Dr. Fletcher said, "then it means that the worms can be *tamed*." She stopped and looked out over us. "Think about it. Think about the possibilities. If we can tame them . . . perhaps we can turn them into an ally. Perhaps we can even use them as the first line of defense against the sentients who put them here."

I doubted that, but she had my attention. You couldn't have dynamited me out of my chair, stomach pain and all. "The question is, how do you tame a worm?

"But let's get even more basic than that. How do you communicate with a worm? Or even, *can* we communicate with the worms? In fact, even more basic than that: How *intelligent* are the worms? That's what we need to know first . . . and that is the point of today's demonstration."

Huh? Demonstration? Had I slept through something?

She lifted her podium and carried it over to the right side of the stage. "I'll open the curtain in a minute and you can see the specimen we're currently working with. We call it 'Tiny'—you'll see that it's anything but. I think you'll also see that the question of intelligence is very clearly answered by this demonstration.

"Tiny was captured near Mendocino last year. At that time, the specimen massed four hundred and fifty kilos. It is now twice that weight. Tiny is living proof that the gastropedes have an incredible rate of growth. By the way, you'll notice that we try to be very careful not to use 'he' or 'she' when talking about the worms. We're still not certain of their sexuality and we don't want to accidentally prejudice our own perceptions."

She touched a button on her podium and the curtains behind her slid open to reveal a pink-lit chamber. The theater overlooked a deep room, large and almost featureless; we were staring down into it. "The color of the light is halfway between Earth-normal and what we believe to be Chtorr-normal."

Dr. Fletcher touched another button and a panel on the opposite wall of the chamber slid open. There was darkness beyond. "This is Tiny," she said. A medium-sized worm slid out of the darkness, sniffing the air as it moved. It was thick and red. The brain case hump on its back was very pronounced and it held its eyes high and alert. They swiveled back and forth, up and down, scanning the entire space. The worm hesitated, blinked and paused, and looked toward us.

I'd seen worms in viewing theaters before. I always had the impression that they could somehow see through the glass—that they knew we were out here. This time was no different. Tiny looked *curious*. Its long dark arms were still folded against the brain case, but the claws were twitching gently. At a guess, I'd say the creature was a little impatient.

"Now," said Fletcher, "you need to know that Tiny is essentially a child, a youngster, and like all youngsters Tiny likes an occasional treat. With dolphins you use fish, with chimps you use grapes—with Tiny, we use rabbits."

She touched another button and another panel on the wall slid open. There was a fat brown rabbit in a glass case at Tiny's eye level. Below the case was a complicated assembly of rods and gears and latches. In front of that was a panel of assorted knobs and switches; all were thick and heavy-looking. "That's our test setup," said Fletcher. "It's a puzzle. Each one of those knobs and levers controls a different part of the lock. If Tiny operates them all in the right order, the glass case will open and it can have the treat."

Tiny cocked its eyes sideways and looked at the rabbit. The rabbit was huddling in the corner of the case. Tiny cocked its eyes the opposite way and studied the rabbit from a different angle. The gesture gave the worm a floppy, hand-puppet expression. It would have been funny if I didn't know how dangerous a worm could be.

Tiny hunched around to examine the case and the lock and the panel of switches. Through the speakers we could hear the thoughtful clicking of its mandibles. It made a grunting noise and then moved up to the panel of knobs and switches.

The worm unfolded its arms and arched them over its eyes and down to the puzzle. It let its claws drift thoughtfully over the controls of the locks before it selected one.

"For your information," Fletcher said, "Tiny has never seen this puzzle before. It is not the most complicated one we've assembled, but for the purposes of this demonstration we thought we'd keep it short. All of our puzzles are rigged to keep a record of Tiny's moves—and once Tiny goes to work the life-expectancy of the rabbit can be measured in minutes. The longest Tiny has ever taken was half an hour."

Tiny was already hard at work, turning the knobs and observing what effect they had on the machinery, sliding the levers back and forth and peering cock-eyed at the lock.

"As you see," Fletcher said, "Tiny has a high degree of manipulative curiosity. We think this indicates a pretty good spatial sense for all worms—but again, that's only an extrapolation and not to be treated as hard fact."

"A question—" It was the same grim-looking colonel.

"Yes?" Fletcher asked.

"How does a human being compare on these same puzzles?" he asked.

"A good question," Fletcher acknowledged. "We haven't been running direct comparisons, but I can tell you that humans usually take at least forty-five minutes—even on the easy ones."

"So you're saying that these worms are smarter than men?"

"Not at all, Colonel. They just have a highly advanced manipulative sense. They should be very good with tools, But," she added, "so far, we haven't found much evidence that they use tools. At least, not naturally."

"Mm-hm," said the colonel. He wasn't impressed.

A chime sounded then.

"That means Tiny's solved the puzzle," said Fletcher.

The glass case popped open.

Tiny grabbed the rabbit with one dark claw, lifted it up high—it *squealed*, I didn't know rabbits could scream—and Tiny shoved the creature into its gaping maw. There was a wet slobbery crunching sound . . . and then Tiny uttered a soft trill of pleasure and looked around for more.

Behind me I could feel the room stiffening. It was not pleasant to watch a worm eat. I didn't like being reminded.

Dr. Fletcher touched a control and the panel with the puzzle slid closed. She said, "Tiny took eleven minutes to solve this problem. We are now going to reset the puzzle. It'll take about two minutes. Does anyone have any questions so far? Yes— "

A dark man with an Indian accent. "Your work is remarkably advanced, Dr. Fletcher. I am most impressed. May I ask you, how do the worms reproduce?"

"We don't know. I'm sorry, I can't even give you a good guess. There aren't any. Next? Yes—" She pointed.

"Dr. Fletcher, why do they call these things worms?" asked a broad ruddy-faced man. "It looks more like a big pink caterpillar to me. Hell, I've picked bigger caterpillars off my rosebushes back home in Amarillo." There was good-natured laughter in the room.

Even Dr. Fletcher smiled. She replied, "The first reliable sighting of a worm actually occurred about a year before the outbreak of the first plagues. Some of you may even remember. It happened in northern Canada. A troop of scouts was on a three-day outing. They were on horseback. One of the girls was momentarily separated from the rest of the troop. She had stopped to readjust her saddle straps. Something attacked her horse. The rest of the troop heard her screams and started back for her. They met her halfway. She was so hysterical they almost couldn't catch her to calm her down. The most they could get out of her was that it was big, it was dark, it looked like a giant worm, and kept saying, *'Chtorrrr! Chtorrrrrr!'* "

Dr. Fletcher added, "The troop leader and two of the boys went back to investigate. They found the horse had been half-eaten. They did not see a worm. They did not hear it cry, *'Chtorrr!'* The Royal Canadian Mounted Police later searched the surrounding area as thoroughly as it could—it was near the Canadian Rockies—but they found nothing.

"Naturally, the news media played it for laughs. It was a dull summer, so The Giant Canadian Rocky Mountain Worm filled a lot of space on otherwise slow news days. Of course, once the plagues broke out it was forgotten. It wasn't until much later that we realized that this event, and several others like it, were harbingers.

"We know now that the worms have a fairly thick coat of fur and that the name 'worm' is something of a misnomer. We think that what we've seen is another Chtorran adaptation to the planet. The first worms to appear did have very little fur, and they really did look like worms; but over the last three years, we've seen them developing thicker and thicker coats. But what it means, I can't tell you. Actually, it's not even fur—it's sensory antennae. The creature is coated with nerve fibers. So probably what we're seeing is a more—you should pardon the expression—*sensitive* worm. And yes, you're right; they do look like caterpillars."

She glanced down at her podium display. "I see the puzzle has been reset."

I looked down into the chamber again. Tiny was still positioned eagerly in front of the panel. Apparently the worm had learned to anticipate its second chances at the puzzles.

The panel slid open before it. There was a new rabbit in the cage. The puzzle machinery had been reset. Tiny slid quickly forward and began to operate the levers and knobs. Its claws moved with a certainty that hadn't been demonstrated before.

The chime sounded. The cage popped open.

There were gasps in the room.

"Forty-three seconds," Dr. Fletcher said dryly. Tiny was already eating the rabbit. The sound was hideous. I remembered the feeding room in Denver. And the dogs. And the people who liked to watch.

Dr. Fletcher waited in silence until Tiny was finished, then touched another button on her podium and opened the passage back to its cell. The worm slid obediently into it, She remarked, "We've found Tiny to be surprisingly cooperative. It seems to appreciate the discipline." She checked that the passage was clear, then closed the panel, and then the curtain.

She looked calmly out over the room. "I think that pretty well answers the questions: How intelligent is a worm? The answer is *very*. And they learn fast. As you have seen, incredibly so. Our tests with the second specimen confirm that Tiny's responses are *not* atypical. The other worm is even faster than Tiny. And as other specimens become available for testing, we expect to see the same facility in them as well.

"We're beginning another set of tests next Monday, this time with a completely different type of problem. We're going to further explore the worms' ability to conceptualize. Conceptualization is the key to communication. We're clear that if the worms can conceptualize, they can communicate. But let me caution you, don't confuse conceptualization with sentience. Even a dog can conceptualize; Pavlov proved that. And I think most of you will grant that a dog is capable of a certain rudimentary level of communication. When I talk about communication with the worms, I'm talking about that dog-level of communication. I'm talking about *taming*.

"And in fact, that's the very next question that has to be answered. How can we create a relationship with a worm so that it's *willing* to communicate? In other words, how do we *domesticate* a worm? Your consideration of this particular problem will be much appreciated." She glanced at her watch. "The discussion part of this session will take place this afternoon at fifteen hundred hours. Dr. Larson will be mediating. I thank you for your time and your attention."

I went straight to the men's room and threw up.

Q: What do Chtorrans do in Hollywood?
A: Lunch.

Q: What do Chtorrans do in Beverly Hills?
A: Brunch.

Q: What do Chtorrans eat for brunch?
A: A bagel, cream cheese, and Nova Scotia.

7

The Herd

"The universe is full of surprises—most of them nasty."

—SOLOMON SHORT

I found Dr. Fletcher in her office. She looked up as I came in. "Oh, McCarthy. How are you? Thanks for staying awake this morning." She studied me curiously. "Are you all right?"

"I'm fine." I waved her off. "Just an upset stomach."

"Mm-hm," she said. "A lot of people have that problem after they see a worm eat."

I let it pass. "I have a question for you."

"The answer is, 'I don't know.' What's the question?" She glanced at her watch.

"We gassed a nest of worms yesterday afternoon. Four of them. They were all tied together in a knot."

She nodded. "Your videos came in last night."

"Then you saw? Each time we pulled one off, they reacted as if we were breaking a connection."

She frowned, pressing her lips together. Finally, she pushed back from her terminal and swiveled to face me. She leaned forward intently. "Exactly what did it look like to you?"

"It looked like . . . they were writhing in pain. They cried. It was an . . . eerie sound. And two of them actually opened their eyes and looked at us. It was very disturbing," I admitted.

"I'll bet. What do you think was happening?"

"That's what I wanted to ask you."

"I want your observations first," she said.

"Well . . ." I said. "It looked like—I mean, the way they

42

twisted and turned—it made me think of earthworms. Cut in half. Only this was a giant one, cut into four screaming pieces."

"Mm," said Fletcher, noncommittally. "Interesting."

"What do you think it was?"

She shook her head. "I don't. The best thought anyone around here has is that it was something sexual. Some kind of mating behavior, perhaps. And that's why they reacted so strongly. How would you react if somebody interrupted you?"

I blinked. "The worms have four sexes?"

She laughed, a short sharp bark. "Hardly. At least you can't prove it by their chromosomes. So far, all the tissue samples we've examined are genetic nightmares—we have no idea what we're modeling, but we can identify the chromosome structures, and they seem to be pretty much identical from one specimen to the next. No X or Y chromosomes—or equivalents. By that evidence, the worms have only one sex. It's convenient, I guess; it doubles the chances of finding a date for Saturday night, but . . . it sounds boring. Unless of course you're another worm."

"But . . . then that brings up another question—"

She glanced at her watch again. "It'd better be a short one."

"I'm interrupting something?"

"Mm, sort of. I need to go into San Francisco."

"Huh? I thought the city was closed."

"It is. To most people."

"Oh."

"But I'm on the Advisory," she explained.

"Oh," I said again, disappointedly.

Fletcher studied me speculatively. "Family member? Your mother? No—your father, right?"

"My father," I said, nodding. "We never heard one way or the other. And, uh—I know this is silly— "

"No, it isn't," she said.

"—but my father was always such a . . . survivor. I just can't imagine him dead."

"You think he's still alive somewhere?"

"I . . . just wish I knew for certain. That's all."

"Uh-huh," she said. "The truth is, you want to go there and see for yourself. You think you can find him. Right?" She fixed me with a green-eyed gaze. Her manner was startlingly direct. It put me off-balance.

I shrugged. "Yeah," I admitted.

"Mm-hm. You're not the first one, Lieutenant. I see it all the time. People don't believe until they see for themselves. Well, all right."

"Huh?"

"You want to see San Francisco?" She rolled back to her terminal and start typing. "Let me get you a pass. McCarthy . . . James Edward, Lieutenant—" She frowned at the screen. "When'd you get a purple heart?"

"Denver. Remember?"

"Oh, that."

"Hey!" I protested. "I've still got scars. And a bad knee! And besides, it happened the day *after* I was commissioned. It's legal."

"Hmp," she sniffed. "You ruined a perfectly good specimen."

"It lived, didn't it—?"

"Just barely," she said. "Have you ever seen a deranged worm?"

"Lots of times."

"No. Those were *normal*. This one was deranged." Her fingers tapped at the keys. "Huh?" She stopped abruptly. "That's interesting."

"What is?"

"Uh . . . nothing really. I've seen it before. Part of your file is locked." She resumed typing.

"Oh—that's right." I had a hunch what it was. Something to do with Uncle Ira. Colonel Ira Wallachstein. The *late* Colonel Ira Wallachstein. But I didn't explain.

"All right," she said. "You're cleared—under *my* authority. So you have to behave yourself—and do what I tell you, all right?"

"Right."

"Good. We'll make a human being out of you yet." She shrugged out of her lab coat and tossed it at a laundry bin. Underneath, she was wearing a dark brown jumpsuit. It matched the shade of her hair; it was good planning on either her part or the government's.

I followed her to an elevator. She flashed a key card at the scanner. The door chimed and slid open. The elevator dropped us downward; I couldn't tell how many floors, though. There were no numbers to watch.

Fletcher had to flash her card before two more doors, and then we were on a ramp leading down to the garage. "That one's mine," she said, pointing toward a Jeep. How could she tell? They all looked alike to me. She walked around the front of it while I climbed into the passenger's seat.

"Why all this security?" I asked.

She shook her head. "It's political, I think. Something to do with the Fourth World Alliance. We won't trade information until they open their borders to inspection teams. I think it's a mistake. In the long run, we're only hurting ourselves." She eased the Jeep forward, and pointed it toward the exit. As we rolled out past the final security booth, she added in a quieter tone, "Things are very . . . *cautious* around here. Especially right now." She glanced over at me. "Mm, let me say it this way. The agency does appreciate the cooperation of the military—especially the Special Forces—but, ah . . . there is still a certain amount of individual chafing. The military has everything tied up a little too tight. We're all of us in a great big bag marked TOP SECRET."

I considered what she said. She was being remarkably candid. It was a compliment to me. I replied carefully, "It certainly doesn't make sense from a scientific point of view. We should be sharing information, not hiding it."

Fletcher looked like she wanted to agree. "It's Dr. Zymph's idea. She started out in Bio-War, you know, so her whole career has been about secrecy. I guess she still thinks it's necessary. But it makes it awfully hard to work." Abruptly, she added, "Sometimes I don't know what that woman is up to. She scares me."

Dr. Zymph was the chairman of the Ecological Agency. I looked at Fletcher, surprised. "I thought you admired her."

"I used to. But that was before she became a politician. I liked her better as a scientist."

I didn't reply to that. Fletcher's comments bothered me. I'd first seen Dr. Zymph in action in Denver, and I'd been impressed by her. It was . . . disconcerting to hear this.

The road turned west and then northward. To our left was the metallic wash of San Francisco Bay. The sun was glinting oddly off the surface. The light struck colored sparks.

"The water's a funny color," I said.

"We had an episode of sea sludge," Fletcher said matter-of-factly. "We had to oil and burn it. The bay's still recovering."

"Oh."

"We're waiting to see if it comes back. We think we may have licked it, but it's only a small victory."

"Um . . . you said something before. About the worm in Denver. You said it was deranged. What did you mean by that?"

"Well, wouldn't you be deranged if someone carved you up like that? You shot out its eyes, you turned its mouth into jelly, and you broke both its arms. That does not make for a healthy world-view. And after its fur fell out, the poor thing went autistic—"

"Its fur fell out?"

"Oh, right. That report got squelched. You couldn't have seen it. As if its injuries weren't enough, the poor beast started throwing symptoms. We thought it was infected and put it on Gerromycin. Its fur came out in patches. It was an ugly sight; it really did look like a big red bristly worm."

"*All* the fur came off?"

She shook her head. "No, only the lighter strands. You know that the fur is sensory nerves, don't you? We figured out what happened afterwards. Gerromycin can damage human nervous tissue too. Apparently the pink strands are extremely sensitive. Anyway . . . after that, the gastropede showed as much intelligence as a Terran earthworm. It just lay where it was and quivered and twitched." She shook her head again, remembering. "It was a very queasy thing to watch."

"How come we didn't see that report? That could be a weapon!"

Fletcher sighed and quoted, " 'Information on ways to combat or resist the Chtorran infestation is not to be made available to any nonallied nations or their representatives.' That's the policy—at least until the Fourth World Alliance signs the Unification Treaty."

"That doesn't make sense."

"It does politically. When the worms—or whatever else— become too big a problem for the Fourth World member nations to handle by themselves, a signature on a paper might not seem too high a price for survival. Right now, they'd rather be right. Are you surprised?"

"And you agree with it—?"

She shook her head. "No, but I understand it. The Unification Powers are playing politics with the war. Did you expect us *not* to? Read your history. We have twenty years of grudges to work off. At least. So, now there are people who are willing to let the worms chew on the Fourth World Alliance for a while."

"And in the meantime, the infestation gets a more solid foothold—?"

"Right. Some people have their priorities way up their fundaments. Anyway," she added, "Gerromycin would not be an effective weapon."

"Why not?"

"You wouldn't like the aftereffects. Two or three weeks later, the worm's fur started to come back in—only very dark. Mostly red and purple and black strands. That's when the worm started getting violent. The more dark fur came in, the more violent it became. Obviously, its perception of the world was shifting. We finally had to put it down, it was so badly deranged. We weren't sure we could contain it any longer." She clucked her tongue. "You think the worms are nasty now? Infect a few and see what happens."

I didn't answer. It was too much to think about. I'd known the fur was a kind of nerve. Our gas had been based on that fact. But why should the *type* of nerve cells make a worm peaceful or violent?

"Do you have anyone studying worm fur?" I asked.

She shook her head. "I'd like to, but we're already overextended. There's about fifteen other areas we want to look at first."

"It seems to me that it's important to the question of tamability."

"Mm-hm," she agreed. "That's why we're looking for albinos. . . . The Jeep was slowing as it approached the Oakland Bay Bridge. Fletcher flashed her card at a scanner and the barricades slid open for us. There was a huge advisory sign hanging over the empty toll booths: BY ORDER OF THE MILITARY GOVERNOR OF CALIFORNIA, THE CITY OF SAN FRANCISCO IS HEREBY DECLARED A BLACK ZONE RESTRICTED AREA. ENTER AT YOUR OWN RISK.

"That's reassuring," I said as we rolled under it.

"It's safe," she said.

"What makes you so sure?"

"I told you. I'm on the Advisory Board. San Francisco is currently zoned as unfit for anything but politics."

"I beg your pardon?"

"It's another one of the Agency's good ideas. San Francisco could be a very good Safe City. It's surrounded on three sides by water. Unfortunately, there're a lot of ruins that have to be cleared—and we've got militant preservationists second-guessing every lamppost. So, the governor locked them out. They pay me ten K a month to swear that the city's still a plague reservoir."

"Is it?"

"The truth is . . . yes, it is."

We reached the crest of the bridge then and the city spread out before us—what was left of it. The sight was ghastly. San Francisco was a skeleton. The city had been gutted. The stump of the Trans-America Tower gaped like a broken tooth. Coit Tower still stood, but it was blackened by fire. I didn't recognize many other buildings. Where they should have been there was rubble and ruin. "Oh, my God—" I choked on the words.

"I know," she agreed.

"I've seen the pictures," I gasped. "But—I had no idea—this is *horrible*."

"It gets everybody that way, the first time. I still get a tight throat when I come across the bridge."

"There's . . . nothing left."

"Firestorm," she said. The single word explained everything.

Fletcher unlocked the steering wheel and pulled it into position before her, putting the Jeep back on manual control. Autopilots were fine on paved roads. They had problems with rubble. We rolled down off the bridge in an eerie silence.

"Do you remember City Hall?" she asked.

"Uh-huh. There was a big plaza in front."

"It's still there," she said. "But not much of City Hall."

She steered carefully through the steel and brick canyons of lower Market Street. The fires had burned themselves out here. But even so, there were places where the buildings looked blasted, even *melted* from the heat. I noticed a sign that said, SAN FRANCISCO WARLOCK ADMINISTRATION, and wondered if there were any warlocks left in California at all.

We'd thought the plagues were over. We'd come down from the hills, out of our hiding places. We thought we had vaccines. The government said it was safe. We had all the best excuses to return to the cities.

But the plagues weren't over, and the vaccines only worked sometimes, and the cities still weren't safe. The plagues came back stronger than ever.

There was panic. There were fires.

There was a firestorm.

And when it was over, San Francisco was gone.

It was like driving through a graveyard.

"I thought you said the military was working over here," I said.

"Most of the work is still off the corridor," Fletcher said. "And a lot of it is being done by robots." Suddenly, she pointed. "Look, there—"

"What?" And then I saw. She was pointing at a zombie. She slowed the Jeep.

He was papery and thin, naked except for a ragged blanket he wore like a poncho. There was almost no flesh at all on his bones. He looked like he was a hundred years old; it was impossible to guess what his real age might have been. He was gray and gaunt; his white hair hung down to his shoulders in a greasy mat.

The zombie's face looked mechanically animated; the expression was curiously empty, but the features were in constant motion. The mouth worked continually. The jaw floated up and down, releasing a thin dribble of spittle. The blackened tongue stuck out absently, like a retarded child's, then pulled in again. The cheeks sucked in and puffed out. The face moved as if no one wore it anymore. It looked like a fish sucking the glass wall of an aquarium.

The zombie turned and looked at us then—and for just an instant it was as if whoever might have once lived inside that body was struggling to animate it once again. The expression became momentarily curious, the eyelids fluttered like trapped moths. And then the gaze went confused again. He seemed to be fading in and out of focus, and he had trouble balancing himself as well. He caught himself on the front of the jeep and stared through the windshield, shifting back and forth between Fletcher and myself. He blinked and blinked again as he stared at us. His face wrinkled in puzzlement.

"He looks like he's trying to recognize us," I whispered.

Fletcher nodded. "He can't. He's lost his timebinding ability."

"Huh?"

"A zombie exists only in the present. He only knows something exists if he's looking at it."

As if in confirmation, the zombie's puzzlement was turning to pain. He looked like he wanted to cry but didn't remember how. He fluttered his fingers toward Fletcher, then toward me. Then abruptly he refocused on his hand, a gray claw-like thing on the end of his arm, as if he'd never seen it before. He forgot about us, blinking in confusion. His hand dropped. He turned and moved away without purpose, a soulless thing again. He shambled off toward the west.

"Is that it?" I said. "I've seen zombies before. That's what happens to the walking wounded when they sink to that place below despair. Once they hit the zombie level, you can't bring them back."

Fletcher looked like she wanted to say something in reply to that. Instead, she eased the car forward again.

As we moved up Market Street, we began to see other shambling zombies. Most were heading westward. All of them were thin and dirty. Most wore rags, or less. Their movements were disorganized, fragmented, and surreal. They looked like they'd wandered out of Auschwitz or Belsen or Buchenwald—except for their expression. The concentration-camp survivors had at least had *life* in their eyes, an awareness of the horror and hopelessness of their situation. The zombies had nothing.

The zombies were . . . detached. From the world, from everything—from their own bodies. They looked curious, and their eyes moved in quick, jerky glances; but they had no focus of attention. Their faces were empty. They moved like palsy victims.

Fletcher slowed the Jeep then to steer around the rubble. Most of the zombies were ignoring us. A dirty creature—male or female, it was impossible to tell—shambled by us. It trailed one hand across the hood of the car. Its expression was . . . almost happy.

"That one looks stoned," I said.

"Mm-hm," Fletcher nodded. She angled the Jeep between two piles of bricks and up a side street. I recognized the remains of Brooks Hall on the left. The marquee said simply, SAINT FRANCIS WRITHES AGAIN. I wondered who'd put that message up.

We pulled up facing a wide dirty field. At the far end of it, what was left of City Hall loomed like a broken castle. You could still make out its broad stone steps. This had once been a great plaza; now it was a gray expanse of dust and broken concrete. Nothing grew here any more.

"Okay," I said. "Now what?"

"Now we get out and look around."

"Huh?"

"It's safe." She patted my hand and climbed out of the jeep. I had no choice but to follow.

There were . . . people . . . in the plaza. They were pinker and somewhat healthier looking than the ones we'd passed on Market Street. Zombies? Not quite. Many of them were fairly young—in their twenties and thirties. There were some teenagers, only a few children. There were very few beyond middle age.

Most of the bodies were haphazardly dressed. Or maybe that should have been haphazardly *un*dressed. They moved without regard for their clothing. It was as if someone else had hung clothes on them, or they had draped themselves with whatever was handy. What clothing they did have seemed to be for warmth, not modesty.

"So?" I turned to Fletcher. "I've seen this before too. These are walking wounded."

"Are they?" she asked.

"Well, sure—" I started to say. And then stopped. I looked at her. "They're something else?"

"Go find out," she pointed. "Try talking to them."

I looked at her as if she were crazy. Talk to them?

"It's safe," she reassured.

I turned back and studied the milling bodies. They moved without purpose, but they didn't shamble. They just sort of . . . moved.

I picked out a young male. Maybe he was sixteen. Maybe he was twenty-five. I couldn't tell. He had long brown hair that hung past his shoulders. He was wearing an old gray shirt, nothing else. He had large dark eyes. He'd been very attractive once.

I walked up to him and touched his shoulder. He turned toward me with a halfway expectant expression. His eyes were bottomless. He studied my face for a puzzled moment, then, not finding anything, started to turn away.

"Wait," I said.

He turned back.

"What's your name?"

He blinked at me.

"Your name?" I repeated.

His mouth began to work. "Nay—nay—nay—?" he said. He was trying to imitate my sounds. He smiled at the noises he made. "Nay—nay—nay—nay—nay—nay—" he repeated.

I put my hands on his shoulders. I looked into his eyes, trying to create a sense of *relationship* through eye contact. The boy tried to look away. I pulled his face back to mine and stared into his eyes again. "No. Stay with me," I said firmly.

He blinked at me uncertainly.

"Who are you?" I asked him.

"Bub," he said.

"Bub? Bob?"

"Bub—bub—bub—" He smiled happily. "Bub—bub—bub—bub—"

"No," I said. "No." I pulled his face back to mine again.

"No—no—no—" he said. "No—no—no—" And then, "Bub—bub—bub . . . bub—bub—bub . . ."

I let go of his shoulders and let him wander away, still bubbling. I turned back to Fletcher. "All right. What?"

She shook her head.

"Uh-uh. Keep going."

This time, I chose a little girl. She was wearing only a pair of panties. What was it about these people and clothing, anyway?

She was very thin, very underdeveloped. She could have been a boy.

I stopped her and looked into her face. She was as blank as the others.

"Who are you?" I asked. "What's your name?"

"My name . . . ?" she said. "My name?" She blinked. Like the boy, her expression was uncertain and puzzled.

"That's right. What's your name?"

"My name, my name . . . is Auntie Mame. My game is fame, my game, my name, my name—" She babbled happily at me, smiling with delight at the sound of her own words. She'd figured out the game. "The game is name is fame is lame—"

I let go of her and turned her back toward the crowd.

"All right," I said to Fletcher, "I got it. They're not zombies. You can interact with them. But they've lost most of their sense of speech, so they're not walking wounded either. They're an intermediate step. Is that all?"

"Part of it," she said.

"What is it?" I asked. "A plague effect? Brain burn fever?"

"Brain burn fever is fatal," Fletcher said grimly. "If this is a plague effect, it's something we can't identify. See that fellow there?" She pointed at a tall beefy man. "He used to be one of the sharpest biologists at the university. He was at the South Pole when the plagues broke out. He was never exposed. He was fully vaccinated before he returned. If it's a plague effect, it's a mental one."

"How did he . . . end up here?" I asked.

She lowered her voice. "He was studying them—" She waved her hand to indicate the wandering bodies. "He thought he could see patterns of herding—something like the Emperor Penguins. He spent a lot of time living with them, moving among them. One day, he didn't come back. When we finally got worried, we came down here and found him wandering around with the rest of them. He couldn't talk much more than they could. He'd become one of them."

I thought about that. Before I could ask the question, Fletcher said, "We're not in any danger. It takes prolonged exposure."

"Oh," I said. I was not reassured.

There were several hundred bodies in the plaza now. I stood there for a moment, watching them, trying to figure out why they seemed so . . . *interesting*.

"There's something about them," I said. "I can't figure it out, but there's something going on here. The minute you look at them, you know that they're not *normal*. What is it?" I asked Fletcher. "What's the signal I'm picking up?"

"You tell me," she said. "Tell me what you see."

"I see bodies. Pink bodies. That's part of it, isn't it? They don't wear much clothing."

"By summer, they'll all be naked—but that's not it either. San Francisco has seen crowds of naked bodies before. The average Freedom Day Festival has less clothing than this."

"I wouldn't know. My dad never let me come."

"Too bad. Anyway, nudity is only part of it. What else?"

"Um . . . their skin. When I touched them, their skin felt slick. Not quite oily. Kind of smooth. *Different*."

"Mm-hm, but that's not the cue either. You don't go around touching people to see if they're different."

"Right." I studied the milling crowd again.

"I'll give you a hint," she said. "What's *missing*?"

"Missing? Mmmm. Talking. There's not a lot of talking. A few of them are babbling to themselves, but it's not loud and offensive, not like a street lady. They're babbling like babies amused with the sounds they're making—wait a minute." A thought was beginning to form. "What's missing is . . . *intensity*. They have a quality of innocence. They're like children, aren't they? It's as if they've given up all the stuff they've ever learned about how to be a grownup so they could go back to the innocence of children. Right?"

"Go on," she encouraged, but she was smiling. I was on the right track.

"They can feel pain or anger . . . but they don't carry it around with them. Adults do. We get hurt or angry and we carry it around with us for weeks, handing it out to everybody we meet. Did you ever watch *Aroundabout* on TV? One time they did nothing but photograph faces at random on a city street. Almost every single person they showed looked like they were wearing a mask. Their expressions were all pinchy and tight. But these . . . people—I guess that's what I should call them—these people, their faces are *relaxed*. They've given up the pain—"

I realized something else and shut up suddenly.

"What was that?" Fletcher asked.

"Um, nothing, really. I was just realizing how sad it must be to have to give up your intelligence to be free from pain." I looked at her. Her face was hurting with the same realization. Her eyes were moist. "Is this what you wanted me to see?"

"Oh, no," she said. She swallowed and looked uncomfortable. "It hasn't even started yet."

Make your own Chtorran joke:

Q: _____ ?
A: Lunch.

8

Lunch

"*The great mass of men lead lives of quiet
domestication.*"

—SOLOMON SHORT

I looked at the bodies again. "This is a herd, isn't it?"

"Mm-hm," she said. "Last summer, it numbered over twelve
hundred. During the winter, it fell to about three. Now it's
building up again. We've got about seven-fifty here. This is the
largest herd in Northern California."

"What happened to the others?"

"Most of them died," she said noncommittally. "A few wander
off every night. The pattern is this: You go from shock to being
one of the walking wounded. There's hope for the walking
wounded. But only if you get quick treatment. Otherwise, you just
keep sinking.

"There's an instinct at work here. People seek out crowds,
activity. So, this—" she pointed, "—is inevitable. The walking
wounded gather in herds. I guess it's an illusion of safety. Some
of them, though, are so far gone they can't even survive in a herd.
Dropouts become zombies. The life expectancy of a zombie is six
weeks. I'm surprised it's that long."

I looked at her. "You've been studying this, haven't you?"

She nodded. "You may be looking at the future of the human
race. At the rate this herd is growing, we could hit twenty-five
hundred by July. If that happens, we expect it to split into two
herds." She pointed across the plaza. "See those two trucks over
there? Those are the—you should pardon the expression—
cowboys. They keep the herd under control. We used to keep the
herd at Golden Gate Park, but we were losing too many every

night, so we moved them down here so we could put them to bed in Brooks Hall."

The noon sun was getting warmer. I noticed that more and more of the herd members were discarding what little clothing they wore.

Fletcher followed my glance. "Yeah," she said. "It happens. We used to have a couple of little old ladies who did nothing but follow the herd around putting their clothes back on them. There's one of them now. She finally gave up."

She was pointing at a little wrinkled old lady, wearing nothing but a smile and her varicose veins. She looked like a road map of Pennsylvania. She was carrying a parasol to shield herself from the sun.

"Sometimes, I think Jennie's faking," Fletcher said, "But you'll never get her to admit it. It probably doesn't matter anyway."

"Are any of them faking?" I asked.

She shook her head. "It's not something you can fake for long. Every so often we have civilians sneak in here, thinking they could take advantage of the herd—you know, thinking it would be nothing but a sexual free-for-all. But . . . something happens to them. They don't leave. You can only fake it for so long. Even the faking is part of the process of . . . enrollment." And then she added, "On the other hand, they could *all* be faking—but even if that were true, this would still be a *real* phenomenon. Whatever it is, we don't really understand it yet."

"I'm beginning to see a pattern," I said. "There's something very fascinating going on here. But just standing around watching isn't enough. It's like a . . . an anthropological black hole. The closer you get, the more likely you're going to get sucked in."

"Mm-hm," Fletcher nodded. "That's part of the problem. This herd started out as just another group of walking wounded. But now, it's even pulling in the observers too. Almost everyone who gets close. The cowboys aren't allowed to work more than one day a week, and even that might be too much exposure."

She added, "This herd is one of the main reasons why we're keeping the city closed. We don't know what else to do. We've even discussed . . . euthanasia."

"You're kidding."

She shook her head. "Nope. I'm not. I've argued against it, of course. There's something here we need to understand." She held out a hand to me. "Come on."

"Huh? Where are we going?"

"We're going for a walk among them. It's safe."

I stared at her. "You've just told me that people are getting sucked into this herd every day, and now you want me to walk through it?"

"I'll be with you."

"That doesn't reassure me."

She held up her wrist and pointed to her watch. "Set your sleep alarm. If you start to fade, the buzzer will wake you up. I promise you, it takes more than an hour's exposure to enchant you."

"Enchant?"

"Uh-huh. That's the word. Enchant. You'll see."

I grumbled something about other people's good ideas and cued my own watch. When I looked up, Fletcher was already heading toward the plaza. I hurried to catch up.

"Shh," she said. "Don't run. It upsets them. We had a stampede once. It was awful. Just stand still for a minute and get the feeling of being in the herd. Don't talk. Just look and listen."

We stood there together, side by side, turning slowly and watching the other bodies circling around us. Their faces were *content*. It was unnerving. I felt uncomfortable. I could feel the sweat trickling down from my armpits.

The sun was hot. It felt good. I loosened the top two buttons of my shirt.

There was a naked girl standing in front of me, studying me. She had red hair and a dirty face. She could have been Peter Pan's little sister. She was smiling, but she looked puzzled too. She stepped toward me cautiously and reached out a hand. She touched my shirt. She fingered the cloth. She sniffed it. She looked up at me and sniffed me. She touched my face, let her fingers trail down past my chin to my neck and my chest. She stopped at my shirt buttons and studied them. It didn't take her long to figure it out. She unbuttoned the next button. She smiled with delight at her own cleverness.

She took one of my hands in hers and studied my fingers. She turned my hand over and over. She sniffed it. She must have liked what she smelled, because she licked my fingers. She took my hand and stroked her breasts with my fingertips. Her bosom was small, her nipples were hard.

She let go of my hand; my fingers stayed where they were. She searched my face again, curiously.

Abruptly, she stepped away from me and dropped to the ground. She got down on her hands and knees and presented her rump to me. She looked back at me and smiled and wriggled her butt.

"Uh—" I looked at Fletcher. I could feel myself flushing with embarrassment.

"Go ahead," Fletcher said, nodding in the girl's direction, "if you've a mind for that sort of thing. It's only the first step toward joining the herd."

"I'll pass for now, thank you," I said.

"Most men do. The first time, anyway."

"What do you mean by that?"

She shrugged. "She's communicating on a very direct level. Much more direct that most of us are used to. *That* is very difficult to ignore. It is almost impossible to forget."

The girl looked back at me again, puzzled. She got up from the ground and looked at me again. She looked hurt. She wandered away sadly. I felt sorry for her, but a moment later, she was presenting herself to a teenage boy. The boy mounted her from the rear and took her quickly. She gasped and laughed; so did he.

"From an anthropological point of view—" I began, but my voice cracked suddenly. My throat was dry. I cleared my throat and tried again. "Excuse me. I was going to say that what we're seeing is somewhat atypical behavior."

"At the very least," said Fletcher, tongue in cheek.

"I mean—if you study ape and monkey colonies. Promiscuity isn't very often seen, is it?"

"Not like this. But maybe this isn't atypical for a human-ape colony. We don't know. We don't have enough data on human herds yet. My own theory—" She stopped herself. The boy had finished abruptly, or lost interest. He had wandered away, leaving the girl curled up on the ground giggling softly to herself.

"Go on," I prompted.

"Well . . ." Fletcher said slowly. "I was going to say, my own theory is that what we're seeing here is a . . . distillation, or a reflection, of our own culture, but returned to the ape level."

"Is that why they're all so horny?"

She nodded. "It could be. Our culture tends to be oversexed. These . . . apes . . . have learned the lesson well." And then she said, "I also think . . . that they're still acting out the traumas of culturization—the adaptations that the human animal has had to make for sentience. Even though they seem to have given up sentience, they're still acting the roles, the learned behaviors."

"I'm not sure I understand that."

"All right. Try it this way. Consciousness has goals of its own. Consciousness perverts instinctive behavior to accomplish those goals. On the species level, we're all mad—because we've suppressed our natural tribal behaviors to try to be sentient. Most of us are so busy *pretending* to be sentient that we're deliberately tuning out our own bodies, our own feelings. We're detached from ourselves. Most so-called 'civilized' human beings act as if they're living by remote control. They operate like machines.

"I think what's happening here is a kind of a . . . reaction. The plagues so damaged the world-view of these people that they gave up consciousness. Sentience didn't work any more—so they abandoned it. What we're seeing here is the remaining tribal behavior. The expression of it is no longer covert. It's all out in the open now. They have no past or future, no timebinding. They're just *here*, feeling. When they feel sad, they feel sad . . . until they're through feeling sad; then they stop and feel something else."

She stopped herself abruptly, and looked at me. "In a way, they're lucky. When we're sad, we carry it around with us forever. Most of us are still dragging around the dead bodies of our past." She looked sad for just the briefest instant, then buried it again under a facade of business-as-usual. "Come on—this way."

"Huh?"

She pointed.

Three huge trucks were grumbling slowly into the plaza. The herd began shifting toward them. I thought of cattle heading toward a pasture. The trucks came to a halt. The backs of the trucks opened, and out of each fell a dozen huge bales of . . . something yellow.

I glanced at Fletcher again.

"Lunch," she explained. "You want some?"

"Huh?"

"Come on." She took my hand and led me through the crowd. It wasn't difficult to push our way through the bodies. I noticed they had a strong rank smell to them and mentioned it casually.

"Herd odor," said Fletcher. "I think that's one of the ways they keep together. After a while, you get so you can find the herd by its scent alone."

We pushed up near one of the bales. It looked like it was made out of big pieces of yellow farfel. It smelled yeasty and buttery.

"It's impregnated with vitamins and antibiotics and God knows what else," Fletcher said.

As we watched, the herd members gathered around the bale and began to pull chunks away from it like pieces of bread. They carried their food away with them, not eating until they found a quiet place. Then they sat and chewed quietly. Their expressions remained blank. The entire process was orderly and remarkably quiet.

Some of them sat with their mates or their companions and fed each other with their fingers. I saw a mother feeding her child—at least, I assumed it was her own child, but it might not have been. Two teenage girls shared their meal, giggling. An old man squatted alone and chewed thoughtfully.

A big bear-like man was carrying a piece of the loaf big enough to feed at least a dozen people. Another man came up to him and ripped part of it away. The bear-like man did not protest; in fact, he anchored himself to help rip the piece in half.

There was no hostility or greed or impatience anywhere in the herd. They moved like cattle. They chewed like cattle.

"Is that stuff drugged at all?" I asked.

She shook her head. "Not any more. We tried it once. It only made them crazy. Crazier. They don't need drugs."

One of the cowboys on the back of the truck waved to us then. "Hey, Fletch!" he called. "Are you here again?"

Fletcher grinned and waved back. "Howya doin', Jake?"

"I'm fine," he said. "But you better watch yourself, or your tits'll be hanging out in the sun with the rest of 'em."

Fletch grinned and waved back. "Not till the food gets a little better. I'm not ready to give up my steaks yet."

The cowboy pulled a big chunk off a bale. "Well, here—try it. We've changed the recipe again. Maybe you'll like this enough to join us." He tossed the bread-like mass across to us.

I stepped forward and plucked the stuff out of the air. I turned and offered it to Fletcher. She pulled a smaller piece off the mass and tasted it. "Not bad," she called, "but it's still not sirloin." She held out the rest of the piece for me to eat; she practically pushed it into my mouth. It was soft, warm, fresh, and buttery. And it required just enough chewing to be . . . pleasant. I took another bite.

"Be careful, Jim." Fletcher took the rest of the loaf away. "That's one of the ways people get started," She handed it to a sad-looking boy who'd been hanging back from the main mass of the feeders. He brightened immediately and scampered off to a deserted place to begin eating. "That's Weepy Willie," she said. "He prefers to beg. God knows what he was like when he was human."

She shook her head sadly. "There are a lot of ways to get sucked in. Mostly, you just get tired of day-to-day living. Just being responsible for yourself can be exhausting sometimes." She stopped and looked at me. "This whole thing is dangerous. It sucks energy. Even studying it is dangerous. Any attention at all we give to it just feeds it. It's a kind of social cancer. It grows and it eats. It turns healthy cells into sick ones—and then the sick cells have to be tended, so more healthy cells have to be exposed. It's a never-ending process."

"I've seen the reports," I said.

"There's something else, though. Something that hasn't been in the reports—because we don't know what to make of it. That's what I want you to see." Fletcher brushed her dark hair back from her eyes. She looked grim.

I asked, "All right, so when do I see this whatever-it-is?"

"Not too much longer. But come on, I want you away from the center. It can get a little . . . overwhelming." She led me back toward our Jeep. "You're already a little glassy-eyed."

"Huh?"

"I said—never mind. Stop here. Tell me a joke."

"What?"

"Tell me a joke," she repeated.

"Um, why did the Chtorran cross the road?"

"Because it was shorter than going around. Tell me one I haven't heard."

"Why—?"

"I'm trying to find out if you're still home. Humor is a good test—it requires intellectual ability. Tell me another."

"Right. Uh, what does a Chtorran do when he wakes up in the morning?"

She shrugged. "What?"

"Says grace."

She chuckled once and nodded. "You're okay." She turned me to face the milling herd.

"All right. Now what?"

"We wait."

We didn't have to wait long. Lunch was over. Now, the herd-members were beginning to play among themselves. Some of the younger members were playing a loose form of tag. They reminded me of puppies. Run and chase, tumble and wrestle. But they played in silence, only occasionally yipping or barking. There were no words.

The herd was beginning to be more active now. There was more pairing occurring—some of it was sexual, some of it was not. I noticed that the coupling was remarkably casual. There was little regard for age or sex. A middle-aged female was playing with a teenage male. A male who looked about twenty-five was holding hands with a girl about thirteen. There were several homosexual pairs too, both male and female.

But there were other gatherings that looked to be specifically nonsexual. A cluster of youngish children were milling together and babbling at each other, "Ba-ba-ba-ba-ba-ba . . ." Other groups were beginning to form now, clusters of three or five or even more. Several of the bull males were circling the edges of the plaza, herding the straggling members inward.

"It's starting, isn't it?" I said.

"Uh-huh."

I watched, fascinated, as the herd began to solidify as a mass. The couples who had been initiating sex play were breaking off now to join the clustering masses. I found it hard to see the herd-members as people any more. They were . . . pink apes. Animals.

I shrugged. I was getting the eeriest feeling. I touched Fletcher's arm. "This is . . . weird," I said. "I feel like an *alien* here. I feel like they're the human race and I'm the outsider."

I didn't let go of her arm. I needed to be touching her. The herd was clustering thicker now. They were becoming a milling compact mass.

"Listen—"

The sound was formless at first. They were murmuring among themselves. Individual voices floated above the rest. But the murmuring was starting to blend now and the myriad voices were disappearing into an all-pervasive atonal chorus. There was no pattern to it, no sense of harmony or rhythm. It was just a grand and powerful, all-consuming sound. And it was growing.

It was a fascinating sound, full of hints and meaning. An annoying sound. Reasonless and empty. Steady in its intensity, but uneven in its components. The voices whispered—like the voices in my dreams—if only I could hear what they were saying. . . .

I said, "It sounds and feels like the rumble of the machinery that runs underneath the world. It sounds . . . like . . ." Like the song of the worms.

"Jim, you should hear your voice," Fletcher said.

"Huh?"

"There's a tremble in it—just like that note out there. You're

being affected." She caught herself. "And so am I." I could hear
the excitement rising in her voice too.

"But this is—incredible!" I said, turning to her—

"Are you all right?"

I nodded. "I'm fine. It's just . . . I can feel that note
resonating throughout my whole body." I was still holding her
arm. "I can feel myself rumbling with it. I want to echo it. Do you
feel it? It feels like . . . we're included, like . . . we're a part
of the herd too. . . ."

"We *are* a part of the herd," she said. "We're the part of the
human herd that observes itself. We're the parts of the tribe that
broke free so we could look back from the outside."

"But we can't stay out here forever, can we?" But she didn't
hear me. I let go of her arm—

"That phenomenon"—she was pointing excitedly, "—just
might be the place where we experience *home*. You know, the
home that we're always longing to return to, but we can never
find? That just might be it." She grabbed my hand and forced me
to look at her eyes. "Whatever 'space of consciousness' is being
created over there—it *includes* us too! Just watching is being part
of the herd! And to the extent that we can recognize ourselves in
that mass, we're tuned into it. Do you see now why it's so
dangerous?"

"Mm-hm. Dangerous. . . ." I wondered why she was shouting. Why was she so intense? She didn't have to be. It was nice
out here. The herd seemed pleasant enough.

"It's our sentience—our awareness of self—that allows us to
stay separate. That chorus is a—a calling, Jim. It's a communication without symbols. To listen to it, you have to abandon
concept and listen instead for . . . sensation. It's too powerful!
It upsets, it annoys, it fascinates, it *enchants*. It can't help but
have an effect on us, the way it washes over us. We
just . . . can't allow ourselves to . . . to . . ." she began to
trail off, ". . . let ourselves . . . Jim . . . ?"

I was glad that she had stopped talking. Her words didn't make
any sense any more, anyway. They were just noises strung
together. She was keeping me from concentrating on the sound of
the rest of the herd. It was an incredible noise they were making.
All of them together were making pattering noises. I'd heard this
noise somewhere before, as if from a time before I was born. All
the voices in the world, talking about something in words that
weren't words because words hadn't been invented yet.

My mouth was moving with them. I made mumbling noises of my own, trying to . . . *understand*. Trying to be a part. . . .

What was happening here?

Happening. *It* was happening. Herding. Calling. All the voices singing. Laughing. Boys and boys together. Girls and girls. Boys and boys and girls and girls and all of us. Calling. Someone was holding my hand, I couldn't move forward. Calling. The calling was getting louder. "What?"

Someone was pulling me backward. My feet moved. Moved. Kept moving.

I stumbled. Someone grabbed me, held me up. Someone was saying something. I knew that sound. All purple. *"Shim! Shim!"*

He was calling me—

—face hurt suddenly. Ringing. A slap.

Not shim. Jim.

Me.

"Who?"

"Jim!"

"Who . . . ?" I couldn't finish the thought.

"Stay with me," the voice said. "Jim!"

"Um . . . I have to know who . . . ?"

"Who what?"

"There was someone—I was . . . someone was calling me—"

"I was. I've been saying your name to you over and over."

"No, it wasn't you. It was someone else. Someone from another—" I rubbed my head. Hard. I didn't have a word for the other *place*. I just knew it wasn't *here*. "I almost . . . had it. . . ."

"Jim!"

"If I could just . . ."

"Jim, stay with me. Jim, look at me."

I looked at Fletcher. Her face was red and intense.

I said, "I was—fading . . . wasn't I?"

"You were *gone*."

"I—I'm sorry." I blinked. I looked around. "Where are we?"

"Market Street."

"Market . . . Street . . . ?"

She nodded.

"Oh, my God. . . ." I buried my face in my hands. I was overcome. "I had no idea it was that powerful. Jeez—" I glanced back. "Are they still going?"

"They're just breaking up."

"Oh." There was disappointment in my voice. I could hear it myself.

"Jim, stay here. Stay with me."

"I am. I am."

"What was it—? Describe it." She was forcing me to look at her. Look into her eyes. "Can you describe it?"

"We . . . don't have the words for it. . . ." I pointed in the direction of the herd. *"They* have the words. The words are . . . they . . ."

"Stay with me, Jim!"

"What they're doing . . . it's—" I grabbed her hand. "No, don't slap me again. Let me finish this. There are . . . words beyond words. I know that doesn't make sense, but it does if you've let yourself hear them." I let the thoughts come bubbling up now. They floated clearly in the midst of my . . . fog? No, it wasn't fog.

I swallowed and said, "You're right. They are communicating, but they're not communicating in concepts." I stopped to catch my breath, but I had to get the words out quickly, before they lost their meaning, before I lost the sense. "Over here, we talk in words. Words are concepts. Symbols. We communicate symbols. We exchange agreed-upon symbols. They don't do that. They talk in sounds. No—they talk in . . . music. They make music and tune themselves to the music. They—I'm getting it. It doesn't make sense to me, but this is what I felt. They communicate in experience. They're communicating by creating experiences together and . . . somehow . . . tuning themselves to each other . . . somehow becoming the cells of a . . . larger organism, the herd . . . and . . ."

Oh, God, I could see it clearly now.

"They don't have identity any more," I said. "That's why they've given up. They've given up the ability to remember. They have no memory—and without memory, they can't have identity. The only identity they can have is the herd. They stay together for food and for sex, but mostly for identity. Oh, my God, this is a whole new kind of humanity we're looking at, isn't it!"

The realization was terrifying.

I was trembling. A chill swept up my spine and I shuddered. "Is there a place to sit down?" I asked. I wiped my forehead. I glanced around, confused. I felt dizzy.

Fletcher led me to a blackened stone bench, one of the few pieces that had survived the firestorm. She sat me down on it and parked herself beside me.

"Why didn't you warn me—?" I asked. My voice croaked.

"I didn't know," she apologized. "It affects everybody differently." Her eyes were wet.

I looked away, I looked at the ground. The concrete had bubbled and blistered here. I swallowed hard, and admitted, "I'm feeling . . . very confused right now. And very upset. I felt like I've . . ." I made a frustrated face. "I feel . . . ripped off. Ripped open. Ripped up. I feel like hell. I feel like—I've lost something important—" And then I let the tears come. I sobbed into my hands, and I didn't have any idea at all what the tears were all about, I just couldn't stop crying.

Q: What do Chtorrans call a concrete bunker?
A: Crunchy style.

9

"Break all their legs."

"Probability is a constant."
—SOLOMON SHORT

"Feeling better?" Fletcher asked. She offered me her handkerchief.

I wiped my eyes and looked up at her. "How do you do it?" I asked. "How do you resist the . . . pull?"

She shrugged. "I don't know that I do resist it. I think my way of participating is to watch. To try to understand. Because that's what I do everywhere in my life. I watch. I hold back and watch. Maybe that's why I . . . can move through them the way I can."

I handed back the handkerchief. I still felt empty. Drained. I felt as limp as a wet sweat sock. She offered me her hand and I pulled—tried to pull—myself to my feet. She grabbed my elbow and lifted me off the bench. "Come on," she said. "Just walk."

I looked at her as she guided me. The set of her mouth was firm. "Thank you," I said. We started back toward the Jeep.

The herd had lost its cohesiveness. The *gathering* was over and the members were scattering across the plaza. There were couples copulating on the dry grass of the lawn.

I asked Fletcher, "Is it always like this?"

She shrugged. "It varies. Sometimes they're positively frenzied. The intensity can build to such a peak we've even lost a few to heart attacks. Sometimes it's languid. This is about . . . average, I guess."

"Does this happen every day?"

She frowned. "About three or four times a week now. When it started, it was just once or twice a month. Then it began happening more and more often. Now . . . it's almost every other day. I expect within a month, it'll be every day. I think—and this is just a guess—but I think that it's some kind of . . . enrollment phenomenon. Since it started, the herd has been growing much faster than we expected. Something about the phenomenon pulls people into it—as you experienced."

I nodded.

She added, "*And* I think it also supports the members in *staying* in the herd. Last year, we had dropouts. We had people actually *coming back*. They were confused, and they needed a lot of support therapy, but they were conscious again. This year . . . we haven't had any dropouts. Not since this started."

"Tell me about the dropouts," I said. "How does that happen?"

"Um—usually some kind of shock. We had a young man break his leg. The pain was so bad that he started screaming. And suddenly in the middle of the screaming, he was calling for a doctor. His survival was at stake—he had to do something. None of the herd behavior modes were appropriate, so he dredged up something from his memories. Unfortunately, for him, everything attached to that memory came with it. He had to start communicating with us to tell us where it hurt, and so on. So . . . he had to be self-aware again."

"So, that's how you can break the herd," I said. "Break all their legs."

Fletcher laughed. "I don't think it's that easy, James. I wish it were. You can shock some of them back to self-awareness, but most of them you can't. They're aware, but they're not self-aware, and they don't want to be self-aware ever again."

"Mm," I said. There was something about that thought that deserved a second look. My mind was already holding it up to the light, turning it over and over, looking for the implications in it and the extrapolations that could be shaken out of it.

I stopped and looked at the herd speculatively. There was something *else* here, something still beyond my ability to comprehend, let alone communicate. I frowned. . . .

Fletcher followed my gaze. She asked quietly, "Are you thinking about your father? Do you still think he's alive? In the herd?"

Her question brought me back to Earth. I looked at the thought for a long moment. And then I shook my head. "No. I can't imagine my father giving up his power of reason—not for this. It's easier to imagine him dead." I turned to her. I felt remarkably complete. "I can believe it now. Thank you."

Fletcher touched my cheek. "I know it was a shock, Jim. It's good that you're—" She saw something past my shoulder and her face hardened abruptly.

I turned to see a tall, broad-shouldered man approaching us. He was naked, and he had a chest like a wall. He was muscled like a warrior. His skin was sun-darkened and the sweat glistened on his body. He was a stallion. He was a bull. His eyes were bright—he had a very direct look on his face. He also had a startling erection, impossible to ignore.

"Isn't that your missing scientist—?" I started to ask, but Fletcher pushed me aside quickly.

She stepped forward, baring her teeth at the bull, and growled deep in her throat.

He hesitated—

She growled again.

The bull began to lose his bullishness.

Fletcher began to punctuate her growls with angry grunts. The bull backed away before her anger. She bared her teeth and shouted, "Na-na-na-na!" The bull turned and retreated hastily.

I looked at her. I started to say, "That's very effective—" but her expression was ashen. "What's the matter?"

"Nothing," she said.

"Bullshit," I said. "You're a lousy liar."

She tried to wave me away, but I grabbed her arm. "Hey— you're not fooling anybody."

She yanked her arm free and turned away from me. She put her hands to her eyes and her shoulder shook for a moment. She fumbled for her handkerchief. She turned back to me, wiping at her eyes. "We used to be lovers," she admitted. "I, uh . . . still have trouble seeing him like this. Especially . . . when he does *that*. I'm sorry."

I didn't know what to say, so I didn't say anything. I took her hand and led her back to the Jeep. We climbed in, but she didn't start the engine. "That's why you're so interested in the herd, isn't it?"

She nodded. "I want to make sure that he's all right. I owe him that."

"And . . . ?" I prompted.

She let her breath out. "And . . . I keep hoping that I'll figure it out. The herd. And that . . . I can have him back again." She rubbed her nose. Her eyes were very red.

"He means a lot to you, doesn't he?"

She nodded. "He was—is—very special. An incredibly *gentle*

man." She looked out across the milling bodies. "Sometimes . . ." She didn't finish the sentence.

I followed her glance.

"It's very tempting," she admitted. "They're at peace. And
they have joy." She added, "Perhaps, they're the only ones on the
planet who do."

"I wonder . . ." I said. "How long will they last when there's
no one left to take care of them?" I looked at her. "Their joy is a
very *dangerous* luxury. I don't think we can afford joy any more.
At least, not like this."

She didn't answer. She was looking off across the herd. The
bull had found a mate for the afternoon. A teenage boy who
looked up at him with adoring eyes. Evidently the bull wasn't so
picky. I glanced at Fletcher. Her eyes were hard, so I didn't say
anything.

She started the Jeep and we headed back toward Oakland.

She didn't say anything until we were halfway across the
bridge. "Do me a favor?" she asked.

"Sure."

"Don't say anything about this to anyone."

"I wasn't even here."

"Thanks." She smiled gratefully.

I said, "Besides, I'd just as soon not have Duke know that I
was . . . affected."

She switched the Jeep onto autopilot and pushed the wheel
away from her. "He'll never hear it from me."

"Thanks," I said.

She reached over and patted my hand. We'd traded secrets.
Everything was okay now.

Fletcher dropped me back at the barracks with a wave and a
promise to put me on the permanent pass list for the lab section.
I watched thoughtfully as she drove off. How many times a week
did she cross the bridge into San Francisco?

Well . . . maybe it wasn't really my business.

Duke wasn't in, but he'd left a message: "Go to bed early, we
scramble at six."

There was a new briefing book on my bed. I read it over dinner.
A spotting mission? For this we were pulled out of Colorado?

It didn't make sense.

I went to bed still feeling troubled.

My night was restless and full of voices. But they didn't tell me
anything either.

Q: What do you find in a Chtorran lunch box?
A: Two slices of rye bread and Chicago.

Q: What does a Chtorran use for a toothpick?
A: A jackhammer.

10

Scorpions

"Sour grapes usually make sour whine."
—SOLOMON SHORT

Morning came too soon.

I put the body on automatic and got out of its way. I caught up with it again in the Jeep; the noise woke me up. We were rolling across the cracked and oily tarmac of Oakland International Airport. There was a fully armed Banshee-6 waiting for us at the far end of the runway. Its engines were already screaming.

Duke ran the Jeep right up to the foot of the ramp. Holding my ears, I followed him up the steps at a run. We climbed into the jet-chopper and the door slammed itself shut behind us. The pilot didn't even wait till we were seated; she reached up over her head, released a double-handled lever, and we were rolling. I tossed my bag at the back and scrambled for the seat opposite Duke. The lady punched us up into the air so fast I didn't even have time to finish fastening my safety harness.

She was speaking to her microphone: ". . . Heading three five two. *Enterprise,* you can launch your birds now. We'll pick 'em up over San Pablo Bay."

I knew that voice. Lizard Tirelli! I should have recognized her by that takeoff. I leaned across to Duke. "Remember when Ted and I left Alpha Bravo?" He nodded. I jerked a thumb forward. "That's the same pilot."

She put the ship on autopilot, then swiveled her seat around to face us. She was as pretty as I remembered. I wished she weren't wearing that helmet. I liked looking at redheads. "I'm Colonel Tirelli," she said. "You're Captain Anderson?" Duke nodded. "And Lieutenant McCarthy, of course."

I nodded. "Congratulations on your promotion, Colonel."

She ignored it. She looked to Duke. "I know you're probably surprised at the suddenness of your transfers. I specifically asked for the two of you to be reassigned to me."

"Eh?" That was Duke.

Colonel Tirelli explained. "I like your statistics. You're effective. The Rocky Mountain District is controllable today because of the way you marshaled your resources last year."

"That job isn't even begun," said Duke. I could hear the stiffness in his voice. I didn't know if the Lizard could.

"I know what shape that territory's in. I read your reports. But somebody else is going to have to take it over. You're needed here."

Duke looked unhappy, but he didn't say what he was thinking.

He didn't have to. Apparently, the Lizard could read minds as well as she could fly. She said quietly, "I know, Captain—but this is one of Uncle Ira's jobs."

"Oh," said Duke. The subject was closed.

I'd met Colonel Ira Wallachstein—the day before he died. I'd brought down the worm that killed him. I hadn't exactly liked "Uncle Ira," but he'd been the Godfather of the Special Forces, so I respected his memory.

The Lizard let herself drop into a friendlier tone. "You'll be acting as spotters for this mission. You've been briefed."

Duke said, "We got the mission book last night."

"Did you read it?"

Both Duke and I nodded.

"Good. I'm sorry you didn't have more time with it. Be glad you got it at all. Communications are lousy—and they're going to stay that way until we secure the rest of our ground stations. God knows when we'll do that." She looked strained and frustrated, but not defeated. She continued without hesitation. "Okay, we've got what looks like a major infestation in the lumber regions of Northern California. We're going to take them out—but we've got some anomalies. Second- and third-stage nesting—"

"Third stage?" Duke said.

Lizard looked annoyed at the interruption, but she nodded grimly.

Duke and I exchanged a glance. It was that bad? We'd seen skyball pictures of second-stage nests: hexagonal dome clusters, six around one. Any child with a compass could draw the floor plan. But *third* stage? I couldn't imagine—

Lizard said, "You'll know it when you see it. Captain, you take the left bubble; McCarthy, you take the right. You see anything red, fire a beacon. The cleanup crew will be thirty seconds behind us. They'll be dropping the appropriate detergents. Also short-life radioactive particles, taconite dust, poison vectors, selective X-agents, and degradable biocides. We are not using fire. We will use targeted explosives on medium- to large-scale dome clusters. These will be delivered by the second wave of ships, following sixty seconds after the first. Any questions?"

Duke said, "How far north?"

"An hour and a half."

Duke looked surprised. "That close?"

"It's worse than that. We also have renegade activity in the area."

"Near a heavy infestation?" Duke raised an eyebrow.

Lizard nodded. "It happens."

Duke scratched his head. "If you say so, but I find it awfully hard to believe."

"Most people do," said Lizard. "It started last year. We started finding Tribes in Oregon. Tribes with a capital T. There're pockets of survivors all over. We should have expected that some of them would bounce back at an odd angle. People do whatever they think they have to do to survive. But a couple of these groups were setting up their own governments.

"This one in particular," Lizard said, "had nearly three hundred members. They declared themselves an independent entity. They said the United States was now an 'invalid agreement.'" There was scorn in her voice. "That's what they call a government, 'an agreement of intention.' They said the intention of the United States was no longer valid, so it was their purpose to create the agreement for a new one."

"Did they say what the intention was?" Duke asked.

"It became obvious after a while," Lizard replied.

"It sounds like they were succeeding at something," I said. "At least to the degree that three hundred of them agreed with it. That's a lot of agreement," I was interested in spite of myself.

Lizard shrugged. "Yeah—well, that crap always sounds good to the simple-minded; but I don't buy that jargon. My uniform is still United States green—that's who signs my paycheck. I haven't seen any better offers."

"So you had trouble, right?"

"Both times." Lizard scowled. She rubbed her nose distastefully. "We asked them to move out of the area. For their own protection. They refused. We told them they didn't have any choice. They said that they refused to recognize the authority of the United States. Listen—" Lizard interrupted herself, "I don't care what people want to believe it. My parents were Shamists—Spiritual Harmony Among Mankind—so I've got 'space' to accept just about anything. If people want to paint themselves blue and mate with dwarves and elephants, it's all the same to me. And I tell you truly, you wouldn't believe some of the things these Tribes were up to. The problem was they had 'liberated'—read 'helped themselves'—to United States property. 'In the name of the people,' they said. Naturally, they were 'the people' they were referring to."

"What kind of property?"

"Military, of course. It was not a pretty operation. Somehow they'd gotten hold of some very sophisticated ordnance. We had to call in a major air strike to take them out. I took in the first cleanup crews."

Duke looked startled. "There was no alternative?"

"They had ground-to-air missiles! And tanks! And they were moving toward a nuclear silo!"

Right. No further explanations were necessary.

"I'd heard the Tribes were gaining strength," I said. "I hadn't realized how bad it was getting. It must have been a difficult situation."

"You should have been there," said Lizard. "They'd taught their children how to use machine guns. Have you ever seen the effect on a soldier when he realizes that his enemy is a twelve-year-old girl? It's devastating."

Duke looked startled by that. He looked like he wanted to change the subject. He asked quietly, "Uh, why do they base themselves near Chtorran infestations?"

Lizard said, "We think it's possible they're using the worms for cover."

"You mean they've found a way to coexist?" I couldn't help myself; I had to ask.

Duke snorted at me. "There's only one way to coexist with a worm: from the inside."

Lizard said, "It's very simple. The infested areas are no-man's-land, effectively beyond the jurisdiction of the United States government—at least for now, and probably for a long time to come. The Tribes know that if they come in out of the cold, the minute they step across the barriers and enter a Safe City they're accepting not only the protection, but the authority of the United

States government as well. And that means giving up their 'independence,' " she finished.

"But how do they defend themselves from the worms?" I asked.

"That's one of the things we'd like to find out," she said.

"Didn't you interrogate the survivors?" Duke looked puzzled.

"There weren't any." She said it like a door slamming.

Duke looked at her with new respect. She met his gaze coldly. It was obvious she didn't like talking about the subject; it made her hard. Duke dropped his eyes and studied the floor thoughtfully. He knew what she was going through. He'd been through it himself.

But I knew he didn't know how to say it.

Colonel Tirelli spoke first. She said, "We don't think it's the Tribes. We think it's the worms. There's something going on, some kind of shift in behavior. We're beginning to see a lower proportion of attacks on human beings. Some adaptation may be taking place.

"One of the theories is that now that a lot more of the Chtorran plant life has established itself the worms might prefer to feed on their own ecology rather than ours, so humans might not be number one on the menu any more. But so far that's just speculation. I wouldn't want to test it personally—"

The radio beeped suddenly and she swiveled forward to answer it. "This is Tirelli."

"ELDAVO Banshee-6, we have you on visual. We'll fall in behind like good little children."

Lizard looked off to her left. "I see you." Then she frowned. "How many of you ducklings got into the air?" she asked.

"The whole wing, Colonel."

"How come I see only twelve of you?"

"The second wave is going up 101. We'll pick them up north of Santa Rosa."

"Whose good idea was that?"

"Cap'n Caswell's Colonel."

"I got it. All right, you boys ready to go to work?"

"We're all bright and shiny, Colonel Ma'am, ready to spread death and destruction from here to Klamath."

"Just the target area today, please."

"Roger. Out."

I crossed to Duke's side and leaned down to look out the spotter bubble just behind his seat. I could see six dark gunships just dropping into line behind us. "Hey! Those are Scorpions!"

"Aye-yep," said the Lizard. "They sure are." She swung around to face us again. "You have a question about that?"

"Yes, I do." I looked to Duke, then back to Lizard. "I thought we had to give them up. It was part of the Moscow Treaties. We had to sink our gunships."

"We did. Every last one of them."

"But, how—?" I looked out the bubble again. Those were definitely Scorpions.

Lizard looked very pleased with herself. "Oh, we sank 'em all right. But first we sealed them in acrylic. It kept them nice and dry until we needed them. We started pulling them up last year." She glanced out her side window. "They sure look good, don't they?" She was grinning.

I couldn't deny it. They were big, they were black, and they were mean. With their red spotlights on, they would be terrifying.

"All right," said Lizard. "Let me give you the background. This is *deep* background. Uncredited. But one hundred percent reliable. Denver is getting too vulnerable. The military is looking at moving the federal government again."

"To where—?" I blurted. "Almost everywhere is vulnerable now."

"Hawaii isn't," Lizard said. "So far, there's been no sign of infestation on any of the islands, and we expect it to stay that way. To guarantee it, there won't even be any research labs allowed. Not even on the artificial islands or in the sea-domes."

Duke shook his head. "It'll never sell. It'll look like a retreat."

Lizard nodded. "If it happens, it *will* be a retreat."

"Hawaii's too small," said Duke. "Who gets left behind?"

"Hawaii's only Phase One. Phase Two is Australia and New Zealand. Neither of those land masses has been infested either. The negotiations are already under way. They'll actually be glad to have us, especially if we bring as much of our industrial capacity as we can crate and ship."

She reached down into the cooler next to her seat and pulled out a Coke. She tossed one to Duke and one to me, then took one for herself. "But the immediate goal right now is total centralization within eighteen months. The President will be announcing that before the end of the month. We're setting up a chain of Safe Cities, each one surrounded by a ten-kilometer defensive border. We think we can make each city self-sustaining within a year. We'll be using a lot of robot labor, of course. Each city can then function as a base for military operations in its surrounding district."

I said, "It sounds like you're abandoning the land."

She shook her head. "No. We're saving the people first. We can't fight a war without a front line."

Duke said, "So what does all this have to do with California?"

"Highway 101," Lizard replied. "It's the backbone of the West Coast. We need to keep it clear. Seattle and Oakland will both be Safe Cities. We're hoping San Francisco. Probably Portland too, but that decision isn't final yet. The question is whether it's defensible. We also want to put some fortresses on the route. We're opening up a major campaign here. We need to keep our access to the sea. The Hawaii and Australia options both depend on it. Got it?"

Duke nodded. So did I.

"Good." The radio beeped then and Colonel Tirelli swiveled back to her controls. We were over Geyserville, and we'd picked up the second wing of choppers.

I dropped into the right side bubble and watched the ground stream past. We were flying low, not quite treetop level, but close enough to give me a good case of the queasies anyway. Lizard dropped us even lower, and now we began following the rolling texture of the countryside, up one hill and down the next. California had a landscape like a rumpled blanket.

The hillsides should have been green with April foliage, but they weren't. The trees and shrubs passing below us looked yellowish and sickly. There were patches of pink and red mottling the ground. "I know, it looks like lichen," said Lizard, "But it's not. It's another form of the sea sludge. Needless to say, its by-products aren't friendly to local life forms. The redwoods are especially vulnerable. The stuff grows fastest in puddles. Those bright patches are the places that were slowest to dry after the February storms. We've still got a lot of rain due. If it's bad, this whole area could be red by the end of summer. Denver is already testing specific biocides, but it doesn't look good."

"Thanks," I said. "Any more good news?"

"Yeah," said Lizard. "It gets worse ahead. Stand by. We're about to hit Clear Lake." She thumbed her radio to life. "All right, ducklings, this is Banshee-6. We're going in. Watch for beacons."

Suddenly we were over water. I could look straight down into it. The clear surface was as bright as the sky, a dazzling silver mirror. I could see the dark shadow of the Banshee rippling below us. Not too far behind were the shadows of the Scorpions. They were bigger and more ominous. They roared behind us like flying dragons. From the ground, they must have been terrifying.

We crossed the north shore of the lake and suddenly I was staring down at an animated nightmare. The brightness of it hurt my eyes; they started watering. I blinked in confusion. I couldn't tell what I was looking at. It was all a burning wash of color. I'd never seen anything so garish and bright. I fumbled my goggles over my eyes and dialed them down.

It didn't help.

All the colors were red—all different shades of red, a kaleidoscope of crimson and vermilion blossoms, scarlet trees, and royal fireworks. The eye could not assimilate the information. The brain could not make sense of it. All the possible intensities of red were painted here, all splashed across a pink and almost fleshy looking landscape. There was umber, orange, ochre, and magenta—the colors seemed to hover without shape.

My vision blurred then and I saw the Earth as a gigantic living creature. Its bright pink skin was broken open, scored and lacerated. I looked down into deep and bloody eruptions. Here were open sores and festering wounds. Streams of warm dark blood came bubbling to the surface, ran and puddled into hollows.

I lifted my goggles, rubbed my eyes, and looked again.

Beneath the chopper was a dazzling vision of the floor of Hell. Bright orange bushes leapt upward like flames. Tall sequoias, smothered in red, looked like plumes of crimson smoke. Purple streamers hung from trees like shabby cobwebs. Below were large black spidery growths—they crouched in shadowy places. Red creepers stretched across the ground; they looked like grabbing claws.

The ground was pink.

It looked like it was tufted. It looked like it was made of cotton candy. The hills were sugary dunes. Welcome to wonderland—or insanity. The ground was patched with pallid streaks of blue, or erupting with yellow globular clusters; the colors delineated alien shapes. I couldn't tell what I was looking at. The hills were etched with purple threads—and white ones too; they looked embroidered; they were a crazy quilt of blinding hues.

The pines—what was left of them—were stark black spires, pointing accusingly up from the ground. They looked as if they had been burned raw. I saw the ruins of buildings—a scattering of hollow shells, crumbling beneath their coats of crimson ivy.

We'd crossed into a whole new world, a world from which the color *green* had been entirely banished—and everything else that lived in that green world too.

I looked and I knew. I didn't have to worry about renegade Tribes any more. I didn't have to worry about humanity at all.

I was staring into time. Beyond the bubble was a vision of the future of the Earth. How many years away? It didn't matter. We were not a part of it. Not even bones. There would be no place for humanity. Not here.

The roar of the Banshee's engines shifted then. We were slowing. We'd reached the target area.

Q: What do Chtorrans call a stampede?
A: An interesting challenge.

11

Mandala

"There is only one commandment: Thou
Shalt Not Waste. *All the others are
superfluous."*

—SOLOMON SHORT

We started seeing dome clusters almost immediately.

And many of them were second-stage nests.

The pattern was standard: one central dome, six more the same
size placed hexagonally around it. We'd seen that in the Rocky
Mountain District too, but we still didn't have a sense yet how
many Chtorr a dome cluster would house. A single dome never
held more than four. This was obviously an expansion—but for
how many? These were the first clusters I'd seen where construction looked complete.

We tagged the first few, then gave it up. There were too many.
"Save your markers," Lizard said. "There's a lot more to see."

"Jim!" said Duke. "Directly below us."

I leaned as far forward in the bubble as I could. There were at
least a dozen bright red worms streaming across the ground below
us, more than I'd ever seen in one place before—and they were
huge! That one, chasing the chopper's shadow, had to be at least
as big as a Greyhound Land Cruiser.

I had a horrifying realization. Every time the scale of the
infestation expanded, so did the size of the worms. Was there no
limit to their growth?

It gave me a queasy feeling to realize how puny we really were
in comparison. How big were they going to get? And . . . how
did they perceive *us*? The worms were turning to look up at us,

often raising a third or more of their length off the ground. They waved their arms agitatedly, but I couldn't hear if they were screeching.

The scattered dome clusters were becoming frequent now. I had the sense of a village or a small town. There were domes and corrals and funny looking spires. I remembered the totem pole I'd seen in front of the very first dome I'd ever burned. Were these the same thing? I wished I could have gone down to look at them firsthand. I wondered what a Chtorran town might look like when it was complete. Most of these structures were still in varying stages of construction. There were half-finished domes everywhere, and they were laid out in serpentine courses as often as in circular. There was a hint of pattern in the layout, but it wasn't clear yet. I needed to see more.

But as we flew on, the sense of pattern became *less,* not more, obvious. As the density of clusters increased, so did the number of domes in each cluster, but the careful geometric spacing of the domes seemed to be disintegrating as if under pressure. It was as if some instinctual blueprint had broken down. There were extra domes jammed tightly around every core now, sometimes as many as nine or ten. They were squashed so tightly together, the individual domes were built misshapen, as if pushed out of round by the pressure. I could feel the *wrongness.*

Behind us, I could hear the first of the explosions. The Scorpions were going to work. They were dropping smart bombs to take out the large clusters. I could see the worms moving frantically beneath us. Was that a Chtorran panic? They streamed out of the domes. From the air, they looked like fuzzy pink caterpillars humping and flowing madly after us. I imagined I could hear their warbling cries over the noise of the jets: *"Chtorrrr! Chtorrrrrr!"*

The ship rocked as the blast waves passed us. Lizard hollered something and we bounced up higher. I looked back and saw an ugly yellow cloud spreading across the horizon behind us. A wave of twenty-four Scorpions was spreading a swath of death in our wake. The idea was to sterilize the ground, make it uninhabitable to worms—or anyone else, for that matter.

The truth was, we had no idea how effective any of our measures really were. The Chtorran ecology recovered too fast. Once the short-life radioactives expired and the biodegradables broke down, the Chtorran plants and insect-things were back in force in a matter of weeks. They established themselves faster than any Earth species could. This area would have to be sprayed regularly—until we could find something more permanent. Denver was talking longer short-lives.

Lizard was hollering something at me. "McCarthy! Coming up at two o'clock. What's that?"

It was on my side of the ship—the largest dome cluster yet! A cluster of clusters—the pattern was expanded again! The original hexagon of domes was the core of a larger wheel of hexagons—a Chtorran mandala! A third-stage nest! The sense of pattern was very clear here! There wasn't the same pressured feeling as we had seen elsewhere. It was as if this huge wheel of domes were some kind of model Chtorran village—and the other villages were pushing their growth in an effort to catch up *and were doing it wrong*! The pressure was expressed as cancerous looking domes.

As we came over the mandala, I could see that it was still growing. The central cluster of domes was being expanded into one huge dome, and other clusters were being laid out neatly around the perimeter. The mandala was adding yet another circle.

I hollered back to Lizard. "Bingo! We just found the Chtorran City Hall!" I fired a marker into it, and then another just to be certain. I leaned out into the bubble to watch behind. I wanted to see it explode. I could see the worms streaming out of it as it went up in flames.

The ground was erupting Chtorrans now. It looked like it was bleeding. There were too many of them. All sizes. Larger than I'd ever seen. Smaller than I'd ever seen. And all colors too, from bright purple to flaming orange. I saw everything from baby pink Chtorrans to huge scarlet worms. It was a riot of red! I couldn't see them as individual creatures any more. They were merely crimson streaks on a flesh-toned nightmare landscape. They flowed like oil. They looked like particles of fire. There were so many of them all flowing together that I could see the pattern of their panic as a vermilion river streaking horribly beneath us. It was insanity! Unreal—

The whole camp was on the move; they were a furious stampede. New worms kept joining all the time. In their blind fear, the larger ones tumbled the smaller ones aside, or flowed over them, leaving them writhing and injured in the dirt; the injured creatures disappeared beneath the maddened onrushing bodies of their fellows. I could hear them screaming. All of them. The sound was a high-pitched screech like metal being sheared. I could hear it even over the *whuffling* of the chopper's blades and the noise of its jets.

Now, as we came over them, and as the sound of the Scorpions behind us grew louder, the crimson river swirled in confusion, as if it were caught in the churning turbulence of the chopper blades. The shrieking worms turned this way and that in a bedlam of terrified disorder—until they were enveloped by the sulfurous yellow clouds from the Scorpions. The great black beasts came roaring on behind us like avenging angels of death.

Suddenly the ground below was rockier. The clusters of huts vanished like a dream—as abruptly as if the worms themselves had drawn a border. No more of these crimson horrors poured out of the ground. No more paced the chopper's shadow. The last of them fell behind us and disappeared beneath the Scorpions' wrath.

A few miles farther and the festering red landscape vanished too. The hills gave way to green and brown again. There were pine trees here, and redwoods, and sequoias.

For a moment, there was silence in the plane. Only the steady chuff and screech of chopper blades and the muted whine of jets filled the cabin, and that wasn't a sound any more; it was merely a presence, constant and unpleasant.

Lizard made a sound then—something like a growl, something like a shriek. It started low and quickly rose. It was a release of tension, a controlled scream like the whistle of a steam engine. Her face was tight—

And then she stopped and took a breath. And took us higher.

Q: What do Chtorrans call Harlem?
A: Soul food.

Q: What do Chtorrans call the United Nations?
A: Smorgasbord.

Q: What do Chtorrans call Congress?
A: Inedible.

12

Pink Clouds
on the Horizon

*"Just when you think it's finally settled, it
isn't."*

—SOLOMON SHORT

I turned around and looked at Duke. He looked away. He wouldn't
meet my eyes. Goddammit. He did this every time we came up
against the wall—every time we were reminded just how badly we
were losing. He wouldn't share the pain; he kept it bottled up
instead. He scared me when he got like this. "Goddamn worms."
He said it bitterly.

I knew he'd have to go off somewhere to be by himself for a
while—and then he'd be okay again. Until the next time. But until
he had that chance, he would be bitter. And he'd take it out on the
rest of us.

My own reaction . . .

I felt drained. Every mission only put me more in touch with the
total hopelessness of the job. This one was the worst. I didn't
know what I was doing here.

The worms confused me. I was horrified by them—and at the
same time, I was fascinated. I wanted to know everything I could
about them. I was attracted by the horror—and paralyzed by it.

And there was another feeling too, a darker, more disturbing
one. All that I could sense of it was an occasional hot red flash of
memory, as if there was something I once knew, but had since
forgotten; and yet the resonance of the experience still echoed in
my head.

Whenever these feelings came over me, so did a profound

disgust for my own species. Human beings were turning into something even more monstrous than the invaders.

It was all the killing.

I knew that there were people who looked at me with horror now, because there was death in my eyes. I could see it in Duke's face too. All of us who had met the worms head-on—we all wore the same expression.

We were killing machines. The only difference between us and the worms was that the worms didn't have a choice. We did. *We chose to kill*. We would even kill ourselves if it would hurt the Chtorrans.

I felt the pressure in my chest again.

The chopper bumped me out of my brooding. We were picking up speed. I looked at Lizard. Her face was a military blank. Except for that one moment of screaming release, she was a perfect soldier machine: a pilot-thing, not a human being.

I wondered if she had ever been a real woman, then discarded the thought. Her face was set like steel. I couldn't imagine her laughing, or having a good time, let alone anything more intimate. She wore her body like armor and the effect was inhuman, almost repelling. I couldn't imagine her naked, nor could I see her trusting another human being enough to open up to him. No, she was just another monstrous machine. We all were now.

She was checking her flight plan. "All right, that's the worst of it. We'll let the navy finish cleaning this up. I want to look at Red Bluff before we turn back. Then we'll come back down the coast and look for sea sludge."

"Don't you have skyball overflights?" Duke asked. His voice and expression were normal again, hard and clipped.

"We did. But something's been knocking them down."

"And you want to go looking for it?" I asked. There was incredulity in my tone.

Lizard ignored me. She said to Duke, "We don't have enough skyballs left to schedule regular patrols. We won't until Lockheed starts shipping again."

"How about satellite eyeballs?"

"They can give us pretty good resolution, but they can't get under cloud cover. And they're not mobile on the scene. We need to find out what's going on."

Lizard thumbed her radio to life. "All right, ducklings. This is ELDAVO. You done good. I'm turning east. Fall in behind and keep your eyes open."

"Roger, dodger."

The horizon angled crazily as Lizard tilted the ship eastward. We were over crumpled hills again.

"This area looks green—" Lizard pointed. "But it's red on the map. We're spotting worms in these woods every day now. The governor has pulled the whole lumber industry out."

She added bitterly, "We're going to lose the northern half of the state. It's too wild to control. You won't get anyone to admit it officially, but it's just a matter of time. It's going to be a bitch just to hold the road open. We're running traffic in convoys now and it seems to work, but I don't know what it'll be like in two years. Hell, we don't even know what the worms will be like in two years." And then she added in a quieter tone, "Or even humanity, for that matter. Shit." She flew on in silence.

I looked at Duke. He was leaning forward, staring out of his bubble. All I could see was his back. He had his face in his hands. What was he thinking about? He'd probably never tell.

I turned back to my window and stared out at the ground too. This pervading despair was infectious.

The hills were leveling out now. The slopes were lush and green and heavily forested. Some of the trees looked as if they had a white sheen to them. I couldn't figure out what it was.

"Time to turn north again," Lizard said and banked the chopper to the left. I wondered if we were close enough to see the big meteor crater, now called Red Lake. That was supposed to be around here somewhere. As we angled around and dropped into our new course, I strained forward to look—but the northern horizon was hidden by a line of pink clouds.

I looked back, but I couldn't see the Scorpions any more. I climbed forward and sat down in the copilot's seat. "Are the other choppers still with us?"

Lizard glanced at her controls. There was a screen in the center of the dashboard. She tapped it. "See those red dots. They're five minutes behind us. Don't worry about it, they're just making a wider turn. They'll catch up with us here—" She tapped the screen. "If we have the fuel, we'll take a look around Redding too."

"Oh, I see. Thanks."

"Sure."

"Can I ask you something, Colonel?"

"You can ask anything you want. I don't promise I'll answer."

"It's about Denver. . . ."

Her tone was guarded: "Go on."

"Well . . . I remember thinking that the Special Forces people were all so—well, ruthless."

"Mm-hm," she said. "That's what it takes to win a war."

"I know that now," I said. "In fact, sometimes I think we're not being ruthless enough. But that's not my question. What I want to know is—well, you were one of the first people there to be kind to me. In your own gruff way. Do you mind if I ask why?"

"I don't really remember—" She hesitated, frowning at the approaching wall of clouds. "Maybe I was having a bad day." Then she shrugged. "I used to take in a lot of stray puppies before I found out they all grew up to be sonsabitches." She glanced over at me. "Any other questions?"

"Uh, no—thanks."

Next time, I'd leave well enough alone.

The sunlight had turned a peculiar shade of pink; the sky was a funny bright overcast. "Are we heading into rain?" I asked.

"No." Lizard looked puzzled. "The forecast is for bright sun and strong winds off the ocean." She glanced at her instruments. "That's not moisture, whatever it is. It's too dense."

"Maybe it's sea sludge," I guessed. "Picked up by the clouds?"

"Not possible. There's no sea sludge this far north."

Duke came forward then, leaning into the space between our two seats. "Sandstorm?"

"Couldn't be. Where's it coming from? The northern part of the state is all forest and meadowland." She looked confused.

The clouds were a large fluffy barrier now, only a few kilometers away. They were rolling across the land like a bulldozer. The ground was darkening beneath them. They looked massive. They looked solid. They looked *too* pink.

"I don't like the color of that," Duke said.

"It looks like cotton candy."

Lizard did something to the radar and studied its display. "Whatever it is, it's rolling up awfully high."

"Can you go over that?" I asked.

"It's a little steep—"

"No," said Duke quietly. "Turn the ship around. Now!"

"Huh?"

He pointed past her shoulder. "Look—"

Something was spattering on the windshield. They were little red spots, red and sticky-looking.

"You're right," said Lizard. She angled the ship sideways into a steep turn. My stomach lurched. I grabbed for my seat belt.

More splotches appeared on the windshield. We were in the fringes of a cloud.

"What is it?" Lizard said. "Bugs?"

"I don't think so—" I leaned forward for a closer look. I couldn't see any details in the splotches. They were just little red pustules on the surface of the window. It wasn't rain. They didn't run. The window was rapidly filling up with red splatters. It was becoming opaque.

The sound of the engines shifted then, became a shrill whine. A red light went on in front of Lizard and an electronic voice said, "Engines overheating." Something started beeping. Lizard said a bad word and slammed a double-handled lever down. The chopper lurched as its jets cut back.

She pulled back on her controls and we hung in the air for a moment. The rotor *chuffed* stiffly through the air. "I don't know if we can get out of this without the jets." She checked something on her board. "I'm going to look for a place to set us down—"

Something screeched and went *SPANG!* on top of the ship. We rocked sideways—

"Shit! We lost the rotor!" Lizard pushed the double-handled lever up and pointed the ship skyward. "I'm going to need some height!" The jets roared; a wall of air pressed me into my seat. Behind me, I could hear Duke sliding and skidding toward the tail as we climbed.

Lizard unclipped a safety switch and slapped the first red button underneath it—and then everything happened at once! There was a *BANG!* from the roof of the chopper as the explosive cover blew off the parafoil. The chopper blades went flying away. Then there was a *THUMP* from the right as that side's engine exploded in flames.

Suddenly the ship was enveloped in fire! The air was hot and orange! Beside me, I could hear Lizard's startlement. "What the hell—?" But she was already hitting the release.

There was a *BANG!* that punched the ship like a bomb. I thought for a moment that our fuel was exploding, but it was only the explosive bolts going off as the engines were jettisoned. A smaller bang took off the tail rotor.

We were falling—I was too terrified to scream—Lizard released the parafoil, I heard it pulling away—something went *FWOMP!*—and then it filled with air and a giant hand caught us and we were sailing silently through the air, gliding forward through the reddish murk like a descending eagle.

"Duke! Are you all right?"

There was no answer.

"Worry about him later!" snapped Lizard. "Watch for a clearing!" She was speaking to her radio now. "Ducklings! Turn around! Stay away from *pink clouds*! This is ELDAVO Banshee-6! We're going down! Repeat—turn around! Stay away from pink clouds! It's some kind of dust! It'll seize your engines, and it burns like hell! I'm going in now. Stand by—"

I was pointing. "Sand dunes—I think."

"Good enough," said Lizard. "Hang on!"

She brought the ship around in a tight turn and aimed us at the long axis of the dunes. Too late, I saw the dunes weren't sand at all—they were pink! We hit with a *FOOF* and a *CRUNCH* and a *BANG!*—

Q: What's the Chtorran word for picnic?
A: Rome.

13

Cake

And then everything was silent.

And pink. The light was pink. The windows were pink.

We were canted forward at a steep angle. We'd hit once on the belly of the ship, smacking against the pink drifts of whatever, then bounded up high as the wind-filled parafoil dragged us on. We came down again hard, skidding forward until the nose caught on something and we plowed our way in. But the tail didn't stop; it swung up and forward, tilting the ship even steeper. We were lucky we weren't flipped all the way over on our back.

My heart was pounding like a jackhammer. *That would be stupid,* I thought—*to survive a plane crash only to die of a heart attack afterward.* I counted to ten. Then again. And a third time.

Something smelled sweet.

I wondered what we'd landed in.

The stillness was incredible, as if we were smothered in marshmallow. The sound of my breath seemed unnaturally loud.

91

"Colonel?"

"I'm all right. Yourself?"

"Yeah." I started pushing the still half-inflated airbag away from me. I could hear the air swooshing out of it as I pushed. "Duke?" I called.

He didn't answer.

"Can we get some light?"

"Hang on." There was the sound of switches. I could hear Lizard's hands moving across the console. "Let's try this. . . ."

Whatever it was, it worked. The boards in front of us came back to life. The panel lights lit up, the screens began to glow. Several small alarms started beeping.

"Shut up!" Lizard said. She punched buttons. They shut. "Now, let's do a little fire prevention. . . ."

There was a hissing sound. Suddenly the air felt wet and smelled of menthol.

She thumbed her radio on. "Ducklings, this is ELDAVO Banshee-6. We're down and safe. Possible injuries to one of our party. Do not—repeat, do *not*—attempt to rescue us. The pink clouds are dangerous. Do you copy?"

There was static for a moment, then a military voice came back, "We copy." And then, more personal, "Are you all right, Colonel?"

"I'm a little annoyed."

"I got it. Keep your channel open. We're getting a bearing on you. What happened?"

"We hit a hard cloud."

"Yeah, we can see it. It's rolling south like a big pink carpet. Thanks for the warning. We're heading out over the ocean to get clear of it. What the hell is that stuff anyway?"

"I don't know yet—but it blows up engines. We lost the rotor and both turbines. We came down on the parafoil." She hesitated for a second, then added, "You've got to let Denver know. This is what's knocking down our skyballs. It's just like hitting a wall of cotton candy." She sniffed. "It even smells like cotton candy."

"All right, we've got our fix. We'll be sending a rescue ship back as soon as the candy clouds pass."

"Thanks. I'll keep this channel open as long as I've power. Out."

Lizard went fumbling beneath her seat. "Here—" she handed something across to me—a flashlight. "See what happened to Duke. And be careful. It's steep. I'm going to try to get the emergency power on."

I couldn't swivel my seat backward, not while the chopper was pointed so sharply downward. I guessed we were tilted at a thirty-degree angle. I unbuckled my safety harness and nearly pitched forward onto the controls.

"I told you, be careful."

"Yeah, I will." I angled myself around and swept the flashlight across the rear of the chopper. Duke was sprawled—no, caught—in the right side bubble. I couldn't see his face; his head was below the deck level, he was almost upside down in the seat. I started climbing toward him.

It was hard to find handholds. I had to use my seat and Lizard's to climb. Once I got past them, there were deck rings on either side for securing cargo. I grabbed for the ones on Duke's side of the ship. Halfway up, the chopper lurched—and shifted. The framework groaned. I thought I heard Duke gasp. I froze where I was—

"It's your weight," said Lizard. "You're bringing the tail down. Keep going."

I started climbing again, this time even more carefully. The chopper creaked once and lurched once; then it was still.

"I think that's it," Lizard said. "That last one felt pretty solid." I'd reduced the angle of tilt to fifteen degrees.

Duke's eyes were closed. I lifted him out of the bubble and stretched him out on the floor of the ship. There was blood on his face, streaming from his nose and a bad cut on his forehead—but he was breathing.

"Duke—?"

"There's a red-bordered panel on the floor there," said Lizard. "Open it. That's the primary first aid."

I found the panel she was talking about and pulled it open. There were three plastic boxes stored inside. Once was labeled WATER, one was labeled FOOD. The third simply had a red cross on it.

I took out an ampule of ammonia and broke it under Duke's nose. For a moment, there was no reaction—then he twisted his face away and started coughing. The spasms lasted for only a few seconds. He coughed and looked up at me. Then he lifted his head and looked around the darkened chopper. He glanced toward Colonel Tirelli, then looked back to me. He coughed and said, "I sure hope she can fuck better than she can fly."

I glanced forward to see if Lizard had heard that. She was holding her earphones close to her ears and concentrating on something she was listening to. She hadn't heard. Good.

I turned back to Duke. "I'll let you know when I find out," I whispered.

He grinned at me. "No. I'll let *you* know when *I* find out."

I sat back. "I was going to ask if you were all right," I said. "Obviously, you are."

Duke closed his eyes for a moment, as if he was mentally counting something. "Taking inventory," he said. He opened his eyes again. "All here."

"You sure? It looked like you took quite a beating."

He levered himself halfway up. "I hurt a lot, if that's what you mean. I've been better. . . ." He looked uncertain. "Uh, I think I shit my pants."

"Good. I was afraid I was going to have to tell you."

Lizard came back to join us. She squatted next to Duke and touched her fingers to his carotid artery. "Pulse is good," she said. She plucked a pocket light from her shirt pocket and peered into Duke's eyes. "Reflexes look normal. Hand me the medi-kit, Lieutenant."

Duke frowned as she applied the sensors to his forehead. They looked like little poker chips. "Is this necessary?" he grumbled.

Colonel Tirelli ignored the question; she just pushed him back down onto the deck and continued pasting the chips. She unbuttoned his shirt and applied three more to his chest.

I passed her over the console. "Shh," she said, as she thumbed it to life. She studied its screen thoughtfully. "Mm-hm," she said. She looked at Duke as a person for the first time. "You took a few scratches, but otherwise you're fine."

Duke said dryly, "I could have told you that *without* the medi-kit."

"Yes, but it's nice to have a second opinion, isn't it?" She stood up. "There're clean jumpsuits in the back. I'll get you one."

Duke looked at me and shook his head. "This is not my idea of a good time." He sat up, grimacing, and started peeling off the poker-chip sensors.

Lizard returned with a sani-kit, a plastic-wrapped jumpsuit, and a can of air freshener. Duke thanked her for it. She nodded and returned forward.

"Do you need any help?"

Duke gave me a look that made me sorry I asked.

"Right," I said, and followed Lizard forward. I climbed back into the copilot's seat. Even at this gentler angle, it wasn't comfortable. I still felt like I was about to be tilted out. I looked at Lizard. "How are *you* doing?" I asked. "Are you all right?"

"Only my pride is injured," she said. She was checking her controls with a sour expression. "I've never crashed a ship before."

"Really?" The word fell out before I could catch it.

She raised an eyebrow at me. "Is that a comment on my flying?"

"Um—uh, sorry," I flustered. I pointed to the controls. "How bad is it?"

"We broke the keel of the ship. That took out most of the cables. We have lights forward, nothing aft. There's no power for anything aft. I can run a bypass for the door, or we can pop it manually if we have to. Anything else, I don't know." She rubbed her eyes. For a moment, she looked tired. I felt sorry for her. I remembered what it felt like when I cracked up my first new car two weeks after I bought it. I'd wanted to die then. She probably felt the same way about this chopper.

I looked away politely. There really wasn't anything I could say that would help. Probably I should just keep out of her way for a while. I stared out the front window.

Now that the ship was canted at a gentler angle, we could see out the front windshield. We were staring at a frosty pink landscape. Frosty pink trees and frosty pink bushes—everything was covered by frosty pink snowdrifts. The world looked like the top of some gaudy baroque desert, one of those Valentine's Day surprises my mother used to make; we never knew what was hiding under the thick pink whipped cream. We'd hated them. We thought they were tacky. That's what the frosty snowdrifts reminded me of. I felt there should be maraschino cherries on top of each delicious-looking mound. That made me think of breasts.

I looked at Lizard speculatively. She was studying a radar scan on her screen. She had nice breasts. I wouldn't mind a better look at them.

She looked up and caught me studying her. "What's on your mind?" she asked.

"Um . . . uh, how long do you think we'll have to wait?"

"Depends on the size of the clouds and where they're coming from. We came down right under the leading edge, so we'll have to wait for the whole mass to pass over. I tapped into the weather net for satellite photos, but it didn't show anything we don't already know. I expect we'll have to be lifted out, and probably not before tomorrow."

"Will we be okay until then?"

"Oh sure. This ship will never fly again, but most of her

equipment's still good. She'll sustain us." Lizard patted her console affectionately. "You done good, baby." Then she added, "A salvage chopper can pick her up and take her back to Oakland where they can strip her for parts. Then we can melt down the rest and try again." She slapped a wall with her hand. "Most of this is foamed Kevlar. The frame is the easiest part of the chopper to fabricate. During the Pakistan conflict, the Lockheed plant had ten lines going. They were putting out two hundred and forty frames a day. That's almost two thousand machines a week. Incredible. And they were popping them out for less than five hundred thousand a copy. There'd never been a fleet like that before. You should have seen the dogfights. These birds are light, cheap, and powerful—and quick to build. Most of the parts are modular, designed to be assembled by robots. That's good, because we're probably going to need a lot more of them—and very soon."

"Why do you think that?" I asked.

"Well—" she gestured toward the window. "For one thing the Chtorran ecology doesn't seem to like jet engines. For another, we'll need them to control the spread of infestation. That nest we hit will be back to normal within weeks. We're going to need ten times the number of ships we had today if we're going to hold them back. And that infestation isn't the worst I've seen."

"We don't have enough pilots, do we?"

Lizard shook her head. "No, we don't. Probably we'll have to start flying drones. But these ships are programmable. A good pilot can control a whole wing." She looked annoyed. "I've been recommending it for a month. Maybe today's videos will convince them. God knows it isn't a question of money any more." She snapped off the screen. "Well, there isn't anything else I can do here now. I need to check outside."

We clambered into the back and Duke joined us at the hatch, zipping up his jumpsuit. Lizard opened the hull panel, grabbed a lever, pushed, and . . . grimaced. "Damn! The frame must have bent." She braced herself and pushed again. The lever resisted for a moment, then snapped loudly into position. "All right, we're on manual now."

She closed the panel and hit the large red button next to it with the heel of her fist. The hatch popped open with a bang. It swung out and up and out of the way. The ramp dropped into the fluffy pink dust and disappeared. A puff of pink smoke rose around it.

We stared down at it. How deep was this stuff anyway? We could smell the sweetness of it in the air. It was thick and buttery.

"Mm," Lizard said, "it smells like fresh bread."

"Nope," said Duke. "Too much sugar. It must be cake."

"So?" I asked. "Who wants to be first?"

Neither Lizard nor Duke answered. The intense pink landscape was somehow intimidating. We studied it in silence. The drifts kept sliding and collapsing under their own weight. We were in the middle of a rolling sea of powdery dunes.

I realized I'd been making an inaccurate comparison. These weren't snowdrifts—this was dust as fine as smoke, and piled as delicately as spider silk. The rosy powder was so fine the light glittered and sparkled as if the dunes were made of magic. It was impossible to see them clearly. They were bright and vague and hard to focus on.

There were tiny motes floating in the air. I could feel my eyes starting to water. But I had an odd thought about this stuff—I had to test it.

I stepped down the ramp, three steps, four—knelt and scooped up a handful. It felt like talcum, smooth and powdery—but with a curious silkiness. It was almost liquid.

I sifted a little more, till I was rubbing the last of it between my fingers. "It's very faintly gritty. There must be some larger particles in it too. I don't know." I touched a fingertip to my tongue. It was sweet. I glanced back upward. Both Lizard and Duke were watching me with curious expressions. "It tastes as good as it smells."

I scooped up another handful and blew on it. It puffed away like smoke, like dandelion fur. The motes drifted in the air like snowflakes. I was right in my guess.

I came back up the ramp and stepped back into the chopper, brushing the last of it from my hands. "I know what this stuff is—" I said it hesitantly. The realization was numbing.

Both Lizard and Duke looked at me.

"Remember Dr. Zymph's speech at the conference?" I said to Lizard. "—The one where she listed some of the different creatures in the Chtorran ecology? Well, these are the puffballs! Or what's left of them. They powder like dandelions."

"But so much—?" wondered Lizard. She looked out at the frozen pink landscape again.

I shrugged. "I guess they all blew up at once. The right combination of heat and sun and wind and who knows what else and you get puffballs. But they're practically pure protein," I said. "You can eat all you want. The stuff is harmless."

"Harmless to everything but precision machinery," Lizard said.

"Dammit. The one decent thing in the Chtorran ecology and it knocks airplanes out of the sky."

"Have you got a science kit here?" I asked. "I want to bag some of this."

"Yeah, wait a minute—" I followed her into the back. She opened another panel and dug out a pack for me. I returned to the hatch with a plastic bag.

"This stuff's a mess," coughed Duke, stepping around me. "We're going to need masks."

"I'm already getting them," called Lizard. "And goggles too."

"The puffballs powder as soon as they hit the ground," I reported. I stepped down onto the ramp again. There were fresh puffballs drifting down now; the great wall of clouds was just coming overhead. Some of the puffballs were as large as apricots, but so ethereal to look at they were hardly there. They were just spherical hints in the air, bursting like bubbles if they even brushed against each other, or anything.

"They can't even support their own weight," I called. "The stuff must be compacting under each new layer." I began filling the plastic bag.

"Here's a mask," said Lizard, reappearing in the doorway. I came back up the ramp to get it. She handed me an O-mask with goggles. And an air pack. "That stuff is pretty fine," she explained. "You'd better carry your own air."

"Good thinking," said Duke. He was already pulling his mask down over his head. "What about weapons?"

"What do you want?"

"What have you got?"

"Come take a look—"

Duke followed her aft. I heard the sound of a floor panel being pulled up. Then Duke whistled. "Holy Jesus! This ship is better equipped than a man with three balls!"

"I like to be careful," I heard Lizard say.

I wasn't surprised. I remembered her from my last visit to Denver. The woman was inhuman. What *would* surprise me would be seeing the famous Colonel Tirelli caught *un*prepared. I hoped I'd never be there to see it happen. I doubted there would be survivors.

I stepped out onto the ramp again and looked around.

Something moved.

On the far side of the dune, just behind that pink bush. Something small.

I thought I saw eyes. A face. Staring at me.

I wanted to call Duke, but I was afraid of scaring it off. Instead . . .

I took another step down the ramp. Slowly.

The face didn't move. The eyes blinked.

I wondered what Duke and Lizard were doing. I wished I could warn them not to make any sudden moves or loud noises.

I took another step. Very slowly, I shaded my eyes against the sun and the glittering pink dust.

The eyes behind the bush were large. And gold. The face was pink. And furry. But it wasn't a worm face. Worms didn't have faces. Worms had two eyes, sort of, and a mouth, sort of—but that still didn't add up to a face. A worm had no more face than a snail. This was a face. Almost . . . human. I couldn't tell if the fur was really pink or just covered with dust. I'd bet the latter.

I took another step down. I was on the lowest step of the ramp. One more step. . . .

Q: What's the Chtorran version of the Heimlich maneuver?

A: Eating Dr. Heimlich.

Bunnydogs

"Half of being smart is knowing what you're dumb at."

—SOLOMON SHORT

—And then Duke appeared in the door behind me. "What do you want, Jim—the torch or the freezer?"

The eyes vanished. I caught a quick glimpse of a furry body and that was all. Something scuttled and there was pink smoke.

"Shit!"

"What was that—?" said Duke.

"There was something out there—" I pointed. "Some kind of humanoid!"

"Where—?"

"Over there!" I dropped off the bottom step of the ramp and sank chest deep in the pink powder. A great cloud of it swirled up around me. I ignored it and started pushing toward the bush the creature had been hiding behind. The powder was as light as cotton candy. It pushed aside like cobwebs. It was hardly there at all.

"Jim—wait! It might be a worm!"

"This was no worm! I know a worm when I see one! This was humanoid!"

"Here! Take the freezer!" He came down the ramp after me, but stopped on the bottom step. He was carrying a long nozzled rod and a pair of small tanks. Liquid nitrogen. The rod was almost as tall as I was and connected to the tanks by a stiff silvery hose. I'd used this kind of portable unit before. I grabbed it from Duke and shrugged quickly into the harness. The tanks sat on my back and

I could use the rod to direct a soft-pressure spray of instant supercooling. It was a great way to gather specimens.

Duke reached up behind him and grabbed the flame-thrower. "All right, let's go see—" He jumped into the dust. It came up in a cloud.

Lizard appeared in the doorway carrying a laser gun. Duke waved her back. "No, you stay with the ship! Get on the radio. This might be something." I know what he meant by that. We might not come back. But we could leave a clue for the ones who came after us.

Lizard got it; she nodded. "I'll cover you from the turret."

"Good. Let's go, Jim." We pushed off. The dust was almost waist deep.

I glanced back once and waved toward the chopper. I couldn't tell if Lizard waved back. I had to concentrate on my footing.

I was discovering something interesting about the pink powder we were trying to move through. It was only fluffy on the top. The deeper it was, the denser it got. The more I moved, the lower I sank—and I was sinking deeper with every step. It was like the lunar dust that almost killed that astronaut, "Free Fall" Ferris. The similarity was scary. I began to wonder if this was such a good idea. I started to lift the spray nozzle over my head to protect it—and then I had another thought.

I set the nozzle for wide-spray, pointed it forward, and touched the trigger lightly. A cold white cloud whooshed out, putting a sudden chill into the air. The pink powder snapped and sputtered and solidified.

"Hot stuff?" I shouted.

"Huh?" said Duke.

"I said, 'Hot stuff!' This liquid nitrogen is hot stuff!" I strode forward over crackling ice.

Duke followed me, grumbling and shaking his head. "Liquid nitrogen is anything but 'hot stuff.'"

"You know what I mean."

He grunted something unintelligible in response. I didn't ask him to repeat it.

The liquid nitrogen had frozen a crust in the powder. Where the powder was lightest, it just cracked and crumbled away, but deeper down, where it was almost dense enough to walk on, the supercold had turned the dusty quicksand into a texture more like dry snow—and that we could walk on. There was resistance now. The frozen powder crunched under out feet. Every few steps I stopped and froze another patch ahead of us. We were carving a deep furrow through the high dunes.

We couldn't see anything but powdery drifts all around us. They were piled up like walls. Apparently, we had come down near the center of a large shallow depression, probably an old dry riverbed. We were in the center of it and couldn't see out— assuming, of course, that there was something to see that wasn't pink.

The bush we were heading toward was actually on a high rise of ground. As we climbed up through the dust toward it, we found ourselves climbing out of the powder as well. Toward the top it was only waist deep. This stuff was coming down *fast*.

Perhaps this slope was the western shore of the riverbed, but it was hard to tell. Some of these California riverbeds could be as wide as a kilometer across. This felt like being in a deep desert. Or in a lunar crater. Or on another planet. I wondered if they had places like this on Chtorr.

The air around us was pink with smoke. The wind was stirring up small powdery whorls that rose and dissipated into the air. The clouds of it spread out and became a gentler haze. I looked up. The sky was turning rosy.

And it was impossible to see the horizon. Everything just blurred out in the distance. The only difference was that the sky was slightly brighter than the ground, and the sun was a bright pink glow in the middle of everything.

I glanced back at the chopper. It had carved a long uneven furrow through the pink dunes, I could see where we'd bounced. Already the sides of the soft pink scar were collapsing and sliding inward. The aircraft itself was canted gently forward, its nose halfway buried in one of the highest of the dunes. The silken shroud of the parafoil had draped itself across the slope ahead of the ship. Already the pink dust was sweeping over it, burying it from view. Its lines were barely visible now.

And beyond the chopper—

—there was only more pink. Pink whipped-cream dunes and rosy pink sky, all fading off into an oppressive, bright pink blur. Everything was pink.

We crested the slope—the powder was only knee deep here— and moved around to the other side of the bush. "Look. There're its tracks."

"Looks like some kind of paddlefoot," Duke said. "Four toes. The center two are the longest." He spread out the fingers of his hand and held it over the closest footprint for comparison. "He's a little fellow, whatever he is. My hand just covers this print."

"He went down that way." I pointed. I followed the tracks toward the trees.

"Jim. I don't think that's such a good idea . . ."

"Why not?" I paused and looked back.

"We'd better not get too far from the chopper," said Duke. "If we lose our way, we'll never get back."

"We'll follow our own path," I said.

Duke shook his head and pointed back the way we'd come. "Look—" Already the dust was filling in our trough. "It's still coming down. "We're not aware of it, because we're stirring up so much of it, but if you watch something that isn't moving, you can see this crap is getting deeper. That cloud—" he gestured at the sky, "—is dumping most of its load right here. This stuff can't get past the Sierras. The wind can only carry so much of it. It's got to drop somewhere. This is the place."

"Damn," I said. "We'll have to hurry. Come on."

"That thing could be anywhere by now," Duke said.

"We've got to take the chance. We've got to see what that critter was! You can go back if you want—" I was already heading deeper into the pink forest. The creature had plowed a furrow through the dust, just like us. It zigzagged back and forth through the bushes.

Duke grumbled; but he shrugged, sighed, and followed. There are disadvantages to having a headstrong science officer. We twisted through the frosty trees, Duke muttering quiet obscenities.

"This is what I get for letting them assign you to me," he said.

"You *asked* for me." We'd had this argument before.

He waved it off. "You were the lesser of two evils. The alternative was a morally retarded sociopath who had fragged his commanding officer. The only reason they didn't shoot him was they couldn't prove he had actually tossed the grenade. Frankly, I just don't care to have that kind of man in my command." Duke changed his tone then; he became more serious. "Listen. Whatever it was, it'll turn up again. Someone else will spot one. You don't have to be the guy who brings in all the animals. Besides, it's probably terrified of us and heading for the hills as fast as its fat little feet can carry it."

"I don't think so," I said, following the next turn. "It was studying us. That wasn't just an animal I saw. There was intelligence in those eyes. And where there's one, there're probably many. We're probably being watched from all sides right now." I stopped and pointed. "Look—I was right. There's another track—" A second line of paddlefoot tracks crossed the first. The dustfalls indicated we were following the older set of prints. I turned to follow the newer furrow. It twisted and turned like the first.

"Don't these creatures believe in straight lines?" I asked.

"They must be descended from politicians," Duke replied.

"Or comedians," I said.

I came around what might have been a pine tree and stopped. Duke came up beside me. The furrow we were following headed straight into the center of a wide clearing—

—and into a whole switchyard of crisscrossing paths! It was impossible to tell one from another.

"Damn!" said Duke. "I knew it."

I looked at him. His expression was impossible to read behind the goggles and O-mask. I said, "What are you talking about? This is incredible! There must be a whole colony of these creatures."

"Unless your critter doubled back over his own path."

"Why would he do that?"

"To confuse us," Duke said. "Are you confused?"

"Uh . . . I don't think so."

"Uh-huh." Duke looked at me funny. "Then which way is back?"

I pointed past his shoulder. "That way."

"You sure?"

I looked at him curiously. "Do you know something I don't?"

He turned slowly, studying the dunes. "Remember Shorty? He and I were in Pakistan together. The black pajama boys used to do this exact same trick. They'd let one of their number be seen. As soon as he was spotted he'd take off into the trees. There was always at least one jackass stupid enough to chase after him, so he'd leave the most complicated, zigzag, twisty, serpentine trail he could—but he always made sure it was clear enough to follow. As soon as you were deep enough to be confused about the way back, the trail would stop. That's when his friends would come out to play. We lost an awful lot of jackasses that way."

I glanced around nervously. A steady breeze rustled the surface of the dust, stirring pink wraiths into the air. Everything looked pink. There was no horizon any more, no sky, no ground—just a fine pink haze. We had some bleak-looking bushes and dunes. Nothing else.

I shuddered. For some reason, frosty pink things weren't

charming any more. I looked back to Duke. "Do you think that's what's happening here?"

Duke looked grim. "I don't know. I didn't see your creature and I can't guess what he wants or how his mind works. And this isn't Pakistan. But that's what I keep thinking of. Sorry, son. That's the only thing I have to compare it to—Pakistani Poker."

I considered it. Duke only called me "son" when he thought something was important and he wanted me to listen harder than usual.

"Let's head back," I said.

"I thought you'd agree." He pointed. "It's that way."

"You lead," I said. I fell in behind him.

Our path wound back through the bushes. I didn't remember making this many twists and turns—

Suddenly, Duke stopped and pointed ahead. "Look—"

Our path had been crisscrossed again and again by paddlefoot tracks, until our original prints were no longer visible. Something had been following behind us. "Urk—" I said.

Duke swung the torch around slowly, covering the bushes on all sides. "Well . . . now they know that *we know*." His eyes narrowed behind his goggles. "If they're going to attack, now's the time."

"Well let's not stand here talking about it. Let's keep going!"

"Just a minute." Duke pulled a small plastic disk off his belt. "We're going to need the beeper. . . . " He studied it for half a second, then pushed off at a new angle. "Follow me."

The dust was coming down heavier now. We could see it floating in like snowflakes. The particles were bigger now: big pink clumps, turning as they drifted. They looked like dandelions. I reached out to catch one as it floated down. It disappeared when it touched my hand; it puffed into dust and was gone, it was that light.

"We're in the thick of the storm," I said.

"Uh-huh—and the wind is rising. We'd better hurry. We'll be at the limit of our masks soon."

I nodded and followed him. The visibility was getting worse. I couldn't see more than twenty yards ahead of us.

"Jim, it's getting deeper. You'd better start freezing again."

"Right." I came up even with Duke and sprayed a quick cold cloud of chill ahead. The liquid nitrogen looked like steam when it hissed into the air. The dust crackled and broke as we moved through it. The frozen crust beneath crunched.

Duke checked his beeper and pointed. I moved ahead and sprayed again. We moved forward cautiously.

"You think they <u>can</u> attack in this dust?" I asked.

"It's their natural element," Duke said. "And they don't seem to have any trouble moving around in it. I won't feel safe till we're back in the chopper." He checked his beeper. "More to the left, Jim. We should be almost to the slope—"

"Urk—"

"What's that?"

I stopped and pointed. Duke came up behind me and peered through the pink gloom—

There were three of them.

They looked like flop-eared bunnies. Or puppydogs. They had squat little bodies covered with frosty pink fur. I couldn't tell if that was just the dust or if it was their natural color.

They seemed to have large round faces and short blunt muzzles. The pink frosting that covered everything made it hard to tell. Their noses and mouths were invisible, and their eyes were narrowly slitted against the powdery dust. They were thoroughly covered with it; they stood waist deep in the bright powder. They looked like Chinese bunnies in a cotton candy factory.

Bunny ears. Puppy faces. Not my idea of aliens from space. Certainly not my idea of a Chtorran intelligence.

I couldn't tell if they were friendly, hostile, or just curious. But they were staring at us. There was no question that we were the focus of their attention.

I looked at Duke—and then looked past Duke in horror. Five more of the little bunnydogs were just creeping up behind us.

I whirled around. There were more of them just coming out of the bushes behind me. They were coming out on all sides of us, too many to count.

There were bunnydogs to the left of us, bunnydogs to the right of us—

We were surrounded.

Q: What do Chtorrans call a chain saw?
A: A good kisser.

15

Pinkout

"Every mistake is another opportunity to beat yourself up."

—SOLOMON SHORT

Duke spoke first. "Well . . ." he said, very softly, "here's another fine mess you've gotten me into."

I looked over at him. "I must say, you're taking it rather well."

Duke ignored the remark. He was studying the bunnydogs, trying to figure out which one was the leader. He said, "You're supposed to be a scientist. What's the Chtorran word for friend?"

"The only Chtorran word I know translates out as 'lunch.' "

"Better not," Duke said. "Not until we know what these things eat."

"Well . . . they're not herbivores," I said.

"How do you know that?"

"Their eyes are on the front of their head. Predators need stereoscopic vision for tracking prey. Prey animals need their eyes on the sides of their head for avoiding predators. At least, that's how it happened on this planet. I could be wrong. But . . . if they're meat-eaters, then there's also a potential for intelligence."

"Why?"

"How much brains does it take to sneak up on a blade of grass?" I replied. I'd credit the joke later.

Duke considered the idea and nodded. During all this, the bunnydogs still hadn't moved. They just sat and stared at us.

I added, "Pray that these things are omnivores. According to the Cohen models, intelligence develops first in hunters, but it survives in creatures who aren't totally dependent on the hunt."

"So?" Duke asked. "Are we in trouble here or not?"

"Well . . . they're not carrying any weapons. If they're intelligent, then they could be just as curious about us as we are about them."

Duke turned slowly, studying the circle of little pink eskimo-things. They were remarkably patient little creatures. Duke said slowly, "You may be making a false assumption here, Jim."

I turned in the opposite direction, also studying. "What's that?" I asked.

"You're assuming that these things are sentient. What if they're not? What if this is just a wolf pack?"

The idea startled me. Duke was right. I'd been anthropomor-phizing the bunnydogs from the very first sighting. I'd just naturally assumed that anything with a humanoid form would have to be intelligent. "You're right. I'm sorry."

"Apologize later. Let's get out of here first."

One of the bunnydogs moved then. He shifted his squat to one side, and languidly began to scratch his ear with a hind leg. For a moment he looked just like a fat little puppy. Dammit! These things were too cute to be dangerous!

I looked at Duke. "Still think this is a wolf pack?"

"No more assumptions," he cautioned. He started forward, crunching through the still-frozen powder. Parts of it had started to thaw and were turning muddy. I could hear his boots squelching in the ooze. He took three steps and stopped. The two bunnydogs directly ahead of him stood up, gobbling excitedly and fluttering their hands. Duke glanced at me. What now?

The two bunnydogs looked at each other. They began to gobble at each other like baritone chipmunks. One of them took a hop and a half closer to the other and began gesturing like a little cheerleader. He gobbled and squeaked at his companion. He wrung his hands—they were tiny monkey paws. He put his fists together and shook them as if he were making a martini. He hopped up and down, raising large clouds of pink powder around them both. At one point, he even grabbed his cheeks and pulled them out sideways in a grotesque comical grimace.

His companion made a funny expression and babbled some-thing back. It looked like a disagreement. He waved both his fists over his head and made nattering noises. He thumped his feet in the dust, sending up an even larger cloud of pink smoke.

The first bunnydog flounced its displeasure. He reached over and pinched his companion's cheeks. He pulled and stretched them into a sideways expression. Where he let go, we could almost hear them snap back into place. The second bunnydog was unimpressed. He shook his fingers at the first, waving them like little tentacles.

It was turning into an argument. The pitch and tempo of their voices began to rise, like a recording being speeded up. Then abruptly the argument was over. The two bunnydogs began to make up like a pair of lovers. They touched each other's hands and faces, cooed like doves, glanced at us once, nuzzled each other's cheeks, chittered for a moment longer, but in quieter tones now, then finally turned to face us again.

"And I'm supposed to take them seriously now?" Duke asked. "After that little performance?"

I shrugged. "They do have us outnumbered." I glanced back. More bunnydogs had added themselves to the circle. More were arriving even as I watched. I said, "It's now or never, Duke."

"I agree." He took another step forward—

This time all the bunnydogs started chittering at us. They jumped up and down, gobbling and squeaking. The effect was ludicrous—and terrifying.

"Give 'em a puff of cold," Duke said. "See if they'll back off."

I nodded, pointed the nozzle at the space between us and the forward bunnydogs. I touched the trigger briefly, lightly—and released a *whoosh* of powdery cold into the air.

The bunnies leapt back away from it, startled and chittering, but they didn't panic, and they didn't flee.

They sniffed at the air, wrinkling their noses against the painful coldness of it; then they began to hop forward again, back into position.

"I could freeze a couple of them," I suggested. "But it might not be good for future relations."

Duke considered it. He shook his head. "Maybe a little fire instead." He armed his torch and raised it, deliberately pointing it high—

Something caught my eye. "Duke! Wait—"

Duke froze where he was.

Something large and dark was moving up through the dust toward us. I knew what it was even before it came out of the murk. So that's why the bunnies had held us here. They were waiting for this.

The worm was Papa-sized. It was five meters long, nearly two meters thick at the shoulders. Its eyes were shuttered against the dust.

And then I saw.

There were bunnydogs riding on top of the beast. The largest was perched on the brain-bump, and steering it with chirps and tugs and slaps. He was a chubby fellow, he looked and acted like a fat little bus driver. There were three other bunnydogs riding farther back on the worm. They looked like tourists. All they needed were cameras. If they hadn't been riding a two-thousand-kilo eating machine, they would have been cute.

The worm flowed to a stop and faced us. It blinked—*sput phwut*—and warbled a soft sound. *"Trllp?"* Then it shuttered its eyes again. It looked like it was dozing.

I looked at Duke. I'd never seen a worm do this before. He looked back at me and shrugged. But he kept his torch at the ready.

The bunnydog on top of the worm gobbled something at the bunnies on the ground. They gobbled back. Several of them clambered up onto the back of the worm to confer face-to-face with the newcomers.

Duke lowered his torch just a little bit. "Jim . . ." he said, "what are we looking at?"

"I don't know. I'd like to think that the bunnydogs are intelligent, perhaps even the intelligence behind the worms, but—" I said, "it could be the other way around too. The worm could be the intelligence, and the bunnies could be his dog pack. We might be the guests of honor at a fox hunt."

Duke accepted that thoughtfully. "Well, we need to make up our minds fast. One worm we can handle. We can't take on a whole family."

I nodded. "We're going to have to burn our way out, aren't we?"

Duke didn't answer. He just shifted the torch to his hands and steadied his stance.

Abruptly, the worm woke up. Its eyes popped open and it stared directly at Duke. At the same instant, all the bunnydogs on its back yipped and leapt off. Were they commanding it? Or getting out of its way?

The worm said, *"Chtorrllpp?"*

It looked *questioningly* to Duke. It started to slide forward . . .

"No—!"

—and Duke fired.

It was the dampness in the air that saved him, I'm sure of that. It was the lingering chill from the liquid nitrogen.

For a moment, the flame hung in the air—then it leapt *backward* and enveloped him—he didn't even have time to scream, he was a ball of orange fire—

It was the dust. It was so fine it didn't just burn—it exploded. It couldn't have been more dangerous if it were powdered hydrogen.

I didn't think. I just pointed the freezer at Duke and fired. The flames vanished almost instantly. Great clouds of cold steam whooshed up into the air, crackling and spitting. Duke was somewhere in the center of that.

I had to do it.

If I hadn't, the whole sea of powder would have exploded. It would have been a firestorm. I didn't have a choice.

There was a blackened burned thing standing where Duke had been. It toppled over into the powder.

The bunnydogs were gone, vanished into the bright pink haze; so was the worm, I hadn't even seen it move.

—There was just me and Duke, still crackling in the center of a smoldering black crater.

I started streaming.

"You goddamn sonofabitch!" I was already pushing through the ooze toward him. "I told you wait! Didn't anybody ever tell you about grain elevators? And dust! You stupid asshole!" I pulled his fuel tanks off him and rolled him over on his back. He was still alive. His breath was coming in great rasping wheezes. The O-mask had protected his face and lungs. He had a chance. Maybe.

I grabbed him by the tank harness, looped one of its belts around my forearm, and started dragging him forward. I couldn't carry him through this powder, but I could drag him. It would have to do. I cursed him every step of the way.

And then I stopped.

The whole world had become a fuzzy pink blur, vague and indistinct. Even the sun was gone. The sky and ground had vanished. There was nothing but pink. I couldn't even see my own hands. If I let go of Duke, I wouldn't even be able to find him again.

I'd heard of whiteouts in the Antarctic—this was worse; this was a California pinkout.

I didn't know where I was.

Worse, I didn't know where the chopper was.

Q: What do you say to a Chtorran attacking a battalion?
A: Don't play with your food.

16

The Man Upstairs

*"The trouble with the Ten
Commandments is that there are too
many 'Thou Shalt Nots' and not enough
'Thou Shalts.' "*

—SOLOMON SHORT

I froze. I knew I had to get back. But my sense of direction had totally failed.

I was afraid to take a step in *any* direction for fear I would be going the wrong way. I could be only a few meters from the ship and unable to see it.

The wrong decision would kill us.

I stood there, trembling with the realization, paralyzed by my own terror. I had to do *something*! Duke needed attention *now*. And neither of us had much air left.

I didn't know where the beeper was. It wasn't in Duke's hand or on his belt. I'd looked for it when I grabbed him. That was before the pink closed in. And now it was getting deeper. There was nothing but pink. It was waist-high now.

I had to do something. *Now*.

Even if it was the *wrong* thing to do.

I hadn't turned since grabbing Duke—I should still be pointed in the right direction. I didn't know what else to do.

I held the freezer in my left hand and sprayed it forward. I could hear the whoosh. I saw nothing, but I could feel the chill in the air.

This was crazy. It couldn't work. I moved forward anyway; slowly, I tested each step before putting my weight down.

Suddenly, the pink gave way beneath me. I let out a yell—I hung onto Duke—and we slid down a long slope of powder—

We came to rest at the bottom, buried in pinkness. I couldn't find the place where the ground ended and the air began. We were wrapped in spider webs. I wasn't even sure which way was up any more. I fired the freezer in the direction I thought was forward. The chill woke me up.

I caught my breath. I sat up. Somehow, I stood up. The belt of Duke's harness was still looped around my arm. My God! He was still with me!

I started pushing forward again.

I was frustrated—I was angry!

Dammit! This is Jim McCarthy here! I'm not supposed to die like this! Not this young! I'm only twenty-four! There's supposed to be *more* to my life! I'm important! I'm part of the war against the Chtorr! "Hey, God! Listen up! This is James Edward McCarthy! It's too soon! I haven't had the rest of my life yet!

"Hey, God, come on—let's be reasonable here." I staggered on, dragging Duke with me, spraying the air ahead with chill, and trying to hang onto my footing. I didn't know which way I was going. "Hey, God, give me a sign. Something. Anything. Please. Save me. Save Duke. At least save Duke. I've already got Shorty's death on my conscience. Isn't that enough? Let me save Duke. Then you can have me if you want me. I'm scared of dying, God—" I gulped on that one, "—and I'm sorry, I've been an asshole. Please—God, I thought you had bigger plans for me. This isn't the way it's supposed to work out, is it?" My throat was getting dry. My voice cracked. I didn't know why I was saying all this. It was just something to say while I pushed on.

And then, something happened.

Inside me.

Something shifted.

I realized what I was doing. I remembered something Duke had said to me: "You oughta try it sometime."

I gulped again.

This was stupid. But—

I could feel myself really *caring*. Really wanting to make contact.

If it were possible.

"Um . . . I don't know how to do this, I really don't. I guess I should just talk, shouldn't I? So, um . . . let me start at the beginning. I'm really doing this for Duke. I've been selfish and . . . oh, hell, I know you can't save Duke without saving me too, but—"

My feet moved. My mouth worked. I pushed forward.

And I *prayed*.

"God . . . I don't even know if I believe in you. I don't know that you exist. I never thought about it. So . . . I guess I'm just another goddamn hypocrite only believing in you now when there's no other hope. I'm going crazy here, God. It's just not fair. I'd always thought someday I'd have the chance to find out what it all meant. Are you listening, God?" I stumbled then and fell forward into the pink and somehow the belt to Duke's harness came off my arm. I felt it slip off.

It was gone.

I lay there in the powder, paralyzed.

Duke was only inches from me. If I moved, I could lose him. I had to be careful. Very careful.

I raised myself up to my knees. I reached backward, back and back. I fumbled in the dust. Please, God—let me find Duke. Nothing else. Let me find Duke.

I ignored the sound in my ears. I had to find Duke. Carefully, I turned myself around, praying that I wouldn't slip sideways down another slope, or turn myself the wrong way. I felt around. I sprawled flat and felt ahead—my hand touched something—I grabbed it—

It was Duke's arm. Oh, thank you, God!

I felt around for his face. I found it. I was blind. The world was pink. I didn't care if I never saw again. Just let him be alive! I brought my face close to Duke's and listened. *Tried* to listen. Couldn't. There was too much noise. But his mask was making rasping sounds! He was still breathing! Oh, sweet heaven—thank you, God! Now, please—let me get him to the chopper!

The sound in my ears was getting louder. Annoying. Insistent. What the hell was that anyway? It sounded like a siren.

I stopped to catch my breath. And listened.

The sound was muffled by the dust. It was close by, yet sounded very far away. Some kind of whooping.

It *was* a siren! It came out of the pinkness as a steady series of short sharp rising yelps.

The chopper? It had to be!

What was it doing way over there to my left? I'd been heading wrong! I didn't care. Thank you, God! We could make it!

I tied Duke's belt around my waist again. I stumbled back to my feet. I faced the siren. I pushed. I dragged Duke behind me. I focused only on the sound.

It was whooping like a demon. Like someone beating a bassett hound. The strokes were sharp and steady. A yelping purple sound. It was the only thing in the world that wasn't pink. And I pushed toward it.

I sprayed the liquid nitrogen ahead. I crunched through dust. I pushed through crackling spider-web fluffiness. Everything was pink. But I could hear the siren and I knew that we were saved!

Thank you, God. Thanks!

There is a job here for me, isn't there!

Q: What do Chtorrans call a poodle?
A: Hors d'oeuvres.

17

The Dust

"You'll find it in the last place you look."
—SOLOMON SHORT

I found the chopper by stumbling into it.

I don't know how I found the door. I just started feeling along the side of the ship, pounding and shouting as I went. The chopper was so deep in the powder that I was pounding on the roof of it. "Lizard! Open the goddamn door!"

And then suddenly the door popped open in front of me and I fell in. I couldn't see it, I just fell in. I poured in, dragging Duke with me. The dust poured in on top of us. Somebody was pulling me forward. "Oh, my God—"

"Save Duke!" I was screaming. "Don't worry about me! I'm all right! See to Duke!"

"Wait! I've got to close the door!" Lizard was screaming back at me. "The dust is pouring in—" She coughed and disappeared.

I lay there on the chopper floor, listening to my heartbeat, listening to the insistent whooping of the siren, listening to my own sobs of relief. I couldn't move. I had to move. There was still something to do. I pulled myself to my knees. I heard the sound of the door hissing shut. There was something wrong with the sound. I still couldn't see. But at least it wasn't pink any more. It was dark and blurry. I wiped at my goggles—

"Keep your O-mask on!" Lizard was in front of me again. "McCarthy, can you hear me? Do you understand? Keep your O-mask on!"

I managed to nod and gasp, "Water—"

She put a bulb of something into my hand and was gone. I sucked at the moisture greedily. It was sweet. Everything was sweet. Suddenly I could smell the powder again. Fresh-baked croissants. Bubble gum. Marshmallows. Something buttery. Sweet potatoes. Angel food cake. And cotton candy. Always cotton candy.

"McCarthy!" It was Lizard again. "We've got a problem with the door! I can't close it! The dust is in the way! The door is jammed."

"Shit!" I scrambled around, felt past Duke—"I can't see a thing. Where's my freezer!"

"It's here—" She pushed something long and cold into my hands.

"Point me at the door and get out of the way. Get Duke out of the way too!"

I felt her hands on my shoulders, turning me, aiming me— "Wait a minute!" she said. I heard the sound of something heavy being pulled across the deck. "All right—"

I fired. The spray was too loud. The chill was terrible and bitter. Something crackled. This was not the smartest thing in the world. I could feel the clouds of cold steam billowing around me. The liquid nitrogen always reacted strongly to normal air temperatures.

Lizard pushed past me, moving to the front of the ship. I heard the sound of the door hissing again. This time, I could hear the powder crackling out of its way, even exploding as it came into contact with the warmer metal of the door.

And then the door was shut.

A moment later, Lizard shut the siren off.

And everything was black and silent.

"Is there any light?" I yelled. "I still can't see!"

"Just stay there—wait a minute!" I heard her doing something at the front of the ship. She came back almost immediately. I saw a bright glow in front of my eyes. "Can you see anything?"

"A blur. It's bright. It's moving."

"It's a flashlight." She wiped at my goggles. "Keep your mask on. I'm just blowing some of the dust away. Can you see anything now?"

"It's brighter. . . ."

"Just relax. There's a lot of smoke in here. I can't turn on the ventilators. They'll just jam. Give it a minute, I think your freezer is causing the stuff to settle."

"I think my sight is coming back," I said. "This is the eeriest experience."

"Yeah, a lot of fun—" And then she let out an involuntary yelp. "My God! What happened to Duke!"

I tried to focus. I could just barely make him out.

Duke was a mummy. Duke was a pink-crusted body. Duke was a cocoon. Duke was burned all over and frosted with pink powdered sugar. Duke was lying on the floor and gasping for breath.

My lungs hurt too. Despite the masks, we must have both inhaled a couple kilos of the dust. I didn't want to keep going. I wanted to lie down and die. But I didn't. Not yet. I started crawling toward the back, looking for the box with the red cross on it. Lizard came with me. We both knew the drill.

We didn't try to pull the jumpsuit off him. We had to cut it. Parts of it were burned. Parts of it were still frozen. Pieces of charred skin came away with the material. The dust covered everything.

I couldn't tell how badly Duke was injured. We got his shirt off him and started pasting poker-chip-shaped monitors to his chest. I put the last three on his forehead and temples. Then we wrapped him in a medi-blanket. I found another probe and put it in the crook of his elbow. I attached a pressure feeder to his upper arm and gave him a half-liter of artificial blood. Then I started him on glucose and antibiotics.

That done, I lifted his goggles and mask. His eyes were swollen. His nose was bleeding. Lizard wiped his face gently with a damp towel. I found a clean O-mask and carefully replaced his used one. We'd found the chopper just in time. The tank was almost empty.

The console said he was in shock. The ultrasonic scanner in the blanket gave a very confused reading. Then it gave up and merely flashed a simple red warning: WAIT FOR ASSISTANCE.

His brain waves were steady, though. That was a good sign. So was his heart.

I sat back then, pulled off my O-mask and flung it at the back of the ship. Everything was covered with pink. A puff of dust billowed where the mask hit.

I still wanted to die. "Give me one of those cloths—?"

Lizard peeled open a new packet and slapped it onto my palm. I unfolded it and buried my face in its cool freshness. "Thank you," I said. "Thank you for the cloth. Thank you for the siren. Thank you for being here. Thank you for saving Duke's life." I didn't know if I was thanking Lizard or God. Probably both.

"Thank you." My voice cracked on the last one. Lizard handed me another bulb of water.

"What happened?" she asked.

I sank back against the bulkhead behind me. I sucked water from the bulb for a moment, then looked at her. She pulled off her mask. She was frosted all over with pink powder too, except for her eyes and mouth. The effect was horrible. We both looked grotesque. She sat back against the bulkhead opposite me and waited.

I let out my breath. My chest hurt. I sucked more water. I didn't want to talk. I said, "You are looking at the biggest asshole on the face of the Earth. I screwed it up worse than I have ever screwed up anything—"

"That part is obvious," Lizard said. "Tell me the part I don't know."

"I'm sorry," I said. "I led us into a trap. At least it looked like a trap to Duke. I'm still not sure it was. But the effect was the same." I sucked at the bulb. God, I was thirsty! What was it about this dust, anyway! I looked back to Lizard and continued softly, "Anyway, there *are* creatures out there. We saw them. They surrounded us. They look like little furry men. They're shaped like ducks. They waddle. They have round faces and slitted eyes and floppy ears. They talk like chipmunks. They make faces at each other. They use their hands when they talk. They're too cute to be real. I think they escaped from Disneyland. They surrounded us and wouldn't let us pass. They were keeping us for something. A worm. Three more of them—no, four—came riding up on a Daddy-worm. They held a conference. And then the worm moved toward Duke. It didn't look like an attack to me, but Duke fired anyway. And his torch blew up. It must have been the dust. It's too fine. It explodes—" I shuddered at the memory. I didn't want to talk any more, I didn't want to tell the rest.

Lizard didn't press me. She just sat and studied me quietly.

I studied her back.

I didn't know how to *be* with her. I'd fallen back into this chopper and I'd wanted to bawl like a baby. I'd wanted to cry into someone's arms. That's how I'd always thought of women—that they had an unlimited supply of hugs for the needy—because that's what I thought a woman should be. Because I'd always been one of the needy.

But there weren't any hugs here.

That wasn't Lizard. Lizard was all military. Lizard was as crisp as a brand new bank note. She scared me.

I sucked at the bulb of water again. It was empty.

Lizard went digging in the supplies and handed me another bubble. I took it and bit the nipple open. As I drank, she asked quietly, "Were you scared?"

"That's the *funny* thing. Not while it happened. Now—" I held out my hand to show her, "I'm still shaking—"

She nodded. "I'm familiar with the experience. People who don't know call it courage."

"Yeah," I said. "It wasn't courage. It was just . . . me doing what I had to do because I couldn't think of anything else."

Her eyes were too penetrating. I looked away. At the floor, the walls, the ceiling of the chopper.

Did she see how close to panic I still was? She began to speak again, quietly. "I saw an old air force hangar blow up that way once. I was only ten meters from the place where the fire started. It was just a little thing at first. It started in a trash can; some idiot tossed a lit cigarette into it, but the flames suddenly climbed up the wall. I turned for the door just as the fire touched the first catwalk. There were fifty years of dust on the rafters. By the time I finished turning, the fire had already raced ahead of me. In less than three seconds it had reached across the whole ceiling. Somebody yelled at me, so I ran. By the time I made it to the door there was a hot wind pushing me out. I got out of the building, ran twenty meters, turned around to look, and saw the whole wall explode outward. I turned around and kept running. The next time I looked back, the roof of the building was just coming off in a ball of orange flame. The whole process of ignition took less than ten seconds. I've been terrified of it happening again ever since. I don't remember being scared at the time. But I've been scared ever since."

"Yeah," I said. The bulb was empty. I put it aside. "That's what happened here. I didn't have time to think about it then. Now I can't *stop* thinking about it. It's like a video playing over and over in my head and I'm stuck in the middle of it. And I don't know how to stop it. I keep seeing the flames. And the dust. And the worm. And the bunnydogs. I keep wishing I could have done something."

A flicker of annoyance crossed her face; then she looked at me sternly. "What happened?"

"The flames didn't leap out from the torch like they should have. They leapt *back*. They enveloped Duke in a ball of fire. I didn't think—I just pointed the freezer at him and sprayed him with liquid nitrogen. The flames disappeared almost immediately. So did the worm and the bunnydogs. I don't know how they navigate in that stuff. I couldn't. I was lost. I grabbed Duke and started staggering in the direction I thought was the chopper. And I was wrong again. If you hadn't turned on the siren, I'd still be out there dragging him around. Or dead. We'd have been out of air by now," I added.

Lizard nodded. She said, "Actually, you did the right thing. That jumpsuit is flame resistant. So are the O-mask and goggles. There wasn't anything else you could have done. You're alive. He's alive. You did it right."

I shook my head. "But it doesn't *feel* right. It feels like a replay of Shorty—"

"Uh-huh." She nodded. "That's what it looks like to you. Haven't you ever noticed? Nothing is ever just what it is? It's always like something else. Whatever happens, it always reminds you of something that happened before. Right?"

She was right. "Uh—yeah!" I found myself smiling.

"I do it too." She giggled back at me. Her laughter was liquid—and startling. "You told your story," she said, "—so I told mine. Do you know that most conversations are nothing more than two people telling their stories to each other?"

Something about the certainty with which she said it made me think of Dr. Foreman. But I didn't get a chance to ask her—

Duke moaned.

We both looked at him, then scrambled to see if he was all right.

"Duke?" I put my face close.

He moaned again. "It hurts—"

"That's good, Duke. That's a good sign."

The medi-console beeped and flashed: PATIENT NEEDS SEDATION.

I found a red ampule and plugged it into the pressure feeder. After a moment Duke's breathing eased. "He's out of shock," I said. I didn't know if that was true, or just what I wanted to believe. I tried to convince myself. "The medi-kit wouldn't ask for sedation if he was still in shock. Would it?"

"I don't know." Lizard shrugged. "Let me put that console on-line to Oakland and see what they have to suggest." She climbed down toward the nose of the ship.

I sat with Duke a while longer, wishing there was something else I could do for him. I wondered if he was going to live. And if he did . . . what kind of shape would he be in?

I had to stop that train of thought real quick. That would be another good way to drive myself crazy. "Duke," I whispered to him. "I'm sorry. I didn't know what else to do. I love you, Duke.

I never told you, but I really do. I depend on you. Please stay with me."

I knew he couldn't answer. Probably he couldn't hear me either. It didn't matter. I just knew I had to say it.

After a while, I got up and went down to the nose of the ship to join Lizard. She was curled up in her seat, resting her chin on her fist, and studying a weather display. She looked grim. I sat down next to her in silence. The pink dust had risen almost to the top of the windshield. It was getting very dark in here.

"Did you raise Oakland?"

"Uh-huh. They're monitoring. They'll let us know."

I pointed at the windshield. "It's still coming down, isn't it?"

"Uh-huh. It'll be coming down all night." She pointed at the screen in front of her. "The main body of the cloud still has to pass over us. We're going to be buried in this stuff—and I have no idea how deep it's going to get."

Q: What do Chtorrans call a Hollywood lawyer?
A: Tough.

18

"It sure isn't lobster—"

*"People will go to the most incredible
lengths to make fools of themselves."*
—SOLOMON SHORT

A sudden thought came to me. "Will we have enough air?"

Lizard hesitated. "Yeah. We've got some oxygen tanks with the medical supplies. We can crack those. Theoretically, we should be able to hold out for a day and a half. I wouldn't want to have to depend on it though."

She pulled off her headset and tossed it onto the control panel in front of her. "Shit," she said.

"What now?"

"Oh, nothing. I had plans for tonight. Being buried alive wasn't part of them."

"Oh," I said. I couldn't imagine Colonel Lizard Tirelli on a date. "I'm sorry."

"What are you apologizing for? It's not your fault."

"Um, I was just expressing my regret."

"Yeah, well thanks for the thought then. I was thinking about steak and lobster all day."

"Lobster?"

"Uh-huh. The Arizona farms are producing again. You should see some of the monsters they're turning out. This big—" She held her hands a meter apart. She added thoughtfully, "Arizona is an easy state to keep clean. The southern part, anyway. There's not a lot of forage or ground cover for the worms. That's one place we should be able to hold the line against them for a long time."

"Is that part of the long-range planning?"

"Not yet. It will be, though."

"Are you going to be on the Committee?"

"I've been asked. It's a question of . . . priorities." She shrugged. "What good is long-range planning if you don't take care of the present?"

"On the other hand," I said, "what you do in the present should be a function of your long-range goals, shouldn't it?"

She looked at me sharply. "Have you been talking to Dr. Foreman?"

"Uh . . . no. Why?"

"That sounds like something he might say. That's a compliment, by the way. But you're right. I have to go where I'm most effective." She smiled gently. "Which means I probably will join the Committee. I'm just afraid I won't get to fly as much. And I don't want to give up flying."

"I'd think being on the Committee would let you fly even more—you know, on-the-scene observations."

"It's a good idea," she acknowledged. "But I don't know that it would work out that way." She peered at the window then. "Hand me that flashlight."

I passed it over, and she pointed at the beam at the upper edge of the windshield in front of her. It was completely pink. "Yep, I thought so. The nose is completely covered. It must be coming down faster than ever."

She levered herself out of her seat and started working her way to the back. I followed behind. She dug around in a side panel and produced another flashlight and an emergency lamp. The lamp she hung from a hook in the ceiling. "There . . . that's better." She handed me the second flashlight.

She climbed past Duke and pointed her beam around the tail of the chopper. I didn't know what she was looking for. She stuck her head up into the rear bubble and pointed the flashlight around inside. "Uh-huh. We are now completely buried. I sure hope this crap isn't an insulator. We could get awfully hot in here."

"I thought that Banshees were tiled."

"They are, but if we're buried, there's no place for the heat to go." She climbed toward the back. "You hungry?"

"Yeah."

"Good. Get the emergency rations out."

I checked on Duke—no change—and then pulled out the ration box. We reconvened at the front of the chopper. We swiveled the seats around to face the rear. Better to have the fifteen-degree angle noseward tilt holding you in instead of tipping you out. I leaned back and put my feet up on the deck. The ration bars were chewy and required a little concentration.

Abruptly, she asked, "Have you ever been invited to a Blue Mass?"

I shook my head. "Is that an invitation?" I asked.

She gave me a sour look. "I was just wondering if you knew anything about them."

"Sorry." I added, "I've heard that the members are pretty aggressive in their recruitment."

She nodded. "I was invited last week. They have them every weekend now. Hundreds of people attend, and pay a thousand caseys each for the privilege." Lizard's tone went softer then. She said, "I was just wondering—I've heard stories. But not from anybody who's been to one. Apparently there's some kind of confidentiality agreement. But I hear that . . . there's a lot of release. A lot of abandonment. I'm not sure what that means. There's supposed to be a lot of sex too."

She left that thought hanging between us for a beat, then commented, "I don't know that screwing yourself into insensibility is the best way to handle madness, but obviously it works for some people. So . . . sometimes I wonder if it would work for me. I can't help but wonder if maybe all those people have really found something."

Her voice grew very soft then. I had to strain to hear what she said next.

"Sometimes I get tempted. What if it really does work? Wouldn't I be a jerk not to go? It would be nice to forget—even for a little while. That's why I would go. To forget."

I was embarrassed. I wanted to say something, but I knew that whatever I said would automatically be the wrong thing to say.

"Except—" Lizard continued, "I know that it's a trap. It's like drugs. Another escape. Once you start trying to escape, it isn't long before you're running. I've seen it happen to too many people already. I don't want it to happen to me." Abruptly, she fell silent.

I glanced over at her. She was staring at her ration bar moodily. I looked at mine. "It sure isn't lobster, is it?"

"That's right—rub it in." She sounded bitter.

"I'm sorry." I made up my mind then, I had to ask. "Colonel?" She didn't look up.

"Uh . . . sometimes I get the same kind of feelings. And . . . uh, I figure that I'm probably not the only one. So I figure that the brass must know about it. I mean . . . there must be some . . . uh, outlet. Or something. Isn't there?"

She didn't answer immediately. I was beginning to wonder if she was going to answer me at all, when she said, "Yes, the brass knows that most of the men and women in uniform are this close to the edge. And no, there isn't a solution. At least, not the kind you're looking for—the easy one."

And suddenly, she was Colonel Tirelli again, crisp and military. Under control. "Remember Dr. Foreman? He's working on that problem now. The President asked him to. So far, all he's said about it is that the only answer is an unsatisfactory one. He says that each of us is responsible for what's going on inside our own heads. Therefore, each of us is responsible for maintaining our own balance."

"But, how—?"

She shrugged. "That's what he's working on. I suspect it's a more advanced form of the Mode training, but I don't know. Listen," she added, "you're in Special Forces, the Uncle Ira Group, so you can always call Dr. Davidson in Atlanta."

"Do you talk to him?" I asked.

"Now you're getting personal," she said.

"Sorry."

"There you go, apologizing again." She looked over at me, a funny look on her face. "Do you ever do anything else?"

"I'm sorry—I mean, uh, yeah—I screw up." I looked back at her. "So I'll have something to apologize for. Sometimes I think that's the only social transaction I'm good at." I grinned apologetically.

"It's called Schlemiel," she said. "It's a game. You win by getting people to forgive you. That's the payoff. You can play it forever, as long as there are people to spill soup on." She looked at her ration bar sourly. *"But it bores the hell out of me."*

I didn't know what to say. I opened my mouth anyway. Words fell out. "Well excuse me for being on the same planet with you. Excuse me for being in the same species."

"I'm not so sure that we *are* the same species. . . ." she said. "I'd like a second opinion on that."

I flustered. If I could have gotten up and walked away, I would have; but there was no place to walk to. How was I supposed to *respond* to her? I said, "I don't know what to make of you! Just a few minutes ago we were talking like two human beings. Now you're treating me like I'm some kind of a—a *thing*!"

She didn't answer immediately. She was chewing quietly.

When she did speak, she kept her voice calm. She said, "I'm treating you like you're acting, *Lieutenant*. You're acting like a spoiled little brat. It's boring. I'm tired of listening to you apologize. I'm tired of you taking the blame for everything that goes wrong in the world."

"Well, but—"

"No. Just shut up and listen. You're not giving yourself any credit for the things you did right."

"I don't think I did anything right!"

"That's right. You *don't think* you did! You went out in that dust and got a good look at some previously unknown Chtorran creatures. You saved Duke's life—I grant that you did it with an extremely unorthodox and probably not recommended procedure, but you *did* save his life. You single-handedly dragged him back to the chopper. I know a lot of people who wouldn't have done that; they'd have given up first. You didn't give up! And when you did get here, you didn't stop. You didn't do anything for yourself until you'd first done everything you could for Duke. I was here too. Remember? I saw it! You know, they give out medals for that kind of stuff. You're a goddamned hero, McCarthy—"

"No, I'm not!"

"—but you won't believe it, because you have some pictures in your head of what you think a hero is supposed to be and that's not you! Right?"

"Uh—"

"Right?" she demanded. "Am I right?"

"Uh . . . I know I'm not a hero. Yes, you're right."

"Yeah." She nodded. "So you go around apologizing for being who you are. And in the meantime, you keep forgetting to notice that who you are is not such a bad person. You know, you'd be kind of cute if you weren't such a schmuck."

"Huh?"

She flushed and threw her hands up in the air. "Now you know my secret. I think you're cute. An asshole, but a cute one."

"Cut it out! I don't like being teased like that! I had my fill of it in high school!"

"I'm not teasing." She was dead serious.

"Huh—?" This conversation wasn't making sense. "You mean that? You think *I'm* cute?"

"Yeah." She nodded. *"You."*

"Uh—no. I'm not. I have a broken nose that was never properly set. And I'm too short. And I'm too thin. And I'm—"

"There you go, doing it again. Can't you just let it in and say thank you?"

"Uh . . ." This was very hard. "I'm not . . . used to this. Compliments, I mean. Nobody ever . . . I mean . . . uh—" I stopped. I felt embarrassed. And I felt good. Lizard was really a beautiful woman!

"Thank you," I said.

"Good." She beamed. "Very good." She looked at what was left of her ration bar. "But you're right about one thing, you know."

"Huh? About what?"

"This sure as hell *isn't* lobster."

Q: What do Chtorrans call a midget?
A: Bite-size.

19

A Season of Candy

*"The blind man looking in a mirror
cannot see he has no eyes. So what?"*

. — SOLOMON SHORT

I was awakened by Lizard's voice. My throat was filled with
cotton. I tried to clear it and couldn't.

"—No, we're still buried. It's darker in here than the inside of
a bear."

I opened my eyes. She was talking on the radio again. My chest
hurt. Every breath tickled, then it burned. I didn't dare risk
coughing.

"—No, I can't tell how deep. I think the sun's coming up,
though. There's a faint glow in the turret and at the top of the
windshield. But I'm not sure that means anything. The stuff is
translucent. And when it piles up in drifts it doesn't get very
dense, so it passes a lot of light. We could be under ten meters of
it and not know."

I'd heard this conversation before. Lizard and I had covered the
same material all last night before we'd finally collapsed into
separate makeshift bunks.

I pulled myself painfully into a sitting position. I was stiff. I
was sore all over. Everything hurt. My lungs were the worst;
every breath was an effort. I wanted to cough, but I knew I didn't
dare. If I started I'd never stop. I knew I had to keep my breathing
shallow and my movements to a minimum. The pressure to cough
was incredible.

But—first things first. I had to check on Duke.

He was still asleep.

He looked bad. Most of his hair was burned away. Parts of his scalp were peeling and blistered. The skin looked dead. He looked so bad I didn't want to look at him. I didn't want to know what he looked like under the medi-blanket. I felt queasy.

This wasn't Duke any more. This was burned meat. It didn't look like it would ever be Duke again. A thought crossed my mind: Maybe he'd be better off if he died. I shoved it away. And prayed that God hadn't heard me. I didn't mean it, God, I said silently. I really didn't.

I punched the console for display. The medi-kit was continually monitoring his body functions, and the level of sedative in his bloodstream was automatically maintained. It was probably dangerous to keep him out for this long, but what else could we do? They were reading the same information at Oakland. They knew what our circumstance was. If there was anything else to do, they would call us—or they'd reprogram the medi-kit directly. But for the moment, all we could do was sit.

And I hated waiting.

It made me feel useless.

Duke was starting to smell bad. Very, very bad. The screen said his legs were infected. This couldn't go on much longer.

The chopper had a tiny lavatory at the very rear of the cabin. I stepped into it and threw up. And then I started coughing. My chest felt like it was on fire and it hurt like hell.

By the time I rejoined Lizard at the front of the ship, she was off the radio. She had turned her chair around to face the rear again and had just cracked open a new ration kit.

"G'morning." She grinned. "Want some lobster?" She waved a stick of something gray at me. It looked unhealthy.

"No thanks," I said. I collapsed into my own chair. My chest still ached and I felt itchy all over.

"How about some prime rib instead?" She held up a sickly green-looking bar.

"Please—I've already thrown up once this morning. That stuff is not fit for human consumption."

"It depends on the wine you serve with it," she said over a mouthful. She held up a can of beer to show me.

I looked over at her. "When we get out of this," I said, "I will buy you the biggest fucking lobster in Arizona. And the best bottle of wine I can afford. Until then, I don't want to hear about food."

"You're on," she said. "With any luck, that'll be tonight."

"Really?"

She nodded. "Weather scan shows the cloud has dissipated—or spread out too thin to register on the scope. There were strong winds last night. The main body of the cloud passed us by around three in the ayem. Oakland says the last of it is still breaking up over Sacramento. They got a couple inches of cotton candy—but nothing like we got. There's also a chance of rain. With all these dust particles in the air, it's a very good chance. Weather service is adjusting their model now, but I'm betting that it rains before they can bring the new simulation up and running."

"Mp," I said.

Assuming that the puffball clouds hadn't left a permanent pink haze in the air, we still had to address the real problem. The chopper was buried in this crap. How were we going to get out of the ship? If we were under more than two meters of dust, we might as well forget it.

And that suggested *another* problem. Just how extensive *were* these drifts, anyway? I already knew from experience that we wouldn't be able to move very far through them. No, it was too unlikely that we could get to clear ground. They were going to have to pick us up here.

And then there was the problem of Duke.

I sucked at a water bulb and looked at Lizard. She was lost in thought as well.

She caught me looking at her. "Yes?"

"How are we going to get Duke out of here?"

"You've gotten that far with it, huh?"

"Uh, I haven't gotten anywhere. I just figured that Duke is the hard part of the problem. If we can handle that, the rest takes care of itself."

She said, "I think we're going to have to wait for outside assistance. Right now, the best solution I can come up with is a Sikorsky Skyhook. It could just pull us out—if we could get the grapples in place."

I said, "If any part of the parafoil is accessible, they can hook onto that, can't they? They could use that harness."

"Hey! That's not bad—"

"Thanks."

"—except it won't work." She explained, "It's not your fault. The problem is the Sikorsky. No chopper can rescue us. It'll stir up too much dust. It'll ruin its own engines. They'll come down right on top of us."

"I wonder if this stuff could be washed away? My great-grandmother once tried to teach me a rain dance. You said there's a chance of rain. I'll call it down here."

She smiled sourly. "That'll turn this stuff into mud—and then it'll harden into concrete."

"But it's just . . . cake flour."

"You ever try to eat a stale bagel?"

I threw up my hands in despair. "I concede the point."

"Got any other ideas?" she asked.

"Well, we know we can *burn* it away. . . ." I said it unenthusiastically.

"Now, that's a thought," Lizard replied brightly. "You and Duke have already proved the dust is flammable. And this chopper is tiled. It'll make a wonderful oven." She grinned at me. "Do you like brick-oven cooking?"

"No thanks." I picked up the flashlight, switched it on, and swiveled forward. I stared at the pink barrier on the opposite side of the windshield. "I wonder what they do on the planet Chtorr?"

"They probably don't fly in cotton candy weather."

"Yeah, they probably have candy warnings."

"I can imagine the forecasts," Lizard said. "Tomorrow will be mostly fair with scattered high candy and a twenty percent chance of lemonade."

"Not lemonade," I corrected. "Wrong color. More likely strawberry soda."

"Haven't you ever heard of pink lemonade?" She grinned.

I started to answer—but coughed instead, and then got lost in a paroxysm of coughing and choking.

"You okay?" Lizard asked when I finished. She looked worried.

I nodded, weakly. "Some of your lemonade powder went down the wrong pipe." I managed a smile and she relaxed.

"This is pretty rough weather for summer," Lizard said thoughtfully. She was probably trying to distract me. "What do you think their winters are like?"

I cleared my throat carefully. "Colder and wetter."

"Instead of snow, they get syrup? Sounds like a good way to get your wicket sticky."

"Actually," I mused, "that might not be so far from the truth. Everything is edible to something else. We're just another kind of snack to the worms. Maybe their own planet is one great big smorgasbord to them. It's all point of view. Maybe this is the season of candy."

"Well, we could sure use a couple of worms with sweet tooths—sweet teeth?—along about now," Lizard said.

"Uh . . . I'm not sure they're not already here," I replied very slowly.

"Huh?"

"Turn your seat around and look. I think something's moving out there."

Q: What do Chtorrans call a urine specimen?
A: *Au jus*

20

Out There

*"New problems demand new solutions.
New solutions create new problems."*

—SOLOMON SHORT

"Where?" said Lizard.

"There. Up near the top."

"I don't see anything."

"Keep looking. It was just a flicker—right there. As if something's moving on top of the dust."

We stared and waited. Nothing.

After a moment, Lizard said, "Well, I don't see it."

"I'm sure of what I saw." There was an edge of anger in my voice.

"Yes, I'm sure you are," she replied quietly. "Last time you were that sure, you disrupted a conference."

I ignored the knife between my ribs. "And I was right, wasn't I?"

Lizard shrugged. "Being right is rarely a victory."

"Huh?"

"Never mind." She anchored one foot on the console, grunted, and swiveled her seat to the back again. "If there's really something out there, we'll see it soon enough."

I muttered something unprintable and grabbed the flashlight. I climbed past her to check on Duke again. The medi-console said he was stable. He looked a little less gray. I wished I'd taken more pre-med courses. I wasn't sure how to interpret any of this.

"Uh . . . Colonel?"

"Yeah?"

"Do you know anything about first aid?"

"A little."

"Come here and listen. Duke's breathing sounds funny."

She came to the back and squatted down next to Duke. She listened. Then she smiled. "His breathing's fine."

"But that wheezing—"

"He's asleep," she said. "He's snoring."

"Are you sure?"

Lizard looked me straight in the eyes. "I know what a man's snoring sounds like."

"Uh . . . right. Thank you." I picked up the flashlight and went to the back of the tail to look if I could see anything out of the rear bubble. The cotton candy seemed a little more translucent there. I could feel my face burning.

How long would it be till we *really* started getting on each other's nerves? I wondered if I could get angry enough to kill her. I was afraid I might find out.

I climbed into the bubble seat, folded my arms across my chest, and faced the back.

What is it about women anyway? Why do they all seem to think that life is about challenging men? And then they wonder why the men are so touchy—

I was staring at it for several minutes before I realized what I was seeing. I came out of the chair so fast, I bumped my head on the Plexiglas. "Holy shit!—*Owwww!*"

"Are you all right?" Lizard called.

"No—"

"What happened?"

"I bumped my head—" I could still feel the ringing. "Come here!"

"Why? You want me to kiss it?"

"I want you to *see* something. Come here!" I started coughing then, and couldn't think of anything for a minute. Every choking paroxysm was agony. I forced myself to stop, I don't know how. I just held on. My chest was bursting and my eyes were streaming.

When I opened my eyes again, Lizard was looking up at me with a concerned expression. She was holding out a bulb of water. I took it gratefully. "Thanks."

She came climbing past Duke with a sigh. "All right, what do you want me to see?"

I pointed at the window. "There *is* something out there."

She looked. She frowned. She looked confused. Then her eyes widened—

The entire surface of the bubble was alive.

It was still a solid pink mass—but we couldn't resolve a pattern. As we watched, the movements grew more pronounced than ever. The flickerings became scratchings.

"What is it?"

"I don't know. But it's getting bigger."

"Bigger? Couldn't you have chosen *another* word?"

"How about closer?"

"Not much improvement." She folded her arms around herself as if she were cold. "It's getting lighter in here, isn't it?" she offered. "Could it be the wind? Blowing the dust off?"

"I wish it were. But I doubt it."

I moved as close to the window as I could and still keep my eyes focused. Something was moving the pink powder around. The way it shifted and swirled, it looked like thousands of tiny little shapes, all moving and scrambling at once.

And then it *resolved*.

"*Unghh*," I said.

"What—?" she asked.

"Look close."

She leaned into the bubble, staring. Her eyes widened in horror. "Bugs!"

The entire surface of the bubble was flickering and swirling and seething. We were looking at the bodies of millions and millions of frenzied insects.

"They're feeding on the powder," I said. I dropped back into my seat, shuddering. I was feeling very itchy.

Lizard dropped out of the bubble and scrambled forward. I could hear her stopping at the ports. "They're all over us!"

I levered myself out of the seat and went forward to join her. She was staring at the window. Because this part of the chopper was buried deeper in the drift, the seething movement was still limited to the very top of the windshield. It wasn't as clear as it was at the tail, but it was clear enough.

Lizard shuddered. She couldn't tear her eyes away from that flickering pink wall. "They're all over us!"

I tried to imagine what the chopper must look like from above. A large pink sugary hump in the middle of the pink snowdrift—covered by a billion crawling insects, nature's perfect little machines, all of them feeding. I could imagine them working at the powder, their tiny mandibles flashing. I could imagine them chittering and scraping and jostling—

I grabbed her by the shoulders. "Listen to me! Is this ship airtight?"

"It should be—Oh, my God! The compartment—!" She looked to the floor.

"Does it seal?"

"Uh . . . yes, it should."

"Good. Now, we've got to find every possible breach—every leak, no matter how small, has got to be plugged."

"Plugged?"

"What? Is there an echo in here? When those bugs eat down far enough, some of them are going to get in. That's a feeding frenzy out there! They're going to be coming in hungry! You and I and Duke are the only things edible in this larder. What have you got that'll keep them out?"

"Uh, I don't know. Wait a minute—let me think."

"Come on. I thought these choppers were stocked for every emergency."

Abruptly, Lizard stiffened. She looked at me hard. "I suspect that *this* one isn't in the book. The army hasn't had much reason to bury choppers in cotton candy, so we don't really know what happens when bugs eat them out." She looked angry. That was a good sign. "Obviously," she continued, "you and I have been given the opportunity to research the subject."

"Terrific!" I said. "What an opportunity! What'll we try?"

Lizard looked at the floor of the chopper, frowning. She let her gaze travel slowly toward the back. She looked like she was using her X-ray vision to inventory each separate cargo compartment.

Abruptly she said, "Shelterfoam!" She was staring all the way back. "You'll have to move Duke."

"What's shelterfoam?"

"It's in case you crash somewhere and need to build a shelter—especially in cold-weather areas. First you inflate a big balloon, then you spray it with shelterfoam. You wait a half hour for it to harden, cut a door, and move in. It's like living in a pumpkin. We used it as quick-fix housing in Pakistan." She pointed. "Put Duke all the way in the back. He's lying right over the compartment I need to get at."

Duke moaned when I moved him, but he didn't awaken. The console suggested that I give him another bottle of glucose and I did.

As I settled him in, I noticed that the pink luminescence in the tail of the ship was growing stronger. I glanced up at the bubble. The morning sun was pouring directly down on us; I could see a brighter spot beyond the seething pink. I could even feel its warmth.

The layer of powder on the hemisphere of Plexiglas was growing noticeably thinner beneath the hungry insect-things. This cotton candy stuff was incredibly transparent to light. I could see the swarming bugs as darker bits ceaselessly churning and swirling. I wondered what they were.

But I didn't want Duke to wonder about it if he woke up and saw them. I pulled the shutter closed.

Lizard was busying herself with the shelterfoam. She wasn't paying any attention to me. So I took a moment to apologize to Duke. I peeled open a sani-pak and started cleaning his face with a moist towel. "I'm sorry, Duke," I whispered. "I'll get you out of here, I promise." I wiped the dirt from his forehead.

"McCarthy . . ." he mumbled.

"Yes, Duke?"

"Shut up."

"Yes, Duke!"

But he was asleep again. I didn't care. He was going to live—I knew it!

I scrambled forward to tell Lizard. "Duke's going to make it!"

"How do you know?"

"He growled at me. He told me to shut up."

Lizard grinned. "Sounds like good advice. Here—" She thrust a tank into my arms. "The weak spots will be mostly under the floor, where we hit. Especially where we broke the keel. You'll need to empty each compartment, then foam it. Just point the nozzle and press."

"Does this stuff make fumes?"

"No, it's jellied Styrofoam. It's safe. You do the cabin, I'll get under the controls. I want to open the floorboard and get the nose-wheel compartment. If the bugs get in there, they could get into the circuit-pipes or the hydraulics or underneath the insulation. You ever spray for cockroaches?"

"Yeah."

"Then you know." She looked over my shoulder and lowered her voice. "Better pay special attention to the tail. You might just want to make a big cocoon back there."

I followed her glance. Duke. I realized how helpless he was. "Yeah. I see your point."

"Any questions?"

"No."

"All right, let's go to work."

"Uh—"

She stopped. "Yes?"

"I just had a thought, Colonel."

She waited patiently.

"What if these bugs eat Styrofoam too?"

"Will you stop thinking?" she said. "You're scaring the hell out of me."

Q: What do Chtorrans call a carload of drunks?

A: A jar of pickles.

21

Being Right

*"The amount of entropy in the universe is
constant—except when it increases."*
—SOLOMON SHORT

It took us most of the morning.

Lizard stopped only to check in with Oakland and relay a data
chirp from the medi-console. Then she plunged back into her task.
She opened up the whole floor of the ship and filled it with foam
before replacing the deck panels.

By then, I had finished foaming the cargo compartments and
had begun outlining every seam of the interior paneling. Lizard
came back to join me. We set our nozzles for narrow jets and
sprayed every corner, every crack, every seam, every seal on the
interior of that ship. When we finished, the chopper looked like
the inside of a wedding cake.

By the time we sat down in the nose of the ship again, the sun
was high above us. And the chopper was starting to get warm. We
could barely see the sun through the wall of pale powder, but we
could feel its heat. I felt *trapped*.

And my body hurt worse than ever. My lungs felt like they were
on fire. I was keeping an O-mask close now, and taking frequent
breaths from it. It seemed to help. A little.

And my skin felt itchy and red. The dust must have irritated my
skin. I was prickly all over. I felt like I was living inside a bag of
Angora cat hair. When I put my hand inside my shirt to scratch,
I even felt dirty and dusty and furry.

I forced myself—somehow—to concentrate on the scientific
opportunity here.

The front window was a bright pink glare. It flickered with a million tiny bodies. They were crawling all over it, but they were thickest near the bottom, where the pink was still piled up in drifts. It made me feel incredibly queasy just to look at them. I thought about a hot bath, one with hundreds of little pulsing jets, all throbbing in a steady underwater massage. I decided not to share that image with Colonel Tirelli.

"Brr!" she said. "I can't stand to look at them. What do you think they are, anyway?"

"The Chtorran equivalent of ants, maybe," I said. "But I wouldn't bet on it. I don't think we've scratched the surface of this ecology. Remember Dr. Zymph and her jigsaw-puzzle analogy?"

"Yeah?"

"Well, I think we're still at the point where we're just looking into the box. We still haven't dumped it out. We still don't even know how big the puzzle is or how many pieces there are. We just know there are a lot and none of them seem to make sense." I sipped at a water bulb and watched the seething mass of insects on the windscreen in front of me.

"I hate that analogy," Lizard said. "It's got too much *can't* in it."

"Yeah," I agreed.

Lizard picked up her headset and flicked the radio on. "Oakland?"

"Go ahead," said the radio.

"This is ELDAVO. Checking in. Our situation is unchanged. Except the bugs are getting closer."

"We copy, Colonel."

"Is there an estimate yet when someone can come and get us?"

"Nope. Sorry. Satellite shows that whole area is still hazy. The best we can do is pull a blimp out of Portland and let it glide over you."

"That's a little desperate, isn't it?"

"You want to wait a week for pickup?"

Lizard rolled her eyes. "Get the blimp."

"Oh, we do have some good news for you."

"Yeah?"

"Your patient is stable."

"Uh-huh. And what are you *not* telling me?"

"Beg pardon?"

"Stable can mean a lot of things. How bad are his injuries?"

"Uh . . . is this line secure?"

Lizard looked at me, looked back at Duke. "Is he still asleep?"

she whispered. I looked and nodded. Lizard said to the radio, "Go ahead."

"Uh . . . we're getting some funny readings off his legs. Like static. But we don't think it's infection. The monitor shows the antibiotics are holding. Maybe it's some effect of the dust. We won't know for sure until we get him home. Other than that, he's fine. Avoid moving him. We'll try and have a corpsman on the pickup vehicle."

"I copy," Lizard said. "Any more good news?"

"Well . . . it's official as of ten o'clock. The President's going to run again."

"Thanks. Do we get the ball scores too?"

"Dodgers lead the Braves, top of the third, two-nothing."

"Over and out." She hung up and looked at me. "What are you so unhappy about? You an Atlanta fan?"

"No, I'm worried about Duke." I started crawling toward the back.

"Didn't you hear? Oakland says he's doing fine."

"Yeah, I heard. They also said the Dodgers are winning." I sat down next to Duke. He'd been out all day. I didn't know if that was a blessing or not. Was it better to be unconscious—or in pain? If they didn't pick us up soon, there wouldn't be a choice. We were running out of supplies.

I looked at the medi-console. It was almost time to change his I.V. We had plenty of antibiotics left—those were the blue ampules—but we were on the next-to-last bubble of glucose. I wondered what I could do when that ran out. These choppers were equipped only for basic first aid. The assumption was that the patient would be in transit and wouldn't be on the medi-console for long.

The real question was the red ampule. The painkiller. There was only one left in the kit. And I'd heard that burn wounds were the most agonizing. . . .

I reached for the medi-blanket, hesitated, then pulled it back and looked at Duke's legs.

They were burned and peeling. The flesh was blistered and scabbed.

And then I looked again.

Duke's legs were . . . dusty.

No. They were covered with a light pink fuzz. What the—?

I stretched a finger out, carefully, and touched Duke's ankle. The fuzz didn't brush away. It was growing out of his skin.

And it tingled.

Like worm fur.

I sat down with my back against the hull of the ship and my knees up in front of me. I put my fists up to my mouth and sucked thoughtfully through them, all the while staring at Duke's legs and trying to figure out just what the hell was going on.

I hardly noticed when Lizard came back to join me. She looked at Duke's legs and her face went gray. She pulled the medi-blanket over them again and looked at me with a question in her eyes.

I shrugged. "I don't know."

She picked up the medi-console and studied it. The answer wasn't there, either.

I looked across at her. "How long before we know? I mean—if the foam is going to hold?"

She shrugged. "An hour. Maybe less."

"What if he wakes up? Do you think we should tell him?"

Lizard opened her mouth to say something.

But Duke interrupted. "Tell me *what*?" he said.

"Duke! You're awake."

"I've been awake for some time. Listening to you birds jabbering. What'd you drug me with, anyway? My legs itch."

Lizard shot me a concerned glance. Duke didn't see it. I said, "I don't know the name of it. It's in the red cartridge."

"Oh," he said. "Where are we?"

"Near Red Bluff. As soon as the weather clears, they'll be coming to get us."

"The weather?"

"The dust."

"Is it still coming down?"

"No." And then I added, "But—we're buried. And there's haze."

Duke's face was puffy, but I could still see his eyes narrowing as he looked back and forth between me and the medical bag. "The light in here is pink," he said. "How deep is this shit?"

"Up to our ears, Duke." That was Lizard.

"Mmmm," he said. "Then don't make waves."

"How are you feeling?"

"Cloudy." He reached up and grabbed my sleeve. "Jim?"

"Yes, Duke?"

"Do me a favor."

"Name it."

"Pull the red cartridge. Take me off the sleepytime."

"Sorry, Boss. No can do. Anything but that."

"I can handle the pain. I want to be awake."

"I can't! It's procedure! It might kill you!"

"Jim—" He coughed and for a moment I was terrified. It sounded like a death rattle. "Jim—will you pull that cartridge?"

"No, Duke, I won't."

He closed his eyes for a long moment. I had almost started to think that he had gone back to sleep when he opened them again. When he spoke, his voice was very faint.

"Jim?"

"Yes, Duke?" He was fading fast; I had to put my face close.

It came out a whisper. "Then fuck you. . . ." His eyes closed and he fell asleep again.

Lizard looked up from the console. "The machine put him out. He was straining."

"He hates drugs. I'm going to have a lot of apologizing to do." I realized what I'd said and looked up at her. "Sorry. Force of habit."

She didn't smile. "There's something else you want to watch out for."

"Huh?"

"You could have pulled that cartridge, you know."

I shook my head. "No, I couldn't. It's those bugs. If we're going to be eaten alive, he's better off not knowing."

Lizard looked at me sharply. "That's what I'm talking about. That kind of thinking is the first step."

"What kind of thinking?"

"Making other people's decisions for them. The next step is deciding whether or not they should continue living. And you know where that leads. I seem to remember you had a button on that."

"Yeah, well—" I stood up and climbed into the turret above Duke. "It's different when you're the person who has to do the deciding, isn't it?"

She didn't say anything immediately. She just studied me with an introspective look on her face.

Finally, I glanced down at her. "Well, go ahead. Say it."

She shook her head slowly. "I don't have to. You already know what I would say."

"No, I don't."

"Yes, you do."

"God, I hate conversations like this."

She sighed. "It's not important. I just wondered if you would have accepted that justification."

I didn't answer. I turned away from her and pulled the shutter back. I stared at the uneasy surface of the bubble. The creatures were more active than ever in the afternoon sunlight. I could feel the sweat dripping down my sides. I didn't want to continue this conversation any more. I knew she was right.

And my chest hurt worse than ever. *Jeezis*, did it hurt—

Q: What do Chtorrans call a grizzly bear?
A: A good fuck.

22

The Food Chain

*"All life is based on death. Nothing exists
except by feeding on something else. Even
photosynthesis depends on the heat-death
of the sun. Humanity is not exempt.
Embalming doesn't cheat the worms, it
cheats the system. But only temporarily."*

—SOLOMON SHORT

It wasn't until late afternoon that the bugs finally cleaned off the
turret bubble well enough so I could see them clearly.

The sunlight was slanting directly into the rear of the chopper
and there were only pink streaks left on the clear canopy of the
bubble to suggest that the ship had once been covered with the
dust.

The insect-things were very tiny. Most of them were nothing
more than little white specks. Few were big enough to have
features. I had to strain my eyes to see them at all.

I called to Lizard, "Have you got a surveillance camera?"

"I've got a couple of electronics."

"That'll do. Let me have one, please."

She passed it up.

"Ah, good—it's a Sony. For once the army didn't buy cheap.
I'll show you a trick I learned. You can dial these down for
incredible close-ups. We used to use them in school as portable
microscopes." I braced myself and focused the camera on the
insect-things on the surface of the bubble. The lighting was
perfect. The afternoon sunlight was coming in sideways. The
detailing on the image was perfect. The little bugs were white and

powdery and—when the instant of recognition hit me, I felt my relief like a shot of Irish whiskey.

I started giggling.

"What's so funny?"

I closed the shutter and dropped out of the bubble. I was laughing so hard I started coughing. I had to sit down on the floor of the chopper and wait for the spell to pass. I coughed so hard I thought I could see through my chest. I was on fire inside. The cough aggravated the pain. The pain aggravated the cough. I couldn't catch my breath. The coughing only stopped when I ran out of strength. I came to with an O-mask on my face and Lizard looking at me worriedly.

I held up one hand weakly to show I was all right. My whole body felt pink—but something was happening. I was suddenly feeling at peace. No. I was feeling *high*. Almost hallucinatory. It was like I could see inside myself. Maybe I'd run out of adrenaline. Maybe it was endorphin overload. And maybe there was nothing left to feel. But whatever it was, I didn't hurt anymore.

And it was still funny. I hadn't realized how tense and anxious I'd been. Now it was all pouring out of me at once. My breath came out raggedly in tight wheezy giggles. I must have looked crazy. I probably was.

"McCarthy?" Lizard was getting annoyed. "What is it?"

I rolled over on my side and then pulled myself onto my hands and knees. I waited until I caught my breath again and then straightened up. "Come on up front; I'll show you." Lizard helped me back into my chair. The bugs were clearly visible at the top of the windscreen. I handed her the camera. "Look. Do you recognize them?"

She peered up at the windshield through the eyepiece. "No."

"You should. You saw Dr. Zymph's slides."

"Will you just tell me what they are?"

"Those are baby pipe cleaner bugs! They are absolutely harmless to human beings! These and the cotton candy are the only two Chtorran species that are not directly dangerous to us—and we've been hiding here in the chopper terrified all day! By tomorrow morning, they'll have cleaned this entire ship off. There won't be a speck of pink anywhere on this aircraft." I sat down in the copilot's seat again, feeling terrific, a big silly smile on my face. "We're going to be all right."

Lizard sat down across from me, looking relieved and relaxed for the first time today. "We're really not in any danger?"

"Not in the slightest. I feel like such a jerk."

Lizard laughed. "We should celebrate. You want a beer?"

"You got more beer?"

"That cooler by your feet."

I pulled the top open. "Jeez—you don't travel light, do you?"

She spread her hands apologetically. "You never can tell when you're going to be buried in cotton candy. Hand me one . . . thanks."

We sat back in our seats and watched the bugs work on the windshield. We passed the camera back and forth.

Lizard said, "You're a biologist, aren't you?"

"I never got my degree."

"That wasn't the question."

"All right, yes, I'm as much a biologist as anyone is these days."

"Thanks. So, tell me—what's going on?"

"I can make a guess. The pipe cleaner bugs hatch on the same day as the puffballs explode. The puffballs are their primary food."

"But why so many? The scale of this—it's enormous."

"Uh-huh," I agreed. "It's a good breeding strategy for bugs. Have zillions of offspring. That guarantees that enough will survive to breed the next generation." Another thought occurred to me then. "Of course . . . that's a Terran explanation. The Chtorran explanation could be something else entirely."

"What do you mean by that?"

"Just a guess. Remember how Dr. Zymph said that what we were seeing was really the advance guard—that some extraterrestrial agency was obviously trying to *Chtorra*-form this planet?"

"Yeah, so?"

"Well, I've been thinking. Suppose we humans were going to Terra-form Mars or some other nearby world. Would we take our *entire* ecology? Probably not. No, we'd only take those creatures suited for the kind of climate and terrain we'd be moving into. In fact, we wouldn't even take the full spectrum of creatures, we'd only fill the ecological niches that we need to support our own survival."

"What are you getting at?"

"Okay—we'd take a couple species of grass and grain, earthworms, rabbits, foxes to keep the rabbits in check, cows, ducks, chickens, and so on. That is, we'd take only those species immediately useful to us. We wouldn't bother with mosquitoes, termites, rhinoceroses, or three-toed sloths. I'll bet the Chtorrans have done the same thing. That's why the puffballs and the pipe cleaner bugs have experienced population explosions. There aren't the usual wide range of predators present to feed on them. At least not yet. Maybe they'll be here later."

"Mm," said Lizard. She took a drink from the can of beer, then leaned forward and tapped the window. "What's this?" she asked.

She was pointing at a larger, darker speck.

I looked. The speck was round and black and very busy. "That's the creature that feeds on the baby pipe cleaner bugs," I said.

"Well that didn't take long," she said. "There's your first predator." She peered through the camera. "It looks like a spider—only it's got too many legs."

"If it's Chtorran, it's a mouth on wheels. Here's another. And another. It's nearly dusk—the night feeders are coming out. I'll bet we'll be seeing a lot more of them."

"And this?" pointed Lizard. "What are these?" She passed me the camera.

I looked where she pointed. The creatures looked like red-striped silverfish. They made me think of millipedes; these were the micro-size. Or maybe the larvae. I said, "Obviously, these are the bugs that feed on the bugs that feed on the pipe cleaner bugs. I shifted my attention to a thing that looked like a fingernail-sized amoeba. Incredible. It was enveloping one of the silverfish. "You know what we've got here? Box seats! We're seeing a whole slice of Chtorran ecology."

"I'm not sure these are box seats," said Lizard. "We're seeing it from the bottom."

"Best place to see it from. None of the details are lost." I moved higher up the window. "Look—see that? Remember that one? That's a nightwalker."

"He looks like a little vampire."

"That's how he got his name. He lurks in corners. This one must be a baby."

"What's he eating?"

"I can't tell—but it's pink."

"Oh, here's another one—oh, my God!"

I looked where she was pointing. The creature looked like a tiny elf-child. Its eyes were froglike, but its body was pink and as moist-looking as a baby and its proportions were almost completely human, only scaled down to the size of a baby's finger. It was feeding on the candy powder and the pipe cleaner bugs and whatever else got in its way. it had a tiny red tongue.

"This is incredible. Where are the memory clips for this camera? We're probably seeing a hundred new life-forms today."

"In that dark blue box." Lizard jerked a thumb over her shoulder. "And check the battery packs. You may have to plug it in up here."

I levered myself out of my seat. "Cokes, beers, medi-kits, shelterfoam, oxygen tanks, cameras—how come this chopper is so well packed?"

"All military choppers are, now. It's standard issue. The robots check your supplies automatically and replace what's been used. It's all automatic. Obviously, it's for opportunities like this."

"Um," I said. "Hey! Theres a Pentax-Pro in here! With eighty gigs of Zilog layered memory!" I held it up to show her. The batteries were fresh. "It's brand-new. You know, I used to dream about equipment like this."

"Help yourself. There's more where that came from."

"Huh?"

"The army wants you to have that equipment, McCarthy. Remember? There's a war on."

I grabbed the lantern and came back forward. "Here, hang this up somewhere so the light slants sideways. I'll get better contrast." I started shooting micro-close-ups. The details visible just on the camera's preview screen were startling. "Are there any more of those little naked men?"

"Here's a couple—oops, you don't want to see what they're doing!"

"Yes, I do! No, I don't." I took their picture anyway.

"Voyeur," said Lizard.

"They're just licking the powder off each other," I said. "Besides, they might be female." I kept taking pictures. There was a thing that looked like a tiny pink cauliflower—or a walking brain. It was a gnarly little lump with red veins all over its surface. It looked dreadful. I noticed even the other creatures thought so—they kept out of its way too.

"This is incredible!" I said. I was probably repeating myself. I didn't care. I was too excited. "We're seeing things no other human being has ever seen! This is extraordinary! This must be the day everything hatches at once and feeds on everything else. This is wonderful. I don't think we've seen half of these life-forms before!"

"Lizard said, "If that's true, then the joke's on you."

"Huh?"

"You just finished postulating that the Chtorrans would probable bring only their essential support species. Look at this zoo on the window! Do you still believe that?"

I lowered the camera for a second and looked. The window was totally covered with swarming Chtorran bugs and beasties. Long ones. Thin ones. Short fat juicy ones. Pink and black and purple—and red, all shades of red. They glistened in the reflected light of the chopper. Beyond was only darkness. It was already night outside; when had that happened? I'd been so entranced, I hadn't even noticed when the sun set. This closer spectacle was too overwhelming. The bugs were glittering little bodies now. The window fairly sparkled.

"Yeah," I said. "I do. This is still only a very narrow slice of an ecology. A planet might host a billion different species. We're seeing only a few hundred here. The Chtorrans probably haven't brought more than a few thousand altogether. Just what they need." I started to lift the camera to my eye again, then looked at it, stopped, lowered the camera, and looked at Lizard again. Grinning.

"What?" she said.

"I take it all back," I said. "Well, part of it, anyway. The Chtorrans haven't traveled any lighter than we did. We didn't pack just the bare essentials for this mission. We took everything we might conceivably need." I hefted the camera. "And so far, we've needed everything we brought. They did the same."

Lizard laughed with me. She opened the last two beers and passed me one. She lifted hers high and toasted me. "Well, here's to the bugs. Here's to you."

I returned the toast. "It's a great show."

We watched in silence for a while.

I tried to imagine what the ground outside must look like. If the moon was bright enough, it would be covered by a shimmering carpet of night creatures and insects. I wondered if any Earth life-forms were part of that feast out there, and if they were diners or dinners.

Probably dinners. This was a feeding frenzy. These creatures were all so busy eating that they didn't even notice when something else came along and started eating them. I watched as new creatures kept landing on the windshield, joining the orgy. Where were they all coming from?

Lizard decided to call the little naked men "finger-babies." They reminded her of a set of tiny rubbery dolls she had owned a long time ago. You put them on your fingers and as you wiggled your digits; the dolls would open and close their eyes and mouths in unison. Lizard said they looked like a chorus of little dwarves; she used to pretend they were singing. The finger-babies with their grotesque little faces looked just like them.

The creatures had pale, nearly transparent skin and they crawled along the window with slow deliberate motions. They had big blue eyes. It made them look expressionless—or perpetually frightened. It depended on your mood. They would open their tiny wide mouths and touch their tiny red tongues to the pink powder or to the baby pipe cleaner bugs. They lifted their heads while they swallowed, then they would look slowly from side to side before returning to their feast.

For a while, there were a lot of them. Many of them were licking the powder off each other. The window was covered with naked, squirming pink bodies. "It looks like you got your Blue Mass after all."

"There's something disturbing about the comparison," she responded. "Is that what human beings look like from above?"

As the night grew darker, more of the nightwalkers began to arrive. The little vampire creatures had pale faces and large mandibles. They grabbed the finger-babies with their upper pair of arms and pulled then into a disturbingly erotic embrace. The finger-babies didn't fight, not even when the vampires opened their mandibles and started eating. The vampires ate them like little plump sausages. They bit and chewed, bit and chewed, and the finger-babies died. They waved their little pink arms and kicked their little pink legs, but the nightwalkers kept eating. The finger-babies had bright red blood.

For a while, the window was covered with carnage.

"I think I hate them," Lizard said.

"Careful," I said.

"Huh?"

"You're anthropomorphizing. You're making judgments about these creatures. Your species prejudice is showing. What if the finger-babies are really embryonic worms?"

She looked at me, startled. "You don't really think so?"

"No, I don't—but I just wanted to caution you not to make assumptions. I already made one misassumption about the bunnydogs. I don't want to make any more. These things are probably some kind of newtlike organism with a coincidental resemblance. In their adult form, they could be vicious serpents. Or maybe not. Don't make hasty judgments."

Lizard grunted. That was her only answer.

We both fell silent again.

Something snake-like with a red belly slithered across the side of the window. It had a thousand flashing legs, and it plowed through the other life-forms like a vacuum cleaner. Oh no.

"Lizard," I said.

"Yes?"

"You'd better call for help."

"Huh?" She looked at me. "I thought you said we were safe."

"I may have to revise that estimate. You were wondering what comes next?" I pointed. "See that? That's a Chtorran millipede. If that's what comes next, we'd better get out of here. I don't think the shelterfoam will stop them."

Q: What do Chtorrans call a cemetery?
A: Jerky.

23

Smorgasbord

> *"Life is to the universe as rust is to iron.*
> *"We are, in the final judgment (on a planetary scale, certainly), nothing more than an advanced form of corrosion, just one more way for the universe to wear itself out a little faster."*

—SOLOMON SHORT

We got the call at 22:00 hours.

The radio beeped. Lizard leaned forward and flicked it on. "This is ELDAVO."

"All right, here's the scoop. The blimp is on its way. They left Portland an hour ago. They've got a full rescue and medical team aboard. They should be over you by midnight. They're homing in on your beam."

"What about the dust?"

"They're aware of the problem. We all are. There isn't an engine running in the Sacramento Valley today—at least none that were left exposed. But Portland has the most experience with this kind of problem. You can thank Mount St. Helens for that. They've already got the necessary technology on the shelf."

"I'll send a thank-you note to the volcano," Lizard said.

"They'll be monitoring the air all the way in. When they start hitting ten particles per million, they'll shut down the jets and drift with the wind till they're overhead."

"Drift?" asked Lizard skeptically.

"That's right. But they've jury-rigged a cold-rocket assist for local guidance. They can maneuver, and you won't have to worry about the fire danger. If they have to, they can fly on canned air for a short distance—at least far enough to get out of the pink if they head out over the ocean. It's all been thought out."

"I've heard that one before," Lizard said. "How are they going to hold their position over us?"

"They'll fire grapples into the ground and moor themselves. Then they'll lower a basket and pull you up."

"Listen," said Lizard. "We've got a problem with that."

"What's that?"

"We're in the middle of a feeding frenzy here. Once we pop the hatch, we have maybe thirty seconds. If that. We've got a millipede swarm."

"We know about the millipedes. You're not he only ones down in the dust. We've been getting reports that would curl your hair."

I leaned forward at that. "How bad is it?" I asked.

"You don't want to know."

"Yes I do," I insisted.

"We think we lost Redding. All communications are down. We can't get anything into the area. You think you got it bad! The Northern California Eyeball scan shows nothing but pink desert—and there were some *tall* buildings in Redding."

"*Redding*?" But that was eighty kilometers north of here. A terrible suspicion was creeping coldly up my spine. "Just how extensive is the dust?"

"The whole northern half of the state is out. Everything. It's all been brought to a halt. Sacramento took another five inches this afternoon."

Lizard and I exchanged a glance. From Redding to Sacramento?

"You'll see it from the blimp. If the wind holds up, you might be in Oakland—or Sacramento—by tomorrow afternoon."

"Any more good news?" Lizard asked.

"The Dodgers blew it in the eighth."

"Thanks." She signed off, turned, and looked at me. "So. No lobster tonight, either." Then she noticed my expression and asked, "What's that about?"

"Nothing," I said. I climbed out of my seat and headed toward the back of the ship to look at duke's medi-console. He was stable, but . . .

I pulled the blanket back to look at the pink fur on his legs again. It was noticeably longer. There were red and purple strands too.

Lizard squatted down opposite me. She searched my face. "Nothing, huh?"

"All right," I admitted. "I'm worried about Duke. He smells pretty bad—and I don't know what's going on with his legs. That fur is *growing*. Even if we could get him out of here tonight, we'd still be a long way from the kind of care he needs. And you heard the man. Tomorrow afternoon."

Lizard picked up the medi-console and studied its display. Duke was on the last red ampule. There was no more glucose. I'd been waking him up periodically to give him sugar water laced with blue-series antibiotics. It was the best I could do. I couldn't think of anything else.

I knelt down for a closer examination of the pink fur on Duke's legs. It was growing out of his blackened skin like grass creeping back toward ground zero. Tentatively, I let it brush the palm of my hand. It was tingly. I pressed it gently flat. The tingly sensation got stronger.

"He's waking up—" said Lizard.

I straightened up again and took the console from Lizard. The display said Duke was still sound asleep.

"No he's not—" I looked back at Duke's legs. I stretched over and touched the fur again; I stroked a long length of it. The medi-console display went crazy. It said Duke was running up a hill—no, having a heart attack—no, it wasn't sure. PLEASE WAIT. It couldn't interpret. INCREASED NERVOUS ACTIVITY. And again, PLEASE WAIT.

I pulled open the medical supplies and studied the color-coded chart inside. There it was.

Gerromycin.

I looked at Duke's legs again.

But it was such a long shot. It was a very stupid risk to take.

"What are you thinking?" asked Lizard.

"I'm thinking of doing something stupid," I said.

"How stupid?"

"It's never been done before." I popped the plastic ampule out of the kit. "That's worm fur growing out of Duke's legs. This stuff should kill it. Most of it, anyway. Remember the worm in Denver? That's what happened to it."

She frowned unhappily. "I don't know what to tell you, McCarthy. I'm not a doctor."

"I'm not asking your permission. I know more about this than you do. This is one I have to call."

"You're right," she agreed.

"I know." I closed my eyes. *Please God . . . let me be really right*.

I clipped the ampule into place on the feeder.

The medi-console beeped. GERROMYCIN? It queried. I touched the CONFIRM button.

There was nothing to do now but wait.

We covered Duke up again and climbed back to the front of the chopper. The copilot's seat was beginning to get uncomfortable. It creaked as I sank into it. I picked up a flashlight and studied the bugs on the window again. I couldn't identify even half the creatures I saw. But the ones I could identify were enough to terrify me.

"The *real* problem," I said, "is that I don't know how we're going to get him out of here. I don't know how we're going to get *us* out of here. I don't think it's safe to open that hatch." I pointed the flashlight toward the top of the windshield. The beam illuminated four red-bellied millipedes slithering down its curved surface even as I spoke. One of them curled itself around to point its eyes downward. It peered curiously at us, irising its eyes open and shut in confused blinks.

Lizard followed my stare. "Can you freeze them?" she asked.

I shrugged. "That's what I'm planning on, but that's not the problem. I'm worried about worms finding us. They're next in line at this cafeteria." I pointed at the millipedes. "See those? Those millipedes are the nastiest little monsters you can imagine. They'll attack anything that was ever remotely organic. They're as insatiable as an author at a free lunch, and they're almost impossible to kill. They bite like journalists, and they're as deadly as lawyers. They run in swarms and they can denude a forest in a week. They can strip a horse in minutes. Do you want to hear more?"

"And my point is . . .?" Lizard prompted.

"That," I said, "is worm food. Those are Chtorran delicacies. Maybe it's their equivalent of lobster. The worms just pop them in their mouths and chew. Does that give you some idea about the personal habits of the worms? That's what I'm worried about. A worm could peel this chopper open real easy.

"And," I added, "if that's not enough, we are effectively defenseless. Duke's torch is still lying somewhere out there in the dust—and even if we had it, it wouldn't be safe to use. Neither can we use grenades or rocket launchers—nothing that might ignite the dust. All we have is the freezer—and that is of very limited usefulness as a weapon against a worm. Believe me. I've tried it three times. No more. It is not recommended for people who are planning to die in bed. The first time I tried it, I didn't know any better. The second time, I figured it was just a matter of technique. The third time, I began to suspect it was impossible and stopped trying."

"Are you through, Perfessor?" she said.

"I'd be interested in hearing any suggestions you have to offer," I said. "I just wanted you to be clear about the problem."

"First of all—" Lizard gave me a knee-weakening, blue-eyed stare, "I think you're making up problems that you don't have yet. The last worm we saw was forty kilometers on the other side of the mountains." She jerked a thumb westward.

"That was the last worm *you* saw. You forget the last worm *I* saw was on the other side of that hill out there. Are you willing to bet your life that there aren't a lot more of them in this neighborhood? I'm not." I jerked a thumb at the window. "Not a meter away from us, you have the clearest cross-section of the Chtorran food chain anyone has ever seen. That's a Chtorran smorgasbord out there. There *are* worms around. They just haven't found us yet. But they will."

Lizard didn't answer. She didn't like what I was saying, but she couldn't deny it either.

I said, "A worm has a better sense of smell than a shark. We know that they are attracted to human beings. We don't know why, but we do know that a Chtorran gastropede will head for the strongest human scent it can detect. We've found this out the hard way. They've also learned to recognize the smells of our machinery. Like trucks and choppers. They'll home in on those scents too. I didn't want to say anything about this earlier—because I didn't think we were in a heavily infested area—but the millipedes prove that we are. This chopper is a goddamn neon sign. It says FREE LUNCH to any worm in the vicinity." I realized I was getting a little too vehement and lowered my voice. "Sorry. I got excited."

Lizard still wasn't speaking. She was staring gloomily out the window.

I felt I ought to apologize, but I'd promised I wouldn't do that any more. I shut my mouth.

But silence didn't work either. It just accentuated the feelings of discomfort. "Listen," I said. "We do have one thing in our favor. The dust. Maybe it's so thick it masks our scent. That's a very strong possibility. Really. In which case, we might not be in that much danger. We'd only have to worry about a worm finding us by accident. . . ."

"Like that one . . . ?" Lizard asked slowly. She pointed forward.

I looked. I pointed the flashlight.

Something large and dark and red, with two huge black eyes like the headlights of an oncoming subway train, was peering in at us through the windshield. Its eyes shrank in the sudden light.

"I really wanted to be wrong," I said.

The worm cocked its eyes at us diagonally—a listening pose. It opened its mouth slowly and touched its mandibles to the glass. It was testing the surface.

"Oh, God—let it hold."

The glass creaked in its frame.

But it held.

The worm backed away from the window then and ran its fingers curiously over the surface. Its claws scrabbled politely across the glass, tapping and examining. I held the light steady. I was afraid to move it—or even turn it off."

The worm was huge. Four meters long. The dark purple and red stripes on its sides were definite enough to be visible even under the fine coat of pink dust caking its fur.

The monster put its face close to the glass again.

We stared at it. And it stared back at us.

I hoped to God it wasn't hungry.

Q: What do Chtorrans call the morgue?
A: A refrigerator.

Q: What do Chtorrans call the corpsicles?
A: Cold cuts.

24

"I am not a free lunch!"

"The cat is always on the wrong side of the door."

—SOLOMON SHORT

And then the worm backed away and was gone. There was darkness beyond the window. Where was it?

"Don't move," I said.

"I couldn't if I wanted to."

For a moment, everything was silent. I wondered if this was the same worm that Duke and I had seen before. I couldn't tell—and it didn't really make much difference, did it? Then, from the side of the chopper next to Lizard, there came a gentle tapping, a rapping. A scrabbling scraping sound.

The worm was examining the ship.

Lizard's eyes went wide. This was worse then *seeing* what the creature was doing.

The sound moved down the length of the chopper. Slowly, ever so slowly, the worm tapped and scratched its way toward the hatch. When the horrible sounds reached the door of the chopper, they hesitated. It was as if the worm could tell that there was something different about this piece of hull. The examination went on for a long, long time. I thought of a rabbit in a cage—

"I, uh—want you to know something. . . ." Lizard said quietly.

Our attention was on the noise at the door.

"What's that?" I asked.

It almost sounded like a knock. Or like a dog scratching to get in.

"I meant it, what I said before. About you being kind of cute."

Now it was *rattling the door handle!*

"I know," I said. "Thank you."

Go away, goddammit! There's nobody home! *Please, God, don't let me start coughing!*

"No—listen, what I really wanted to tell you . . ." Lizard's voice was strained, "I *can* fuck better then I can fly. You can tell Duke that—if you get the chance. . . ."

The rattle at the door stopped.

I said, "I, uh—wanted to find that out for myself. . . ."

There was silence again. Lizard and I listened painfully. Had the worm given up and gone away?

No. The scrabbling resumed farther back down the hull. Lizard gasped. She blurted quickly, "Me too."

The worm was at the tail of the ship now.

I said, "When we get back to Oakland . . ."

She said, "Okay . . ."

Something went *bang.* The chopper lurched forward. Lizard yelped. Duke moaned.

And then there was silence. A *long* silence.

"It went away . . . ?" she whispered.

"Wait," I cautioned.

"Turn on the outside lights," I said. "All of them."

"Is that safe?"

"It knows we're here. There's no reason to hide any more. We might as well see what we're in the middle of."

She leaned forward slowly and touched a button on her console. The landscape beyond the window blazed suddenly bright. The ground glowed pink. the chopper's headlights were still under the dust; the light was reflecting upward through the powder. It created an eerie luminescence, a faerie landscape. A deep furrow led out of the trees through the pink dunes, and directly toward the chopper. The track of the curious worm. Where was it now?

The pink dunes were losing their pristine condition and collapsing into muddy looking slush that pulsed and throbbed with swarming life. We couldn't identify the smaller creatures; they blurred into a glittering mosaic. Millipedes slithered through them everywhere, feeding like sharks; some of them were as huge as pythons.

But where was the worm?

Lizard switched on the overhead spotlights then—and gasped.

Outside, the air was filled with fluttery things. They looked like epileptic moths. They darted back and forth through the light pouring from the chopper. They dipped and dove and picked at the bugs in the powder. And now there were larger things that sailed through the fluttery things. They curled and swooped like silver ribbons. They rippled through the air in perfect sine waves; they were bizarre and graceful and beautiful to watch. Something like a kite darted through them, snatching them out of the air. What kind of creature fed on the kites?

The creatures in the powder were clearer now, too. There were nightwalkers the size of terriers. There were things that looked like spiders on stilts. There were pipe cleaner bugs the size of rats. There were pink hairballs with mouths creeping through the dust, humping like inchworms.

Lizard stared in fascination. Almost without thinking, she switched on the outside microphones—

Cacophony!

Chirps and whistles! A thousand chattering, cackling, buzzing, warbling voices clamored in at us. The noise was horrendous!

Lizard turned the volume down, but that the only made the sounds *more* ominous, not less.

Now, it sounded like chewing.

A million mandibles crunching, a noise like sizzling fat.

The night had brought out the biggest and the worst. The creatures beyond the window were functioning with a single biological imperative carried to its most horrifying extreme: Eat as much as you can before you are eaten yourself.

It was hideous. And it was fascinating.

I glanced over at Lizard. She was pale and trembling—but she had the camera up to her eye again. I started climbing toward the back.

She yelped, "Hey—where're you going?"

"I've gotta find that worm. " I climbed past Duke.

She followed me back. "What in hell are you thinking?"

"I don't know yet." I was already pulling the weapon bay open. "Have you got any cold explosives?"

"No—wait a minute. See what kind of rockets they packed with the rocket launcher." She pointed.

"I found it." I studied the warning labels.

"You're not going out there?" she said.

"If I have to—"

"That's crazy! You know what's outside."

"Yeah—and I also know how worms like to solve puzzles with bait in 'em. Yeah, this'll do. " I pulled out the "peace-pipe" and one pipe-filler, handed it to her to hold, then closed the compartment again.

"Just one?" she asked dryly.

"I'm only going to get one shot." I took the rocket launcher and loaded it. "You're going to have to cover me with the freezer. You know how to work it?"

"Point the trigger and press—?"

"That's close enough." I was checking the safeties on the weapon. Everything came up green. Good.

"Wait a minute," she said. "Just wait a minute." She held her hands in front of me. "Have you considered all your options here?"

"Yes—and I am not a free lunch! That leaves only this." I hefted the pipe meaningfully. I stopped and looked at her. "Maybe I'll be lucky. Maybe the worm has already gone away." And then I added, "But I'll bet it hasn't. Here, hold this again."

She took it and said, "I could order you not to do this, you know."

I was already climbing past her and pulling myself up into the bubble turret. "Go ahead—but court-martials are very time-consuming." I opened the shutter.

She called up to me. "We don't court-martial lieutenants for insubordination any more."

"Oh—?"

"No, we just shoot them on the spot. It's cheaper."

I dropped down out of the bubble and jerked my thumb up at it. "Well, before you shoot, you better have a look yourself."

She handed me back the rocket launcher and climbed up into the turret. As she brushed past me I couldn't help but notice that she smelled . . . interesting. Had this woman *really* promised me a lobster dinner in Oakland?

"Oh!" she said; and then, after a horrified pause, "But what's it doing?"

"I don't know. Maybe it's considering all *its* options."

"It's just sitting there—staring at the hatch. . . ."

"Uh-huh. And it can probably hear every word we say."

Lizard dropped back down out of the turret and stared at me. "Will this kill it?" she whispered.

"There's only one way to find out, isn't there?"

"Wait a minute. I have to think this out. Just wait a minute."

"I can. It *won't*—"

The radio beeped.

We both looked forward.

Lizard looked at me. "It's waited this long, you can wait too—*that's an order*." She scrambled down to the front of the ship to answer the call. "This is ELDAVO." I let out a loud breath and followed sourly.

"ELDAVO, this is the *Paul Bunyan*," came a male voice, "on loan from Oregon Air-Lumber. Captain Peter Price at your service. You called for a tow?"

Lizard smiled grimly. "We'll be happy with just a lift. Of *any* kind. The sooner the better."

"Well, lift is what it's all about, ma'am. The *Paul Bunyan* has eighty tons of lift. How much of it do you think you'll need?"

Lizard glanced at me, then back at Duke, did a quick mental calculation, and said, "Oh, two hundred and twenty-five kilos ought to cover it." I shouldered the rocket launcher and dropped impatiently into the copilot's seat. How long was this going to take?

"Puttin' on a little weight there, ain'tcha, gal?" came a new voice. A deep male voice.

Lizard yelped, "Danny! What are you doing there?"

"Came along for the ride. How's my favorite redhead?"

"I can't tell you on an open circuit," she said with a laugh. I wondered who this Danny was and what his relationship was with Lizard. I wondered if I should be jealous. His voice boomed like a foghorn. He was too friendly.

Lizard glanced over at me, saw my eyes, and turned back to the radio. "Listen, Danny . . . what's your ETA?"

The man's tone shifted then, became more businesslike. "Well . . . your beam is loud and clear. We should be overhead sometime in the next two hours. How's your patient?"

"Not good."

"He can't ride in a harness?"

"No, we're going to need a basket."

I leaned forward then. "Ask him if they've got a zip line."

"Who's that?" boomed Danny. "Hey, hon—you got a new boyfriend?"

"Don't be silly," Lizard said. "He's only a lieutenant." I felt myself reddening in reaction.

"Cradle-robbing again, I see." Danny laughed heartily. I decided I didn't like him or this conversation.

I leaned forward and spoke to the radio. "Can you rig a zip line?"

"Sure, we've got one, Lieutenant . . . uh—?"

"McCarthy, James Edward."

"Right," said Danny crisply. "McCarthy."

"And have you got a crab?"

"Excuse me," Captain Price interrupted, "are you a blimper?"

"No—"

"Then why don't you let us handle the mission?"

"—but I did seven search-and-destroy drops off of gasbags in Colorado, so I had to learn this stuff the hard way. We've got some problems here—"

"And we've got some problems up here too."

"Are your problems bright red?" I snapped back. "Do they weigh three tons? And can they rip open a chopper with their teeth?"

There was silence for a heartbeat; you could almost hear the two men exchanging a glance. Then Captain Price come back on the radio.

"You have worms?"

"We have one sitting right outside the front door."

Another quick silence.

"Uh . . ." That was Danny. "Lieutenant—" He was speaking very carefully now. "Whatever you do, *don't* annoy it."

"Colonel," I replied, equally carefully. "I have no intention of annoying it. I am going to *kill* it." Before he could argue with me, I added, "That worm is going to do one of two things. Either it's going to peel this ship open or it's going to go and get the rest of its family—and *they* will peel this ship open."

"Lieutenant—" the blimp captain interrupted. "Are you an expert on the worms?" There was skepticism in his voice.

"As good as you're going to find in California," I answered matter-of-factly.

Lizard put in then, "Captain Price, he is. I specifically asked for Lieutenant McCarthy to be assigned to me because of his expertise with the Chtorran ecology. If he says the worms are going to shit soup, you'd better bring your bowl and crackers."

"If you say so, Colonel. My apologies for any offense. None intended. But we've had a few bad experiences with goundhogs today, so you'll understand if we're a little testy."

"No problem," Lizard said. She looked at me. "McCarthy?"

"I'm fine," I said to the radio. "But I've got a worm to kill and you're using up my time. Of course, if you've got a better idea, I'd love to hear it. But I'm still the guy whose ass is on the line—"

"Hold it, Lieutenant," came Danny's voice, very calmly. "Nobody's arguing with you any more. You've made your point. It's your call. I just want you to be certain—"

Something went *thump* at the back of the ship.

Lizard and I both glanced back. "I'm certain," I said.

Again, a *thump*—this time louder!

Lizard said to the radio, "Danny—it's knocking on the door."

"Go do your job, Lieutenant. We'll keep this line open if you need to talk—"

I was already scrambling.

"—and Lizard, keep an eye on your patient for me." But she was already following me toward the back.

"Grab that freezer!" I pointed. "And a mask!"

"Here—" She tossed goggles at me.

Something *banged* loudly against the door. The handle rattled and clanged. Duke yelped in his sleep. I pulled the goggles down over my eyes, fitted the mask over my nose and mouth, then turned to help Lizard with the tank harness. "Who's Danny?" I asked.

"Colonel Danny Anderson. Northwest Liaison." She grunted as she pulled the harness into place. "And whatever he says, he is *not* just along for the ride."

"Anderson?" I glanced over at Duke. "Duke's last name is Anderson."

Lizard nodded. "Danny's his son." She stepped away from me to connect the freezer hose.

Duke was moaning now. He was half-awake, half-delirious. He was breathing very raggedly, and he looked worse then ever.

"Oh God—no."

And then the scratching at the door began again—

Q: What do Chtorrans call a blood bank?
A: A juice bar.

25

Bright Red Problems

"Distrust everything sold at check-out stands."

—SOLOMON SHORT

"What's it doing—" Lizard asked.

I wasn't sure. "It sounds like it's chewing."

It was a quiet, steady sound, but it had too much *crunch* in it. The door protested loudly in its frame. It bulged and squealed. Something black broke through—a mandible? Pink dust floated in the air.

I motioned Lizard to the side. "Give me a clear shot." I braced myself against the opposite wall. "When I give the word, you pop the door—and then freeze it. The whole frame. Ready?"

She nodded.

"Go!"

She hit the release. The door banged outward—

A very surprised looking worm reared up and back and away. *"Chtorrrrr!"*

Lizard stepped in spraying; the worm disappeared behind a cloud of cold steam. "Get out of the fucking way!" I screamed. She stepped back—

The steam cleared just enough for me to see the worm dropping down into a charge—

What did they say in the comic books? *"Eat cold death, you purple slime!"* I squeezed the trigger.

The rocket streaked forward with a high-pitched scream and a cold white smell. The wall behind me *crackled*. I could feel the burning chill on the back of my neck.

There was a muffled *FWOOMP!*—

The worm's body puffed up for just the briefest of instants. It froze in surprise—and then it simply stopped and collapsed where it was. Within seconds, tiny white ice crystals were forming all over its fur.

And then there was silence.

"Did you get it?" Lizard peered out cautiously.

The body of the creature was trembling and twitching. A dark ichor was flowing from its mouth and there was the faint sighing sound of air escaping from somewhere.

"Get the door closed!" I leapt forward and grabbed the handle—the door was stuck in its hinge!

Lizard grabbed too. "Goddamn worm pulled it out of shape—"

"Keep pulling!"

The door came unstuck with a bone-rattling *BANG!* It swung shut with a slam and we tumbled backward on the floor.

"Oh, God—we did it!" Lizard was laughing. She sat up and looked at me. "We really did it. Didn't we?"

I gulped air and nodded—and started coughing again. I held up a hand—

"It's one thing to bomb them from the air. . . ." she marveled—she was almost delirious— "but it's quite another to meet one face to face! Oh, God!"

I was gasping too hard to speak. I pointed at the door.

She followed my glance. "Oh, no."

The hatch had a hole in it large enough to stick your head through—and you wouldn't have to remove your helmet first either.

"Shelterfoam?"

She managed to shake her head. "No good. The hole's too big. There's no support. We need a patch." She looked around the cabin—

"No. You stay there with the freezer! Dust that hole and keep it dusted!" I scrambled to the back of the ship to a place where the frame had bent. Several of the floor panels had popped off in the crash. I'd had to shelterfoam the hull back here.

I scooped up the largest of the panels and the shelterfoam canister and headed back toward Lizard. As I passed Duke, he reached out and grabbed me. "Wha's 'oing on?"

"It's all right, Duke." I patted his arm, tried to disengage his fingers.

"My legs 'urt. M'legs. Feel all red. Burr'ng."

I pried his hand loose. "I'll be right back. Hang on." He didn't hear me. He kept on moaning.

"All right. Dust it again!" I screamed at Lizard. She loosed a fine spray of liquid coldness at the hole in the door; she directed it all around the edges.

"All right! All right!" I screamed to stop her. I sprayed the edges of the hole with shelterfoam. It crackled against the frigid surface of the hatch. I waited ten seconds, then sprayed again, outlining the break three times over. I slapped the panel over it and held it in place, bracing myself for maximum pressure. "How long does it take for this stuff to harden?"

"Fifteen minutes, half an hour. I'm not sure."

"Terrific. Grab that canister. Spray the hatch. The hinges. The handles. Everything. Outline it."

"Right."

She had to work around me, but she was thorough. By the time she was finished, the foam over the break was already hardening. Gingerly, I took my hands away from the panel I was holding. It stayed put. I took the canister from Lizard and gave it another *shpritz* around the edges. Good.

I turned around and looked at her. She was giggling. She pointed at the door. "I always wanted a window—"

"Huh?" I turned back to the door. The patch had a glass window in it. And a warning: CAUTION. DO NOT OPEN THIS PANEL WHILE— The rest was obliterated.

I was too tired to laugh. I pointed toward the front of the ship. "Call whatsisname. Tell him we're okay. And—" I lowered my voice, "—tell him Duke's in pretty bad shape."

She searched my face. "As in 'Duke's on the roof and we can't get him down'?"

"Yeah. Better start preparing him."

I pulled off my O-mask and goggles, and climbed into the back to see what I could do for Duke. He was still moaning about his legs being red and burning. I pulled back the blanket and looked. The Gerromycin had done its job—the pink strands were gone from his legs—but the purple and red strands were longer. It *was* worm fur! But—why? How?

Duke's whole body was hot. The console said his temperature was 102. His face was dry. His skin was red and cracked. His eyes were puffed up so badly, I was sure he couldn't see out of them, but he turned his face toward me and managed to croak something.

I didn't understand. I had to put my face closer. "What?"

"Ho . . . go ho . . . tay ho . . ."

"Home? Right, Duke. We're on our way. Just hang on a little

longer, okay?" I squeezed his arm in what was meant to be a reassuring gesture, but he writhed at my touch. "I'm sorry. Just hang on, Duke. A little longer. Danny's coming to get you. Your son."

He turned his head away from me.

There was nothing more I could do for him. I climbed back down to the front of the ship. Lizard was just signing off. She nodded to me. "They're rigging a crab and a zip line."

I grunted and sank down into my seat.

"Everything okay back there?" she asked.

"Yeah," I replied. I wasn't very convincing.

She reached over and patted me. "You're doing fine, McCarthy. Hang on just a little longer."

I looked at her sourly. "That's what I just told Duke."

"Sorry," she said.

"We're gonna lose him. I know it."

"Jim—"

"I am tired of all this dying!" I said. "I hate it!" I could hear the raggedness in my own voice and how loud I sounded in the cramped cabin of the chopper, and abruptly I realized just how close I was to the edge.

I turned away from Lizard and buried my face against my arm, trying to create even a small private space for my frustration. I hurt so badly. My throat tickled, and when I tried to clear it I stated coughing again. I couldn't *stop* coughing. My lungs were trying to climb out through my throat. My chest heaved and hacked until I was nauseous—and I still couldn't stop. Everything hurt at once. Jeezis, God, what a terrible way to die. There was blood and saliva and phlegm and pink frothy syrup dribbling out of my mouth. Lizard was trying to clamp an O-mask over my face. I grabbed at it, but it hardly helped. For a moment I even blacked out. Or something. Everything flickered. Somehow I waved Lizard away. She was hovering over me like a mother, but I turned away bitterly, motioning for her to just keep her distance and please not say anything. "No. Just leave me alone for a while. Okay?"

"Sure. Okay."

And I was alone with the aftermath of the pain. Its resonance was a dark red fire crawling around the inside of my lungs. This attack was the worst yet. I wiped the froth from my mouth. I probably couldn't survive much more of this. I was probably dead already. I rubbed my chest uncomfortably. My hand tasted dirty and salty.

The chopper was cold. There were tiny patches of frost on the walls where the freezer had sprayed—and ice crystals. It smelled of cotton candy and shelterfoam. There was a faint pink haze in the air, but it wasn't strong enough to cover the smell of our sweat—and the other smell too. The smell from the back of the ship.

We sat in silence. We listened to the eternal sound of the Chtorran ecology eating. We watched its myriad tiny forms scuttling across the windshield of the chopper. There were a lot less of them now. They probably didn't like the light and had gone elsewhere. The only critters left were the ones that didn't care.

One of the pink furballs was humping right across my field of vision. Almost mechanically, I picked up my camera and began photographing it. The creature had a tiny puckered mouth and it vacuumed up everything in its path. Maybe this was a larval worm. I wondered if I'd live to find out. I wondered if this would be my legacy—these pictures.

"Hey." I lowered the camera and looked at Lizard.

"What?"

"I just realized. Duke's only a captain. How come Danny's a colonel?"

"You want the truth?"

"Yes."

"Do you know much about what happened in Pakistan?"

"Not a lot, no. That was a long time ago."

Lizard sighed. "Fifteen years is not a long time ago."

"I was only nine years old," I protested.

"I was in high school," Lizard replied. "Anyway, did you ever hear of The Rawalpindi Incident?"

"That I heard of."

"Well . . . your Captain Anderson back there—only he was Lieutenant Anderson at the time—was . . . ah, actively involved."

"How actively?"

"They gave him orders. He followed them."

"I must be stupid," I said. "I don't understand what you're trying not to say."

"Captain Anderson did his job. People got killed. A lot of them. Mostly on the other side. That happens a lot in war. Captain Anderson deserved a medal. Instead, they gave him a court-martial."

"Duke?"

Lizard nodded. "He was acquitted, but then, so was Lizzie Borden, and look at how most people remember her."

"Jeez, I didn't know any of this."

"Not many people do any more. I had to look it up myself. It's very interesting reading. Captain Anderson can have a promotion anytime he wants. All he has to do is retire."

"No way. Not Duke."

"Mm-hm. A lesser man might have resigned his commission. Captain Anderson didn't. You ought to look up his statement to the court. That's the most interesting part. It's about the real meaning of service; he said, 'Commitment means not quitting just because the job got tough.'"

"But they never promoted him after that?"

"Right."

I thought for a moment. Her explanation made sense—except it didn't. I looked at Lizard sharply. "There's something else you're not telling me, isn't there?"

She didn't answer.

"Well . . . ?" I prompted.

"All right," she sighed. "You'd better hear it from me, I guess."

"Hear what?"

"The *other* reason you were pulled out of Colorado is that Danny asked me, off the record, to find something a little less *dangerous* for Captain Anderson. You know, he's almost sixty."

"Duke?"

"Yeah, Duke."

I glanced to the back of the chopper. I'd never thought of Duke as *old*.

"I told you I looked up his record. It's impressive. So I asked for him to be assigned to me. You were part of the package, so you got pulled too. But it could have happened anyway. We're pulling a lot of personnel out of the Rocky Mountain District right now for California."

I grunted a polite acknowledgment. I didn't like the implications.

Lizard reached over and put her hand on mine. She waited till I looked up at her. Her eyes were incredibly blue. "Listen, stupid. I did mean what I said about your expertise. I could have put you and Duke anywhere, but I asked for you in my section because the two of you are exactly what I need right now. I especially appreciate your sense of the Chtorran ecology. I've learned to appreciate it even more in the past two days."

"Thanks," I said grumpily. I even meant it.

"Are you unhappy about that?"

"Listen," I said. "As long as we're telling the truth . . . the only reason I'm the best worm expert in California is that there aren't any others. You think too much of my abilities."

"You haven't done too badly here."

"There's no trick to that."

"Oh? Really?"

"Sure. You just ask yourself what could make this situation worse. Then plan for that. If it happens, you look like you know what you're doing. If it doesn't, you're still better prepared to handle whatever does happen."

"You're kidding."

"Nope. Try it." I gestured toward the windshield. "What could make *this* situation worse?"

She said, "Looking out the window and seeing a whole family of worms surrounding the chopper."

I glanced at my watch. "Probably within fifteen minutes."

"You needn't be so cheerful about it."

I shrugged. "It's hard being right. You get cocky. Besides, what *else* can go wrong?"

She looked at me sharply. "You don't want this transfer, do you?"

"No, I don't," I said candidly. "I don't like the way it was handled. It's been too abrupt. And I don't like leaving a job unfinished. We were making real progress in Colorado."

"Uh-huh." She nodded. "You want to know something about that?"

"What?"

"Nobody's ever going to pull you off an important job unless the one they're putting you on is even *more* important. You might want to remember that. It's true even when there *are* other considerations."

She meant Duke.

Behind us, his breathing had gotten painfully loud. And it seemed even more ragged and uneven then before. I wondered if he was even going to last until the blimp arrived.

We sat in silence for a while.

Suddenly, Lizard said, "You son of a bitch."

"Huh?"

"You did it again." She pointed. I looked.

Outside the chopper, there was something moving through the edges of darkness—something just beyond the warm circle of our lights. Its eyes glimmered and flashed as it glanced toward us. It was that reflection that had given it away.

"Is the spotlight working?" I asked.

"The nose light is out, but I've got one overhead. Hang on." She touched her control panel. A bright beam sprang out across the clearing, catching the little silvery-pink figure in sudden surprise—it was centered in a rosy pool of light. The creatures blinked and froze in the sparkling glare. It was round and furry and as cute as a baby abominable snowman. Pink dust hung in the air around it.

"Oh—" gasped Lizard. "Is that a bunnydog?" Her eyes widened in wonder.

"Yeah," I said sourly. I lifted the camera to my eye. The creature was only thigh-deep in the powder. That meant the cotton candy was settling.

"He doesn't seem scared of the light, does he?"

"No. Just curious. These creatures don't display much fear of anything. Do you see the others?" There were more bunnydogs in the dimness behind it. We could see them in the reflected glow. They were motionless too.

Lizard was grinning. "You just blew one. These aren't worms."

"I've still got ten minutes."

The bunnydog blinked and unfroze then. It scratched behind one ear, rubbed its face with its paws, made a face at us, then turned and ambled out of the spotlight.

"Well, I guess he told you," said Lizard.

"Yeah, but what?"

The other bunnydogs were getting curious now. One at a time, they began taking cautious little hops toward the chopper. They pushed through the powder in quick spurts of motion, stopping often to look ahead and ponder. They cocked their heads sideways to listen, their ears flopping open as they did so. I held my camera steady and recorded every moment of it. I thumbed the controls and zoomed in for close-ups. These pictures were going to be *important*.

There was something funny about the shape of their mouths. They seemed permanently pouted; their muzzles were oddly blunted. As I watched, one of them straightened up and turned to its companion, pursing its lips as if kissing the air. The other replied with a kissy-face of its own. They looked like puppies who'd been pulled off mama's tit. Of course! Their mouths were shaped more for sucking than for chewing!

How very . . . odd.

I watched—and photographed—as the bunnydogs continued sniffing closer to the chopper. Every so often, one or another of them would lower its muzzle to the dust and suck and chew. Were they going for the powder—or the creatures feeding on the powder? I couldn't tell. But I knew it was important; it was part of the bigger question. Were these creatures intelligent? Were they omnivores? Were these the sentients we were looking for?

Their nostrils and eyes were slits against the powder, but every so often one of the creatures would pause and straighten and look at us, blinking its eyes wide for a quick curious instant; then we could see that the bunnydogs actually had very large round eyes. Puppydog eyes. Probably that was their normal configuration—when they weren't rump-deep in dust.

I said, "This is very, very bad news."

Lizard glanced at me. "Huh?"

"We've been telling people that the Chtorran ecology is extraordinarily vicious, right?"

"Uh-huh."

"And we've got pictures to prove it, right?"

"Go on. . . ."

"So—how long do you think we'll be able to sell that story after *these* creatures are seen by the public?"

"You're right," she said. "This *is* bad news."

I continued recording the bunnydogs' cautious inspection of the chopper. "We're going to have to put a lid on this. At least until we know what we're looking at. These creatures could be the most dangerous of all. And we might not find out what the danger is until it's too late, because we're so distracted by how cute they are."

The first of the bunnydogs reached the windshield then. It climbed up the side of the chopper and peered in at us, blinking owlishly. With its paws flat against the glass, it looked like a small child peering in the window of a candy store. It sucked at the surface—tasting it, no doubt.

"I keep wanting to saw *awww*," whispered Lizard.

"It's a fucking teddy bear—a goddamned fucking teddy bear!" I growled. "What a dirty trick."

The bunnydog licked its chops politely. I wondered what that meant.

There were other bunnydogs climbing up the side of the chopper now. Within minutes, the window was full of tiny little faces peering in at us.

"I, uh . . . hate to say this," said Lizard, "but I'm starting to get scared."

"Me too. I never thought I'd be afraid of a herd of teddy bears."

"They just keep staring at us. What do they want?"

"I don't know." I was still recording. "I think maybe they're just curious." I lowered my camera. "I want to try something. Will you record this?"

"Sure." She took the camera from me. "Okay, go ahead."

I leaned forward in my seat and placed my hands up against the glass, opposite the paws of the first bunny. Its paws were no larger than a baby's.

The bunnydog blinked. It tried to sniff my hands through the windshield. It sucked at the glass. Then it stopped and frowned. It looked puzzled. It blinked and tried again. This time, it licked the glass. Its tongue was soft and pink. The other bunnydogs watched curiously.

"That doesn't seem very intelligent," Lizard said.

"It is if you've never seen glass before. It's testing."

The bunnydog blinked at me again.

I blinked back at it, a big oversized gesture.

The bunnydog showed its teeth.

I showed mine. As wide as I could.

The bunnydog—there was no other word for it—smiled.

I smiled too, a big ridiculous grin.

"I think you're communicating," Lizard said.

I wonder what we're saying to each other?"

"It looks like, 'for better or worse, for richer or poorer, in sickness and in health . . .'"

"Bite your tongue," I said. But my face was frozen. I was still smiling broadly at the bunnydog. "Maybe we're negotiating a peace treaty. . . ."

The bunnydog made a face. It pulled its cheeks out into a grotesque expression. And held it.

"I dare you," Lizard said.

I swallowed. "The things I do for my species." I made a face back at the bunnydog. I hooked my fingers in my mouth and stretched it wide. I crossed my eyes and stuck out my tongue and touched the tip of it to my nose.

The bunnydog fell off the window in surprise. So did all the others.

"Oh, God—I think I've insulted them."

The bunnydogs were rolling around in the powder, stamping

their feet and drumming up big clouds of pale pink dust. They looked like they were having a collective seizure.

"Or something," Lizard said. "Maybe they're laughing themselves to death."

I looked at Lizard; she had the camera still recording. She pointed it straight at me. "This—" I said angrily to posterity, "—is *not* the way Captain Kirk always did it!"

Q: What do Chtorrans call cremation?
A: Wasting food.

26

Beyond Adrenaline

*"It is almost always dangerous to be right
too soon."*

—SOLOMON SHORT

The bunnydogs climbed back up on the windshield and stared at
us for a while longer. I made some more faces at them. They made
some more faces at me. Gradually, they lost interest in that game
and drifted away to explore other parts of the chopper. We heard
them scrabbling across the top of the ship and scratching at the
observation bubbles.

"I'd better see what they're up to—" I grabbed the camera and
headed for the back. I stopped and peered up into the turret. One
of the little cutenesses was peering back down at me. I waved at
it facetiously—it waved back—then I closed the shutter in case
Duke woke up again.

On a hunch, I peered out through the tiny accidental window in
the door patch. "Holy Hannah!" I jammed the camera against the
glass and started shooting. There were bunnies all over the dead
worm! The ice had evaporated from its fur—now it was just a big
collapsed bag of dead pudding—but the bunnies were climbing up
onto its back, patting it curiously and chittering at it. They looked
like they were trying to wake it up. One of them was even peering
into its mouth.

Lizard called me then. "Hey, McCarthy. Something's happening."

"Wait a minute—"

"I mean it! You better get down here!"

She was right. Something *was* happening. The bunnies were
suddenly dropping off the dead worm and moving forward again.

I swung down to the front of the chopper and climbed back into my seat.

Lizard pointed off to the left. "Over there. Look. The bunny-dogs have all stopped to listen."

She as right. The little round creatures had fallen still. They were *listening* for something. They had their heads cocked sideways and their expressions were expectant.

Beyond the darkness, something was stirring up the dust. Clouds of it rose brightly in the glare of our lights.

The bunnydogs stiffened expectantly. . . .

I could feel my heart rising. This was it.

And then the first worm poured over the dunes and down into the drifts.

And then a second worm, and a third.

There were more bunnydogs riding on their backs.

Lizard lifted her camera and started shooting. "Well, you got the worms right," she said, "but you missed the time."

I barely heard her. The worms were still pouring over the dunes. I gulped. "Win one, lose one."

Lizard was scanning the groups with her camera. "I see six, seven, eight . . . no, make that ten, eleven—urk, fourteen worms."

They were all different sizes. The smallest was no bigger than a pony. The largest was the size of a bus. They swiveled their big black hand-puppet eyes at us, cocked them back and forth, up and down, locked them into place, and stared at the chopper. If they had expressions, they were unreadable.

We could see the coloring of the worms vividly. They were bright red and orange, striped with purple, and frosted all over with pink powder. They left trails of glittering dust in the air. They sparkled as if they were made out of magic.

"I hate to say it," whispered Lizard, "but . . . they're beautiful."

She was right. As horrifying as the worms were, they were also *fascinating*. Each worm was a gaudy calliope of color. Their stripes had the confusing effect of seeming to shift even as we watched. If there was a pattern to the markings, I couldn't tell.

Despite the dust, this was the clearest and closest view of worms in the wild we'd had yet.

The monsters were shaped like stubby cigars, but with a bulge at the front like the nose of an old Boeing 747. That was the brain case, a thick shell of bone shielding the creature's gray matter (or whatever color it was—more likely purple). The monster's arms were anchored here. Mostly the worms kept their peculiarly double-jointed arms folded flat against the brain case, reaching up and over the eyes only to grasp or hold something. Or some*one*.

The creatures' eyes rose up just in front of the brain case. The two eyes moved independently of each other, as if they were mounted on separate swivels, but both organs were enclosed in the same rubbery bag of skin.

At the very front of the creature was the mouth.

When it was closed, it looked like a sphincter; but when it was open, it was hideous—it was a maw, a grinding hole, a pit. It had two sharp-looking mandibles that folded back into the skin, almost disappearing, but which could slice out in an instant. The creatures rattled their mandibles nervously while they waited. No, nothing godly was responsible for this beast. Lizard was wrong. The gastropede was not a beautiful creature. Never could be. The mouth spoiled it.

The worms were moving around the chopper now, inspecting it, looking at it sideways, but always keeping a cautious distance—at least three lengths away. Several of them began moving toward the rear—

"Oh, my God—the dead worm!"

Lizard followed me back. I leapt over Duke toward the weapon bay; she climbed into the turret. "They've found it! McCarthy, look at this!"

I grabbed the box of rockets and scrambled back. I shoved my face up to the accidental window. Three large worms were inspecting the body of the dead one. The bunnydogs moved to keep out of their way.

One of the worms slid around then, bringing itself directly alongside the body. It rolled up to it as if it were . . . cuddling? That didn't make sense. Another worm was doing the same thing on the opposite side.

"What are they doing?" Lizard called quietly.

"I don't know. I've never seen this before. Are you still carrying your camera?"

"Yeah. I'm getting it!"

Abruptly, one of the worms lifted its eyes and looked straight at me. It was studying the door—the same door its colleague had been trying to open when we'd killed it.

The worm slid forward—

I yelped and leapt for the peace-pipe. I fumbled a rocket into it, then looked out the window again.

The worm was peering in at me.

I jumped backward, almost tripping, slamming into the opposite wall. I braced myself and aimed the rocket launcher straight ahead.

Something tapped at the door. It sounded *exactly* like a knock.

"Don't answer it. . . . " squeaked Lizard.

The tapping continued for a long . . . long moment. And then it stopped abruptly.

I could feel my heart beating like a jackhammer. The silence was terrifying!

Abruptly the door squeaked and groaned.

The worm was trying to work the latch!

It didn't rattle. The shelterfoam held—

And then silence.

"What's it doing?" I whispered.

"It's backing away from the door."

I jumped for the window. She was right. The worm was retreating a meter at a time. It was still studying the chopper door curiously. And then it—scratched itself right between the eyes. It looked . . . *puzzled*!

"Are you getting all this?"

"Uh-huh. I don't believe it either. McCarthy! Look at the other one!"

The second worm to cuddle against the dead one had lifted its eyes to study the door now. It shifted its glance to the worm that was backing away, as if considering. Then it looked to the door again and apparently made a decision. It slid off toward the nose of the chopper.

Several of the other worms approached the dead one now. They looked like they were sniffing and inspecting it, but none of them moved up alongside it. "Nobody else wants to cuddle . . .?" I guessed.

"Would you?" Lizard asked. She dropped out of the turret. "Come on! Something's happening up front."

The worms were forming themselves into groups. There were two groups of four and two groups of three. The bunnydogs looked like they were directing them, but I wasn't sure. I never listened to the person guiding me into a parking place either; why should a worm? The creatures were settling down quickly.

"Now what are they doing?" Lizard wondered.

"I don't know," I whispered back. "Always, before, we've seen worms only in groups of three or four. We've assumed those were family groups. We've never had a chance to observe a really large gathering." My voice cracked on the next-to-last word. I swallowed hard. My throat hurt. I was afraid I was going to start coughing again.

Lizard looked over at me. "How are you doing?"

"You mean, am I scared?"

"Yeah."

"I'm petrified. How about you?"

She said it matter-of-factly: "I guess you could say I'm handling it as well as can be expected."

I heard the quaver. I reached over and touched her hand. "Under the circumstances, there's not a hell of a lot of other options."

She squeezed my hand in hers—almost a little too hard. Then she let go quickly, as if she were embarrassed at having admitted the feeling.

I covered my own reaction by picking up the Pentax again. When in doubt, take care of business. I popped the clip and dropped the memory cassette into my lap. I reached down for a new one and snapped it into place.

I'd filled eighty gigabytes of memory with two hours of high-resolution video. No matter what else happened, what we'd photographed here tonight would make an incredible difference to the war effort. We'd seen things that no other human beings had ever observed—and we'd made a record of them.

I expected the next hour to be even *more* interesting."

If we survived.

That thought hovered oddly.

I knew that we were very close to death here—

—and it didn't matter.

I realized I couldn't be scared any more. I'd moved beyond fear.

I'd passed into a kind of free-floating euphoria. It was the strangest feeling; I'd used up all my fear. All that was left was *interest*.

I supposed I'd run out of adrenaline. That was probably the medical explanation; but it *felt* like the freedom of madness.

And I didn't mind.

It was all right to be crazy. It was the best thing to be. I didn't have to be responsible any more. I was tired of being *responsible*. . . .

I floated. I photographed the Chtorran worms, and floated above the land of fear.

The bunnydogs were gathering in front of the worm groups

now. They were absolutely unafraid of the worms. The two species were obviously in partnership.

The question was . . . *which one* was the dominant partner?

The four groups of worms were arranged in a large arc in front of the chopper. Now, several of the bunnydogs hopped into the focus of that space and began stamping out a large circle, an arena several meters across. A cloud of pink dust rose around them as they moved. It glittered and sparkled in the air. They didn't act as if they noticed. They rabbit-thumped their big paddlefeet and pounded the powder into a hard-packed surface. They moved around and around the circle, spiraling out and then in again.

There were at least a dozen of them, and they went about their task with an almost grim determination. They were little round pink warriors trying to invent a war dance. As they continued, more and more of the bunnydogs entered the circle and joined the task, until all of them were there, determinedly stamping out an arena.

I glanced to the worms. They were paying very close attention to what was happening here. One by one, they were shifting to face forward. They moved up to the very edge of the circle, but did not enter it. Instead, they settled into positions of quiet readiness. They looked like giant red meat loaves; they folded their arms back and swiveled their eyes forward, and focused their attention on the bunnies in the circle.

They were *waiting* on the bunnydogs.

They were a monstrous tableau. Their large black eyes blinked rapidly against the spreading dust in the air. They watched dispassionately. If they had expressions, they were impossible to read.

Very quickly, the bunnydogs finished preparing their arena and stopped. As each one finished, he/she/it? moved to the center of the circle and waited. Finally, they were all of them gathered silently in the center in a loose jumble. For a moment, nothing happened. The bunnydogs were still. The worms might have been statues. The dust hung in the air, a silent pink haze. Everything was frozen.

"Now, what?"

"Shhh."

We waited.

The first movements were imperceptible. We saw the dust, not the motion; it rose around the bunnydogs in a fresh pink cloud. They were stamping their feet again, but this time it had a *ritual* quality. They were trembling. They were shivering and shuddering. And finally, they were moving—all as one now—turning slowly around and around among themselves.

The cluster began to expand. Still stamping, still turning, they began to move outward toward the edges of their circle. At the same time they began to expand the size of their movements. They brought their arms out from their bodies. They lifted their hands over their heads. They opened their mouths wide and a shrill keening rose from their throats.

They had the *sweetest* voices.

The keening went on and on—and then suddenly, one of the bunnydogs let loose a rapid, high-pitched series of yelps. The other bunnies froze for just an instant and—

—then began to *dance*.

It was a wild and frenzied performance, an explosion of bright pink energy. The bunnydogs stamped the ground beneath their feet as hard as they could. The dust rose in thick billowing explosions, sparkling and churning around them. The bunnies whirled and pounded, jumped and bounced. They chittered and shrieked and whooped.

They flung their arms out wide and leapt into the air, screaming like sirens. They bounced like popcorn. Where one came down, five more leapt up. It was a chain reaction of giggling joyous energy. We could hear them growling like teddy bears and yelping like Indians.

There was no pattern to it that we could see. The dance was a celebration, an exuberant demonstration of enthusiasm and delight. I couldn't help myself, I could feel the grin spreading across my face. I glanced over at Lizard and she was smiling too. The bunnies were *funny*.

By now they must have been out of control. They caromed off each other like Ping-Pong balls in a wind tunnel. The bunnies were shuddering and shaking and waggling their fat little butts like ecstatic puppies. I wanted to run out there and join them. I wondered if Lizard was feeling the same way. I glanced over at her.

"It's marvelous!" she said. "But what does it mean?"

"It looks like a *wraggle*."

"A . . . what?"

"A dance. A communication dance. That's how bees tell other bees where to find the tastiest flowers. Maybe that's what's happening here. Maybe this is how you control or communicate with worms—by dancing. Dr. Fletcher is going to want to see this."

But—

No, it didn't make sense.

This dance couldn't be just for the fun of it—not here. Not now. *Not with all these worms watching.*

There was something else going on here, something I couldn't even begin to understand—and I knew I should.

It felt too *familiar*.

But the connection refused to complete; it hovered annoyingly beyond the edge of recognition. I could feel the frustration growing like a knot in my chest.

The bunnydogs were whirling now, not leaping. They twirled and spun like little fat dervishes—like plump pink pigs. They bumped into each other, fell into the dust, sputtering and gobbling, then bounced back up into the smoke and kept on twirling. They looked like chipmunks trying to describe a tornado.

A communication dance.

And then I realized—

"Oh, my God."

"What—?"

"I've seen this before," I said.

"What!"

I added quickly, "Not exactly this, but something enough like it." I swallowed hard. "In the herd. In San Francisco. Dr. Fletcher took me. The herd members do a kind of dance. It looks like this." I shook my head. "I don't know. Maybe it's a coincidence."

"Why does the herd dance?" Lizard asked.

"Dr. Fletcher thinks that it has something to do with communication. Nonverbal communication."

Lizard didn't reply immediately. She was studying the bunnydogs again. They were still bouncing. Their energy seemed inexhaustible.

"How do you decode it?" she asked.

"I don't know. I'm not a worm."

"You think the dance is for the worms?"

"Who else? Maybe they're telling the worms about us, about what they saw when they peeked in the windows. I don't know. Maybe—" I hesitated, then added, "I don't want to worry you with this thought, but—"

"Worry me," she said.

"Well . . . obviously, there's some kind of partnership here. And, uh, it seems pretty obvious to me—by the shape of their muzzles—that the bunnydogs are meat-eaters, or at least omnivorous. Their mouths look like they're good for sucking too.

Maybe they use the worms to kill for them. Maybe they're telling them right now that this is a picnic basket."

"Right," said Lizard. "Listen, if you have any more thoughts like that . . . you don't have to worry me."

Outside, the frenzy was ebbing now. The dance was slowing. One by one, the bunnies whirled into the center and collapsed exhaustedly into the dust. They fell on one another, rolling and tumbling. The dance was deflating into a big pile of pink fur.

There was silence. The ever-present pink dust hung in the air.

"Now what?" Lizard wondered.

I didn't answer.

The worms had watched the entire dance without reaction. Now, they slowly turned their eyes toward each other. They almost looked . . . uncertain, as if they were waiting for the emperor's reaction before they allowed their own.

Only . . . which one was the emperor?

One by one, the worms were turning their attention toward the largest—*and most patterned*—worm in the group. It had narrowed the apertures of its eyes; it looked like it was brooding thoughtfully.

Caesar Augustus? Or Caligula?

Abruptly, its eyes bounced open.

And then it moved.

Ponderously, majestically, it flowed forward. Straight toward us.

And then *all* the worms flowed forward.

They surrounded the chopper—and began to examine it. All fourteen of them. They scratched and tapped and thumped the hull of the ship.

The chopper pitched and bumped ominously—

Q: Why did the Chtorran cross the road?
A: To eat everything on the other side.

27

God Came Out at Midnight

"Space is not the final frontier.
"The final frontier is the human soul.
Space is merely the place where we are
most likely to meet the challenge. The
victory will occur in the continual process
of challenging and testing our
limits—both as individuals and as a
species—and not in the amount of
territory conquered."

—SOLOMON SHORT

Lizard was on the radio immediately, *"Houston! We've got a problem!"*

Colonel Danny Anderson replied immediately, "Go ahead, ELDAVO."

"We've got worms. More than a dozen of 'em——" Lizard screamed, "—and they're reading the label on this package. Canned people!" She yelped again as something rocked the chopper.

I scrambled out of my seat and crawled back, looking for the rocket launcher or the freeze gun. Maybe I could hold them off until the blimp arrived.

There were scrabbling sounds at the door. Something was scraping across the roof. The chopper bumped as if something else were pushing it from behind. It lurched so hard I stumbled against the wall.

Duke was moaning! He was waving his arms, trying to get up. He was mumbling and reaching. "Torsh—whah mah torsh?" A pair of giant black eyes was peering in at him through the left side bubble.

I didn't think. I grabbed the shelterfoam gun and sprayed the window. Did the worm looked surprised? Did it back away? I didn't see. I turned and sprayed the other bubble.

I crawled over to Duke, pushing him back down onto the deck. "Stay still," I commanded.

"Huh . . . whuh?"

"Stay still! That's an order, Captain!"

"Yessuhm—" and he lapsed into unconsciousness.

As I scrambled back to Lizard, she tossed me a sideways glance. "Gave yourself a little promotion, huh?"

"So court-martial me. Where's the goddamn blimp?" I looked at the clock. "They're overdue."

"I don't know—"

"We're eight minutes away," boomed Colonel Anderson's voice from the radio. "Keep your pants on."

"Why?" I snapped back. "Will that taste better to the worms?"

"Listen up, Lieutenant!" Colonel Anderson had his father's same angry tone. "Anchoring a blimp is tricky. How you *feel* about it is irrelevant. It's going to take the same amount of time whether you're calm and rational or panicky and screaming. So it's up to you. How do you want to play it?"

Something in the rear of the chopper creaked ominously. It sounded like a Kevlar strut crackling under pressure. Something else went *thump* against the door. The door *bulged*. A piece of shelterfoam *sponged* away and ricocheted off the opposite wall.

I turned back to the radio. "That's real reasonable, Colonel, sir—but you don't have several tons of worm trying to climb into your ship. We do."

"I'm aware of your problem, Lieutenant. But we don't have any more time to talk about it. You'll have to have your little hissy-fit *after* we pick you up."

A worm was staring at us through the windshield, but it didn't push through. It just goggled its eyes and blinked. *Sput-phwut*. A second worm slid up beside it.

I opened my mouth to reply to Colonel Anderson—and then shut it. I realized how stupid I was about to be. I was going to argue for my right to be terrified and upset. The worms were still only inspecting us. If they'd wanted to come in, they would have. Time enough to scream then. "Go ahead," I gulped.

"We've got you on our horizon now. Stand by." There was a pause. "Nope. There's still too much *schmutz* in the air. We'll have to do this on instruments." Another pause. "All right, we're dropping the crab. I'll give you the video—"

Lizard reached out and switched on the main display. She punched through the channels quickly. A bright clear image came up on the screen.

We were looking down from the blimp. A round, spidery looking robot—it had a lot of arms and legs and attachments—was dangling from four lines that looked too slender to support it. It was caught in the spotlights of the blimp and it flashed with spotlights of its own. The only indications of motion were the pale and luminous clouds sweeping past below.

Lizard touched her controls again and a second screen lit up to show the view from the crab's camera. There were pink trees swinging wildly below us.

I leaned forward to peer out the front windshield. "Shouldn't we be seeing them soon?"

Lizard asked the radio, "Can you eyeball us?"

"Not yet. Stand by. We'll give you the computer scan. Channel three."

Lizard punched up a third display screen. The image was plastic looking, without detail; the blimp's computer had compiled all its sensory data—sonic, infrared, radar, visual, and who knew what else—into a single three-dimensional portrait. The landscape looked rippled and uneven; the computer had painted it a dull orange. A wide depression angled diagonally through the image; we were sliding toward it.

There! Just left of center—that bright white object! That was us! A tiny gunship half-buried in a furrow of red. There were dark shapes crawling all over it. I wished I hadn't seen that.

Lizard studied it for a moment, then pointed back over my shoulder. "The blimp'll be coming in from that angle. You'll see them first from the turret."

I climbed back to the turret and pulled myself up into it. I pulled the shutter back—

—and I was suddenly staring into the large round eyes of a large round worm. It blinked. I blinked. It blinked again. I made a face at it. It blinked a third time. I shined my flashlight at it. It blinked.

But it didn't attack.

Why not?

What was going here?!

"Shoo!" I shouted. "Shoo!"

The worm blinked at me again.

"Goddammit! Get out of my way! You big fat hairy bag of pustulant pink pudding!"

The worm backed away from the turret.

I stared in surprise. I didn't know my own strength.

I swiveled around quickly. The worms were all over the chopper—and all around it on the ground. They were huge dark shapes in the night, moving quickly and silently across the pale glow of the dust drifts. The lights of the ship struck highlights off the powder crust on their sides.

Another worm raised itself up to peer at me—one of the biggest. It leaned its weight against the chopper—and pulled us sideways! Lizard yelped. Duke moaned. I heard it over my own scream. The worm loomed ominous and huge outside the turret. It swiveled one eye high and the other eye low to look at me from a very cockeyed angle. It only wanted to *study* me. It was *curious*.

These were not *ordinary* worms. They weren't hungry.

I'd never met a worm before that wasn't crazy with hunger—or rage. This was a whole new mode of behavior. We were going to have to rewrite the book.

We'd always assumed that the worms were like the millipedes—so much a victim of their own hunger that *everything* was perceived as food. But these worms were beyond that.

How did that happen? How much food did a worm need to eat to be *satisfied*?

How much did it take to *stuff* a worm? Seattle? North Dakota?

Or maybe the answer was all around me. First, you bury California under two meters of cotton candy powder so the worms are surrounded by food. Then let them out for a walk. Every time they take a step they get a mouthful. Feed them faster than they can eat. The issue of hunger is taken care of.

Maybe.

Maybe we were safe for as long as there was pink snow on the ground.

Or maybe that was just a false connection. Maybe there was something else going on here too.

We just didn't know.

A pink light in the sky pulled me back to the present. It looked like a warm glow behind a veil of smoke.

"I can see the blimp!" I hollered.

As I watched, the glow began to assume brilliance and color and even a hint of size and form. Then it became a cluster of lights. They grew brighter. The glow moved out of the darkness and became a gaudy, cigar-shaped, rose-enveloped *presence*. The air glowed pink around it. Its brightest lights were banked along its belly; rows of spotlights, swiveling and pointing in all directions. The crab was a smaller cluster of beams and auras hanging just below.

The ship hung in the sky like a vision—like an angel. Its rays came sweeping through the pale haze like fingers from heaven, turning everything *luminous*. The beams poured from the sky. They were beautiful! One of them touched me in passing and it was almost too bright to look at.

The whole world glowed with the light—the land, the drifts, the stark and barren trees. Everything looked ghostly and iridescent. Even the dark worms and the darker body of the chopper. A line from something floated through my head. *God came out at midnight. I could see him floating in the sky.*

All around us, the worms were stopping what they were doing, turning and looking upward. Some of them even backed away from the chopper for a better view. They were puzzled at the light in the sky, trying to make out what it could be—but there was no focus there. No edges, no shapes, no lines—only the light. The beautiful, brilliant, dazzling *light*!

I felt a surge of joy in my chest and in my throat. It made the pain all that more exquisite. My eyes started to water. "It's beautiful," I said.

"What?" asked Lizard.

"It's beautiful!" I called. "I can see the lights of the blimp! It's the most beautiful sight I've ever seen."

"How far are they?"

"Uh—" I brought myself back to reality again. "It's hard to tell. Maybe a kilometer. Maybe two."

"They're past the trees," Lizard said. "They can fire the harpoon any time now."

Something puffed from the bottom of the crab. It hit the ground with a muffled thump, and a large cloud of pale powdery smoke rose from the point of impact. The crab slid down the line and disappeared into the cloud, leaving four thin lines hanging in the air, stiffening against the pull of the blimp.

"They got it!" I called. "They've moored."

"Not yet!" Lizard called back. "Two more to go."

The crab released the anchor line and scuttled sideways across the pink drifts. Almost immediately it disappeared into them, marking its passage by the three lines still anchored to it. They cut through the powder like fishing lines through water, only they left a trail, a moving cloud of brightly glowing dust.

Abruptly, the crab appeared again, coming up suddenly on a rise. Its motion was mad—even comical—but it was *fast*. It scrambled quickly across the ground, varying its gait to match the terrain; it bounced, it crawled, it scuttled sideways; it paused, it backed up, it dipped and tilted; it *tiptoed* around a pink lump that once had been a bush, then dashed down the opposite side of the slope in a rapid spurt of action.

The bunnydogs were frozen. The worms *stared*.

The crab picked its steps like a ballet dancer. It moved like a lunar walker. It raced like a thoroughbred. If it could have cooked, I'd have married it.

It stopped inside another pink drift. The whole powdery area *glowed* with its light. There was another bright puff—another harpoon—and another line was anchored. This time when the crab came scuttling out, it was trailing only two lines back up to the blimp.

It headed directly toward the chopper now, directly toward two of the largest worms. Their eyes blinked as it approached.

It hesitated only a moment—then dashed directly between the two of them. Their eyes swiveled to follow this small presumptuous machine. It passed between them so rapidly they nearly twisted their eyes off. Only after it passed their tails did they remember to be surprised, and leapt around to stare at it again. Was that a Chtorran double take?

One of the worms cocked its eyes curiously—the "hand-puppet expression" was getting very familiar—and started to follow the crab tentatively. The crab swiveled a spotlight toward it, and the worm backed away quickly. I started to giggle. It was *funny*. These monsters had to mass several tons apiece, and they were startled by a hyperkinetic machine?!

The crab had already scuttled sideways around the chopper. I swiveled around to watch it disappear over—no, through—one of the steepest drifts of all. Its powdery light gleamed in the distance. It was moving as far from the chopper as it could to provide a long third leg for the tripod of mooring ropes. After a moment, I saw the now-familiar puff of smoke, and a few moments later the crab scuttled back, trailing only a single line. Our lifeline.

"All right," called Lizard. "They're ready if we are."

"Wait a minute," I called.. "Something's happening."

The worms were swiveling their eyes upward again—to stare at the blimp. The airship was moving onto station directly overhead.

Mother! That thing was huge! And bright! The air around it didn't just glow—it *shimmered*.

The blimp was a giant pink egg that filled the sky. It hung there like a gorgeous UFO, pouring light down on all of us—the pale powdery drifts, the stubby bunnydogs, the darkened chopper, and the curious worms.

The worms—

I couldn't tear my eyes from them. They shone incredibly in the glare from above; they looked luminous. They looked like they were made of electricity. Their fur rippled in waves; the stripes on their sides seemed to shiver and shift with red and purple iridescence. They looked as if they were lit from within. They glowed with pink auras.

The airship was pulling itself into position by adjusting the length of its mooring lines at the source. It was a tricky maneuver because the pilot also had to keep the ship pointed into the wind. The display boards on its sides were flashing with bright stripes and colored patterns and even a crawling message. HEAVY LIFTING IS OUR BAG. OREGON AIR-LUMBER. Then a moment later: PAUL BUNYAN RESCUES U.S. ARMY. PICTURES AT ELEVEN.

The worms were fascinated by the sight. They turned around and around under the blimp; their eyes were angled upward, blinking furiously. They circled in the clearing, oblivious to everything else; they bumped into each other again and again as they tried to track with the airship. The bunnydogs had to scramble to keep out of their way.

"They're going crazy," I called. "Something about the blimp—"

And then one of the worms *stood up*. It raised itself almost its entire length. I wouldn't have believed it if I hadn't seen it with my own eyes. It *reached* futilely, frantically for the blimp. It stretched its arms upward in a pleading gesture—

I thought of pictures I'd seen of New Christians trying to touch the robes of The Apostle.

—and then the worm opened its mouth and let loose the most incredible sound I'd ever heard from the throat of any creature—a long high-pitched, warbling-wavering, strung-out-forever wail of hope, desire, and *despair*. The sound was *maddening*.

And then the worm fell back down into the dust. It toppled backward, writhing, its two rows of pitifully tiny feet waved in the air for a moment, and then it scrambled around madly trying to right itself, trying to reach for the blimp again.

I felt sorry for it.

The other worms were trying to lift themselves toward the blimp too. They stretched their arms and cried. They wailed. They *worshiped*.

"I don't get it," Lizard said.

"I do. The blimp looks like a worm. A big bright friendly worm—" and then the second, *deeper* part of that realization hit me, "—a giant, floating, dazzling, *vision* of a worm! An angel hanging in the sky! Pouring light! In their own image! It looks like *God* to them!"

"Oh my God," said Lizard softly. She saw it too.

"Tell the blimp to cut their lights!" I called forward. "It's the lights that are doing it. We're going to have to do this in the dark."

I looked upward again myself. The blimp was beautiful. I could see why the worms were so crazy underneath it. How would you feel if an angel opened the sky and shone its light down on you?

And then the blimp doused its lights and disappeared. It vanished *completely,* cloaked by the night and the thick powdery gloom in the air.

The worms *shrieked.*

They screamed like all the tortured souls of Hell. The sound was hideous.

"Oh, no—" I'd made a mistake.

How would you feel if an angel opened the sky and shone its light down on you? How would you feel if, when you called to that angel, it disappeared and left you behind? *Alone*.

You'd feel damned.

Outside, the worms were raging.

Q: Where does a 500-pound gorilla sleep?
A: Inside the Chtorran.

28

"—what could be worse?"

*"If you want to bring a centipede to a
crashing halt, ask it in which order it
moves its legs."*

—SOLOMON SHORT

We were left with only the lights of the chopper and the crab.

The worms were dark shapes in the night again.

The blimp was a darker shape overhead—not seen, just barely
sensed.

The worms were moving again.

They circled and shrieked and raged at the sky. They raged at
each other. They raged at the chopper. Something bumped us—
hard. Duke began to moan again. I wondered if the worms were
going to vent their fury on us.

A long dark shape flowed *over* the chopper just a few meters
away from me. It startled me so badly, I tried to leap back in the
turret and banged my head on the Plexiglas. The chopper creaked
with the weight of its passage. The hull cracked and *complained*.
Oh, God—

The monster poured down the opposite side and charged at the
largest worm in its path. I wished for a spotlight. It shrieked and
leapt. It attacked the other worm in a raging fury. The two great
beasts wound themselves around each other like serpentine
wrestlers and rolled across the powdery dust in a furious tangle.
The smoke rose around them.

They broke apart once, then wrapped themselves up in each
other again and wrestled off into the darkness, quickly disappearing in the ever-present haze.

I'd never seen that before. I'd never seen a worm attack another worm.

All around the chopper, suddenly *all* the worms were attacking one another. Or, at least, trying to.

They rushed at each other, then jumped away. They circled warily, all the time shrieking and moaning and making low rumbling sounds. They were hellbeasts. They were terrifying.

There was a pattern to their battles. Two by two, they paired off, writhing into the gloom. It didn't look like an attack any more—it looked like a ritual of some kind. It looked like . . . communication. The worms were withdrawing into each other's embraces, as if no one single one of them could figure this out by itself, as if they had to pool their brainpower.

And then, suddenly, all the worms were gone. And there was silence.

Stillness.

Nothing moved. Even the dust seemed frozen in the air.

The bunnydogs had disappeared. The millipedes were gone. There was nothing but the pale pink dust again.

"Is it over?" asked Lizard.

"I don't know." I made myself let go of the turret handles I'd been gripping. My fingers ached with the sudden release of tension. My chest was hurting again—so bad I could barely move.

"What were they doing?"

"I don't know, but let's get out of here now. Quickly! Before they come back!"

Even as I spoke, the crab was scrabbling up the side of the chopper. It poised itself next to the turret and pointed two spotlights and a double-eyed camera at me. One mechanical claw snapped upward in a crisp salute. Automatically I started to salute back, then pulled my hand down in embarrassment. The crab bobbled its lights as if it were laughing—and waved. I glared back.

"That's cute, McCarthy. Real cute!" Lizard called from up front. She could see me through the crab's eyes—the video was relayed.

"Just what I need," I said. "A crab with a sense of humor. I'm going to kill the operator." I dropped to the cabin floor.

"All right," Lizard was saying, "get your ass out of the way—and Duke's too. I'm going to blow the turret."

I pulled Duke as far forward as I could. I had to ignore his moaning—there was nothing else I could do for him now—and fitted a clean O-mask over his face. Then I climbed up front again to join Lizard. She was just unlocking the trigger. I handed her a mask and hung my own around my neck.

"All set?" she asked the radio.

"You may fire when ready, Grisly."

There were three switches. Lizard flipped the first one. A quietly mechanical voice said, "The explosive bolts are now charged. You have three minutes to arm."

I glanced out the front of the chopper. Two of the worms were returning. They were moving solemnly back into our arena of light. They looked . . . thoughtful.

I pointed silently.

Lizard looked. She glanced sideways at me. "Will they move?"

"I don't know."

"Well, think. What could be worse?"

I didn't answer. I shook my head. I couldn't think of *worse* any more. We'd already gone beyond my capacity to imagine worse.

Lizard flipped the second switch. The mechanical voice said, "The explosive bolts are now armed. You have three minutes to fire."

Two more worms returned. Their eyes were blinking steadily, a sure sign of interest. I started to point—

"I see 'em," Lizard said, without looking up. "Put your mask on. We're getting out of here." The screen in front of her with the radar scan from the blimp was showing a ragged circle of cigar shapes closing in on the chopper again. *All* the worms were returning.

Lizard started pulling her mask on. She paused and grinned sideways at me. "Don't forget. You owe me a lobster dinner, buddy."

She threw the third switch.

The turret blew off the back of the chopper with a BANG!

Almost immediately, a swirl of dust came filtering down through the hole. I started scrambling back. The crab was positioning itself over the escape hatch. Its lower eyes peered into the chopper, swiveling forward. Then two of its claws dropped the fourth and last line into the cabin. Someone had painted ANCHOR ME on the grapple at the end of the line. I grabbed it and hooked it it under one of the seats.

"Zip line's on its way down," said Lizard.

I looked up and saw something dropping from the sky. It was illuminated by a single red beacon. The crab stepped back out of its way. The object—it was a gurney basket and a couple of harnesses attached to a cable-rider—banged onto the roof of the ship. The crab grabbed the gurney basket and fed it down through the turret, then the harnesses.

I pulled the basket forward. "Come on, Lizard. I need your help." Duke's moans were louder now. We lifted him as gently as we could into the basket. I checked the seals on the medi-blanket while Lizard strapped him in, then I hung the console in the slot provided for it.

The crab was lowering three connector cables into the cabin. I snapped the first to the head of Duke's basket. I tossed a harness at Lizard and grabbed the other for myself. "The cameras—" I said.

"I've got all the recordings right here," Lizard said, patting her flight bag. She passed the second connector cable through its handles before snapping it onto her harness. "They're safe."

I finished shrugging into my harness and connected the third cable. "All right," I said. "Duke first, then you. I'll bring up the rear."

"Sorry, Lieutenant," she said. "The captain is the last to leave the ship. You go second."

"I'm going to cover your rear," I insisted.

"You'll wait until after dinner—and that's an order. All right—" she said to the crab, "—let's have a little help lifting this basket."

The cables began to retract. The basket pulled back, then upward toward the turret as the cable continued tightening. We guided it carefully up through the hatch. I climbed up after it, then turned and pulled Lizard up after me. Then I started shivering. The night air was *cold*.

There were worms all around the chopper, sitting and watching us. Their black bulks were huge in the gloom. I couldn't tell how many there were, but there were more than fourteen of them now, that was for sure. There could have been thirty or fifty, I couldn't tell, but I could hear the sounds of their eyes blinking. *Sput-phwut. Sput-phwut.*

Lizard steadied herself on my arm, then leaned over and gave me a quick kiss on the lips. "Thanks," she said. She turned to the crab and gave a thumbs-up signal. The crab returned it with one mechanical claw.

And then the worms screamed again— "*Chtorr! Chtorr!*"—and swarmed in toward the chopper. One of them flowed up the front of the craft, the chopper's windshield cracked under its weight. It kept on coming anyway. It was on top of the ship now, pouring toward us—

—the crab swiveled all its spotlights and hit it with its brightest glare. The worm recoiled, blinking. The crab scuttled toward it, waving all its arms and legs and everything else—all its cameras, lights, and attachments—in as threatening a manner as possible. The worm backed away, uncertainly—

—and then, suddenly, the cable-rider was screaming up the line, yanking us with it! Duke screamed at the jolt as the basket leapt upward; he must have been in incredible pain. I gasped in surprise—I was hurting too hard to cough—and Lizard yelled like a kid on a roller coaster. The chopper dropped away below us. It was an oasis of pink light in a sea of ink.

The worms were swarming up onto it now, more and more of them. The crab retreated before their onslaught. It clamped itself to the line and followed us up. A worm grabbed for it and missed.

And then the chopper was too far below to see anything else clearly.

I glanced upward. The blimp was an ominous hole in the night. Its lights were still off and we were hurtling toward a gigantic darkness. A square of yellow warmth opened directly overhead. The color of the light was startling. After two days of nothing but pink, it looked *alien*.

The square expanded, it became a hatch. We rose up through it and suddenly we were *inside* the blimp—first the basket, then me, then Colonel Tirelli.

There were men and women in jumpsuits to pull us aboard, to swing us away from the hatch, grab us, and disconnect the cables from our harnesses. They were applauding and cheering. It was all a blur of faces and hands. I couldn't hear. I couldn't focus my eyes. They were too wet.

Someone was helping me out of my harness and O-mask. I kept blinking in confusion. All the light—all the noise—all these people! It was too dazzling!

And the room—it was *huge*. We could have put the chopper in it and we'd still have room for a dance floor. I saw the dust-covered crab come lifting through a great hole in the floor. The last of the line came up after it.

The hole closed up and a man with a headset said, "A-2 is aboard and the hatch is *closed*. Retrieval is *complete*." There was more cheering at this. Even I was cheering now—between paroxysms of coughing. It was starting again. I was having trouble breathing—and standing too. Somebody grabbed my arm and held me up. Two of them kept me from toppling over. The pain was roaring—

"Release the mooring harpoons," the man with the headset said. "Let's go to Oakland." he grinned at me. "The lieutenant wants a lobster."

I looked at Lizard and blushed.

She *winked* at me.

Q: What do Chtorrans call a political convention?
A: A wild party.

29

Paul Bunyan

"I try not to pay too much attention to the news. It's always full of other people's problems."

—SOLOMON SHORT

Four men grabbed the basket with Duke and disappeared through a door. Lizard could still walk, but I had to be half-carried out. It was all catching up to me. I moved in a pink fog. We went down a long corridor and into a medical facility. They split us up then, putting Lizard in one cubbyhole and depositing me in another.

Somebody clamped something around my right arm. Somebody else attached a tube to my left. They pulled off the O-mask I was wearing and replaced it with a larger one. I sucked at it eagerly.

"Don't suck! You'll start coughing again. Just take it easy."

I blinked against the pain. My eyes were thick with crusty pink crud. I tried to wipe at them, but somebody pushed my hand away. I heard the hiss of a spray and felt something damp and wet across my face. It dripped coldly and smelled medicinal. Somebody dabbed gently with a cloth. Then they irrigated again and dabbed again.

When I could see—I was looking at a teenage girl in a white jacket. She was studying me concernedly. "How are you feeling now?" There was a medi-kit console beside her. All its lights were blinking blue, yellow, or red. There were no greens. Uh-oh.

She saw my glance and switched the panel off. "Don't panic," she said. "It's not connected. Can you talk?"

I held down a cough—I thought my chest would burst—but I managed to report, "Hoarse. Sore throat. Pressure in my chest.

Itchy all over. Trouble breathing. Lots of coughing. Pain. Eyes hurt. Ears hurt. I want a bath. I'm still cold. I feel great!" I grinned at her.

She smiled sweetly but impersonally. "Okay, take off your shirt." She was already opening the kit.

"Huh? Where's the doctor?"

"I'm the doctor. Take off your shirt."

"Uh—" I shut up and took off my shirt. She gasped. My skin was all red and prickly looking. Even I hadn't realized. She pursed her lips and stared thoughtfully.

"What is it?" I asked.

"I was about to ask you the same question." She extended a finger tentatively—

"Careful!"

"Does that hurt?"

"No—it just tastes funny."

"Tastes?" She frowned. "What do you mean by that?"

"I dunno. It just—that was the right word."

"Mmm," she said. "It's probably just a dermic reaction of some kind. Maybe you're allergic to something in the dust or maybe it's an irritation caused by the particles. They'll know better in Oakland. I'm just a . . . I mean, I don't have the equipment to know more."

"It's all right," I croaked. She was lying about something— either the stuff on my skin or her own inexperience. Or both. But I didn't have the strength to challenge her on it.

"It's on your back too," she said. "Take down your pants, let me see your legs—here, I'll help. Mm, not as bad. That's good. All right, let's see what Mr. Silicon says—although I don't think I'm going to get very reliable readings through this shit. Sorry." She bit her lip and began sticking poker chips to my chest, my arms, my back, my neck, and my temples. "That doesn't hurt, does it?"

I shook my head no.

She studied her read-outs, nodded, and blanked the screen before I could peek over her shoulder. She peered into my mouth, my nose, my eyes, and my ears. She nodded and said, "Mm-hm. Wait a minute. I'll be right back."

She returned with a tray. On it was a pressure injector, a glass of orange juice and a small plastic container with a handful of capsules. "Antibiotics and vitamins," she explained apologetically. "I don't want to do anything risky. Sorry, but this is one for the Oakland boys."

She touched the pressure injector to my arm. It hissed. I felt an icy wet sensation—it spread throughout my body and turned into a shuddering chill that left me shivering and shaking and dripping cold sweat. The fire in my thorax and lungs and stomach took on a whole new dimension of agony. It burned *cold* now. I couldn't breathe—

She waited until the spasm passed, then handed me the capsules and the orange juice. I took them without complaint.

"What else . . . was in that shot?"

"I don't know what you're talking about," she said. I almost believed her. "Drink that. It's very expensive."

I drank. The juice was sweet and fresh. I'd forgotten that there were things in the world that could taste this good. It was an all-too-brief hole in the firestorm.

"All right," she said. "That'll hold you until we hit Oakland. Try not to do anything strenuous. You can put your shirt back on now. I'd give you something to put you out, but they want to talk to you." She peeled off all the poker chips and tossed them to one side with a look of annoyance. Whether it was annoyance at me or *them* or simply at the fact that she couldn't do anything more, I couldn't tell. And I didn't have the breath to ask before she left.

The whole process had taken less than five minutes.

As I fastened my shirt, I wondered if I should wait here—or what?

Somebody stuck his head into the cubbyhole. He was wearing a jumpsuit with a *Paul Bunyan* patch on his left chest. "Lieutenant McCarthy?"

I nodded.

"Colonel Anderson requests your presence in the forward lounge. Follow me please? Oh—will you need help?"

"I can walk—I think." Apparently the drugs were starting to take effect. I was even beginning to hallucinate a little. I felt like I could *hear* through my chest—everything *twinged*. But somehow I stood up and with a little help from the crewman, I even managed to walk. We made our way to the forward lounge.

He made sure I was carefully seated before he let go of me. "Make yourself comfortable," he said. As if I had a *choice* in the matter. I could barely move. "Colonel Anderson will be along in a minute. The bar is open if you want anything." I waved him away. I just wanted to be left alone; I wanted to die in peace. The crewman seemed grateful to leave.

The lounge seemed almost as big as the loading bay; it extended across the width of the ship. I marveled at the sense of luxury. I could imagine the board of directors entertaining in here. The furniture was elegant. It was true; the heavy lifters had space to *waste*. This room was the whole bottom half of the nose of the airship. The windows were tall, slanting outward, and circled the cabin in a great dark horseshoe. I was sitting near the very front. I swiveled in my chair and leaned my forehead against the cold hard glass and just let the fatigue and the resonance of the ebbing pain in my chest wash over me. After a while, I opened my eyes and peered out into the night.

The airship's running lights had been turned on again. There must have been a huge bank of spotlights just above the lounge, because the whole sky ahead glowed with the reflected light. It looked like we were plowing through pink fog. There was nothing else to see.

I could feel a faint vibration beneath my feet. We were under power. Captain Price must be using the cold-rocket assist. No other engine could function in this weather.

There was a well-stocked bar at the back of the lounge. I thought about a drink. My throat *demanded* a drink. But the effort necessary to lever myself up out of the chair, crawl to the back of the lounge, summon up the wind to tell the robot bartender what I wanted, and then crawl all the way back here to my chair was intimidating. Walking was out of the question. There weren't enough things to hang onto between here and there. If this chair had rollers, I might be able to roll back there—but no, it hadn't.

If this was *Derby* and if I were T.J., then I'd probably be able to just saunter back to the bar. "Make me a Staggering Buffalo. Go easy on the soy." Hell, if I were T.J., I wouldn't even be here. I'd be on my yacht in the Bahamas, plotting to take over another bank or a country or something—

"Lieutenant McCarthy?"

I looked up. And up.

The man had shoulders the size of Ohio. He had a broken nose and a beefy grin. He stuck out a paw at me. I stared at it for a few seconds before I realized what he wanted. I leapt to my feet and saluted. "Sir?" And almost fell down. I'd forgotten I was trying to die.

He returned my salute with something that looked more like a wave than a salute, then stuck out his hand again. I offered mine and he shook it gently. When he let go, I wanted to stare at my fingers. He *hadn't* crushed them.

"I'm Danny Anderson," he said. His voice resonated like the inside of a hangar. He had a smile as wide as the door. The smile flickered out just before I collapsed. He caught me and levered me back into my chair.

"Are you all right?"

"No," I gasped honestly, but I waved his help away and concentrated on my breathing.

He studied me concernedly for a moment, then grabbed a chair and pulled it over to face me. He perched on the edge of his seat and waited while I stared at my shoes and counted six long breaths. Damn. I wasn't dead yet. I looked up at him wearily.

"I want to thank you for the job you did on my father. You saved his life."

"Uh . . . I hate to disagree with a superior officer, sir—" *Especially one as big as you.* I took another breath. "—But I didn't do half the job I should have."

"Oh? Could you have done better than you did?" He raised a bushy eyebrow at me.

"Sir, I did the very best I could. It just wasn't as good as I could have done if I'd had the proper supplies. We ran out of everything."

He started laughing. I stared at him. He caught himself and stopped, but the grin remained.

He reached over and put one gigantic hand on my shoulder. "I'm not laughing at you, son. Colonel Tirelli told me you would do this. I'm trying to thank you and you're too busy devaluing your contribution to hear me. You're going to have to knock that off, Lieutenant."

"Uh—" I was doing it again. "Right. Thank you, sir."

"Good. Now, let me tell it to you again. You did a good job. You saved Captain Anderson's life. Colonel Tirelli is putting you in for a medal."

I hardly heard the last. "Uh . . . thank you, sir. Uh, can I ask, how is Duke—Captain Anderson?"

Danny Anderson hesitated. He looked embarrassed, and his voice went curiously flat. "It . . . uh, looks like he's going to make it. His vital signs steadied out as soon as we got him on Code Blue maintenance. But it's still too early to say what kind of shape he's going to be in." And then he added quietly. "He might lose his legs."

The last balloon inside my chest suddenly collapsed. I lost the last of my air. It just wheezed out of me and I sank way back into my seat. I was through inhaling. It was all over. And then I did anyway, so I could say, "It's that red furry stuff, isn't it? I've got it all over me too. It feels like I can see through it. It's worm fur or something. I don't know. But it was really hurting him. Oh, shit. I was afraid of this. I gave him Gerromycin, but I didn't know what else I could do."

Danny Anderson pulled his chair closer. Our legs were touching. He put his hand on my shoulder again. "Hey!" he interrupted. "I told you to knock that off."

I gulped. "I'm sorry, sir. It's just . . . so damned frustrating! I mean, he's been like a dad to me, and—" I looked up at him. "Well, you know what he's like—"

"No," he said coldly. "I don't."

"Huh?"

"Don't worry about it, McCarthy." There was something hard in his voice. "That's not your concern."

"Oh. Uh . . . yes, sir. I—" shut up. And wondered.

"Listen to me," he said. "What's done is done. This is it. This is how it turned out. Like it or not. So stop arguing against me inside your head and let me congratulate you. The video that you and Colonel Tirelli brought back with you may be the most important recordings we've got. Those bunnydogs are incredible!"

I swallowed hard. I said, "I think they may be the next step of the invasion."

"I won't argue with you, Lieutenant. You've had more opportunity to observe the creatures than anyone else."

"Yes sir."

"Now, I know you're tired and sore. I know you're probably hungry for a decent meal, a hot bath, and a bed. We've got all of those waiting for you. But we really want to debrief you first while it's all still fresh in your memory. Can you manage that?"

I nodded. "Get me a pitcher of coffee and a straw, and I'm yours. No, better make that an I.V. bottle."

"Sorry, no coffee. We have tea and cocoa."

"No coffee?"

He shook his head. "Not at thirty caseys for a half-kilo of beans."

"The bean-rot?"

He nodded. "Congress closed the border. The only coffee you're going to get from now on will be greenhouse bean. If you can afford it."

"I'll have the cocoa, thanks."

"Good. Now look, I was going to set you up in one of the cabins, but I think we'd better do it here. There's more room and I think we can make you more comfortable. And I don't want you moving around any more. We have a terminal and the new Hayes-6 debriefing program, and we've got a couple of eco-techs who are hitching a ride down to Oakland who have some questions of their own. If you get tired, you can stop anytime. I'll try and check back every so often too. Will that work for you?"

I nodded.

"Good. We really appreciate this." He patted my shoulder gently. "Something else?"

"I'll need something for my cough. And a fresh O-mask."

"I'll have the doctor bring whatever you need."

"Thank you, sir."

I made it almost three-quarters of the way through the debriefing before I started coughing and passed out.

Q: What does a Chtorran call Moby Dick?
A: Sushi.

30

Dust Poisoning

"There is no such thing as justice. There is only the desire to see the pain spread around equally."

—SOLOMON SHORT

I woke up again in the ambulance. We were slowing. There was something happening outside.

I could hear someone with a bullhorn trying to give instructions to a crowd. They weren't listening. Scattered voices were hollering their defiance. I wondered if they were turning into a mob.

I wondered where I was.

I was flat on my back, staring at a plastic ceiling. I turned my head. A curtained window. I raised a hand. My chest was numb. There was something wrong with my lungs. My whole body ached, but I couldn't feel my thorax at all. And I could. The sheet tasted white. The air tasted red. There were tubes all over—in my nose and in my arms and in my mouth. Somehow I pushed the curtain aside. Just a little. We were slowing.

The day was still pink, the air, the sky . . .

There were frightened people everywhere. On the lawns, on the driveways, and most of all, crowded around the emergency entrance. Some of them must have been waiting all night for treatment. They looked tired and drawn. Their eyes were red, their faces were puffy. Was this turning into another plague? Would this be the one that finally destroyed our ability to resist?

And then the ambulance was stopping and the orderlies slid me out like a side of beef and onto a cart. Somebody in white grabbed hold behind me and then we were moving—quickly—through a sea of painful, anxious faces. Somebody else was parting the crowds ahead of us. I turned my head to look at them. The people were huddling in the entrance hall, five deep. They were lined up in ragged formations, waiting. I thought I saw military guards. Were we under attack? No, those were riot helmets.

The hospital was a nightmare.

It was a wall of noise—children crying, people arguing, somebody screaming. The sound pressed in like an assault; each component voice was edged with hysteria. A woman was shrieking with rage—

—the cart lurched. And nearly toppled. The shrieking woman had grabbed it. She was screaming in my face. I wanted to hurt her back. She yanked the blanket off me. "See! Another goddamn soldier! I knew it! The military is getting preferential treatment! They're going to let the rest of us die!" And then they were pulling her off of me and the cart was rolling again, faster than before.

I heard voices. They were arguing about me. We were stopped again.

"—I can't do anything more for him than has already been done. Give him a shot and an inhaler and send him home to rest—"

"With third-degree pink lung?"

"When it turns into dust poisoning bring him back—"

"I'm not paid to take them home. I only deliver the meat—and this one's already signed in. He's got an army triple-A-plus priority and your chief of surgery already accepted delivery."

"Did they also tell you where the hell we're going to put him? The halls are already full of air mattresses—"

"That's not my problem. Here, read his chart—"

"I can't do this! I'll have to pull the plug on someone else—"

"That's not my problem."

Suddenly, someone bent her face close to mine. She looked tired and angry. "Open your eyes!" she demanded. "Can you move?"

I couldn't speak. I made a noise—not even strong enough to be a moan. It turned into a cough. It came out pink.

I think I won the argument.

Now the cart was rolling again, this time faster than before—

—came awake again as they were sliding me onto a bed. I blinked through tears of pain, turned my head, and squinted at the light.

This was a private room!

I tried to protest, but I didn't even have enough air to croak. I pointed toward the door, the unseen crowds, and waved my hand frantically, despite the roaring agony it cost me.

The nurse just pushed me back down and said, "No, you don't. Your job is to be here now." He was a chubby little man with a well-scrubbed face. He could have been anywhere between thirty and fifty. He looked like someone's maiden aunt, but he had surprisingly strong arms. He held me down and pushed a breathing mask onto my nose and mouth. "Now, just relax," he said. "I'll be right here the whole time."

I was dimly aware that something was happening. There were other people in the room now.

Something bit my arm. I let go and floated.

And waited to see if I was going to die.

I watched from above while they poked, they prodded, and they scanned. They set me up for DX studies and the Kelley series of broad-band vaccines, processes, and affirmations. Then they "vacuumed" my lungs—which turned out to be nowhere near as painful as it sounded—and put me in an oxygen-helium tent.

And then they left me alone.

I floated and waited.

The reaction set in the next morning.

I woke up somewhere on the other side of death. I was trying to fight my way back, but I was smothering in marshmallow. I couldn't breathe.

There were alarm bells ringing all around me. I was trying to scream, but no noise was coming out of my throat; there was no air to scream with. Even as I thrashed on the bed, I knew I was doing the wrong thing.

And then something cold touched my arm—and something bit me on the chest—and something wet was sliding down my throat.

I faded out.

And in again.

I still couldn't breathe. I faded out again—

And in. And out. I lost count.

Q: What are the ingredients in Chtorran mouthwash?
A: Kerosene, nitric acid and 32 lawyers.

31

Stargasm

I was sitting on top of a tree.

It was a red tree and I was a red monkey with red fur, sitting under a red sun on a red planet. Above me, there were red clouds in a red sky. Red overhead. Red on the ground. Red all around.

My fur was red, shading to pink in the tenderest places, and I could see backward for a thousand generations. At least a thousand generations. Behind that, it all became a soft pink blur. And behind the blur, I could feel the warm red presence at the edge of the universe, throbbing and pinging softly under everything. It was a shell around us all, it was the edge of the womb. It felt so smooth against the naked skin of my soul. And beyond that—behind that warm red shell—I could feel God. She felt *deep*. She was singing too. To herself. She was happy about something, so we were happy too. I was happy.

I was sitting on top of a tree.

The stems were thick and ropy. Through my hands, through my feet, through my buttocks, I could feel the earth-blood pulsing through the vines. The sweet black syrup flowed through the veins of the world and nourished us all. It throbbed in orgasmic surges that tickled and delighted and made me giggle.

I was sitting on top of a tree.

I was sitting inside one of the giant red blossoms. They were all around me. Our fur mingled. They were open mouths, they were soft kisses, they were sensual and enveloping. The blossoms were

211

velvet and cruel; they were delicious ecstasy. I could feel them eating the air. I could taste their eating from inside. The soft whirr of a whirligig, the tumbling drift of the puffballs, I could taste it all. I could taste *myself*.

I was the insect being eaten; it was ecstasy. I could taste the insect through my petals; it was exquisite. I could taste the tree all the way down to the roots. I could taste the soil, rich and dark. I could taste the cold air and the alkaline rain and all the different oils on my skin, on my bark, on my wings, and on my leaves. I could taste the weather through the tree and I could taste the forest and the land and the world all the way out to the sea.

The air was dry with promise. I could burst soon. There was red dust in the west. It tasted salty. The silk veils of the north were turning sweet. I shuddered in anticipation.

The soil was sweet and rich and full of rotting things and fresh things and things that nestled and grew warm. There were red things growing in me and other red things crawling through my veins, through my tunnels and arteries and passageways. They crawled and crept and slithered up and down my branches, across the linking vines, up to the top of the atmosphere and down again.

The top of the tree was so high.

The world below was a pink and gaudy landscape, tufted with cotton and blossoms, spotted with swirls and curls of forest and color. The talltrees that circled the edge of the world stood crimson and black, orange and yellow. They stood like a wall; they marched out to the horizon and faded into ochre haze. Things were moving in them, things red and gold, blue and purple, black and pink. They crawled in and out, up and down, all around.

The land below was pink and streaked with red and purple and black. I was so high, I could see the pattern. It was just the tiniest part of the pattern, but it whorled and turned upon itself like the red lightning in a mating storm. So beautiful, I surged again in my groin.

We were rising. Rising higher.

The throbbing was growing more intense. Almost painful, but too pleasureful to stop.

I liked sitting here in this tree.

We were surging higher.

I saw beyond my eyes. I saw with the eyes of the trees, the eyes of the sky. I marveled at the world-pattern, at all of its tastes and smells and colors. I rose above the mandala of life, laughing and singing in the cold, cold air.

The world curved away into blackness, the mandala curling

across its surface. The foothill trees were black. The anchor trees were darker still. The great supporting arteries flowed across them all, wove across the surface, gave the world a dark striated texture.

So high.

The air beneath me. The sun before me. The world behind me. The sky around me.

High above the dust, reaching toward the stars, the world so red and bright, beneath, above, below. I floated, I swam, I sang to God and waited for her answers. She lived behind the shell behind the stars.

I could feel the godsong rising up inside me now. It was time. We'd waited oh, so long. So very long. And God was so very happy now.

I could taste the stars, so faint and faraway. The radio-bright one—so sweet it hurt. I reached toward it with my tongues. All my tongues. The tongues in my mouths and the tongues between my legs. All were stiff as life, as hard as the future, as towering as my trees. I ached upward. I shuddered and ached—

—and cracked.

And came.

The great trunks of the world began to break apart. The blood of God poured out, a great black spray that boiled into mist. The dust turned the sky pink, and streaks of fire left blazing trails across the lines of shadow.

I surged and screamed and bled. My life pulsed out of every broken branch. The world fell away, all black and bottomless.

I died in ecstasy.

I gave birth.

I was alone.

In darkness.

Tumbling.

Falling.

And finally . . .

. . . fell asleep.

Q: What do Chtorrans call a thousand worms in one big pile?
A: A race to eat your way out.

Q: What does the winner get?
A: Seconds.

32

Soup

"A full bladder is the best alarm clock in the world."

—SOLOMON SHORT

And then one night, I woke up gasping. My throat was raw. And dry. I wanted water. I managed to holler—and my lungs screamed in agony! That was a mistake. My chest felt like it had fossilized. I wanted to die just to end the pain.

Somebody was saying something to me. "It's all right, Lieutenant. Just relax. See if you can relax." I tried to focus on the voice. All I saw was a blur. The room was too dim.

"Don't talk," he said. "Don't try to breathe, either. The machines are breathing for you. Don't make their job harder. Wait—"

I couldn't see what he did, but after a bit I floated away again. Away, but not out. And after another bit, he asked, "Are you ready to try eating?" For some reason, I nodded. I wanted to please him so he wouldn't leave me.

"Okay. Here we go—" He held me gently across his lap, cradling my head and feeding me soup in small delicious doses. "Just eat. I'll talk." It was the nurse with the very clean face.

"Mnnf," I said, splurting soup.

He wiped my mouth with a napkin. "You're at Oakland General. It's Monday evening and you've already missed tonight's episode of *Derby*. Too bad. It was a good one. Grant is still looking for the missing robot, but now he knows it's still in the plant. Carrie found out about the last DV sale—T.J. told her, of course—and now she's demanding a stockholders' meeting. Everything depends on Stephanie, but now she's suddenly refusing to leave Hong Kong and nobody knows why. Ready for more?"

"Mmfl."

"Good. Open wide. So, compared to that your problems are nothing, right?"

I didn't answer. My lungs hurt too much. Besides, Grant should have known from the beginning that T.J. couldn't risk having that robot's memory dumped.

"All right, one more slurp and we're done. There you go. Dr. Fletcher will be in to have a look at you in a little bit."

Dr. Fletcher was wearing gloves and a mask. All I could see were her eyes. They looked tired.

The first thing she said to me was, "Don't talk. You run the risk of destroying your vocal cords." She sat down on the edge of the bed and looked into my eyes, my ears, my nose. She studied the medi-console on her lap. Then she looked at me and said, "Congratulations."

"Mm?"

"You'll live. We didn't expect you to. The tissues of your lungs were so swollen, there was no room for air. We had you on lung support for a week. You're one of the lucky ones. There were more than two thousand others who didn't make it—because we didn't have the machines for them."

I wanted to ask, but she put a finger across my mouth before I could speak.

"I said, *don't talk*." She hesitated, then added, "You had one of the worst cases of dust poisoning in the state, Lieutenant. We should have pulled the plug on you—we needed the bed space—but your commanding officer wouldn't allow it. She said you owed her a lobster dinner and you weren't going to get out of your obligations that easily.

"Besides, we needed to discover something, and you helped us do it. We now know that dust poisoning is reversible in even the *worst* cases. If we can save you, then we can save anybody. We're already preparing for next year."

"Umf," I said. I held up a hand to stop her from going.

"You're going to be all right," she said. "Don't worry. The worst is over."

I grabbed her arm. "Mmf?"

"Colonel Tirelli is all right too."

"Dmk?"

"*And* Duke. He's in intensive care and his condition is

stabilized. We're watching him closely. You did a good job on him, Lieutenant. You can be proud."

"Mp."

"I'm going to put you back to sleep now," she said. "And then I'm going to put you back on maintenance. It'll be easier for you." She touched a button on the medi-console.

And I went out again.

Q: Why don't Chtorrans take Alka-Seltzer?
A: Indigestion is how a Chtorran knows it had a good time.

33

The Personal Physician

"I'd feel a lot better about doctors if it weren't called practice."

—SOLOMON SHORT

The next time Dr. Fletcher came in, I was more coherent.

She picked up the console and studied it. Did all hospital personnel do that automatically?

"How am I?" I asked.

"You're fine," she said. "And I can say that with authority, because I am your personal physician. Only the President and movie stars get better treatment."

She sat down on the edge of the bed and put her hand on mine. "The truth is, all medical personnel in the Science Section were moved over to help with the emergency, but even if that weren't the case, you'd still be under my care. You are not so much a medical case as a scientific one."

"Because I had the worst exposure to the dust?"

"That's part of it," she said noncommittally. She let that sink in.

It took me a blurry moment but I got it. "What's the *other* part?"

"You don't remember, do you?"

I shook my head. "I had a lot of *weird* red dreams. Whatever stuff you had me on makes *great* hallucinations."

"Gerromycin," she said—and waited.

For some reason I touched my chest. My skin was cold and dry and just a little bit rough, but otherwise it felt normal. I couldn't taste my hand at all—

"The fur?" I asked.

"You had it all over you. They're little parasites. On the gastropedes they're symbiotes—on us they're parasites. Science Section is calling them *quills* for now. So far we've identified twenty-three different subspecies."

"Last time around, you told me the fur was nerves."

"And it is. They are. That's the function that the quill-creatures provide. The symbiote burrows in head first until it finds a nerve connection, then it grows outward and lets its tail hang outside the host's skin. Anything that stimulates the tail gets reported to the host. Very effective, really. Without the quills, the worm is just a big naked slug. Very ugly to look at."

I tried to imagine a naked worm. I couldn't.

"That's why you were getting all those strange feelings," Fletcher added. "You were a human pincushion. Something in the dust encourages the parasites to burrow and grow. But you were right to remember the Gerromycin. It's a very effective agent. Too bad you didn't think to take any yourself, you'd have had an easier time of it; but you'll be all right now."

"Thanks." I said hoarsely. I had to think about this. *Worm fur?*

"You were very lucky," she said. "We all were. Fortunately the dust is about as benign as a Chtorran life-form can be. The death toll is expected to remain below three thousand."

"You sound disappointed."

"Not at all. You've turned into a very interesting case—and I've learned a lot more about the Chtorran ecology than I expected to. But, yes, I am impatient to get back to my worms."

"Worms? Plural?"

She nodded. "Uh-huh. We've got two more live ones."

"Have you put them together yet . . . ?"

"They're in the same tank. Why?"

"How often do they—I don't know how to phrase this—roll around together and act like they're making love?"

She looked surprised. "How do you know about that? We've only had them together for a few days. The whole thing is still very secret."

"I've seen it in the wild. Haven't you seen the videos we brought back?"

She raised an eyebrow at me. "In all my spare time? In case you hadn't noticed—"

"Right. Sorry. Well, we also saw the wrestling behavior when the blimp arrived. The worms got frantic. At first I thought they were attacking each other but they weren't. They came back. They looked confused—but I wouldn't even begin to guess what was going on."

"Mm," she said. She looked like she was considering something.

"I want to see your worms," I said.

She nodded. "I want to see your videos. As soon as you're ambulatory again, okay? I'll set it up." She stood up to go. "There's a wheelchair in the closet if you want to get out of bed. Please ask a nurse to assist you. Don't be proud."

"Thanks. What room is Colonel Tirelli in?"

"She checked out last week. But Captain Anderson is upstairs and you can visit him any time." She remembered something. "Oh—you have messages, quite a stack of them. Please read the priority ones first. And I think your mother wants to visit you. Handle that, all right?" And then she was out the door.

After a while, I buzzed for assistance and got myself bathed, shaved, and transferred into a wheelchair. I found my way up to the twelfth floor without too much trouble.

Duke was still in an oxygen tent.

He looked dreadful. He looked like the guest of honor at a Texas barbecue. I couldn't look and I couldn't look away. His face was swollen. His eyes were blistered shut. His skin was blackened and peeling. His arms looked wet and putrefying. And he smelled bad.

I almost fled in horror. Human beings should not look like this. Human beings should not *smell* like this. But I didn't know how to put the wheelchair in reverse, and the little voice in my head was already bawling me out for being a coward. I steeled myself and stayed.

I rolled around to the foot of his bed and picked up the medi-console.

Duke was on maintenance. He was beyond consciousness.

For that I was grateful. There was not a lot to say. And I wasn't sure I could talk to him yet. Not with him looking like something out of a horror show. This wasn't Duke. I couldn't rectify this monstrous piece of meat with the man I had spent so much time with.

I didn't see how he could ever be human again. He might live. But his life was over. I don't know how I knew it. I just knew it.

My mind brought up memories. Duke had taught me almost everything I knew about how to be a military man. He'd made it very simple, he'd boiled it down to two words.

Be certain.

"Here's how to know if you're certain," he'd said. "Can I rip your arm off if you're wrong? If you can't give me an unqualified yes, then you're still not certain.

"That thing that you ignore—that thing that you let yourself be unaware of, or unconscious of, or uncertain about—that's the thing that's going to kill you. So your job, whatever it looks like, is really this. You have to know everything about *everything* that you have to deal with.

"There are no accidents, Jim. If you get killed the game is over. You lost."

Simple.

Except . . . what would you call lying in a hospital bed looking like a bride's first roast?

Duke had screwed up somewhere. He'd trusted *me*. It didn't matter what Colonels Tirelli and Anderson said. This was my fault.

I wished I could wake him up long enough to ask him to forgive me.

Except I knew he wouldn't.

Q: What did God say when He made the first Chtorran?
A: Oh, shit.

34

Crimson Death

"Christ was grandstanding when he chased the moneylenders out of the temple. Yes, he made his point, but he also ruined his credit rating."

—SOLOMON SHORT

Eventually my chest scan came up clean and they checked me out of the hospital. They needed the bed space. I still coughed a lot and my chest still hurt with the echoes of larger agonies, but I was ambulatory and getting stronger every day. I would live—and I was actually looking forward to it.

Most of it, anyway.

"Go visit your mother," Fletcher told me. "She's been bugging us every day for almost a month."

Mom was in Santa Cruz doing something with maps—I wasn't sure what. She said she'd explain when I got there. I checked out a Jeep from the motor pool and headed south on I-117.

It was over an hour's drive but I barely noticed. The whole way there, all I could hear was the argument inside my head.

I was considering resigning my commission.

It was something that Dr. Fletcher had said; it still rankled. "You and I have two different jobs. Your job is to kill worms. My job is to study them." I was looking at myself in a mirror and wondering how the hell I'd gotten *here*. This wasn't where I'd *wanted* to be.

What I really wanted to do was what Dr. Fletcher was doing—study the worms. But how could I do that with stripes on my sleeves? They kept putting weapons into my hands and that guaranteed that all I could do was kill worms. That was the thing about being in the army—there weren't a whole lot of options.

But killing the worms—at least the way we were doing it now— was *not* working.

The Chtorran ecology was eating us alive.

Its microorganisms alone had killed billions of people. Those of us who survived the plagues still had to deal with the sea sludge, the stingflies, the bladderbugs, the red kudzu, the oilworms, the "grabgrass," the binnies, the libbits, the meeps—and of course, always and inevitably, the worms.

Our ancestors had killed the dinosaurs. We'd sucked their eggs and eaten their children. We still ate their descendants today: chickens, ducks, and turkeys. If tyrannosaur and hadrosaur and deinonychus still walked the Earth, we'd find a way to eat them too. The Chtorrans would do the same to us. They couldn't see us as anything more than food. Do you talk to your sandwich?

And if this was only the first wave of the invasion—as Dr. Zymph kept saying—what horrors were *still* waiting to manifest themselves?

How long did it take to Chtorra-form a planet? How many waves of infestation?

There *had* to be an intelligence behind this madness, but it might not show up for centuries, perhaps not until long after the last human being was . . . what? In a zoo? In a museum? Did we figure at all in the equation?

I didn't think so.

But—

—if I really felt that way, then why did I bother to keep on fighting? If the situation was that hopeless, why not just lay down and die?

Because—I had to smile at myself—I still didn't really believe it. I *knew* it, but I didn't believe it.

But none of this had anything to do with the army anyway. The army was irrelevant. We were holding back the worms by sheer brute force because we couldn't think of anything else to do.

No, it wasn't the futility of the situation that was making me think about resigning. I'd fight the worms forever, no matter how ugly the odds.

No. This was really about Duke.

I felt responsible.

Damn it anyway!

It was Shorty all over again, but with a vengeance. I'd burned

Shorty—and the worm that came down on top of him. Shorty had been lucky, he'd died quick, but Duke might take years—

If I did resign, I could probably go to work immediately for Dr. Fletcher. I already had the security clearance.

It was very tempting. I even went so far as to unclip my phone from my belt.

But I didn't call. No. I might be able to resign from the army—I'd fulfilled the basic obligation over a year ago—but I'd never be able to resign from the pain.

And that was the real issue.

I pulled off the freeway in Santa Cruz, but inside my head I was still in the same place. Stuck.

And I wasn't looking forward to seeing my mother, either. I knew what that was going to be like.

She had an office-apartment in a private (read *fortress*) community called Fantasy Valley Towers, a sprawling complex of bubbles, domes, and spires like something out of a Hollywood fairy tale. The style was called Apocalypse Baroque. Inside the walls, it was a maze of arches, terraces, and balconies. Before the plagues, it must have been very expensive. Now it looked run down—and even a little *wild*.

The front doors of Mother's apartment were twice as tall as I was, and they looked like they were made out of crystal. But the effect was spoiled by the unswept leaves piled up against the portico.

Mother answered the door with a flourish and a wild laugh. She was wearing a gaudy concoction of bright silks and feathers; she was a cascade of pink and scarlet. And around her neck, she had a silver and turquoise Navajo squash-blossom necklace, with twelve jeweled squashes on each side. It looked heavy. So did the rings on her fingers.

"Ahh . . . here's my baby now!" she cried. She presented her cheek for a kiss. It tasted of powder. She had a glass in her hand. "I'm sorry we didn't come and visit you in the hospital, but they wouldn't let us."

"It's all right. I wouldn't have been very good company anyway."

She took my wrist and led me out onto the terrace, calling loudly, "Alan! Alan! Jim is here! Jim, you remember Alan, don't you?"

"The surfer?"

"No, silly. That was Bobby." Bobby had been only two years older than me; when I met him he still hadn't decided what he wanted to be when he grew up. "This is Alan Wise. You remember, I told you about him."

"No, you told me about Alan Plaskow."

"I did?"

"Uh-huh. I don't think I know this Alan."

"Oh, well—"

This Alan was tall and blond and graying at the temples. When he smiled, his eyes crinkled. His handshake was just a little too hearty, and his chest was in the process of migrating south toward his stomach.

There was another man on the terrace too. He was short and dark and of Japanese descent. He wore thick glasses and a dark gray business suit. He looked like a lawyer. Alan introduced him as Shibumi Takahara. Mr. Takahara bowed politely. I bowed back.

Alan slapped me on the shoulder and said, "Well, son, it must feel good to get home for a little old-fashioned cooking, eh?"

"Uh . . . yes, sir. It does." Except this wasn't *home* and my mother hadn't cooked a meal herself since the *Hindenberg* went down.

"What are you drinking?" he asked. He was already at the bar, dropping ice into a glass. " 'Nita? Do you want a refill?"

"Do you know how to make a Sylvia Plath?" I asked.

"A what?"

"Never mind. You probably don't have the ingredients anyway."

Mom was looking at me funny. "What's a Sylvia Plath, Jim?"

I shrugged. "It's not important. It was just a joke."

"No, tell us—" she insisted.

Mr. Takahara answered her. "It's a layer of mercury, a layer of salad oil, and a layer of crème de menthe. You drink only the top layer." I looked at him sharply. Behind his glasses, his eyes were twinkling.

Mom frowned. "I'm afraid I don't get the joke. Do you get it, Alan?"

" 'Fraid it's a little too deep for me, hon. How's about a Crimson Death?"

"Uh, no thanks. I've had enough Crimson Death this month. I'll just have a beer, if you don't mind."

"Don't mind at all," he said. He ducked behind the bar, muttering to himself. "Beer, beer . . . where's the beer? Ah!" He came up with a slender green bottle. "Here we go—private stock. Imported especially for you from exotic, erotic, exciting . . . Topeka!" He poured with a flourish.

"Down the side, please—" I pointed.

"Eh?"

"You pour beer down the side of the glass, not the center."

"Oh, well—it's too late now. Sorry." He handed me the glass of beer suds and the still half-full bottle. "I'll know for the next time, right?"

"Yeah, right." There wasn't going to be a *next* time.

"I guess I'm just not used to pouring my own drinks," he said, sitting again. He patted the couch next to him and glanced toward my mother. She came over and sat down—a little too close. "I'm too used to being taken care of." He grinned and slid his arm around my mother's shoulders.

Mother said, "Alan, Jim's been off fighting those awful Cha-torrans—"

"Oh? Really?" He looked interested. "Have you actually *seen* any—?"

"Uh . . . first of all, it's pronounced 'Ktorran.' The *Ch* is silent. It's sort of a click before the *T*. Just say the word 'victor' and leave off the *vi*."

"Oh, well—" my mother said, excusing herself with a wave. "I never watch the news. I only read about them in the morning papers."

"And, yes," I said to Alan of the hearty handshake; I said it coldly. "I *have* seen a few. Quite a few, in fact."

"Really?" he asked. "They exist?"

I nodded. I sipped at my beer. I wiped my mouth with the back of my hand. I was debating inside whether I should be polite or tell the truth. My mother had the "dance for Grandma" expression on her face, Alan Wise wore a big plastic smile, but Mr. Takahara was watching me quietly. The truth won out.

I looked across at Alan Wise and asked, "Where have you been, that you don't know what's happening?"

He shrugged, "Right here. The good old U.S. of A. Where have *you* been?"

"Colorado. Wyoming. Northern California."

"You're kidding! We have—how do you say it?—Torrans right here in California?"

"One of the worst infestations I've ever seen. Just north of Clear Lake."

"Well . . . I'll be damned." He looked at my mother and gave her a little squeeze. "I didn't know that. Maybe we should drive up some Sunday and have a look. What do you think, 'Nita?"

I blinked. He couldn't really have meant that! I put my glass down on the end table, and said quietly, "That area is sealed off. And even if it weren't, that wouldn't be a very good idea."

"Oh, come now—" He dismissed me as casually as if I'd just told him the sky was pink. This far south and this close to the coast, it wasn't. "I think you're exaggerating the case, son. It's just some more of that same military thinking that got us into Pakistan twenty years ago. Of course, you probably don't remember that. You were just a little tyke then—"

"I know about Pakistan," I said. I'd had time to do a lot of reading in the hospital.

"Well—let me tell you something, Jim. You're too close to the forest. You don't have the perspective. You don't have objectivity. Y'see, this thing with the Ch'torrans, K'torrans, whatever— it's overrated. Oh, now—" He held up a hand to keep me from interrupting. "—I'll *grant* that there's really something out there. I'm sure that some old lady somewhere was actually frightened out of her panties by a big pink caterpillar; but when you look at the *whole* picture—like I have—you'll see that a young man like yourself needs to be looking toward the future."

"If there is one," I said dryly. Mr. Takahara's eyes narrowed thoughtfully.

"Oh, now, don't give me that liberal-defeatist crap. That song and dance may work on a congressman—but you're talking to Alan Wise here, and you know your mother doesn't hang out with dummies."

"Mmmm, if you say so."

"Listen, I know how the game is played. The military has to make the war look serious to justify all those heavyweight appropriations. Read your history, son! The more money they want, the worse the war gets. It's all about John Q. Taxpayer and his hard-earned Labor Standard Kilocalorie banknotes. The truth is, this is a terrific time for a smart man who knows how to read a newspaper."

"I beg your pardon?"

"I'm talking big money, son. Corporations, licenses, federal grants. I want you to know, there's an incredible opportunity here!"

"Huh?"

"It's raining soup!" he said. "It's time to grab your bucket! I'm in the reclamation industry—and people are making fortunes every day! It's all there for the taking. There are huge areas still waiting to be reopened—whole cities. Somebody's got to go in and do the job—and whoever does it is going to get rich. *Very* rich. The government knows this. The *army* knows it. But all this war-scare stuff is keeping people from seeing the real problem— that big government has got its hands in our pockets again. *And* it's a very good excuse for the army to go in and nationalize the unclaimed property. You pay attention, son. Read the papers! Not just that K'torran stuff. You'll see what's going on."

Mother gave his arm a squeeze and said, "Alan works so hard—" She looked across at me with an expression that said, *Don't start an argument.*

"Mr. Wise," I said.

"Alan," he corrected.

I ignored it. "Mr. Wise, I am a lieutenant in the United States Army, Special Forces Warrant Agency. We take care of those *special* challenges that are beyond the duties of the regular army. As such," I explained, "we are under the direct command of the President of the United States. The Special Forces is currently assigned to one task and one task only: the eradication of all Chtorran gastropedes—we call them worms—from the continental United States and Alaska. Hawaii is not presently infested.

"In the course of my duties, I have come in contact with over a hundred of the monsters. I have been personally responsible for the deaths of twenty of them. I have one of the highest kill ratios in the Special Forces. If we had such classifications, I would be considered an ace. So I will tell you this about the worms—"

"Jim," his mother interrupted. "I don't think this is the time or place for war stories."

I caught myself. I looked at my mother, and at Alan Wise. And realized something. They were both a little red-faced and happy looking. They were both drunk. I couldn't tell about Mr. Taka-hara. He was a silent enigma.

What was it Duke had told me once? When a drunk and a fool get into an argument, you can't tell which is which. You have to wait until the drunk sobers up; the other one is the fool. How do you know when a drunk and a fool are in an argument? Easy. Anyone who argues with a drunk is automatically a fool.

Right.

"No, no, hon. Let him talk. I want to hear—" Alan Wise turned and nuzzled my mother's cheek, her neck—he nibbled her ear. She squealed and protested, but she didn't push him away.

I said, "Actually, I don't think we can have this conversation at all—"

"Eh?" He looked up at me.

"—because you don't really know what you're talking about, Mr. Wise. When you've done your research properly, then we can talk." I stood up. Their faces were gaping. "If you'll excuse me, I have to go to the bathroom."

Q: What should you make when you invite a Chtorran to dinner?
A: Your will.

35

"I'll take Manhattan—"

"Anything worth doing is worth doing for money."

—SOLOMON SHORT

My mother was waiting for me when I came out of the bathroom. I'd have been disappointed in her if she hadn't.

"What is the matter with you!" she whispered angrily. "All I wanted was a quiet little evening with the two men in my life! Is that too much to ask! Do you have to ruin *everything?* Now, I want you to go back in there and apologize—"

I headed for the front door instead.

Her voice went up an octave. "Where are you going?"

"Back to the military-industrial complex for a little more brainwashing," I growled.

Alan Wise of the hearty handshake was leaning up against the front door. I guess he thought that would stop me.

"Son," he said.

"I am not your son—" I warned.

"Whether you apologize to me or not is unimportant. But I certainly think you owe an apology to your mother. You're being rude in her house."

A half-dozen possible replies flashed through my head, most of them having to do with the inhabitants of my mother's bedroom. I discarded all of them as being unworthy.

I opened my mouth. I closed it. I realized that whatever I said would only make it worse. The situation was a zero-sum game. I could apologize and be wrong, or I could remove Mr. Wise from the door and leave—and be wrong. It was a question of how wrong I wanted to be. I knew I sure as hell wasn't going to apologize. I only apologized to people I *liked*.

I started to turn away. The hell with it. I turned back. I said, "Listen—I didn't mean to infer that you don't know anything. You may know quite a bit about your field, but you don't know anything about *my* field. I know the Chtorran ecology. I just spent three days buried up to my ass in it and three weeks in a hospital recovering. I know what we're up against. You can tell me anything you want about anything else, but I've seen the worms. I've see what they can do. I've seen—"

And stopped in the middle of my tirade.

And realized something.

Three days buried in pink dust—and I hadn't seen the most obvious thing!

Those worms—every single one of them—from the first worm that Duke and I encountered to the congregation that clustered around the chopper to worship the blimp—those worms were the first ones I'd ever seen that had not *immediately* attacked a human being on sight.

I turned away from Alan Wise and my mother and my anger and walked out onto the terrace again. I held up my hand as a signal for them to leave me alone.

What if he was right—?

Not about all that political crap—but what if he was right about the worms? What if the truth was, they were *not* hostile?

I picked up my beer and carried it to the balcony rail. I looked out toward the Santa Cruz mountains. Were there worms up there? I wondered.

Look—I told myself—every worm I've ever encountered, I've had a torch in my hands and I've burned it. And that was because all the worms I'd ever seen—until the episode in the dust—had been hostile.

But then, I'd always had a torch in my hands. The episode in the dust was the first time I hadn't. And that was the first time I saw nonhostile worms.

Could it be that the worms were somehow sensing and reacting to my own hostility?

It was a fascinating idea.

If I could meet a worm in a situation with no hostility in it, would it still attack?

There was no way to test it. No, scratch that. There was no *safe* way to test it.

We'd made up our minds that the worms were a threat, so we

were burning them. What if the worms were only a threat to us because we were a threat to them?

The other factor in that equation, of course, was the bunnydogs.

Based on the evidence I'd seen so far, you could make a very good case that the bunnydogs controlled the worms. If so, then we knew that the worms *could* be controlled. Now if we could find out *how*—

I needed to talk about this with Dr. Fletcher.

"Jim—" That was my mother. "Are you all right?"

I turned around. Alan Wise was standing behind her. They both looked concerned. Mr. Takahara had discreetly absented himself.

I nodded. "I'm fine. I really am. It's just—I just realized something very important." I looked past her to Alan Wise. "You were the catalyst. Something you said. It triggered an idea. Thank you. And"—What the hell, Lizard said it was the one thing I was good at—"I'm sorry I flew off the handle, I really am."

"Apology accepted." Alan waved magnanimously. He was still a jerk, but at least I didn't have to hate him for it any more.

I turned back to my mom. "I need to get back to Oakland."

"Without eating? You just got here!"

"Won't it wait?" Alan asked.

"Um . . . this is really important."

"Well, so is dinner. There's something Alan wants to talk to you about. I specifically invited you so he could."

We started off with fresh tomato juice, pâté, and a spinach salad. Where had she found *spinach?* Obviously, somebody had spent some money on this meal. This was *important*.

So I praised every course, and waited for the punch line. Had he proposed? Was that what this was about? And who was Mr. Takahara?

Alan kept his dinner conversation polite. Apparently my earlier outburst had given him a healthy fear of the United States Army—or at least of my commitment to it.

He was also talking much more obliquely than before. "Listen, Jim—I wasn't kidding about the money to be made. For instance, do you know what July dollars are selling for right now? If you had bought July dollars last December, you could turn them over for a thirty percent profit right now. The market is galloping. It's a whole new ball game—and it's the best one yet. Now that the banks have been reorganized, this country can show a profit on the inflation of its currency. And thirty percent is a very healthy rate. It's good for us. It guarantees a lot of economic growth."

I shrugged. "I guess you're right, Alan. I don't really know that much about economics."

He nodded at me enthusiastically. "That's the point. If you were to start turning your caseys into future dollars, you could double your money every eighteen months."

"So . . . ?"

He looked over at my mother. She looked at me. "Dear— " she said, "—don't they pay you some kind of bounty for every Chtorran you kill?"

The punch line.

The United States government would pay one million caseys for every worm killed, ten million for every one captured alive. I'd collected six bounties as an individual and was owed a seventh. As a member of a team, I'd participated in 106 others. Last I'd looked, I was worth 22.2 million kilocalories. So what? What was I going to do with it?

My mother had an idea.

I looked at her. I looked at Alan. I was incredulous. "I don't believe this. That's what this is all about?"

Alan held up a hand. I held back. "Jim, wait a minute. Hear me out."

"No," I said. "Absolutely not. Not half an hour ago, you were telling me you didn't even believe the worms were a threat. Now you're asking for the money the government pays for killing them. Excuse me, but that feels a lot like hypocrisy." I could feel my tantrum shifting into high gear.

Alan said, *"Jim!* I didn't know that was the source of your money. I apologize."

I looked at him. "Really?"

"Really. I apologize. I was out of line before. I didn't know." He looked a little desperate. "You had every right to get angry with me. If you have twenty-two million caseys in bounty money, I guess that's proof enough you know what you're talking about."

"How did you know it was twenty-two million? I never said how much I had."

"Your mother told me you had a credit account. She didn't tell me where it came from. I'm sorry, Jim. Really."

Two apologies. The man *was* desperate. I sat down again, curious.

Alan looked to my mother. " 'Nita, honey, would you serve the coffee now?"

My mother nodded and left the table.

"Coffee? *Real* coffee?"

"No expense has been spared for the number one son." He grinned nervously, then allowed himself to relax a little. "I'd like to offer you an opportunity, Jim. I'd like you to listen, if you will."

I shrugged. "I'll listen, but I'm not lending any money."

Mr. Takahara cleared his throat politely.

We both turned to look at him.

"If I may," he said. "The opportunity is actually mine to offer. Mr. Wise—" he bowed modestly, "—invited me here tonight specifically to meet you."

"Sir?"

"I am not going to ask you to lend me any money, young man. I already have all the money I need. May I tell you how this works?"

"I said I'd listen. . . ."

He took that as an assent. "My company is bidding on a major reclamation project—I can't tell you what—but it's one of the biggest ever. Now, I don't know if you know anything about the Reclamation Laws, but they're very strict. You cannot just set up a company and start bidding."

"Any gang of looters can do that— " interrupted Alan.

Mr. Takahara looked at Alan Wise politely.

Alan Wise shut up.

Mr. Takahara smiled and turned back to me. "This is the way it works. You have to put a deposit in escrow equal to one percent of your claim. So the amount of money you bring in determines the amount of money you can take out."

My mother returned with the coffee. Alan and I waited while she poured it. The aroma was intoxicating. I'd forgotten how much I missed real coffee.

"So," said Alan, resuming—yanking me out of my reverie over coffee. "Do you see what a terrific opportunity this is for you? You can put your money into a protected escrow account—and our company can then claim a very large and important piece of property. That's why I was suggesting that you invest in dollar futures. The federal government will accept that as a continually expanding collateral. You put it in a rotating account."

"Uh-huh—and what happens when I want to take my money out again?"

Alan nodded. "But you won't want to."

I said, "It sounds like I take the risk and you take the profits."

Mr. Takahara spoke again. He said, "This is a very good coffee. My compliments."

My mother smiled and nodded and looked uncertain. "Why . . . thank you."

Mr. Takahara looked to me then. "There is no risk to you. You will own a pro rata share of the operation. That is better than you can get from any other reclamation company."

Alan Wise added, "You stand to turn your twenty-two million caseys into a hundred million." He looked at me expectantly. "That's quite a deal, isn't it?"

I hesitated. "If you say so. Um . . . what do you get out of it?"

Alan Wise spread his hands modestly. "I'm what they call . . . a participating agent. I put the package together and I take points."

"Points?"

"A piece of the package."

"Oh."

"Jim," he added, "it's not just your money we want. It's your expertise as well. It's *you* we want. And . . . there's something else. I didn't want to bring it up, but it wouldn't be fair not to." He glanced over at my mom and then back to me. "Your mother asked me if I could get you out of the army and into someplace a little, well . . . safer. Your being in the hospital and all . . . well, you know how mothers are. She worries. I don't know what your present commitment is; but I know you've completed your basic obligation, so I know that *something* can be worked out. I know some people in Denver, and . . . well, you know; maybe it can be arranged. And certainly, if these worms, as you call them, are as dangerous as you say, then you *ought* to give serious thought to this. It's a safer, far more lucrative alternative. You've done your part for your country. Now it's time to do something for yourself, and for your mother too."

I glanced over at her. Too much makeup, too much jewelry, too much perfume . . . and too much hope in her eyes. There was too much desperation in this room. It made me very uncomfortable.

"This coffee *is* very good," I said. I put my cup down thoughtfully. All of them were watching me carefully. I picked up my napkin and patted my mouth. "I, uh . . . I'm going to have to think about this." My father had taught me that, the *polite* way to say no: "I have to think about it." Just keep repeating it until they get tired. It works on everyone except used-car and encyclopedia salesmen.

"Absolutely!" Alan Wise agreed, a little too enthusiastically.

"You have to be sure that it *works* for you. I wouldn't want you to do anything that you're not absolutely sure of. But I just want to give you one more fact. Now, it's completely off the record, and you didn't hear it here—but it just might be the one piece of information you need to hear—" He looked at me, he looked at Mr. Takahara, he looked at my mother, he looked back to me. "Are you ready?" he asked dramatically.

"I think I can take it," I said.

"One word." He whispered, *"Manhattan."*

"No way!" I protested. "Denver has been denying access to that real estate for three years. They say they won't even consider reclamation for another three. Even the Mothball Corps has to be bonded before they can go in. There's no way you're going to get a piece of that rock!"

Alan spread his hands wide in front of him. "Be that as it may. That's the word you need to keep in mind."

I realized my skepticism was showing. I picked up my coffee cup, but it was empty. I put it down again quickly. "Well . . . like I said, I need time to think it over."

Mr. Takahara patted his mouth with his napkin and said, "I understand your position perfectly."

Alan Wise I didn't trust—but Mr. Takahara was another story. "Is this true about Manhattan?" I asked him.

"I would be violating a confidence if I told you all that I knew," he replied.

"Yes, of course. But that doesn't answer my question."

He smiled—and he looked like Buddha. "What I can tell you is that there are extraordinary developments coming to fruition in the next eighteen months."

"Mm," I said. He'd told me nothing. "Thank you."

"I'm sure you understand what he *really* means," Alan said a little too quickly.

"Yes, but like I said, I have to think about it."

"Yes, of course. I don't want to push you." He wiped his nose with his napkin. "Here, let me give you my card. If you have any questions, call me—any time, day or night."

I slipped his card into my pocket without looking at it. I turned instead to my mother. "You said you were working on some project with maps?"

She shook her head. "I've been working with the refugee relocation office. We're looking for places to establish colonies, that's all. We're using Family as the model—that's the one that takes care of the children, remember?"

"Uh-huh. That's off the new peninsula, right? How is that doing?"

"Very nicely," she said. But she didn't really want to talk about it, I could tell. The light had gone out of her eyes. She excused herself abruptly and went into the kitchen and clattered the dishes around.

Alan and I and Mr. Takahara looked at each other embarrassedly. "So when will you let us know?" Alan asked.

"Oh, in a day or two. I just want to take a little time to think it over, that's all."

"Sure. Take all the time you need, but remember, this is one opportunity that isn't going to wait long."

"Yes, thank you. I'll keep that in mind." I smiled politely at them both. The subject was closed. In fact, it was dead.

We adjourned to the terrace then, Alan and I and the enigmatic Mr. Takahara. We talked about *Derby* for a while. The conversation was deliberately casual. Mr. Takahara advanced the theory that the missing robot was hiding on the assembly line. After all, who would look there? I admitted it was an interesting idea. I couldn't think of a better place.

When my mother finally came out to join us, I made my goodbyes and left quickly.

I realized I was humming all the way to the Jeep. I felt oddly satisfied. I had a brand-new thought about the worms—and my mother and her boyfriend had solved my other problem too.

Resign my commission?

Hell, no!

Q: What's meaner than a Chtorran with the clap?
A: The lawyer who gave it to him.

36

Mother

> *"How successful were your parents?*
> *Well—how quickly did you forgive them?"*
> —SOLOMON SHORT

Mom was furious.

I could tell, because she was being so charming.

And because she called me *James*.

Uh-oh.

She hadn't called me James since I was fourteen and she'd caught me making nitroglycerin in the bathtub. It isn't that hard to make nitroglycerin. The hard part is getting rid of it quietly. But, boy—was she pissed. She called me James for six months. I was afraid I was going to have to change my name, until Dad finally told her to knock it off. He said she was stunting my growth.

"James," she said; her voice was so cold and polite that the telephone was icing up. "I'm driving up this morning. We're having lunch. Don't tell me you have *other* plans. I've already talked to your commanding officer. I'll meet you at the Overlook at 12:30."

"Yes, Mom. Are you bringing the creep?"

"It'll be just you and me. And I want you to remember your manners for a change. This is a grown-up restaurant." She chimed off.

On my end, it wasn't a chime; just the sound of ice crackling. The glaciers were restless again.

The Special Forces do not have any classes in swearing. You're supposed to learn that in the regular army. By the time you get to Special Forces, it's assumed you're an expert.

"Shit," I said. I couldn't think of anything better.

The thing is, I already knew what to expect. She was going to come in wearing her weepy, disappointed expression. She was going to tell me how hurt she was, how she had no one else to depend on and I was always letting her down. She was going to tell me again how she needed me and I was never there for her. She would remind me at length how she never asked me for anything. That was always the preamble to her next sentence, the one that began, "Just this one time, I'd like you to—"

And of course, Mom's requests were never *really* unreasonable. Not after she pointed out that the state of motherhood was the only state in the Union specifically exempted from certain key provisions of the Fourteenth Amendment to the Constitution of the United States of America. Roughly translated: *"I'm your mother! Doesn't that mean anything to you?"*

The long version: "I raised you from a baby. I diapered you. You used to pee in my face. You're still doing it now!"

I didn't have to say a word. Mom was so skilled at running this performance, she could manage the segue from Disappointed Mother to Avenging Harpy all by herself. All I had to do was sit across from her and say nothing. She didn't need me to feed her the cues; this was a monolog. My job was audience.

This is how Mom knew she wasn't crazy. As long as she wasn't talking to herself, she was still one of the sane. That's why my attendance was mandatory.

Nothing would be settled, of course. After she'd unloaded her burden of injuries, then she'd begin to demand reparations. A mere apology would be insufficient. The apology was only phase one of the negotiations; it would establish her moral right to whatever it was she was going to request next. The request would be punctuated with great weepy sighs, much nose sniffling, and if necessary—depending on the size of the request—a great wallow of tears, like a hippopotamus flubbering about in the mud.

Shit. I already knew what the punch line was. I could hear her saying it: "Jim—*dear* Jimmy—I'm not asking so much, am I? All I want you to do is just *consider* the opportunity Alan is offering. Here, I brought some of the brochures. For *my* happiness. Please?"

I would be lucky to escape with a non-committal mumble.

If I said no, she'd hear maybe.

If I said maybe, she'd hear yes.

If I said yes, she'd have me sign the power of attorney before the dessert was served.

I knew my mother.

She was the best agent Dad ever had. In fact, Dad ended up *owning* one of his publishers because of Mom's skill in making deals over lunch—and then watchdogging every crossed *I* and dotted *T* in the fine print.

I was doomed.

Mom was an expert.

My only hope was to fall on a grenade and die instantly. Failing that, I would order the most expensive lunch possible. Mom hated spending money.

I dressed in civvies. Silk shirt. Levi kilt. Only a couple stripes of warpaint. Just enough to make me look angrier than usual.

I was deliberately late arriving at the restaurant. Mom hated it when I was late; that's why I did it.

The maître d' showed me to a table on the terrace. Mom was already waiting. She had a half-finished drink in front of her. As I approached, she looked me up and down coldly. She made a moue of distaste and said, "I have always hated the idea of men in dresses."

"I love you too, Mom."

She offered one powdered cheek for a kiss. I closed my eyes and did my duty, then sat down opposite her.

"How are you feeling? Do you want a drink?"

"No, thanks—yes, I will." To the maître d', I said, "Bring me a glass of buttermilk." I had to give him credit. He didn't flinch.

After he left, she looked at me skeptically. "Buttermilk?"

"Oh, I'm not going to drink it. I'm just going to leave it on the table in front of you and watch you make faces at it."

"Cute, James. Very cute."

Uh-oh. She called me James again.

She picked up the menu and began studying it carefully, making tiny sucking noises of displeasure through her teeth. "Hm . . . hmmm. I don't know. You can't tell what's safe to eat any more, can you? I wish they'd put the confidence ratings on the fish—" She turned the page. "Hm. Lamb is probably safe enough. . . ."

"Why don't you have the veal?" I offered.

Mom's response was instantaneous. "Do you know how they make veal? *They torture calves.*"

I smiled with deliberate nonchalance. "I shouldn't think that would make a difference to you."

"James," she said sweetly. "I am not going to let you anger me. I have something to say to you, and we're going to discuss it calmly and in a civilized manner, like rational human beings."

"I find that difficult to believe, since neither one of us has been rational for years."

"That's precisely what we are going to discuss. I am tired of living in a state of warfare with you— " She stopped herself from saying any more as the waiter came up to the table with my buttermilk. She flinched.

"Are you ready to order?" the waiter asked.

"No, not yet." Mother started to wave him away.

"I'll have the Hothouse Salad," I said quickly.

She glared at me, turned her attention angrily to the menu again, and snapped, "Crab. I'll have the crab." She handed the menu to the waiter without taking her eyes off me.

As soon as he was gone, she said, "All right, let's get straight to the point. You've embarrassed me for the last time."

"I doubt that."

"I'm trying to do things for you. For *us*."

"Mom, don't do anything for me. Please. I don't want your help."

"You are all I have left, Jim—I'm not going to lose you too."

"You still have Maggie."

"Maggie's moving to Australia."

"So? Australia isn't death."

"It might as well be! Jim, you're all I have left. I can't be alone!"

"Mom, everybody's alone."

"Not *me!* I'm not *everybody*." She added, in a softer tone, "You don't know what I'm going through, Jim."

"I'm sorry, Mom. It's hard on all of us. You don't know what I've been through either."

"How could I know? You never tell me anything."

"It's all classified. If I told you anything, I could be shot."

"Oh, don't give me that. The army doesn't shoot people anymore. I don't understand you. How can something be a military secret anyway? It's us against the Ka-torrans. Who talks to them? Do they have spies? Don't be silly. Who are you keeping a secret from? If we could talk to them, we wouldn't have to fight them, would we? We could negotiate."

"First of all, Mom, it's pronounced (K)torran. The *K* sound is sort of silent. It's just an extra little click in the sound of the *T*. Think of the word *cut*, but without the vowel. Say the *K* and the *T* at the same time."

"That's what I said. Cut-torran."

"(K)torran," I corrected.

" 'Torran, Cut-torran. Whatever."

I sighed and gave up.

"Anyway, you didn't answer my question. Have you tried talking to them?"

"Mom, do you know what a Chtorran calls a negotiator? Lunch."

"Jokes. Always with the jokes. With you, it's either a nasty joke or a rude remark. Thank God your father's dead. To see you like this, with the dress, with the makeup, with the attitude—it would have killed him."

It was no good. She had me surrounded. Plan B.

"I don't know," she said. "I thought if I came and talked to you, maybe we could work something out. Alan doesn't think so, but I said, 'No. Give me a chance. He's my son. I'll talk to him.' Now, I see. Alan was right."

"Mom?" I waved a hand to catch her eye. "I'm supposed to do some dialog in there—to motivate your anger at me. Remember how it works?"

"Mr. Smart Mouth again. You think you're so clever, don't you? We'll see how smart you are."

"What are you talking about?"

"You'll see," she said. She noticed the waiter coming and shut up. She looked very smug and very pleased with herself while the waiter unloaded the cart. He uncovered her plate, then mine, then retreated politely.

"All right." I spoke first. "What are you up to and what do you *really* want?"

"James," she began. Uh-oh. We were back to James. "I can see that trying to reason with you is a waste of time. So yesterday morning—Jim, you have to understand, this is for your own good—"

"I have *always* hated that phrase. Whenever you've said, 'It's for your own good,' it's always been for your good, not mine."

"James, this is exactly what I'm talking about. You're totally out of control. You don't listen to anybody. You don't respect anybody. And ever since this goddamned Cut-torran business started, you've been absolutely impossible. That's why I had to do what I did. I know you're not going to like it now, but someday you'll see I did the right thing. I'm only thinking of you and your future."

"*What* did you do?"

She sighed. Loudly. "I filed some papers—"

"*What* kind of papers?"

She stiffened. "A request for power of attorney."

"Don't be silly. I'm twenty-four years old."

"Based on diminished capacity. I think we can show a pretty good case. All that . . . worm dust you've been eating or breathing or whatever—" She wouldn't meet my eyes. "We don't even have to win. We can get an injunction and tie your money up for years while the whole thing drags through the court system. I know how to do it, James. You know that."

I couldn't believe I was hearing this. "You're trying to blackmail me!"

"No, we're not. We've already filed the papers, Jim." She reached across the table for my hand. I pulled it back. I didn't want her touching me, ever again.

"Listen to me," she said. "You're just a baby. You don't know how to handle all that money. I do. I handled your father's finances for years."

"That's a good point," I said.

"Then you agree with me."

"Where is Dad's money?"

"I've invested it."

"With the creep?"

"James— "

"*I* should file papers on *you!* Jeezis! Why didn't you just hire a male courtesan? It would have been cheaper—and safer. And probably more satisfying too."

Her face reddened. She picked up her napkin and patted at her mouth politely. "If you're going to talk like that to me, then perhaps we shouldn't talk at all. At least not without attorneys in the room."

I ran both my hands through my hair, all the way down the back of my head to my neck. I stared at her across my elbows. "I don't believe this. I don't fucking believe this. How could you do such a stupid thing? First you give him all your money, now you want to give him all of mine. Mom, if you need money, I'll give you all you want. Honest. You don't have to do this. But, please—get rid of that creep."

"Please stop using that word."

"All right. Get rid of that scumbag, that parasite, that cretinous scoundrel, that scuttlefish, that blood-sucking worm. Stop me when I get to a word you like."

"We're going to be married. He's going to be your stepfather."

"Like hell he will!" I realized I was getting too loud. I lowered my voice to a roar. "I'll divorce you first."

Her face paled.

I realized I had said the wrong thing.

Or the right thing—maybe.

"Mom, listen to me." One last chance. "You don't have to be alone. I haven't abandoned you. But you don't need this louse either. There are better men in the world. You're a treasure. You don't have to demean yourself. You don't have pay for this man's affection. Look, the army has some of the best legal software available anywhere in the world. I can probably even get Special Forces lawyers to handle your case. We can get your money back. And if not, we can put this liar away once and for all. But please, don't throw yourself at this bastard this way. You deserve better."

For a moment—for just the briefest of instants—I thought she heard me. And then the wall slammed down again. "Who are you to decide how I should live my life?"

"I could say the same to you."

"You're just a baby, Jim. You don't know. You don't understand. You'll see. Someday you'll thank me."

"No. I won't. Not for this. This is betrayal. You've decided that he's more important than I am. You keep telling me that you don't want to be alone anymore. I got it. I got how desperate you are. You're so desperate, you'll sell your children. No wonder Maggie's going to Australia. Now I understand. This explains everything."

"How dare you talk to me that way!"

"He's going to leave you, Mom. When you run out of money, when you run out of resources, he'll be history. And where will you be then? Alone. Because in your desperation to keep him, you'll have chased away both Maggie and me. That's when you'll really be alone. God, I hope I have it in me to forgive you then—because I sure as hell don't have it in me now." I stood up and threw my napkin down on the table. "Thanks for lunch. It was terrific."

"James, if you leave me now—"

"Do your worst," I said, and left.

I swore all the way out to the parking lot.

Not for her, for me.

Because she wasn't the only one who was alone now.

So was I.

Q: What's the difference between a Chtorran and a lawyer?
A: There are some things a Chtorran won't do.

Q: Why won't a Chtorran eat a lawyer?
A: Even a Chtorran has some taste.

37

Baby Cooper

"There is no such thing as overkill."
—SOLOMON SHORT

I had to do something about Mom, and I had to do it right away.

Actually, I had to do something about the money.

Worst-case scenario: Mom gets me declared incompetent. What can I do to put my money beyond her reach before that happens? Someplace where I can get at it, but she can't.

Interesting thought.

Mom had made a serious mistake. She probably hadn't realized it at the time—it hadn't occurred to me either; but her papers weren't legal until I acknowledged notification. Until I logged on and picked up my mail—

But how long could I avoid doing that? And that was only a temporary escape. If I didn't acknowledge receipt, in seven days the paper went legal anyhow.

"Shit," I said to myself. I was very annoyed. "Your mother boots army software."

And then I realized the irony of that old joke. I had it backwards. She *didn't* have access to military software. But I *did*.

Bingo.

There was that flyer from the Special Forces Workers Alliance—our union—that I had received a couple of weeks ago, something about a Total Financial Management Service. The AI was up and running on the new 99ers with optical ganglia; it was networked across a seven-dimensional linkage guaranteed to be the most sophisticated service intelligence available anywhere in the world. The ad had said, "Not yet available to the general public." I remembered that. I remembered thinking that it would be pretty good if it were true.

Hmm.

First thing I did when I got back to my room, I logged onto the Special Forces Net. My mail flag was chiming red. I knew what that was; I ignored it. Found the flyer in the *save* bin and retrieved it. Studied it thoroughly.

My major objection to the plan was that I was giving an agency of the United States government control over my money. By any rational standards, this act alone would prove me totally incompetent to take care of myself.

But—the advantage of the idea was that Mom couldn't challenge the legality of that without challenging the entire Financial Trust Act, under which the program was authorized. Heh heh. There was no way she could win that one. She'd be up against the entire United States government. That was the attractive part. The Justice Department was the world's largest contractor of legal software. In fact, according to *NetWeek Review*, Justice had the largest research division this side of the ABA.

It might work. . . .

Mom was good. (I'd seen what she'd done to Paramount.) But I'd still bet on the army. The new 99ers were too good. They outclassed everything. You'd have to have access to a matching installation of your own just to keep up with them. I was pretty sure Mom couldn't even afford a software search for loopholes.

Actually, I had no idea how much money I'd earned in worm-bounties. At one time, I'd kept a running tally in my head, but after a particularly confused and nasty burn, I'd lost count. I figured I was worth maybe twenty-five or thirty million caseys by now.

The problem was that all that money was only valuable on paper. You could rent stock with it, you could buy leverages, you could turn options, you could purchase exchange-rate futures, you could invest in reclamations—or if you were conservative enough (read paranoid), you could convert it to *real* money.

Except the casey was still falling.

Dr. Foreman had predicted it, over a year ago. He'd said that with a steadily shrinking labor force the casey was doomed to inflate. These big bounties were proof enough. I hadn't paid too much attention at the time because I didn't have enough caseys to worry about. Now, however . . . .

The exchange rate had topped 100 to 1 and was still climbing. As of this afternoon, thirty million caseys was less than three hundred thousand dollars. This was probably due more to the rising value of the dollar than the falling value of the casey, but the effect was the same. Neither had it escaped my attention that more and more stores were demanding payment in plastic dollars only. A very bad sign, that.

It meant Mom was right about one thing. I had to do something substantial with all this money—while it was still worth something.

For some reason, I thought of *Derby*.

Hm.

Leverages.

That was why T.J. was so scared of Stephanie—and why Grant had to find the missing robot. Only the robot had the access to the three percent leverages. And now that Carrie had called a stockholder's meeting, those leverages were more important than ever.

Leverages. Yes.

Forget the silly TV show. Think of corporate leverages instead. Think of the money you can earn—if they follow through.

Okay, so it was risky. Very, very risky.

But hell, that was how I'd earned those bounties in the first place—by taking big risks. I was betting the farm every time I went out into the field. Why not bet the farm all over again?

I could think of a lot of reasons not to do it—cowardice was one of them—and two very good reasons why I should.

One: I did not expect to live long enough to spend a single penny of it.

Two: It would make Mom crazy.

And, yes, the SFWA Financial Management Service could handle leverages of all flavors. Including insurances, cautionaries, blowbacks, and feed-arounds.

The question was, what did I want to leverage?

Leverages were tricky things—and much more difficult to explain than to use. Essentially, it derived from Election Theory; that is, in any given election some votes are more important than others. The block votes can always be predicted, but the swing votes are the ones you court. The swing votes are usually the smallest part of the electorate—but they're also the most powerful because they determine the outcome. This particular fact of life annoys everyone, especially block voters and idealists. It also makes for some fascinating politics.

Now apply Election Theory to a stockholders' referendum. Who really controls the direction of the corporation? Right. Now if you could rent those shares of stock—the holders get a guaranteed profit, you take all the risks—and you now have a lever with which to control the company.

Sounds easy? It is—but only if nobody else is renting anyone else's stock. Then it turns into a free-for all. So now you start buying cautionaries on all the other stock in the company and this is where the paper starts piling up.

Whatever it is you want the corporation to do, it had better be *worth* all this trouble.

And even then, there's no guarantee that you'll succeed.

Leverages are not for the squeamish.

Well, hell—neither were worms.

If I'd had access to some of my dad's accounts, I probably could have done an opportunity search through the netware, but I'd bet a nickel that Mom had already locked me out of that access. And even if she hadn't, I didn't want her to be able to follow my track.

Okay . . . I studied the options on the screen.

Probably a long-term plan would be best.

That was overly optimistic of me, I knew, but what the hell? Why not plan for the future? I just wanted to do something with the money that made sense, something that would help the human race win the war.

Except . . . I already knew better than most people that human beings could not possibly win this war. We'd already lost. Most of us just didn't know it yet.

No, the best that humanity could hope for was not victory, but survival.

Hm. . . .

I punched for DIRECTORY. Yes, there was a local office of Lunar Five Enterprises in Berkeley. A white-haired woman answered the phone. Yes, she said, the Lunar Colony was officially reopened—and yes, construction on the two L-5 stations had resumed. As a matter of fact, the project was operating under the authority of the North American Unification Treaty, and as such was able to draw funding from public corporations in Canada, the United States, the nation of Quebec, both Mexicos, and the Isthmus Protectorate.

Did I care to invest? she inquired. She flashed me a list of the companies currently involved.

I could have climbed through the screen and kissed her.

I studied the list for half an hour, did some exploring through the network for background information, and eventually decided to buy a nice large piece of a Boeing Olympus-class high-orbit shuttle. The more spaceships we had, the better. There was stock available in the *Apollo*, the *Hercules*, and the *Vulcan*. No, those were already funded to the point of construction. I wanted this investment to make a difference. It cost just a little under three million caseys to start a new shuttle. Here was one of the few places where caseys could be more effective than dollars.

I decided to spread my cash three ways. I started construction on the *Pegasus*, the *Athena*, and the *Ganymede*. I swept half of the rest of the money into the Kilimanjaro catapult and the other half into The Beanstalk Project. The latter looked like a long shot to me, there were technical problems that I didn't think could ever be solved—something to do with the strength of molecular bonds— but the payoff was very attractive. If the orbital elevator worked, the cost of lifting one kilo of mass into orbit would drop from five thousand caseys to five. All you'd pay for was the electricity, and you'd get most of that back on the way down.

The paymaster's office could handle the necessary paperwork. The advantage to using the U.S. Army brokerage is that the commission is held to a scale rate, and your taxes are paid automatically. These particular investments, though, fell under the Resource Incentive Program and no taxes could be assessed on reinvested funds, so almost all that cash got put to work immediately and Uncle Sam's share was limited to the handling charge. I set up a recycling trust with instructions that any and all future bounty payments were to be automatically invested in the same areas, as appropriate, on a pro-rata basis, subject to availability of resources and priorities, etcetera, etcetera.

I spent another half-hour assigning priorities to the management software.

Priority One: Invest in space—shuttles, platforms, colonies, mines, catapults, beanstalks, satellites, factories, and anything else that I'd forgotten to list. Initiate construction projects wherever possible; if not, invest in them to keep them going.

Priority Two: Invest in payloads, particularly gene banks and seed farms; upload as much of the Terran ecology as possible. We'll need it. Also the World Library Project. We had to save our cultural inheritance too, especially the scientific libraries. If and when the space fleet reaches critical mass and becomes a self-sustaining economic threshold, priority two becomes priority one.

Priority Three: Invest in biological research, development, and deployment. If necessary, training and educational programs could be included in this priority. Translation: Kill the worms.

Yes. That was what I wanted to do with my money. I sat back in my chair, satisfied. I grinned at the screen.

That was the easy part.

Now I had to put a shell around all this to protect it from Mom.

I needed a self-sustaining trust. No, a foundation; even better. The Brass Cannon Foundation, a private investment trust. Not to be liquidated without the permission of James Edward McCarthy, or, failing that, before the death of James Edward McCarthy. Additionally, all windfall earnings, whether McCarthy's or the Foundation's, from any and all sources, are hereby assigned to the Foundation, without condition, qualification, or reservation. I used standard legal boilerplate throughout. Despite what the high-priced lawyers say, it's still the safest way to go; in the past two decades, this particular software had already withstood three hundred million man-years of legal challenges. You couldn't upset this boilerplate without also destroying half the financial agreements operating our economy—and, assuming you could, you'd still have to deal with a possible Protection of Intention ruling from the Supreme Court, which would throw your whole case into the bit-bucket anyway.

But just to be baroque, I hired a rider: Should any attempt be made to set aside these financial arrangements, as much of the assets of The Brass Cannon Foundation as are necessary to the task shall be *continually* invested in the most powerful legal software available for the sole purpose of resisting all challenges and attempts to subvert the purposes of the Foundation, using any and all possible legal means—until such time as such challenges are defeated or withdrawn, or until such time as the Foundation has no further assets available to be liquidated.

In other words: Sue me and this fortune self-destructs as fast as you can litigate. The harder you sue, the faster it goes. The Brass Cannon Foundation would transform itself from an aggressive and well-protected investment entity into a single-minded, totally paranoid survival entity. It would literally destroy itself before it would surrender its assets. In fact, it *couldn't* surrender. It would eat itself alive to avoid surrendering. Mom would have to match the Foundation's access to software if she even hoped to get into court—which meant she'd have to spend *more* than the total worth of the Foundation just to get on the calendar. And even if she got that far, the software would stall the case for a thousand years if it had to—as long as it took to win the case or self-destruct, whichever came first.

I supposed that if Mom wanted to be particularly vicious, she *would* sue . . . simply to keep me from my own earnings. But if she did that, the software was intelligent enough to file an aggressive barrage of countersuits for damages. If Mom knew she couldn't get her hands on the money, the reasoning went, then the only justification she could have for suing would be to damage the assets of the Foundation; therefore . . .

That was the nice thing about software entities. You could create the most interesting legal monsters and turn them loose upon society, where there would be loose cannons for decades to come. The Baby Cooper Dollar Bill, for example, was only fifty years old—and the lawyers would probably be fighting over that trust until the turn of the century, by which time it would probably be worth more than the entire planet.

The short version: Grandpa Cooper thought he was being cute. He bought a one-dollar investment trust, the proceeds of which would be delivered to the first-born child of his only daughter (who was at that time only four years old) on the occasion of his/her twenty-first birthday. Then he died, leaving an investment-oriented software entity (which was quickly dubbed a "fairy godmother") to operate the trust without human overrides. The software entity invested the dollar first into Chinese labor contracts, shifting to optical leverages three weeks before the Pakistan Agreement, and then micro-biotechnical futures eighteen days before Apple announced the Pippin development project. And so on. Within fifteen years the electric-Scrooge had cascaded the yearly earnings of the Baby Cooper Dollar Bill into the millions. Well, hell, if all you had to do was study upwardly directed catastrophic trends—at the rate of 16 billion neurological operations per second—you'd probable make some pretty good decisions too. Then Wilma Cooper gave birth to twins. Caesarean. The doctor would live to regret it. Mommy and Daddy Cooper, thinking to be responsible and wanting to protect their children if anything awful happened to them, created "guardian angels" to watch over their children's interests—specialized software entities to monitor and protect the twins' legal, financial, and investment needs. As it happened, the accident that killed Daddy Cooper left Mommy Cooper a quadriplegic; the guardian angels were immediately activated and within three days had filed massive lawsuits on each other's client. The guardian angel for Twin B was now suing Twin A for half the money, claiming that Twin B would have been firstborn if not for the intervention of the doctor. The guardian angel for Twin A was suing Twin B for slander, alienation of affections, attempt to subvert, violation of intention, and malicious litigation. Both guardian angels were also suing the doctor who had delivered the twins, the hospital where they were born, and the now-crippled Wilma Cooper who had signed the Caesarean consent form in the first place, claiming massive damages on the grounds that they were being forced to litigation because of the incompetence of the doctor, the hospital, and Wilma Cooper. The twins themselves were unaware of these battles being fought on their behalf because they were only two years old at the time. Still following this? Good. Because now it gets baroque. Turns out that the ever-cautious Mommy and Daddy Cooper, fearing accidents, infertility, premature spousal termination, etc., had also deposited three viable eggs and six vials of sperm with the Northridge Community Creche. The death of Daddy Cooper automatically turned loose three more guardian angels upon the legal network, each one claiming that its "client" had prior claim on the Baby Cooper Dollar Bill despite not yet having been conceived. The argument here was that conception was *implied* by the storage of sperm and egg despite not yet having occurred in actuality; therefore under the Protection of Intention Amendment, one of these three would-be children was the rightful recipient of the Dollar Bill Trust. Now the religious groups got involved and the case was aiming straight for the Supreme Court. (Already two justices had resigned rather than be forced to rule on the issues involved. The guardian angels had resisted all attempts to break the case into its component parts and were demanding total resolution, not particle resolution.) The Fundamentalist Judeo-Islamic Baptists were claiming that the whole case was a blasphemy because of Mommy Cooper's high school abortion. *That* had been the first-born child, they claimed. Therefore, upon its death, the money had to revert to the estate of Grandpa Cooper—who, it turned out, had at one time signed an agreement of financial support for the Ministry for the Salvation of Lesser Souls (meaning cats, dogs, horses, cows, sheep, and pigs; but not apes). Grandpa had not yet honored his pledge (of $5) before he died and therefore the ministry had filed a lien on the earnings of Grandpa Cooper's estate. The aforesaid Ministry for the Salvation of Lesser Souls was one of the subdivisions of the Christo-Baptist Coalition, which just happened to be now affiliated with the—are you surprised?—Fundamentalist Judeo-Islamic Baptists. Since filing its lawsuit that group had splintered into six separate schisms, but not before it had created its own software entity to pursue its claims. This particular software harpy was being pursued by six harpies of its own, each created by one of the splinter factions. Then the woodwork *really* got porous. Turned out Grandpa Cooper owed *everybody* money. And they were all filing claims against his estate. The legal software churning the net had become a zooful of monsters. Grandpa Cooper's single fairy godmother had given birth to a whole host of guardian angels, harpies, demons, imps, whirlwinds, berserkers, trolls, and ghouls—not to mention several particularly vicious nameless horrors—all prowling through the system, looking for a throat to rip out. It was a legal firestorm looking for a place to happen—and sure enough, it did. . . . It turned out that the original Baby Cooper Dollar Bill itself—which was still in the vault at McBroker's, sealed in a glass case—was *counterfeit*. Somebody had passed it to Grandpa Cooper. Unthinkingly, he'd passed it to the broker. The discovery that the bill was counterfeit was accidentally made during the course of a video feature story about near-sentient software entities. The shitstorm that this triggered made everything that had gone before seem like a fart in a tornado. If the original contract was invalidated because of Grandpa Cooper's failure to provide one legal dollar, then who owned the resultant fortune? McBroker's? The McShareholders thought this was a good idea. McBroker's immediately sued the Baby Cooper Trust for fraud. The Baby Cooper Trust countersued for breach of contract, claiming that McBroker's original acceptance of the counterfeit dollar validated the deal. True to form, the United States government adopted a schizophrenic position: The Justice Department argued that to invalidate the original contract would violate the Protection of Intention Amendment; the Treasury Department argued that to *not* invalidate the contract would legalize the counterfeiting of plastic dollars. Justice argued that the statute of limitations had expired and therefore the dollar had to be treated as legal tender. Treasury argued that under the Seizure of Illegal Profits Act the entire Baby Cooper fortune now belonged to the government. The original counterfeiter came forward and claimed that the fortune was his, arguing that his dollars were works of art and he was only leasing them, not selling them. At least two presidents had considered revaluing the dollar to zero for about twenty seconds, so as to force the Baby Cooper software to self-destruct in its own economic starvation. The doctor who had delivered the Cooper twins committed suicide; his family promptly sued everybody in sight, claiming that the mental stress of the years of legal harassment had driven him to his death. The twins themselves—remember them?—had been separated shortly after the first lawsuits were filed and reared separately.

Neither had spoken to the other nor to their mother since their fourth birthday. By the time they turned twenty-one, the Baby Cooper Dollar Bill was worth the better part of a billion dollars, but not a single one of the lawsuits had yet made it to court. On the day that the Baby Cooper Dollar Bill Trust surpassed the Zurich Lottery in value, a class-action lawsuit on behalf of the members of the International Monetary Council was filed against the United States Justice Department for impeding the resolution of a case which would significantly affect the world's economy. This particular action guaranteed an additional twenty years, at minimum, of legal maneuvering—which was the intention all along; the Baby Cooper assets had to be kept frozen. Should that much cash turn liquid all at once, there was no way to predict what kind of hydrostatic shock waves would resonate through the world economy. Meanwhile, an international community of software vampires was already looking for ways to buy into the donny-brook. Even though Baby Cooper futures were rated a very high-risk investment, shares of all seven of the major corporate entities involved were being traded on the New York Stock Exchange, not to mention more than a score of remora corporations riding on their earnings or echoing their investments. At least most of the software entities involved were smart enough to hedge their bets against an adverse court ruling; they were starting to expand into other investment areas—including the creation of several new Dollar Bill entities. . . . Rumor had it that the Supreme Court was reluctant to rule on this case for fear of crashing the market. That more than half of the human participants in this Byzantine affair had died in the plagues was irrelevant to the software entities battling on their behalfs. It just triggered a whole new class of software ghouls pursuing beneficiary claims; the filing rate for these set a three-day record for the New York network. Unfortunately, the record was short-lived. When the National Resource Reclamation Act was passed, so many claims were filed on the first day of business that the system was down before lunchtime. The commisioners refused to bring the system back online until they could rule the Baby Cooper Trust exempt from further actions. The Federal Appeals Court refused to uphold this ruling and the commissioners promptly allowed the system to crash three more times. (Yes, this also triggered a spate of suits and countersuits—everybody from the court and the commission to the bystanders whose transactions had been lost in the disaster.) Wait, it gets better—Congress's refusal to grant an exemption opened up *everything* that had gone before to the entire range of possible Reclamation actions. Yes, this was an open invitation to several hundred thousand more would-be players to leap into the mayhem—and it was deliberate. The Baby Cooper Dollar Bill was now generating more lawsuits per day than any action in human history. The whole thing had become a legal black hole, but the United States govenment was generating almost as much income off the legal fees—these were all pay-as-you-go cases—as the Dollar Bill itself was generating in interest; so the Secretary of the Treasury had a very real stake in continuing the uproar for as long a time as possible.

Now *that* was software.

I doubted very much that my meager fortune would ever be worth enough to trigger that kind of a feeding frenzy—for one thing, the Baby Cooper millions were all dollars; mine were only caseys—but I was sure that the precedent of the Baby Cooper abyss would give Mom serious pause to think. The protections I had put around my money would be sufficient to tie up more resources than she had to spend.

Yes, I was that angry with her.

She'd hate it. She'd kill me.

Ah, good thing I thought of that. I'd have to amend my will, too. Easy enough. Only an extra few minutes of work. In the case of my death . . . etc, etc.

She'd never forgive me.

I double-checked my work, authorized the insurances, the cautionaries, and the Protection of Intention guarantees; then I set the whole package up for continual multiple loophole detection. I finished off by assigning powers of attorney and appointing the software of the Financial Management Service to full executor status, with a three hundred percent liability penalty, the maximum possible.

Good.

My money was locked up so tight now that even I couldn't get at it without my own permission.

I reviewed my work, authorized and confirmed, signed off, and put the whole thing out of my mind.

Alan Wise be damned.

Q: What do you call a Chtorran who eats its children?
A: Well adjusted.

38

"Bfllshmt!"

"There's always someone willing to disagree with me; but I'm the one who's called controversial."

—SOLOMON SHORT

There were voices in my sleep again.

They dropped out of a hovering pink sky, a wall of brightness—like God—and danced in circles around me. When I looked, they were bunnydogs. When I turned with them, they were men again. We took off our bunnydog suits and danced naked. We were happy there. When I looked at the singing sky, it was a worm.

There was something I wanted to know. I floated up toward the worm, but it sailed away and I couldn't catch it—and the dance was over now. I'd missed it. The herd was breaking up—

I woke up trembling.

I knew something.

There weren't words. I had this overwhelming sense that there were connections underneath the world, as if I'd heard the heavenly music, the great chords of reality, and the sound was still reverberating in my soul.

The weird feeling stayed with me all morning. It meant something. I knew it. There was something I had to do . . . something about that dream . . .

And maybe too it was another fit of delirium; but when they checked me out at the hospital, my readings came up green. "Forget it, Lieutenant," the doctor said. "You had a bad dream. Considering what you've been through, you're entitled to a few nightmares."

Except, it hadn't been a *bad* dream. It had been an extraordinarily *good* one. That was what troubled me so. I wanted to return to it.

I sighed, shrugged, thanked the doctor, and headed upstairs to Intensive Care.

This time, Duke was conscious.

They were keeping him in a sterilized environment, so he was still inside a big plastic tent with odd little ventilation tubes and ultraviolet lights plugged into it.

He turned his head to look at me when I came in. His face was starting to look like a face again. But I wondered if plastic surgery would be able to make it look like a *human* face.

I dropped my gaze embarrassedly. I looked around for a chair, snagged one, and pulled it up to the bed. "Hi, Duke—"

He didn't respond. He turned his head back to look at the ceiling. His breathing sounded labored. The shape under the sheets was disturbingly short.

Just to have something to do, I snagged his medi-console off the foot of the bed and studied it.

And then I wished I hadn't.

They'd taken off both of his legs and his left arm. Dr. Fletcher's notes said there was too much nerve damage for prostheses.

Embarrassedly, I replaced the console. I looked to Duke again. "Uh, they said you were still having trouble talking . . . so, uh, if you don't want to talk, you don't have to. I'll do the talking . . . if you want . . ."

I waited a moment to see what he would do. I couldn't read his expression, so I continued. "I don't really know where to start. Um, I guess I should tell you that we brought back some truly astonishing videos. They're being examined frame by frame. I've been debriefing almost every day since I was released. We really did discover something. I mean . . . nobody knows what to make of those bunnydogs.

"One theory is that they're worm tenders, kind of like tickbirds and crocodiles. Or lieutenants and captains. The bunnydogs handle the paperwork."

He shifted his head slightly to look at me through the plastic. I wished I knew what was going on inside that skull. What was he feeling?

"Um . . . the other theory, Duke, is that the bunnydogs are the worm-controllers. We don't think that the bunnies are the intelligent species behind the invasion—although they could be—but we're wondering if perhaps they mightn't be the managers of this phase. Maybe they're some kind of sub-Chtorran intelligence.

"And . . . um, there's another theory—it's just a thought, nobody's advocating it seriously yet, it's just something to think about—that perhaps we're dealing with several different intelligences, or a compound intelligence. The worms are one part, the bunnies are another, something else is still a third part. What we're trying to do now is figure out how the bunnies and the worms communicate. If we can do that, then maybe we can find some way to . . . talk to them and negotiate or sue for peace or something."

Duke made a rumbling noise in his throat.

"I'm sorry," I said. "I didn't get that, Duke."

He turned his head toward me and said it again. I had to strain to make it out. "*Bfllshmt*," he said. The meaning was clear.

"Uh, yeah. I think so too. Listen, um . . . a lot of people have been asking me about you. I heard from the guys in Colorado. They send their best. And Dr. Fletcher says hello too. And—uh, I saw your son—"

Was it my imagination or did his expression harden? He turned his face back to the ceiling.

"I guess it's none of my business, but I think he wants to come and see you, Duke—I mean, he didn't say anything, I just sort of got the idea that he wanted to; he called me and asked how you were. But he didn't want me to say hi for him, so I don't know if I'm messing where I shouldn't. I just . . . well—"

"Shft fp."

"Huh?"

He didn't repeat it.

"I'm sorry." I said. "I guess I should go."

"Wfft."

"What?"

He struggled to make himself heard. "*Wait*—" he rasped. "I want . . . oo t'do smmfing. . . ."

"Anything, Duke!"

"Write 'own co'nummer."

"Write down a code number?" I was already fumbling for a pen. "Right. Go ahead; I'm ready."

He cleared his throat, coughed, and began hoarsely reciting digits. He was giving me his personal military code—and password!

"Duke—I don't think you should—"

"Shft fp, McCarfy."

"Yes, sir."

"I want'—yoo ge' me . . . a grenay."

"A . . . grenade?"

He nodded; the gesture was difficult for him. "Sfuicide grenaye. Ffoice-activiated."

"Duke, I don't think—"

"Fmk what you fhink!" he said. He glared at me. This time there was no mistaking his expression, even through the plastic. "I don't want—be helfless—" He was interrupted by a spasm of coughing. It went on for a long moment. I wondered if I should signal for a nurse. No, if he was in real trouble, the medi-console would alert the nurses automatically. Duke caught his breath and continued, "—nft helfless . . . against wfrms—"

"Worms? Duke, there are no worms in Oakland."

Somehow, he managed to turn halfway toward me. He tried to reach for me through the plastic of the sterile tent. His hand looked like a worm claw. "*Ge' grenay, Jhm!*" he rasped. "I don' wan'—to die—helfless!" There was terror in Duke's eyes.

I studied the code number in my hands. By rights, I should tear it up and forget it. This was insane. Duke wasn't being rational. A suicide grenade in a hospital? Defense against the worms *here*?

"McCarfy—promisf?"

"Duke, I *can't* do this—"

"Promisf me!" He looked wild. He couldn't hear a refusal.

I nodded. I swallowed hard. "I'll figure . . . something out, Duke. I promise."

He seemed to relax then. He sighed and sank back into his pillow.

"Duke—? Sir?"

"Mm?"

"Remember once, I asked who you cleared with—and you said you checked in with the boss upstairs? Do you remember that? Um—have you checked in recently . . .?"

"Fmk'ff."

"I didn't get that, Duke. Could you say it again?"

He rolled his head toward me and rasped, "Ghod isf a lie—ge' grenay."

I sat there in silence, wondering what I should do. Should I tell his doctors—or what? I was churning up inside.

Damn it! This was Duke—

I owed him!

But—this was crazy! Where do you draw the line?

You son of a bitch, I thought. *Haven't I got enough guilt already?*

Q: What's Chtorran Planned Parenthood?
A: Tactical nukes.

39

Lucky

"—and those who cannot teach, criticize."

—SOLOMON SHORT

I probably should have discussed it with my commanding officer.

Except I hadn't seen her in three weeks.

But she'd assigned me a terminal in the Science Section, so I knew she hadn't forgotten me. I guessed she wanted me to catch up on my paperwork.

There was a note from Danny Anderson thanking me for keeping him posted on Duke. I wondered if I should tell him about his father's request and decided not to. This was something I was going to have to handle myself.

And there was a letter from Dinnie, that nurse in Denver, asking me how I was doing and if I'd heard from Ted recently. No, I hadn't.

General Poole had sent me a congratulatory note. I'd been awarded a Silver Star. I wondered if I was supposed to send him a thank-you note. I decided to play it safe and did.

Dr. Fletcher had forwarded me a copy of her section's schedule. She'd highlighted the session on "Gastropede Communication." That was only an hour from now. Obviously, she meant that as an invitation.

And—*new orders from my colonel*! A search-and-devour mission. Two lobsters! Nineteen hundred hours. Jack London Square. I logged my confirmation with a grin. She hadn't forgotten!

And one last item. The paymaster had authorized the bounty check for the worm I'd flash-frozen from the chopper. One million caseys. The money had already been paid into the account of The

Brass Cannon Foundation. The Brass Cannon Foundation was now worth . . . fifty-six-point-six million caseys.

Huh?

I guess I really *had* lost count of how many worms I had killed.

The breakdown showed that I had twelve full bounties of my own and pro-rata shares in nearly a hundred and fifty more, plus royalties in nearly a thousand other kills that had used information or techniques that I had developed. It added up. There was also an asterisked entry marked *parallel account,* but no numbers were displayed. When I clicked on it for explanation, the screen opened a box that said simply, "Occasionally parallel accounts will be created for internal bookkeeping purposes. Please disregard." When I finished reading it, the box disappeared.

Huh? I thought I knew financial software. I'd never heard of that before. I'd have to ask what it meant. It must be some kind of military procedure—or maybe it was related to the Financial Management Service. Or maybe it was an echo account. Some services set up matching fund accounts for you, which you could only claim if you left the principle untouched for a set number of years. Or maybe it was for internal bookkeeping purposes, a phantom account for double-checking against software embezzlements, viruses, worms, core-crawlers, and sentient hacks. Or maybe it was . . . just something they put there to confuse me.

The important thing was the fifty-six-point-six million caseys. . . . No, I still wasn't a millionaire; not in dollars. But this was a nice healthy slice of a million dollars. Give me another year or two and I'd make it. Not bad for a twenty-four-year-old with an incomplete college education.

No recruiting officer had ever told me about this, and the irony didn't escape me. The last place I expected to get rich was the United States Army.

I supposed I should feel guilty about all that money. It was too much. But no, the money didn't trouble me at all. The bounties were necessary.

According to the newspapers, the economy was in dreadful shape. Everybody said so—and they had the numbers to prove it. All I knew was that the President was committed to getting as much dead cash back into circulation as possible—and that meant lots of bounty and reclamation programs. It also meant a lot of complaints from the neoconservatives. They said this was one more example of big government looting the private sector.

Translation: They weren't getting their share.

But, hell—the worm bounty wasn't limited to members of the

military. Anyone who wanted a million caseys could go out and kill as many worms as he could find. The government would cheerfully pay up. The Montana office even paid in cash. All you had to do was deliver the mandibles. In fact, several mountaineers had done just that.

Hmm. Maybe Alan Wise should join the Special Forces.

Nah.

The only position he was qualified to fill was bait.

I turned back to my mail.

I finished by dropping a quick note into my mother's mailbox letting her know that I had named Maggie as my beneficiary. That would go down well. I wondered if she'd respond. Well, she hadn't given me any choice.

I logged off, realized I was already late to Dr. Fletcher's session, and headed down to the lab section. I slipped quietly into the back of the theater; all the chairs were filled so I found myself an inconspicuous place on the side to stand. There were a lot more uniforms in the audience than last time. This must be important. There were a lot of brass present.

Down below, Tiny was already hard at work. The worm's claws moved *thoughtfully* over the controls of the problem. This particular puzzle had a lot of interlocking rods and sliding blocks. It was almost too complex to visualize.

According to the outline Fletcher had sent me, these problems were designed by a computer program and could be manufactured to almost any degree of difficulty. So far, they had not come up with a problem that Tiny could not solve. The longest the worm had ever taken had been six hours.

Right now, an overhead clock showed the elapsed time was seventeen minutes. According to the agenda, this was supposed to be an "easy" problem.

The chime sounded, the cage popped open—and Tiny grabbed the rabbit. A white rabbit. Seventeen minutes, thirty-seven seconds. The rabbit did not have time to squeal.

Dr. Fletcher touched her controls, and the panel with the puzzle slid closed. She said, "I know that many of you have seen our earlier demonstrations; you know what Tiny is capable of. If we were to give it this puzzle again, Tiny would remember exactly the sequence of moves to open it, and would probably take no more than thirty seconds. Now—" She typed something into her keyboard, waited, frowned, typed again, and looked up.

"Our second specimen," she continued, "was captured near Superstition Mountain in southern Arizona last month. It was close to death from dehydration and hunger. That area is not particularly kind to the gastropedes. We've found a number of their carcasses in the area. We think they wander down from the northern part of the state; there have been sightings in the high country. Had this one not been so weak, capture would have been out of the question, as the creature already massed nine hundred kilos. As it was, two men were killed and three others injured— and the creature was almost destroyed. We call this second specimen 'Lucky.'"

She added, "We think that Lucky may be a female, but we aren't certain." She touched a control and another panel in the chamber below slid open. "I am now going to introduce Lucky to the chamber."

There were audible gasps when Lucky appeared. According to the briefing book, this was the biggest worm in captivity. The beast slid into the chamber like a bus filling a row of parking places.

The two worms goggled their eyes at each other, chirruped, and trilled. They circled each other like boxers—

"We believe this is a ritual behavior," said Fletcher. "Perhaps a kind of meeting dance."

The two worms suddenly leapt at each other and writhed together like snakes, turning and tumbling across the floor of the chamber. First one, then the other, was on top. It looked almost like a combat to the death.

"The first time we put them together," Fletcher noted, "we thought they were trying to kill each other."

Suddenly, the two worms froze in position. They were wrapped rigidly around each other. They held like lovers at climax; their bodies were as tense as steel.

"We call this state *communion*. It is as close to a sexual behavior as we have yet seen in the gastropedes." She looked like she wanted to add something else, but was holding back. "The length of communion tends to vary. So far, our experience has been that the more often two worms are exposed to each other, the shorter any individual episode of communion will be. We have four worms we're working with here. We've found that the first exposure is usually the longest. We have some theories about this, but none that we're willing to discuss at this point, let alone endorse." She glanced down into the chamber. "Ah, I see that they're complete."

Lucky and Tiny were disentangling. They curled and chirruped, rolled sideways, trilled, and broke apart.

Now Fletcher opened the passage to Tiny's cell and the smaller worm slid obediently into it. She remarked, "As I've said before, we have *not* tamed the worms. The creatures appear to cooperate, yes; but we rather think that they're learning the routine of our operations more than anything else. Even a kitten can learn to identify a refrigerator as the source of milk."

Fletcher checked that the passage was clear, and then closed the panel behind Tiny. Lucky was now alone in the chamber. It twitched its hands impatiently—the *same* gesture that Tiny had used the first time I'd been here. The big worm slid up to the panel that concealed the rabbit puzzle and waited.

"You want to notice what Lucky's doing now," said Fletcher. "Every time we change the puzzle, we also put it behind a different panel. Lucky already knows exactly where this one is going to appear."

Lucky looked up at the glass then and issued a rapid, high-pitched trill. There were chuckles in the auditorium. "That's as clear a hurry-up as I've ever heard," someone remarked. Lucky repeated its cry, then returned its attention eagerly to the panel.

"What you're seeing now," said Fletcher, "is a very clear indication that the gastropede has learned not only to anticipate, but to actually *enjoy* these tests."

She opened the panel for Lucky then. The puzzle had been reset, this time with a spotted black-and-white rabbit. The rabbit was trembling in the cage. Lucky burbled in delight and moved immediately to the panel. It unfolded its arms from its upper back, reached forward over its eyes, and began to work the knobs and switches of the puzzle with a swift deliberation. There was no uncertainty in the creature's movements.

Almost immediately, the puzzle chimed and the glass case popped open. There were gasps in the auditorium. Fletcher looked satisfied. So did Lucky. The worm grabbed the rabbit and popped it into its mouth. Again, the wet slobbery crunching.

Fletcher opened the passage to Lucky's cell, waited to see that Lucky was returning to its cage, closed the panel, and then closed the curtain of the theater. She paused for just the briefest moment, as if studying her notes, then looked out over her audience. The scientists looked excited. The soldiers looked grim. I could understand both reactions.

"There you have it," Fletcher said. "A very clear demonstration that the worms *do* communicate." She added, "I want to stress the importance of what you've seen here. Without this demonstration, a very good case could be made that a large part of the behavior of these creatures is instinctive and ritualized. We now have proof that they're capable of a lot more. How much more, we're still investigating.

"We do know that the communication between the two specimens—the transmission of information about the puzzle— occurs *in the communion state*. When the worms have visual and auditory access to each other, but are prevented by physical barriers from achieving communion, the transmission of information does *not* occur. It only occurs in the presence of communion.

"But," and she paused to consider her next remarks carefully, "we still don't know what the mechanism of transmission is. We have extensively analyzed the chirps and trills of the creatures— and there is not enough patterning or modulation in the cries to indicate even a rudimentary language. At most, the chirruping calls are emotional indicators. We have identified a few calls to which we have assigned values corresponding to curiosity, interest, delight, impatience, anger, rage, anguish, and despair; but we have not found any calls, patterns of calls, phonemes, or patterns of phonemes that are ever repeated with any correspondence to events in the physical universe.

"We have tested for chemical communication. The gastropedes have a very sophisticated set of pheromones which vary with their moods, but again, there is no pattern, and the bandwidth of the channel is too narrow to carry the necessary transmission. You don't send stereovision images by Morse code.

"We have measured the radio emissions of the worms, and the gastropedes *are* low-level transmitters. While the bandwidth of this particular channel *is* wide enough, all that we have been able to detect so far is static and noise. It may be that worms in the wild are capable of radio transmission, but these specimens are unconscious to it. We've tried broadcasting signals to them, but the only effect we've been able to produce is a nervous rigidity. It looks like—but we're not yet willing to say it is—a kind of insane terror."

She looked up at someone in the back of the room. "No—hold your questions for a minute. This may answer some of them. We wondered ourselves why the worms would have this potential if they don't use it. Our best guess is that it's a by-product of the way the creature's nervous system is structured, and that it's too recent an evolutionary event for the species to have turned it into either an advantage or disadvantage. Just because the Chtorrans have a half-billion-year evolutionary head start on us doesn't mean that their evolution has stopped. In fact, we are very likely seeing their ecology in a state of severe chaos as it tries to adapt to this world.

"But I've strayed from the subject—the mechanism for communication. We've noticed that the worms begin every communication by touching their antennae at some point. We're not sure what this means either, but we've monitored the electrical pulses at the creatures' antennae and found some patterning, but again, it's not a communication pattern. It's too rhythmic and there's not enough variation. It looks a lot like an alpha wave.

"But we do know that communication *is* occurring during communion. We've attached sensors to both animals and discovered that all of their body cycles synchronize during the act. When that moment of synchronicity occurs, the creatures demonstrate a rigid and frozen posture. Our best hypothesis is that the mechanism of gastropede communication is multi-channel. The trilling cries might indicate the context of the information to be transmitted. The radio noise might contain some modulation we've missed. The physical gestures may mean something, as might the creatures' pheromones. We don't know yet."

A hand from one of the scientists went up. "If you could identify the channel of communication, would it be possible to jam it in some way?"

Fletcher shrugged. "Maybe. It depends on the channel. We've identified the problem here. We're still a long way from the answer."

"Can you give us a time frame?" asked one of the general's aides.

"No, I can't," Dr. Fletcher replied.

The general, with a thick Southern accent, spoke up then. "We wuh told, Doctuh Fletchuh, that you had infuhmation to present heah today that could be of vital military importance. Was that it? The wuhms talk to each othuh?"

"Yes, General, that was the point of the demonstration." She met his gaze with equanimity. "Was there something else?"

"Ah'm sorry, ma'am, Ah guess Ah would have preferred somethin' of *real* military importance. Like a weapon."

That was a mistake. Fletcher's eyes flashed angrily. "General," she said, looking directly at him, "I know you're here for answers. I wish I had them to give to you. But right now, the very best this section can do is give you intelligence about the enemy. There's still too much we don't know about the worms; we still have a long way to go before we can start suggesting ecological countermeasures."

She raised her voice to include the rest of the room. "Listen, the purpose of these demonstrations is to give you all a better idea of what you're up against." And then she focused on the general again. "I don't claim to be knowledgeable in military procedures. I'm a scientist. But I asked you to be here because I think it could be important for you to know that our enemy is capable of a very sophisticated level of information transmission. It may be possible for the worms to spread the word about our procedures almost as fast as we disseminate our information about theirs."

The general smiled broadly, and a little too easily. He stood up and bowed a gentleman's bow. "Ma'am," he said with a shade too much graciousness, "Ah was raised nevah to ahgue with a lady. So ah'll just accept all of this at face value. Ah'm sure that the wuhk you're doin' heah *is* very important to the war effort. Ah guess *Ah* just wanted to see somethin' a little more immediate, a little more he'pful to mah own needs. So if there's nothin' else you want to show us, we do thank you for yoah time, but we do need to be gettin' back to ouah desks—" The man was *smarmy*. He'd just blown her whole demonstration right out of the water. He nodded politely and started for the exit. His aides followed quickly— as did most of the other men and women in uniforms. Several of those in lab coats assumed the session was over then and also started up the aisles.

Dr. Fletcher looked annoyed and frustrated. "If there are no further questions—" she began, but nobody was listening any longer. Most of the audience was already filing out the door.

She switched off her console, took a deep breath, and said, "Shit!"

Q: What's a Chtorran abortion?
A: A hungry rat on a string.

40

Networking

*"The human brain is the only computer in
the world made out of meat."*

—SOLOMON SHORT

Duke had once given me a very interesting compliment.

It was after a burn, after the debriefing, after the usual bull and beer session; he and I had retired to the office to "hoist a jar" privately.

Duke didn't usually say much after a burn; he just sat and sipped. This time, however, he looked like he had something on his mind, so I nursed my drink and waited.

He had turned his chair to face the window and put his feet up on the little filing cabinet. He was holding his glass against his forehead, as if he had a headache and was enjoying the coolness of the ice.

"You know," he said, "You really impressed me this afternoon."

"Uh—thanks. What'd I do?"

"Amy Burrell."

"Oh," I said. "Yeah." I'd been wondering if he was going to say anything about that.

"You did right," Duke said. He lowered the glass from his forehead and glanced over at me.

I shrugged. "If you say so."

"I do say so. You didn't have a choice. You've known it for months that she's your weak link. I've seen it in your planning. And you knew it this afternoon. You did what you had to do."

"But I still feel bad about decking her."

"If you hadn't, it would be worse next time. Or it would be someone else. Think you can knock down José Moreno?"

"No way."

"Well, you'll probably never have to," Duke said. "Not now. Not after today."

"I hope so," I said. I shook my head. "But I keep seeing the look on her face—"

"You mean the tears? That's just the racket she runs on men. That crap doesn't work on officers."

"No, I mean when I jerked her back to her feet and shoved her at the dome. If she'd been carrying a weapon instead of a camera, I'd be dead now."

"That's precisely why she's carrying a camera instead of a gun. Because she can't be trusted with one." He sipped at his drink thoughtfully, then added, "Let me tell you something about integrity, Jim. It's like a balloon. It doesn't matter how good the rubber is; the air still goes out the hole."

"Uh . . . right," I said. I still wasn't sure where he was going with this.

"Integrity means airtight. No leaks. No holes in the balloon. A hundred percent."

"So, what you're saying is—"

"What you did was appropriate. You closed up a hole. It was a good lesson for all of them. You showed them that there's no alternative to doing the job. Your team will be a lot tighter the next time out. You'll see the difference."

"Thanks," I said, and I meant it. "But the truth is, I did it without thinking. I just got pissed off at her continual whining."

Duke raised his glass in my direction. "Absolutely. And you administered the appropriate response. I congratulate you. I salute you." And he drank to my health.

I remembered that now. I wondered what kind of a salute Duke would give me if I punched out a general.

Well . . .

At least, I could think about it.

I strode down to the front of the room and said, "Hi."

Fletcher looked up at me with a weary smile. "Hi, yourself."

I plunged right in. "I have a question for you."

"The answer is probably 'I don't know.' What's the question?"

"Well, your demonstration here was very impressive, despite General Whatsisname's reaction—"

"General Poole."

"That was General Poole? I didn't know they were so hard up for generals."

Fletcher allowed herself a hint of a smile. "What's your question, James?"

"Well, I was remembering something you said before, about the gastropedes' fur. You said it wasn't fur."

"Right. The quill creatures serve as nerve endings."

"Uh-huh, that's my question. When two worms go into communion, isn't it possible that they're experiencing direct nerve-to-nerve contact?"

She nodded. "They very definitely are."

"Well . . . couldn't that be your mechanism? Maybe they're passing nerve impulses directly from one to the other."

She raised an eyebrow at me. "You think so?"

"You don't think much of the idea, do you?"

"As a matter of fact," Fletcher admitted, "I like the idea very much. It would explain a lot of things."

"But—?" I prompted.

"But—" she agreed, "it was one of the first things we tested for when we started putting Lucky and Tiny together. And it was one of the first hypotheses we had to discard. We kept finding arguments against it. Too many arguments."

"Really?"

"Really." She glanced at her watch. "All right, I'll have to give you the short version. Here's what we know. Most of the Chtorran symbiotes are sensory receptors of one type or another. We've identified at least seventeen distinct types of quill creatures—each with a different apparant sensory purpose. Each of those types is further divisible into categories of shade, length, and specialization of function. So far, we've identified over five hundred different subcategories of nerve strand. We presume that there is considerable overlap of function among the strand types, but we don't have the people available to do the necessary research.

"Most of the nerve strand creatures serve as sensory receptors of one type or another: temperature, smell, taste, touch even light and color—but some the symbiotes also work as 'tickler nerves.' Like little transmitters, they can trigger any nerve they touch. That accounts for the tingly feeling of the fur. So, yes—it does look like a very good mechanism for communication. Pat yourself on the back for recognizing the possibility. Now here's the bad news. It can't possibly work. Do you want a minute to figure it out yourself?"

I thought about it. "It's a connection problem?"

"Not quite. The worms have no problem connecting. When they're in communion, they're connecting at least twenty percent of their surface area. But you're on the right track. It's a networking problem."

"Huh?"

"When you plug one computer into another, how many lines are you connecting?"

"Just one—oh, I see what you mean. There are one thousand and twenty-four individual channels in a standard lux-cable."

"Right. Now suppose you were working with wires instead of light and you had to connect each wire by hand—and suppose also that you didn't know which one went where. What are the chances of you plugging each of those lines into the right socket?"

"None, and less than that," I said. "There're billions of wrong combinations, and only one right one."

"That particular problem," she said, "would take longer than the life of this universe to solve. Now, raise it to the power of itself, and you have the odds against two worms forming a direct nerve-to-nerve contact for communication. Don't take my word for it," she added. "Run a simulation on the nearest terminal."

"No, it's all right. I'll take your word for it. But couldn't the worms have some kind of internal decoding?"

"We thought of that too," Fletcher said. "We had two fellows from the Minsky Foundation looking into that very problem. They said it was possible only if the creature was almost entirely brain and very little else. So far, we haven't found the evidence of that. Have you had the opportunity to see any of the photo-isotomographs?"

"I've seen the demonstrations, but I haven't had the opportunity to poke around on my own." A photo-isotomograph was a three-dimensional map. Easy to make. You thin-slice a frozen worm, taking a picture of the cross section after each slice. You store all the pictures in a computer; the computer holds the data as a three-dimensional matrix which can then be explored as a visual display. You can examine any part of the worm's body, inside or out, from any angle. With a joystick you can move around through the entire body, tracing the paths of blood vessels, nerves, and other structures. So far, most of what we'd seen still fell into the category of "other structures." There were organs inside the worms with no apparent function. Were they evolutionary leftovers, the equivalent of the human appendix? Or were they something else, on biological standby and still waiting to be activated?

"I'll get you lab time if you want," Fletcher said. "If you can prove they have the computing power to do that kind of encoding, I'll dance naked with a big pink worm."

"You're that sure, huh?"

"I'm that sure, yes."

"Hm," I said. "But that still raises another question—"

She glanced at her watch again. "It'd better be a short one."

I said, "If not for communication, then what *are* the tickler nerves for?"

Fletcher smiled. "Stimulation. Very *intense* stimulation. Probably very sexual. Communion is a kind of hug. The density of the strands, plus the tickler nerves, must make it a very intense experience. You saw the rigidity of their 'climax,' didn't you?"

I nodded, but I asked, "Now is that one a theory or a fact?"

A flicker of annoyance crossed her face. I was immediately sorry I'd asked the question; it was the kind of thing General Poole might have said. But Dr. Fletcher let it pass. "It's an *extrapolation*," she corrected. "In our own ecology, we know that as life-forms become more sophisticated, the sexual experiences become more intense. So do the rituals; so do the mechanisms of communication. Humans are the best example of all. The worms may be a good half-billion years further down the evolutionary line than anything that's evolved on earth, but it doesn't necessarily mean they're more intelligent; however, it *does* imply several orders of magnitude of adaptation. Who knows? The worms could be what Terran earthworms might evolve into. You ought to know that sexual reproduction not only encourages evolution, it also self-selects for more sexuality in the species."

I grinned. "Okay, I concede the point."

She looked at her watch once more, looked annoyed, but didn't leave—not yet. "Listen, James," she said to me. "You're asking all the right questions. If you ask enough of the right questions, you'll probably retrace most of the steps we've taken in the last eighteen months. Right now, we're bang up against this communication thing—and I'm terribly afraid we're overlooking something so obvious that even a lieutenant could see it." She gave me a speculative smile. "Have you been noticing anything?"

"Well . . . " I began cautiously, "there is something. Um—you've seen our videos, haven't you? The ones from the chopper?"

"I have, yes."

"Did you notice anything about the bunnydogs and that little dance they did?"

"You mean, did it remind me of the herd?"

"Then you recognized it too."

She said, "It's an obvious comparison."

"I think it's more than that. You were the one who gave me the clue. Remember what you called the clustering phenomenon in the herd? You called it an 'enrollment process.'"

"It's a lot more than that," Fletcher said. "It's an essential way for the herd to mortar its identity. It's the glue that holds the members there."

"Yes, of course—but to someone who isn't a member of the herd, it's something else. It's an . . . invitation."

"All right. So?" And then it hit her. She looked up at me in surprise. "The bunnydogs?"

"Uh-huh. Exactly. I'm thinking that their dance was an invitation to Colonel Tirelli and myself to come out and join them!"

A thoughtful expression appeared on her face. "Wait a minute." She unclipped her phone from her belt and punched a number. "Jerry? Fletch. I'm going to be late. Can you handle—?" She listened a moment. "Oh, good. All right. Thanks." She refolded the phone and reattached it to her belt. "All right. You've obviously been thinking about this. Give me the rest."

"Well, while I was in the hospital, I did a lot of reading. I looked up Dr. Foreman's essays on communication." She frowned when I said the name. "Is there something wrong?" I asked. "I thought you were one of his students. You once told me that you'd done the Mode Training."

"Yes, I did—and I got a lot out of it—but . . . I don't like what it's become. I don't like the—never mind. Go on with what you were saying."

"Well . . . the point of his study seemed to be that human beings don't very often experience true communication. In fact, most of us don't even know what true communication really is. If you look it up in the dictionary, communication is defined as an exchange of agreed-upon symbols. Foreman says that's an inaccurate description of communication. He goes on at some length to demonstrate this—"

"I'm familiar with the essays," Fletcher interrupted. "You don't need to do the whole recap."

"All right, well—Foreman makes the point that true communication is actually the transmission of experience. If I could take a feeling out of my head and pour it directly into yours, that would be true communication. He says if we could function with that kind of communication, our perception of ourselves, the universe, everything, would be transformed. A race like that would be like gods. That's why I was thinking about the worms."

Fletcher nodded. "We went down that tunnel. So far, we haven't found any cheese. But go on."

"Well, that was only my first thought. The thing that really blew me away was what Foreman said about language. He said that language is ineffective for transmitting experience. A language is really just a set of concepts, so while it's terrific for describing the *physical* universe—that is, things that can be measured and tested; like the wavelength of light, the temperature of water, stuff like that. But it's totally insufficient for describing the *experiential* universe; that is, the universe of individual perception. I mean, try to describe love, right? The best that language can do is *evoke* experience. That human beings do so well is testament more to our commitment to communication than to our ability.

"What he said absolutely has to happen before a transmission of experience can occur is a *relationship* of communication. Communion—right? Well—that's what the herd clustering is, isn't it? A relationship? It's a willingness to be together. And that's what the bunnydog clustering is too, I'll bet." I studied her face eagerly. "What do you think?"

She said slowly, "I think . . . you've done very well." She took my arm. "Come on, let's go for a walk. I'll buy you a cup of coffee. *Real* coffee. My office."

"Uh—? Sure." I was a little puzzled. Usually she answered a scientific question right away.

She made small talk as she brewed the coffee. "Remember those eggs you brought in to Denver, the ones that hatched into millipedes?"

"Yeah?"

"We kept them alive because they were the only red-bellied millipedes we'd ever seen—at least until recently. The ones up north all had red bellies. Do you take milk? Sorry, I don't have any sugar. Anyway, you might be interested to know that the red-bellies aren't as voracious as their black-bellied cousins. They grow a lot slower too. And—if you'll accept an undocumented opinion—I suspect they're also smarter. We were going to do some maze tests, but we never had the chance, what with the hassle of moving the whole operation here. I think we brought your three bugs—I'd have to check—if you want to see how they're doing." She handed me a heavy white mug.

"Later," I said. "What about my idea about the bunnydogs?"

She sat down opposite me. "Is the coffee okay?"

I tasted it politely, then started to ask the question again—then stopped and looked back into the mug. The aroma was *heavenly*. I inhaled deeply. "Mmmm . . . this is terrific. Thank you." I decided to shut up and just enjoy the terrific smell.

There were loose strands of hair hanging down over Dr. Fletcher's forehead. She brushed them back and I realized how tired she looked. There were tiny lines around her eyes. She must have been under a lot of strain these past few weeks. She sipped at her coffee and said, "We've been planning another mission, James—up north, the same area—specifically to try to establish contact with the bunnydogs. We think there's a chance that we're looking at the next step here—we're not sure. There's been a lot of discussion about that clustering dance and what it might mean. We've spent a lot of time looking at those videos." She paused, swirled her coffee mug, took a careful drink, and then said, "And we've covered a lot of the same ground you have. . . ."

I could feel my balloon deflating. "So, this isn't news, is it?"

She shook her head. "No, it isn't. The thing about the dance being an invitation, though—that's very interesting. We hadn't realized that." She studied my face.

I sighed and looked into my lap. I rolled my coffee mug between my hands. "You're trying to let me down easy, aren't you?"

"Not at all. The fact is, you not only saw the resemblance, you also did the appropriate research—and you came up with a pretty damn good hypothesis. It makes more sense than even you may realize." She scratched her head bemusedly. "I think I'd better offer you a job, James."

"A job?"

"Mm-hm." She nodded. "We're going to need a mission specialist. I think you might be right for the position."

Q: What do Chtorrans call a hospital nursery?
A: Hot canapes.

41

The Communication Gap

"You don't need a lid on a basket of crabs. If one of them tries to climb out, the others will pull it back down."

—SOLOMON SHORT

There were eight people in the room all seated around a huge shiny-topped conference table. I knew Colonel Tirelli, Colonel Anderson, Jerry Larson, Dr. Zymph, and Dr. Fletcher. General Poole was flanked by two of his aids. The three of them looked about as pleasant as a bowl of cafeteria chili.

"Based on the evidence of your video," Dr. Zymph was saying, "we have to assume that communication with the bunnydogs *or* the worms may actually be possible." She still looked like a truck driver—she was a squat barrel-shaped woman with the expression of a bulldog and jowls to match. There was more gray in her hair than I remembered from Denver, but her voice was as fierce and gravelly as ever. "We were able to identify over a hundred and forty-three specific interactions among the creatures we are now calling 'bunnydogs' and another eighty-seven interactions between the bunnydogs and the worms."

"And based on that evidence, you want to drop a man in their midst. Is that correct?" I asked.

"The mission specialist will be given every protection possible," grumbled General Poole. "You'll have two full squads behind you."

"But . . . essentially, what you're asking me to do is step out of a chopper and walk up to the first bunnydog I see and offer to shake hands, right?"

Dr. Zymph admitted it. "We want to put a man and a bunnydog face to face and see what happens."

"And if I don't get eaten, then you'll know it's safe for the real scientists to come out and talk," I finished.

"Not exactly, but—"

"But exactly?" I interrupted. "You want to stake me out like a goat. That's what you've outlined here."

"Lieutenant," said the general warningly.

"Excuse me, sir. I think it's time I said something about this idea. It's not going to work. At least not the way it's been explained here. I know I'm only a lieutenant, but I've had more experience with the worms and the bunnydogs—face to face— than anybody else in this room. That makes me the expert."

"That's right," said General Poole. "That's what makes you so important to the success of the mission. We want the benefit of your experience." He was wearing his plastic smile.

"If you really do mean that, General, then you'll listen to what I have to tell you. I've seen a lot of cute ideas come down from Denver and everywhere else about how we should deal with the worms. Some are . . . interesting. Most are dangerous. A few are damned foolish. But almost all of them require some dogface like myself to go out there and put his ass on the line to test somebody else's theory. If the mission fails, you don't lose anything but face, but the asshole who trusted you finds himself on the inside of a giant pink appetite with hair."

"So you're sayin'—?"

"—That if someone has to put his head in the lion's mouth, he should be allowed to choose his own lion."

Dr. Zymph cleared her throat. We all looked toward her. "I think you're exaggerating the situation a bit, Lieutenant—"

"No, I'm not! I'm the guy who froze three worms before we found out it was impossible. This makes even less sense than that. I admit I'm unpopular, but couldn't you find something a little less transparent?"

"Are you through?" she asked.

"For the moment. If I think of anything else," I growled, "I'll interrupt you again."

General Poole said quietly. "Lieutenant! Ah'll be glad to acknowledge the contributions of the Uncle Ira Group any day or night—but let me remind you that you are still part of Uncle *Sam's* army. When you took your oath you were signifyin' your willingness to give your life, if need be." He gave me his famous intimidation stare.

I gave him my defiant look. "I took an oath, not a suicide pact. Sir."

"Ah'm talking about service and commitment, Lieutenant."

"I hear you. And if I'd wanted to talk about service and commitment, I'd have joined a Tribe and played follow the leader."

"Ah take it that's your answer? You don't want this opportunity, after all."

"On the contrary, sir. I want this opportunity very much. But if I'm the guy who's gotta get out of this chopper and say howdy to the bunnies and the worms armed only with my good looks and sparkling personality, then it's my responsibility to make sure this thing is actually *doable*."

General Poole looked around in disgust. "This isn't getting us anywhere. Who else have we got? Preferably someone with balls."

"No one else who's qualified—" said Dr. Fletcher. "If we don't use McCarthy, then it'll have to be me or Jerry here—"

"That's out of the question," said Dr. Zymph.

Lizard said, "Excuse me—but I've seen McCarthy in action. He's neither a coward nor a fool. I'd like to hear what he has to say."

Poole glowered at her—

"General," said Colonel Danny Anderson, "so would I."

The general shifted his glower to me. "All right . . . if you have something else to say, Lieutenant, let's hear it."

"Sir—you have me at a disadvantage. I've only had a half-hour with this proposal, just enough time to recognize that it's seriously flawed. My apologies to those who wrote it." Jerry Larson looked grim. I mushed on. "But I don't think it takes into account who or what we're really dealing with."

Larson raised his hand. "If I may—" General Poole nodded; Larson continued, "I disagree! This proposal takes very much into account who or what we're dealing with." He opened his copy of the briefing book and turned it around for me to see. "We know how dangerous the worms can be. We're sending in enough firepower—"

"That's the *first* mistake," I said. "You've set this up as a *military* operation. You want to put men and machines down in the thickest part of the infested region to see who'll come and say hello. The worms have got to have some very bad feelings about choppers by now. We spread death from the sky. You're not even going to get close to them or the bunnies until you've demilita-

rized the mission. You're going to have to put the team down and
get the choppers out of there fast—or hide them. And hide
anything that looks like a weapon. Maybe take no weapons at all.

"What if the bunnies or the worms are telepathic or have some
other way of sensing hostile feelings? We're doomed before we
start."

General Poole looked at Dr. Zymph. "Is that possible?"

Dr. Zymph pursed her lips sideways in a thoughtful grimace.
"As a matter of fact, it just might be."

General Poole made it clear by his reaction that he did not like
that answer. "Would you clarify that, please?"

"Yes, of course. This information has not been made generally
available yet, because we're not sure how to interpret it, but there
is some kind of communication going on between the worms that
we cannot explain. I believe you've seen Dr. Fletcher's
demonstration—"

General Poole made an affirmative sounding snort.

"Well," said Dr. Zymph, "you should find this very interesting.
In January of this year, we introduced three new weapons against
the worms on the Cumberland Plateau in Tennessee. That's a
fairly isolated area of infestation, so it gave us a pretty good test
of the effectiveness of our operation.

"We tested three kinds of biocide capsules, two types of gas
mines, and four different worm barriers. Within two months, the
worms in the region had learned to recognize and avoid the
mines—even when they were buried. They learned to ignore the
heifers wearing the biocide collars, and they learned how to
neutralize two of the fences.

"We then moved our region of testing to western Canada.
Within one *week,* we had established that the worms in the
Canadian Rockies already knew how to recognize our gas mines
and how to neutralize two of the test barriers. They did not take a
single heifer we staked out. They took two ponies wearing biocide
collars and none after that. When we went back to Tennessee, the
worms there would not take ponies. They learned to recognize the
biocide collars and they learned to pass the information on. Would
you call that pretty fair intelligence, General?"

General Poole scowled. I could have kissed Dr. Zymph.

I said quickly, "So, the point is—we don't dare bring in
anything that is identifiable as military hardware. That's one. The
second point is—"

"Wait a minute. Ah still haven't digested the first one," said

General Poole. He frowned at me. "First you tell me that it's your butt on the line, then you tell me you don't *want* any protection—"

"I don't want it *visible*," I said. "That's my second point. This proposal makes too many assumptions about the behavior of the worms and the bunnies, and I don't think we should even try to structure a contact like this proposal suggests. It would make sense only if we were trying to contact another *human* species. It doesn't make sense here."

"Ah'm sorry, Lieutenant." General Poole looked annoyed. "You've lost me. Ah understand the proposal clearly. Set down and talk."

My annoyance must have shown visibly because Dr. Fletcher reached over and stopped me with a touch on my arm. "I think that what Lieutenant McCarthy is saying is that we're not completely sure about the relationship of the bunnydogs and the worms. It's clear that we're seeing a level of partnership that doesn't exist on this planet, because there hasn't been enough time on our evolutionary clock for this kind of thing to happen.

"In our lab experiments, we have been able to *train* worms. We have not been able to talk to them. This suggests that we are dealing with an essentially *un*intelligent life-form. But the other side of that argument is that we may have been dealing with immature or feral individuals, so there is as little possibility for communication as there would be with a three-year-old baby or a wolf-boy. So that whole area of investigation is still unresolved.

"Now, as for the bunnydogs—well, the evidence of Lieutenant McCarthy's very extensive video record is that the bunnydogs do exert considerable influence, perhaps even *control,* over the worms. We very much need to know the source of that relationship and if it is possible for human beings to create a similar relationship with the worms. That's *our* goal here. Lieutenant McCarthy is suggesting that the bunnies and the worms may have goals or methods of their own that could be way beyond our best ability to extrapolate, and we need to allow for that in our planning. We need to be flexible."

General Poole looked around the table. He rubbed his jaw thoughtfully. The rest of us waited. Finally, he returned his attention to Dr. Fletcher. "For once, you make sense," he said.

Dr. Fletcher did a better job of concealing her annoyance than I would have. She merely said, "General, it's the same thing I've been saying all along."

General Poole shook his head and looked around the table. "When Ah walked in here, Ah thought this operation was all settled and needed only a Go-date, but the more Ah let you people talk, the more Ah wonder."

Dr. Zymph looked like she wanted to interrupt, but General Poole held up hand to stop her. "No—it's mah turn now! Rank still has *some* privilege. You people are the most confused operation in this entire effort. So Ah have to give you what you need; but Ah can't work like this. You people don't know what you want. First you want military backup, then you don't. Next you'll be telling me that the Lieutenant here has to dance naked with the furballs—"

"That's not a bad idea either," I said softly.

The general heard me and shot me a withering look. "Before this goes any further, Ah want to see some agreement about what you want to do and *how* you want to do it. Now Ah'm through listenin' to you people squabble. Ah've got some *real* work to do. Don't come back to me until you're sure about what you want to do. Understand? This meetin' is adjourned."

The general stood up and walked out, followed by his aides. Lizard traded glances with Danny Anderson and then the two of them followed quickly. "General Poole—" She hadn't even glanced in my direction.

Dr. Zymph looked across the table at me. "You know, Lieutenant, you're even more deadly *without* a gun in your hands." Then she got up and walked out. Jerry Larson muttered something unintelligible and followed.

I looked at Dr. Fletcher. "I don't get the job, huh?"

She touched my arm again. "James—you said what had to be said. Thank you for saying it."

"But—?"

"But I think you'd better make yourself scarce. This is going to take a while."

Q: To a Chtorran, what's the difference between a baby and a bowling ball?

A: The bowling ball needs salt.

> *"TINSTAFL—There Is No Such Thing As*
> *Free Love."*
>
> —SOLOMON SHORT

Jack London Square in Oakland was not square.

It might have been square once, but now it was a great sweeping arch that encircled a sheltered lagoon. Along the shore, tall trees strung with glittering lights overlooked wide lawns bordered with pink brick paths. Beyond the lawns was a long row of elegant three-story neo-Victorian buildings. There were clusters of tiny shops and open-air restaurants, all bathed in soft gaslight. I felt as if I'd stepped into another world, an old-fashioned fantasy of another era. It looked like a fairy tale. Everything was too beautiful. There were wide avenues for strolling couples, shaded arcades, and even a summery gazebo. The only vehicles were occasional pedicabs. Silvery music—like faint fairy-bells—came drifting across the water.

I was staring at a big bronze plaque set in a concrete marker. It had a huge arrow pointing directly at the ground, and the legend above it said: YOU ARE THERE!

Below, in smaller letters, it said, FOR GERTRUDE STEIN. I guessed I was going to have to have someone explain it to me.

I shouldered my rifle and started walking.

The restaurant was at the end of the strand. It was called This Crystal Castle and it was a gaudy pastiche of baroque gables and cupolas, gingerbread ornaments, and stained-glass windows. It shimmered in a glow of opal, golden, and rose-red light. It looked like something out of a dream. As I approached, I could hear the gentle sound of a playful string quartet. Mozart? I wasn't sure.

Inside, the lobby was done in shades of emerald and gold. It was deliberately overdone to let you know that it was elegant; but I already knew this place was expensive—it had human waiters. The maître d' was wearing a green Doorman-of-Oz suit. He asked me to check my rifle, but I glared at him and told him I was on twenty-four-hour duty; he bowed subserviently and got out of my way. Lizard wasn't here yet, so I stepped into the bar. It was interesting the way people reacted to the red beret of the Special Forces.

The bar was subdued and suggestive. The walls were polished oak and purple velvet wallpaper. The chandeliers glowed with the soft golden color of candlelight. The mirrors behind the bar were smoky, so you couldn't see yourself getting drunker.

While I waited, I studied the cocktail menu. There were drinks here I'd never heard of before. What, for instance, was a Rubber Worm? Or a Leather Helper? Or a Plumber's Revenge?

My phone beeped.

I pulled it off my belt and flipped it open. "McCarthy," I said.

"Jim?" Lizard's voice.

"Hi. Where are you?"

"Stuck in a meeting, thank you." She sounded annoyed. "This is going to be resolved tonight."

"What time will you be out? I'll wait."

"No good. They're sending out for sandwiches. We'll be here for hours. Unfortunately, you've opened a real—you should pardon the expression—can of worms. We're gong to have to cancel our date."

I couldn't think of a single polite thing to say.

"Jim—? Are you there?"

"Uh . . . yes. You've just won the undying gratitude of a couple of very large lobsters."

"I'm sorry, Jim, I really am." She didn't sound sorry.

"How about tomorrow night?"

"Um—no, that won't work. Listen, let me call you. All right?"

"Yeah. I guess so."

"It's not all right, is it?" she said. "I can hear it in your voice."

So I admitted the truth. "Yeah, I'm disappointed. I was really looking forward to this."

"Jim—I've gotta run now," she said quickly. "I promise you, we'll work it out. I do care." She clicked off.

I stood there marveling at my peculiar mix of feelings. I felt disappointed and wonderful at the same time. I refolded my phone and stuck it on my belt. I replayed her words over and over in my head. "I promise you, we'll work it out," she'd said. "I do care."

I could feel good for a long time on those three words.

Except—what was I going to do *tonight*?"

Me and my big mouth.

I turned to the bartender and ordered a Green Slime. It was tall. It was green. It was tart. It turned my knees to jelly. I had to sit down. I wondered how many it would take to turn the rest of me into a slimy green puddle. I ordered a second one. While I waited, I looked around the bar.

The Chinese girl had shining eyes.

That's what first attracted my attention—the way she was looking at me. Then I noticed her waist. She was deliciously slender. And her hands—as delicate as orchid blossoms. Then I noticed her eyes again. She looked as if she knew something I didn't.

She floated in my direction. My heart popped and missed a beat. Every male eye in the bar—and several female ones as well—swiveled to follow her. She was wearing a silk dress so red they'd have to retire the color after tonight. Just the way she walked was illegal in thirty-seven states. One fellow leaned out so far he nearly fell off his stool.

She stopped directly in front of me. I wondered which of the gods was smiling on me. "Something I can do for you?" I asked.

Her smile grew sweeter. She wet her lips and said, "I was wondering what caliber your gun was . . . ?" She touched the barrel suggestively with one exquisite finger.

My mouth went dry. My throat wouldn't work. My tongue was paralyzed. "Uh," I finally said. "Well—uh, properly speaking, it doesn't have a caliber. It fires eleven-grain needles, four thousand per minute. The focus isn't as precise as the two-eighty—" My mouth kept making words—automatically. I was impaled on her smile. She never took her eyes off me. She was *fascinated*. "Uh—it tends to shred the target, but that's more effective— against the worms, I mean."

"You have the *greenest* eyes," she said.

"I do?" I swallowed.

"Mm-hmm." She slid onto the stool next to me. Somebody at the end of the bar moaned. I wondered if I was about to pass out from lack of blood to my brain.

The bartender rolled up to her immediately and beeped. "Your order, ma'am?"

She didn't even glance at the robot. She said, "I'll have

a . . . *Pink Butterfly*." She held her eyes on me—I was paralyzed by her spell. I wondered if I was drooling on myself.

The robot returned and put something pink and frosty in front of her.

I didn't know what to do, so I just grinned embarrassedly, and said, "You'll pardon me for saying this, but all of the Chinese girls I've ever met in the past have been extraordinarily . . . ah, demure. I mean—not quite so . . . uh, forward. Are you sure you're Chinese?"

"Chinese?" She blinked in sweet confusion. She flipped open her purse and looked into her mirror. Her eyes went round. "My God—you're right! I *am* Chinese!" She closed her purse again. "Wow!" she said wonderingly. "Chinese! Wait'll I tell my mom!"

"Your mom? Right. She doesn't know?"

The girl laughed. "Well, how could she? I mean—I just found out myself."

I stared at her. This was too confusing. I felt as if my reality were starting to shred. I said, "I—ah, don't think that I know what's really going on here, Ms. . . . ? I mean, maybe—that is, I was just going—"

"No, wait—" She touched my arm to stop me. "I'm sorry, Jim."

"Huh?" I stopped. I looked at her again. "Do I know you?"

She met my puzzled stare with embarrassing directness. "We've met."

I studied her face. It was almost a perfect oval. She had high cheekbones and bright almond-shaped eyes. Her mouth was wide, but not too wide. Her hair fell to her shoulders like a wave of sheer black silk. I'd never seen her before. I'd have remembered this face. And yet—I couldn't shake the feeling that there was something else going on here. "Who are you?"

She smiled. "If I'm Chinese, I'm supposed to be mysterious. You know, inscrutable. You figure it out." Her smile was impish.

All my alarm bells were ringing now, and I still didn't know why. I said, "What's your name?"

"You can call me Tanjy."

"Tanjy. Is that Chinese?"

"No," she said. "I'm not Chinese."

"You're not? I think you need to look in that mirror again."

"You still haven't figured it out, have you? I'll give you a hint."

For just the briefest moment her face went blank, then she was back again. She said, "Do you get it now?"

I pointed at her. "What was *that*?"

"I was communicating with my terminal."

I frowned. "You're a—?"

"Telepath, yes. Something wrong?"

"Uh, no. You just caught me by surprise—" And then I realized—

She said, "You ought to have your face checked. It does the most curious things when you're caught by surprise."

The realization was still sweeping over me. I grabbed her by the shoulders. "*You son of a bitch!*"

"Hi, Jimbo!" she said broadly.

"I should have known!" My mouth was working like a fish out of water. I managed to make some words with it. "*Ted!* Tanjy! Theodore Andrew Nathaniel Jackson! You creep!" People were staring at us. I didn't care.

She—he?—grinned at me. "Don't you even kiss an old friend hello?"

"Kiss you? I oughta—" I unclenched my fist. I sputtered helplessly. I didn't know what to say.

"Gee, Jim!" He—she?—twinkled. "You're *cute* when you're angry!"

Q: What do Chtorrans call the afterbirth?
A: Dessert.

43

How To Be a Telepath

"It's a good thing money can't buy happiness. We couldn't stand the commercials."

—SOLOMON SHORT

Listen, I'm no bigot.

At least, I don't think I am.

But I was raised old-fashioned, so I never held much with people shifting their sexes around—but then again, whatever one or more consenting individuals wanted to do in the privacy of his or her own body was his or her own business. Certainly not mine.

I was able to achieve the enlightenment of this position by dint of an adolescence uncontaminated by any experience other than theoretical. That is, I didn't know anyone who had ever changed sex—or even gender-identity.

It is one thing to hold an enlightened position in a vacuum. It is quite another to be confronted by your ex-best friend wearing a body that can turn parts of men to stone.

I hadn't realized the Telepathy Corps worked like this.

"Um—" I couldn't find the words. "This—this is going to require a lot more explaining than usual, Ted."

The way I'd always understood telepathy, it was like having a computer terminal in your head; the same microtechnology that made it possible to graft the artificial nerves in a prosthesis also made it possible to graft a prosthetic lobe into the human brain, a lobe that could be programmed for any multitude of data-processing and communication functions. I'd heard that the new generation of implants made full-sensory transmission possible, but I'd thought it worked like a mental movie screen—like looking through the remotes on a spider.

Ted—Tanjy?—corrected that misperception quickly. "The transmission of experience is *total*—at least it *experiences* that way. I think they drop out a lot of the hash at the bottom, because the experience feels somehow cleaner, *purer*. When you become an operator—like I am—control is also assigned. That's when your soul moves out of your body. It feels just like being here. It's like being able to change bodies as often as you change your underwear. Or, in your case, even more often."

He—she?—I really was going to have to figure this out—was a kind of courier. Sort of. There really wasn't a word in the language yet. His (her?) job was to gather experience and put it into the telepathy network, where it was recorded and made available to the—again, there was no word—*synthesists,* the people who experienced the data, assimilated it, and looked for patterns. It was so high-level even Ted/Tanjy didn't understand it. Yet. Perhaps eventually, she said.

Over dinner—well, it would have been stupid to waste the reservations—I asked her, "Where's your own body now?"

"You mean the one you think of as Ted?"

"Yeah."

"It's in Amsterdam. I think. I'll have to check."

"You're not sure?"

"Jimmy," she explained, "when you get certified, you donate your body to the network. In return you get access to every other body in the network. Pretty soon, you give up the *attachment* to the body you grew up in. In fact, attachment is considered . . . disloyal. That's the closest referent. Um—individualism is disloyal to the massmind in that it makes fragments. Hidden agendas pull the mass off center. Never mind—these are experiences that are beyond your referents. I'm sorry. I'm not used to communicating in such a narrow bandwidth."

"Uh—right."

"Well," she said, "hard work must agree with you, Jimmy. You look terrific."

"I uh,—wish I could say the same for you, Ted— "

"Tanjy," she corrected.

"Uh, yeah, Tanjy. As a matter of fact, I can. I think I can truthfully say that I've never seen you looking better. Um, didn't they have any male bodies available?"

"Sure. But then you wouldn't have been willing to buy me

dinner." She added, "Except for that, gender is really a very arbitrary definition."

"Not to the gend*ee*."

"Not sex," she said. "Gender. Mundanes have trouble with that one, I know. Trust me. Gender is merely a role to play. Like all the other roles. A large part of the telepathy training is about overcoming your gender identification, your age identification, your racial identification—and all the other *arbitrary* identifications that you've wired up while you've been trapped in a single body. By the way, you'd love the section on personal hygiene. I discovered things I never knew about the female body. And the male."

"That must have been quite a revelation."

She ignored the jibe. "It's part of the basic agreements. You have to leave the body in as good condition as you found it. Proper food, proper exercise, enough rest, and so on." The Chinese girl grinned, but it was Ted's grin on her face. "It also means I'm not allowed to get pregnant or go out with sadists." She looked at me speculatively. "You want to keep that in mind?"

I could feel my face reddening. "I uh, think—that you can trust me," I said.

So, of course—naturally—we ended up back at her place. The body's place. The apartment was furnished with surprising luxury. An indoor garden. A lawn. A pool. An overhanging bedroom. A bed the size of Rhode Island.

"Well, why not?" Ted/Tanjy asked. "Think about it. Money is irrelevant to a telepath. It's difficult—not impossible, but difficult—to take it with you. But you don't become a telepath for the money anyway. All that's left are the local perks and privileges. A silk dress is easier to experience than a thousand caseys." He ran her hands up her body. I stared at the gesture. I'd never seen anyone fondle a woman from the inside.

Ted/Tanjy seemed to keep shifting from male to female. The body remained the same, but the personality inhabiting it was a chameleon, sometimes male, sometimes female, sometimes neither. It gave me a peculiar double vision. There were moments when I was conscious only of the person, not the body—and there were moments when I was *acutely* conscious of the body. It was gorgeous. I could have watched it for days. My erection was killing me. I would never wear tight underwear again.

Ted/Tanjy sat the body down on the couch. She left room for me.

I sat down on the chair opposite. "I have to admit, this is still very unnerving."

"I really do understand," she said. "The first time I found myself in a girl's body, I was so caught by surprise, I started to cry."

"You? Really?"

"It happened during my training," she explained. "Mostly, you spend the first part of your training in the body pool. You're always on call. They loan your body out to whoever needs a body to wear. Sometimes you get to ride along, most of the time not. Sometimes they turn you loose in the library. You get to play a lot of recorded experiences. Pretty soon, you start to get a sense of the range of human experience that's available to you. It's mind-stretching, Jim. It really is. You're never quite the same afterward."

"I remember how you were at the bus stop in Denver," I said. "You were a little dazzled."

"That's an understatement, Jim. I was mindfucked. Everybody goes through it. You have to. It's part of the process. Suddenly you find out all kinds of amazing things. You get to look at the same incident from a hundred different points of view and pretty soon you start to get a holographic perspective. Your whole mind-set is destroyed and reformed and destroyed, over and over and over—and each time, it's more exhilarating. It's like the first time you learned how to masturbate. It feels so good, you can't help but suspect there has to be something wrong with it, but you sure as hell aren't going to stop. You are definitely not the same person afterward."

"You certainly weren't," I said. "Not then."

She nodded. "It's one of the very first tests. Becoming a telepath is like running an obstacle course. You have to make it past all the barriers. The first one is to simply find out if you can handle it. I nearly blew it. I almost disappeared into the network. It happens. People get lost, leaving their bodies behind. I was lucky. I came back.

"Somehow, I got past the initial exhilaration. You have to do that on your own. There's no help for that. If you do, that's when your *real* training starts."

"The *real* training?"

"Mm-hm. They put you in a training class with thirty other men, and you start trading bodies with each other for short periods. This goes on for three or four weeks, and you still return to your own body at the end of each training session. That's so you can begin to appreciate what happens to a body when it's worn by someone who's unfamiliar with it. That teaches you respect for the equipment real fast.

"Then they start leaving you in your traded bodies for longer and longer periods, so you can start to learn how to fit into a new body comfortably, how to work with it instead of against it—and also so you can begin to give up the attachment you have to your own body. After all, you may never see it again. You end up being *everybody* in your training class. Once—after we'd had a chance to get to know each other—they scrambled us around and we had to figure out who was wearing whose body. It was really eye-opening. We disclosed a lot about the signals that we project unconsciously. One boy gave himself away because he didn't realize how often he wiped his nose—even when it wasn't running. We always knew which body he was in.

"Anyway, I guess I got cocky. I started to think I could handle anything they threw at me. After all, I'd already experienced so much in the library, I thought I was an expert. God, I was a jerk."

"No!" I said, grinning.

"Oh, yes!" she laughed back. "I was even a bigger jerk than you." She grabbed my shoulders and stared into my eyes. "Listen to me, Jim—there is an incredible difference between being the recipient of an experience and the author of it. They really set me up to discover that.

"It was my first prolonged solo, although I didn't know it at the time. They just told me I was to take a walk through the woods and smell the flowers. I didn't think anything about it; they had started bouncing all of us around on odd little errands. They never told us the purpose of the assignments until afterward. Sometimes it was a test, sometimes they wanted to record a specific experience, sometimes they wanted to see what we could discover on our own.

"Anyway, you're going to laugh when you hear this. I found myself on a hillside. I was alone. I was wearing a sweatshirt and jeans and tennis shoes. The background feel of the body was different, of course—it always is—but this one felt funnier than usual. I had a lower center of gravity and I felt kind of soft. I'd had the opportunities to wear a lot of different bodies by then, so I knew it took a little while to get adjusted, so I didn't think too much about it. I just sort of took it for granted. I assumed they'd given me one of those flabby effeminate little-boy bodies that we used to call capons. I figured they wanted this body exercised and that was the purpose of this assignment. I was so *naive*.

"So, I started walking. It was a beautiful day. The air smelled of flowers everywhere. I think I must have been in Hawaii or the Bahamas, or someplace tropical. The closer you get to the equator, the more intense the light is . . . well, the colors were just incredibly bright and beautiful.

"The day was hot, a little muggy, and I thought I could smell the sea. And my skin was darker than I was used to—and smoother—so I figured they'd given me a native body. Once, I reached into my shirt to scratch a nipple and I was amazed at how soft and sensitive I was. But I still didn't put it together. Still not yet. To be fair, the body was young—maybe thirteen or fourteen—and not all that well developed. In fact, it was quite boyish. But still, you'd think that I, one of the great breast-strokers of our time, could have figured it out, wouldn't you? Well, I didn't. Not from the inside.

"The body was wearing a pack. There was food in the pack, and a canteen, but no mirror or ID card. Nothing to let me know who or what I was. That's part of the training too. You can't take on the identity of the host body. You have to create a new one, all your own.

"After a while, I realized I had to pee. There was no one around, so I just unzipped my jeans and reached in—and reached in—and felt around and felt around. It was funny, I still hadn't quite figured it out, I thought I was tangled in my underwear. You know how you'll think anything to avoid confronting the truth? I finally got annoyed; I figured there was something wrong with this body—I yanked down my jeans and my underpants—and just stared at myself. I can still remember the feeling of . . . there's no other word for it—horror. Everything contracted at once. It was like something squeezing me in the balls—except I didn't have any balls! No penis, no nothing! Just hair! I forgot who I was, where I was, everything! I felt betrayed! It must have been terribly funny to the monitors. I started feeling around in my crotch looking for myself; I still couldn't quite accept the truth yet. There was all this loose skin—and it was all wet and skwooshy—and it was so sensitive—and then I touched my own clitoris—and I *knew*—

"I think I yelped in surprise. I can't tell you the *shift of identity* I experienced, Jim. It wasn't just the body that was female—*I was*! When I realized it, I nearly *came*! My nipples came instantly erect, I could feel them hardening against the material of the sweatshirt. My skin flushed. My face got hot. It was an incredible wave of feeling that swept up through me. I felt dizzy. I nearly fell down. It was the most exquisite flash of excitement and discovery and shock. You can't imagine it.

"They hadn't told me on purpose. It was a setup. The point of the exercise was for me to discover the assumptions that I brought to a circumstance. Oh boy, did I feel stupid—and flustered. The physical waves of shock—and pleasure—were still sweeping through my body. That's when I started to cry. It was such a *basic* mistake! I felt so *embarrassed*. I'd wanted to be the perfect trainee and instead I'd just demonstrated how pompous and naive and airheaded I really was. The monitors were probably laughing their heads off over me.

"After I stopped crying, I started feeling silly. And after that, I realized that they wouldn't have done this to me if they hadn't had a purpose. So I tried to figure out what the purpose was. I decided they'd wanted to teach me a little humility. Well, they'd certainly done that. Learning how to pee from a squatting position doesn't sound difficult, but if you're not familiar with how the equipment works—well, never mind."

"So what happened?"

She shrugged. "I cleaned myself up and waited for my recall. I thought that now that I'd figured it all out, the exercise was over. Only it wasn't. Nothing happened. They left me waiting. After a while, I figured it out again. They *weren't* going to recall me. There was something else I had to discover. Are you sure you want to hear the rest of this?"

I said, "If you don't finish this story, I'll kill you."

"Right," she said. "So I took off my clothes and started examining the body as thoroughly as I could."

"Huh?"

"Well, wouldn't you?"

"Uh . . ." I thought about it. "I guess so."

"Of course," she said. "So soon as you're sure it's safe, the first thing you do is explore the most unknown thing in your environment." She added, "But there was something else going on here too. I didn't want to be caught by any more surprises. You see, I'd heard stories about people flunking out during training—"

"I didn't know it was possible to flunk out of the corps," I interrupted.

"It isn't possible. But it happens. What they do is, they put you in 'maintenance.' It means they transfer you into some old body that they're not currently using, or have no place to use, or no need for, and let you stay there. Your job is to maintain it. Right? It puts you out of the way.

"Anyway, we were in that part of our training where we were starting to lose some of our fellows, and they never told us why, so I couldn't help but wonder. I'd had a little run-in with a captain during my training and she'd threatened to send me to a leper colony—or something equally unpleasant. Maybe she'd made good her threat, I didn't know. This could very well be my body for the next umpty-leven years. I'd already made one mistake with it. I didn't want to make any more. I figured I'd better find out exactly *who* I was—or who I was wearing, that is. You know, Jim, the English language is really inadequate for this kind of discussion."

"You're doing okay," I said. "Go on."

"Well—it was like being a kid again. You know how when you reach a certain age, a certain point in life, you start getting really curious about your body and what it can do. Some of it is sexual, some of it isn't. You explore all your nooks and crannies. You find out what you feel like. You see what parts of you are smooth and what parts are hairy. You touch the places that are sensitive to find out just how sensitive you are. You do a lot of masturbating for a while. You have to do it. It's part of the job of moving in and getting comfortable and finding out how the body works.

"We'd had that in the training—we'd had to trade bodies and then explore ourselves from the inside. You can't imagine how silly it looks to see a room full of naked men sitting on the floor and playing with themselves, examining their hands, their fingers, their toes, their etceteras. But it's part of the job of developing your sensitivities.

"This was the first time I'd ever really been a female, so I went through the steps as completely and thoroughly as if I had a manual in front of me. I knew I was being *really* tested now, so I explored that body as if I were going to spend the rest of my life in it. I found out everything I could about what it meant to be a female. I supposed someone who'd grown up in a female body would think most of what I discovered was terribly naive, but I was excited. I felt like I was discovering a new continent. I guess, in a way, I was.

"Of course, I did all that stuff you see in the movies. I pinched my nipples, I stroked my breasts, I rubbed the insides of my thighs—do you know the inside of a woman's thighs are extraordinarily sensitive? Most men don't. That's why they're such uninspiring lovers. There's a lot you can learn if you just listen to the body.

"It was a remarkable afternoon for me, Jim. My whole sexual

identity was destroyed—and rebuilt. You see always before I'd been a guest in a woman's body, a visitor. Now, I was the . . . host. Hostess! I gave myself permission to do everything I'd always been curious about, but too polite to ask. It was like being given a wonderful, delicious toy to play with.

"I spent the whole afternoon playing with myself, Jim. I had a great time. It was terrific. I found out later that almost all men do that the first time they're turned loose in a female body. They can't resist their own curiosity. The women tend to be a little bit shyer their first time in male equipment. You figure it out. But it was an incredible experience, Jim. Do you know that female bodies don't experience orgasm like male bodies? A female orgasm comes in waves—wave after delicious wave—that sweep up inside of you. It was incredible. I fell in love with myself five times over." Her face was glowing, her eyes were shining. Even the retelling of the experience had roused her.

I felt momentarily embarrassed at her—his?—revelations. It wasn't just the information, it was the candor with which he shared it. It was *too* intimate. I was embarrassed because I was aroused—and fascinated. I wanted to hear every bit of his story. Her story.

"Do you know what they did to me?" she asked.

"What?"

"They left me in that body for three weeks."

"In the forest?"

"In the forest," she said.

Q: What do you call a Chtorran with gas?
A: A showoff.

44

In the Forest

"Chastity is its own punishment."
—SOLOMON SHORT

"There was an old navy weather station nearby," Tanjy continued. "The Telepathy Corps used it as a retreat. Robots ran everything now, so the human quarters were completely available. It was the perfect place for this kind of exercise. We were on an island somewhere, completely isolated. There were three male bodies and four female bodies besides the one I was wearing. They greeted me as I came up the path.

"They must have been able to recognize that I was a new operator. Before I could even say hi, they led me inside into the main lounge. One wall was painted white and was covered with big black lettering—the ground rules for the retreat. They were very simple. The first one was that you couldn't tell who you were. You couldn't tell your name or anything from your past experience. You had to make up a new name for yourself that didn't have any gender attached to it—I used my initials.

"You couldn't say anything that might reveal any past identity you might have held. No personal histories were allowed. Also, you couldn't speculate on the purpose of this assignment, and you couldn't ask other people how long they had been here, or any other questions the answer to which would break any of the agreements.

"The point is, you couldn't go around explaining, 'This isn't my *real* body, you know. I'm not really like this.' That's hiding out. That's pretending it isn't really happening to you. You had to be a person in the body you were wearing—nothing else. The only identity you could have was the one you created in this situation—

whatever you made up in the here and now. I tell you, it was a very crazy time. I knew I wasn't really a girl, at least not inside—but I had no way of knowing I was a boy either, except by my own say-so. I didn't know what I was for a while. And neither did anyone else, I think. I gave off a lot of conflicting signals; come-hither mixed with bug-off, please-help-me, and I'm-all-right-Jack. They were real patient with me, though—or else they knew what I was going through.

"Eventually, what I found out was that I had an incredible investment in my sexual identity—and I had to give it up. Not the identity, the investment. I had to stop being a visitor in the body and start being the owner. I had to *be* a girl, as completely as if it were the only thing in the world I knew."

Abruptly, she shivered. "I still get cold chills thinking about it. It was an adventure. And the others—they were so . . . supportive. Because they knew. They were going through it too. I think at least one of the other women had been a man before. I'm pretty sure—because of the way she spoke, the way she taught me how to be a woman, she was almost clinical—and by the way she made love. Oh, yes—there was a lot of lovemaking. A *lot*." She laughed and added, "There wasn't much else to do on the island. So we played combinations. The first time a man entered me I wept. I still don't know why. It was very intense. He was extraordinarily gentle."

She fell silent, remembering.

I was at a loss for words. I picked up my drink and held it in my hands. I looked at Tanjy, I looked at my glass again. I felt embarrassed—and I felt privileged. I'd never heard a telepath speak so candidly about his or her experiences before. And I felt even a little envious.

She looked up at me with those large Chinese eyes and smiled. The expression on her face was mysterious, as if she were looking at me from far, far away. It gave me a weird feeling of transparency—as if she were reading my mind. As if there were no secrets I could keep from her. I could feel myself stiffening. I wanted to be known—and I was scared of it too.

And then, abruptly, she grinned with Ted's old grin, and I knew it was all right.

"Hey—mix us a couple of Crazy Marys," she said. "I want to get out of this dress." She came back in a black silk wrap that revealed more than it concealed, and sat cross-legged at one end of the couch.

I handed her a drink and parked myself at the opposite end. I wanted to hear the rest of her story.

"It was that *willingness to experience* that they were looking for," she continued. "That was the whole purpose of the retreat. They were tapping into me. They knew when I had broken through. When they picked me up again, they told me I'd graduated to the next level of my training. I'd demonstrated that I could assimilate. Now I was ready to be *trained* in assimilation.

"You can't imagine the classes, Jim. We wore the most incredible bodies, different bodies every day, bodies we'd never seen before. The paradox was that it was so we could be trained as *beings,* not identities. You see, identities and bodies are all tangled up together. You can't detach from one unless you also detach from the other.

"Do you know—no, of course, you couldn't—but after a while, when you know your body is just a transient phenomenon, you realize that bodies are *irrelevant*. Very quickly, you get detached from the physical universe that way; you lose all identifications and you begin to exist only in an experiential universe—a universe of pure beingness. I mean, the physical stuff is still there, of course, but it doesn't have any significance any more. It's just another piece in the game.

"And then after that, they started making us stay in the assigned bodies for longer and longer periods of time, so we wouldn't get too detached. Sometimes we had bodies as young as six, sometimes as old as seventy. Once I wore a Down's syndrome. Another time, I wore a little-girl body that still wet the bed. Once I was a football player. I felt like I was made out of bricks. They wanted us to know—and appreciate—the operating equipment that the rest of the human race is . . . trapped in. So we could . . . sympathize with their condition.

"Then, and only then, did we start the classes in how to act like a male or a female in different cultures. I was amazed at how much I didn't know about how to be a man. I knew I didn't know how to be a woman—but there's a lot about manliness that most men don't know, either. And we don't take the time to learn because we think we already know it by the mere virtue of having been born male. The roles that we play—including *gender*—are almost all learned behavior. We make it up. Really! It's all an act, a performance. We had to learn those performances. We had to learn how to be actors putting on our parts so thoroughly we became them. Just like you mundanes do— except you mundanes don't know you're doing it. That's the trap—and we escaped. We learned how to let go again too, so we could move onto the next identity.

"They told us we would probably change sex so often that we'd eventually lose any identification we had with either gender. And with that we'd also lose whatever investment we might have in a specific sexual identity. They said that ultimately we'd become *omnisexual*. I think I'm beginning to understand that now. Sex has become a totally different experience."

"I can imagine . . ." I started to say.

"No. Unfortunately, you *can't*. I'm sorry, Jim—I feel like I keep excluding you. But this is beyond imagination."

"Try me," I said.

She sighed and waved a hand in frustration. "What I've experienced, Jim, is so . . . incredible, I *can't* put it into words. It's that *different* when you don't have an identity attached. See, Jim, that's what I really learned—that I don't *have* to have an identity!"

"I beg your pardon?"

"Normal people need identities. Telepaths don't. We're detached!"

"Uh—" I said. "I'm sorry, Ted. I don't get that."

"Oh." Her mood collapsed. Her effervescence disappeared. "You missed a step along the way, huh?"

"I guess so."

"Sorry." She scratched her head, a very unfeminine gesture. "Um, let's see—I guess I'm going to have to define my terms. Look, Jim," she said patiently, "the problem is the word 'identity.'

"See if you can get this. Your identity is really a concept that you carry around. It's all attachments. You attach yourself to your name, to the cards in your wallet, to your job, to everything in your life—the car you drive, who you live with, who your parents were, what your rank is, where you come from, what school you went to, what your ambitions are, what your zodiac sign is, what church you go to, what branch of therapy you're currently in—did I leave anything out?"

"Doesn't sound like it."

"But that's not who you really are, is it? You could change any of those things—or all of them—and you'd still be the same self, the same person experiencing. Right?"

"All right, yeah. I got that."

"The self is what *experiences* the identity, Jim. Identity is only memory. It's the cumulative sense of all that stuff in your data banks. If I were to take away your memories, I'd be robbing you of your identity, but you'd still be the same person experiencing."

"But . . . I know I'm me *now*," I said, tapping my chest. "I know who I am—"

"You know your attachments. When I ask you who you are, where do you go to look? When I ask you where you went to school, who your parents were, what kind of terminal you work on, where do you look?"

"Uh—oh, I see. In my memory."

"Right." She grinned. "So if I took away your memory, you wouldn't know who you were, would you?"

"I'd be awfully confused."

"Sure. In your case, that'd be just like normal. But you see the point. If you had no memory, you'd have no identity. You'd have to build a whole new one, wouldn't you?"

I shrugged. "Yeah, sure."

"Now if I gave you all of my memories, if I could just pour them into your head you'd think you were me, wouldn't you?"

"Yeah. I can see that."

"But you'd still be you, the same person experiencing it all. You'd just be experiencing a different identity now, right?"

"Okay, I got it."

"Good." She leaned back against the sofa and relaxed. "Well, that's what this whole thing is all about. The *self*—that being inside—that's who you really are. A telepath needs to know that or he'll go crazy. That's what all that training is really about. I had to experience my identity as a thing apart from my *self* so I could know my *self*. Jim," she said, with frightening candor, "I can never be my old identity again—because I know how artificial it was in the first place. In my training, I learned how I made it up. I looked at all my old memories. I saw how it all happened and it freed me!

"They tell you when you start your training that you're going to have to give up that thing you'd rather die than give up. I didn't know then what they meant—but it's the attachment to your identity. I had to give up being Ted. I am not Ted any more. I will never be Ted again." She stopped abruptly and looked at me, as if waiting for a reaction.

I stared at her. For a moment, I had the bizarre sensation that I was sitting with a total stranger again. "But I know who you are—" I protested. "Or do I? Is there any of Ted left?" I asked.

"All of me is left," she laughed. "What's gone are the

'foofoos'—the false connections—the arbitrary attachments to being a *specific* person."

"This is very confusing," I admitted. "I keep thinking they've done something *weird* to you. I mean, weirder even than you're telling me."

"Of course it's weird!" She laughed. "That's the only reason for doing it." And then she turned serious again. She took my hand in hers. There was a hint of—was it sadness?—in her voice now. "The difference between us is that I *know* that identities are *all* artificial. That's a terrifying thing to know. An identity isn't just threatened by the fact—it's *destroyed*. Of course, you're going to resist knowing that. Because then you have to start being responsible for the identity you've created, are continually creating!"

"Uck," I said.

"That's exactly what I said when I found out, but there's something else on the other side of that: a whole new way of experiencing people. It was like discovering a new species! I stopped seeing—that is, I stopped focusing on all the shallow, physical, temporal attachments that people surround themselves with, and started seeing beyond the identity to the *being* who'd created it in the first place! It is an eerie—and wonderful—experience."

"You did that to me before, didn't you?"

She nodded.

"Yeah. I had the strangest feeling that you were reading my mind. Or something."

"I was. Sort of. Only not quite the way you think. I was reading the physical expression of your mind."

"Huh?"

"Jim." She put her hand on my arm. Her tone was serious and intense now. She captured me with her eyes. "People build identities out of fear. You build an identity because you think you need it for survival. You use it as a wall. Telepaths know how to read the walls. You think your life is a secret? It never has been. We can see how it turned out on your face."

I didn't know what to say. I felt as if I'd been slammed against the wall—my wall. Why was she telling me this? What did she want from me?

She must have seen it in my expression. She stroked my arm gently. "A telepath has to know all this, Jim, because part of the job of the telepath is to *build* new identities. Every time I shift into a new body, I have to create a persona that's appropriate. It's not about acting—it's about *being*. I know this is hard for you to understand, Jim. I'm trying to condense months of training into a single conversation."

"I really do want to understand," I said.

"I know. I can see it. That's what makes this so hard for me. All I can tell you is that when you lose your body *and* your identity, what you gain is an incredible *freedom*. You can't imagine it. Really. There's a—a thing that happens, a point you reach, like an airplane racing down a runway, where you become airborne, and then you're flying. You know when you reach it; nobody has to tell you. That's the experience, Jim. I wish I could take you with me. I wish I could share it with you."

I said, "So do I."

She didn't reply. Neither of us spoke for a moment. The moment stretched out, became an uncomfortable silence. I looked at her eyes again. I felt myself drawn—and I felt uneasy too. She was my boyfriend who'd become a goddess, and I didn't know what that made me.

"What's the matter?" she asked. She touched my hand gently.

"I, um—" I shrugged and pulled my hand away. "I'm a little overwhelmed, I guess." I took a breath, I exhaled loudly, I put my drink down. I wondered if I should say good night and go.

She sat up a little straighter then, became more purposeful. She said quietly, "I'll tell you the truth, Jim. I had a very simple intention for tonight. I was going to bring you up here and fuck your brains out. Nothing more. I didn't really intend to have this conversation. I just wanted to complete some old business for myself and have a little fun with an old buddy and pay you back for all the hard times I gave you in the past. Stupid me. I guess I really do love you too much to take that much advantage of you."

"Huh?" I picked up my jaw and fitted it back in place.

"Well, yeah," she admitted. "Hell—the one time we did it, you were so intense, it was like touching a high-voltage line. Don't you wonder why I kept trying to get you back in the sack—or the shower? That was my hidden agenda for tonight. But then we started talking. And there was just too much to talk about. And I realized how much *mis*information there was between us. And I wanted you to just know me as I am now."

Her face was shining again. I thought of Ted. I remembered how he was always like a big silly kid, and the whole world was filled with fascinating toys. He was always grinning—like this. I'd never realized before how *innocent* his grin had been.

That smile was so sweet, so infectious . . . and Tanjy's eyes were incredibly fascinating. I could look into them for hours, years, the rest of my life. I forgot all about Ted. That was a couple of lifetimes ago. This was a beautiful woman; this was now—

Something . . . happened. A throb of dizziness and—

The way I saw her *shifted*. The easy personality that was Tanjy was gone—the *performance* of Tanjy, but not the *self*. It was like a veil being pulled aside, revealing the light behind as clearly as a rosy vision hovering in the sky. The smile was a window—and her drowning eyes were bottomless; I fell upward into them. She glowed like a goddess—she was radiant. And I felt beautiful, just basking in her reflection. The delight rose like a bubble; I surged with it—

And suddenly, I knew what she meant.

I had to blink and pull myself back out of her eyes. I didn't want to, but I had to ask. "Tanjy—there's a kind of telepathy that doesn't need an implant, isn't there—?"

Without taking her eyes from mine, she nodded slowly. "The corps thinks so. We know there's something that happens between two people that can't be explained." She took my hands in hers and held them warmly. Her face was angelic. I wanted to drown in her eyes again. "It's a kind of communication without words . . ." she whispered.

"I've heard of such a thing. . . . I've never really experienced it . . . until now."

For a moment, we sat there looking at each other. She wasn't Ted; she wasn't Tanjy. She was just . . . beautiful.

The room, the world around us, ceased to exist. We were alone in an island universe, just the two of us. Her bright eyes had swallowed me. I had the weirdest feeling that the person opposite me was a mirror of my own soul.

In that moment, I loved her. Him.

I shook my head slowly. "None of this makes any sense to me," I said. "I don't understand any of this—and at the same time, I think I know exactly what you mean. There's a kind of tension between us, an electricity in the air. And I don't think it's just my hormones either."

"Uh-huh." Her eyes were immense. "Don't try to explain it," she said. "Just . . . enjoy it."

"I have to know—"

She placed a finger across my lips. "Shh. Let it be mystical." And then she added, "Non-telepaths might call this love. It is, of course—but not the kind of love you think of when you use that concept-symbol. It's the experience of love without the attachments."

"I do . . . love you . . ." Or did I? Who did I love?

"Listen to me—" she said abruptly. "You're going to be involved with some very big stuff, very soon now. I want to tell you something about communication. *True* communication. You're going to need to know this. It's not about talking—it's about *listening*. Listening with your *whole* soul. It's about listening so hard that you *become the person you're listening to*. Like you're doing right now. Can you remember that?"

"Yes, I will. I promise."

She looked thoughtful then. Even a little sad. She was Ted—or Tanjy—again. It didn't make any difference. She allowed herself a small smile and touched my hand. "Good. Your life may depend on it. And . . . I love you too much to want to see you wasted."

And then there was nothing else to say. We just sat and looked at each other until the clock beeped. Three in the morning.

"It's late," I said.

"Do you want to spend the night?" she asked.

"Sure."

She stood up then and offered me her hand. I got up off the couch and she led me into the bedroom.

I was surprised at how easy and natural it was.

Q: What do you call a Chtorran with the clap?
A: I don't want to call one and neither do you.

45

Carpetbagging

*"Gay people are at their most brilliant
when one of them leaves the room."*
—SOLOMON SHORT

The first part of me to wake up was my smile.

I said, "Mmmmm," and curled affectionately around the warm female body next to me. I slid my hands around her waist and up to cup her breasts.

She said, "Excuse me," and slipped out of bed. I heard her pad barefoot across the floor and into the bathroom. I heard the sound of a toilet flush. I waited for her to come back.

Instead, there was the sound of water running. A bathtub?

I opened my eyes. I sat up. Wasn't she coming back?

She came back into the room, wearing a long dark robe suitable for a convent. She glanced around and made an expression of distaste. "What happened here last night? What is this—? Marshmallows?" She gave me an odd look. Almost hostile.

She wasn't beautiful any more. She was small and mean-looking. She seemed scrawny.

She wasn't Tanjy.

"We had—a marshmallow fight," I explained. "We were going to pick them up—"

She looked at me as if I were a cockroach in her bed.

"Um—I'm sorry . . . It wasn't *my* idea."

"Mm-hm," she said, picking up marshmallows from the floor. "It never is."

"Are you the, uh—owner here?"

"The host? yes, I am." She was making no secret of her annoyance.

"Oh," I said, feeling suddenly very weird. Like an intruder. I felt like I should pull the blanket up in front of me. Like a shield. "I uh, guess I should be going, then."

"Yes, you should."

I still didn't move. I said, "I'm sorry for the mess. Can I help you clean up?"

She stood up then and faced me. "No, I'd rather you didn't. I'd rather you just got out. Now, please."

I slid out of bed. I stepped on marshmallows. I started gathering up my clothes and pulling them on as quickly as I could.

As I was buttoning my shirt, I looked over at her. "Can I ask you something?"

She dumped the marshmallows into a wastebasket and straightened, brushing the powdered sugar off her hands. She waited for me to continue.

"What happened to Tanjy?" I asked.

She shrugged. "She went on to the next."

I said, "Look—I know this is difficult for you, but I get the feeling that there's something very wrong here, and I don't understand."

The Chinese girl said, "Wait a minute." She stepped into the bathroom and shut off the running water. When she came back, I was just tying my tie. She said, "Do you know what we call telepaths like Tanjy?"

I shook my head.

"Carpetbaggers."

"Carpetbaggers?"

"Mm-hm. They take over your body, your house, your life for an evening. They get your body drunk, they take your body to bed with strangers, they get stains on your best silk dresses, they get sticky marshmallows all over your sheets and rugs, and then they disappear in the middle of the night, leaving you with a hangover, scraped legs, chafed elbows, a sore back, and three days of cleaning. Not the least of which is explaining it all to last night's trick."

"Can I help pay for the damages?" I asked, reaching for my wallet.

She stiffened. "I am not a whore, thank you. No, you may not. The service will cover any costs. Besides, it's not your fault. You're as much a victim of the carpetbagger as me."

I shoved my wallet back into my pocket. "Can I ask you one more thing?"

"Go ahead."

"Well, maybe this will sound stupid, but I thought—that is, Tanjy said that telepaths don't have much identity. That is, you don't have much attachment to body, house, clothes, that kind of stuff. But, you . . . ?" I pointed around the room and shrugged and looked at her.

The Chinese girl looked annoyed again. "Right. That's the carpetbagger's justification again." She said, "The truth is that some telepaths do and some telepaths don't. My duties require me to stay local. Twice a month, I rejoin the network and go worldwide. I have work that has to be done on-site. That's the limit of my telepathic participation. I hate leaving my body in the pool, because I never know who's going to be in it while I'm gone or what damage they're going to do."

I stood there, feeling very guilty. I wanted to apologize, and at the same time . . . I didn't want to. I didn't want to admit that Tanjy—Ted—and I had been like two small boys playing with a girl's body while she wasn't home. I felt like the time my cousin and I had been caught looking in my sister's underwear drawer—only this was worse. Far worse. This time I didn't have a cousin here to share the blame. And we'd been playing with far more than her underwear.

I said, "Um, I understood—I mean, I was told that there were certain . . . agreements between telepaths."

Her eyes narrowed. "You don't understand anything, soldier."

"I guess not," I said. I picked up my hat. This Chinese girl was *nasty*. "Well, I'm sorry," I said. "I really am."

"Yes, you said that. You boys *always* say that. Now, if you don't mind, I'd like to take my bath. I want to feel *clean* again."

Outside, on the street, I could feel my anger smoldering. Dammit!

I felt dirty now too.

I should have punched him when I'd had the chance—except it still would have been the Chinese girl who woke up with the bruise.

It wasn't fair!

Dammit! He'd done it to me again!

Q: How do you housebreak a Chtorran?
A: With a flame-thrower.

Q: How do you teach a Chtorran to sit?
A: Holler "sit!" and kick its hind legs out from under it.

46

A Letter From Mama

"Resorting to lawyers is proof of failure."
—SOLOMON SHORT

There was a letter from Mom waiting for me.

Hardcopy. A big fat envelope.

Uh-oh.

I used my pocket knife to slit the edge of the envelope. Several thick documents slid out.

Certificate of divorce. Dissolution of familial relationship. Filed this day, 18th of July, etcetera, etcetera . . . and officially confirmed by the office of the State Registrar in Santa Cruz. Signed. Sealed. Stamped. Notarized.

I'd been *disowned*.

I sank down onto a chair.

Wow.

She was angry.

No. She was *beyond* anger.

This was irretrievable. This was *permanent*.

I flashed between rage and grief. I didn't know what I felt. How dare she do this to me? Yes, I deserved it! But how could I have been so stupid? She shouldn't have demanded so much of me! But I should have realized—but then, so should she! How had we stumbled into this, goddammit?

I *knew* how we'd stumbled into it. I wouldn't let her have the last word and she couldn't let me have it either. That's how all our arguments got started—and that's why they never ended. I didn't know who to be angrier with—her or me.

Me.

No. Her. She could have waited till she cooled off. She didn't have to do this—this was *forever*.

But then again, what else could she have done? What I'd done had been pretty damned permanent too.

She couldn't have interpreted my actions as anything else but a rejection. I really hadn't left her any choice, had I?

But this—?

It still hurt.

I unfolded the second paper. It was an injunction. I was forbidden to call her, to write her, to approach her in any way. Not even through an attorney. My attorney could contact her attorney if there was anything I had to say to her or anything I wanted to ask of her. Oh, yes—and before you ask, the answer is *no*.

I had to give her credit. She was as good as I was. Better even. After all, everything I'd ever learned about legal software, I'd learned from watching her.

The third paper was a financial statement—with a check attached. $193,076.13. *Dollars*. My pro-rata share of Dad's estate. Mom had exercised the buy-out option. I had no further claim on the McCarthy Investment Trust. I was effectively frozen out.

Good for her. She didn't miss a trick. She *meant* it.

But, if Mom had access to this kind of money, then why did she want *me* to invest in Alan Wise's damned fool scheme? Unless she'd already liquidated her share of the trust for him and he'd already spent it?

No. Mom couldn't have been that stupid.

Yes, she could.

She'd disowned me.

That hadn't been her idea. That had been *his*. I was out and he was in—and I had no way to protect her from him any more. My own stupidity had guaranteed that. I couldn't even sue for protection of common assets, because she'd bought me out.

If I wanted to protect her, I'd have to kill the bastard.

The question was, did I really want to help her? Maybe she *deserved* the creep.

And maybe I deserved this.

Damn.

I couldn't even apologize to her. She'd never get the message.

"This is not fun," I said. I stared at the empty walls. "I've had fun. This isn't it."

Nobody answered.

I was alone with my hurt. This was about as low as I'd ever felt.

"Okay, universe," I said, looking up at the ceiling. "What else are you going to do to me? Whatever it is, do it now—while I'm ready for it. It could only be an improvement."

Nothing happened.

Q: What do Chtorrans call two people having sex?
A: Making lunch.

47

"—it has to be *your* choice."

"A human being is a computer's way of making another computer. Yes, we are their sex organs."

—SOLOMON SHORT

After a while, I noticed the lockbox sitting on my desk.

It was a large gray security lockbox, the kind the Special Forces used. It opened to my thumbprint. Inside were three very fat mission books.

Somebody had done a lot of work last night.

I spent most of the morning going through the books, my astonishment growing as I did so.

They'd listened to what I'd said.

The first book outlined how the military would deliver the presentation team to the target site and provide protection without being a physical presence. The choppers would be extensively camouflaged.

The second book described the duties of the observation team and how they would keep the physical presence of their monitoring devices to an absolute minimum.

The third book discussed what was known and what wasn't known about the worms and the bunnies.

But it didn't say much about how to contact them.

I had an idea about that. It was something Ted/Tanjy had suggested. Listen with all your soul.

I tried to imagine sitting down and talking to a bunnydog. I couldn't. The best I could imagine was joining their cluster.

Finally, I went to see Dr. Fletcher.

I stuck my head in her office door and knocked, "Got a moment?"

She looked up from the report she was studying. She had a sandwich in one hand. "Oh, James. Come on in. Did you read the books?"

"Yeah, that's why I'm here." I snagged a chair and sat down opposite her. "I assume I got the job."

"That was never a question," she said. "Do you want some tea?"

"Oh, today it's only tea, huh?"

"Hey—coffee's for special occasions. You're on the team now. I don't have to be nice to you any more." And then she asked, "What's the problem?"

I explained to her about the briefing books. There was nothing in them for me.

She put the last bite of sandwich into her mouth, nodded thoughtfully, waited until she finished chewing, and wiped her fingers on a napkin. "Uh-huh—and how would you make contact with the bunnydogs?" she finally asked.

"This is going to sound weird, but I think General Poole was right. Dance naked with the bunnydogs."

"An interesting idea—" she said. She patted her mouth and tossed the napkin aside.

"I can justify it—"

"You don't have to. I know the reasoning."

"Huh?"

"We talked about this for a long time last night. We pretty well explored the subject."

"Really?"

"The military sat the meeting out. We accomplished a lot. I didn't put it in your book because I wanted to see how much of it you'd figure out yourself. You did good. Now let's see if you can get the second half of it. How would you prepare for such a dance?"

"It's obvious. Go into the herd."

"Mm."

"You're not going to argue with me? I've given this a lot of thought."

She shook her head. She stretched over to her desk and picked up her clipboard. She settled it in her lap and switched it on. "When do you want to go in?"

"The sooner the better, I guess."

"Mm-hm. Tomorrow morning?"

"Sure, I could do that."

"And how long do you want to stay?"

"Two days, three. Just long enough to get the sense of it."

"Mm." She was writing all this down.

"I figured I could wear a beeper collar, so you could track me."

"And—" she looked up, "—how do you figure we're going to bring you back?"

"Well, you could always break my leg?"

Fletcher smiled. "As a matter of fact, we might just have to do that. Let me give you some bad news about the herd, James— some things we've been finding out.

"We've been doing enzyme analysis on various herd members, and we've found that the brain chemistry is slightly skewed. There's a shift in the body's ability to produce certain memoreceptor activators. In other words, there's a chemical basis for the lack of timebinding. To some degree, it's a self-induced drug experience. But—" She hesitated. "It's the permanence of the effect that we can't understand. We have a . . . theory, but—"

"Go on," I prompted.

"Well, you're not going to like this. We think it's another plague, only—not quite. It's not a fatal one. We think that there are some low-level Chtorran viruses spreading through the biosphere. The suspicion is that these viruses do not produce diseases as much as they shift our body chemistry—and as such shift our state of consciousness."

"Like a drug experience?"

"Mm, maybe. Maybe not. We think that the human species has always had this herding potential, but we've always been so acculturated that we've been able to channel the herding instinct into the service of the culture; but this viral effect so damages our chemoreceptors that we're—all of us—functioning right on the edge all the time now. The slightest stimulus can push us over. In other words," she said somberly, "—it is now an act of deliberate will to be an intelligent and rational being."

"Hasn't it *always* been?" I asked.

She smiled. "I appreciate your cynicism—but, James, you need to appreciate the danger here. The process may be irreversible."

"Isn't there a counterenzyme or a vaccination or something—?"

"We don't know. We don't have the people to do the research. Listen, I've given you the bad news. Now, let me give you the worse news. We suspect that the viral agent that unlocks the herding capacity is already so widespread in the human species that for all practical purposes it's transparent. We're all infected. Did you see the news this morning?"

"You mean the cleanup after the Capetown riots?"

"Mm-hm. There was no reason for that madness, all that rage. It was as if all those people just went berserk at the same time. Could that have been another effect of the same virus? We don't know. I'd love to do a dozen autopsies, but with the political situation the way it is—anyway, you get the point, don't you?"

"We could all fall into herds tomorrow, couldn't we?"

She nodded. "Just waking up human is a victory."

"So . . . what you're saying is that if I go into the herd, you don't know that you can bring me back, right?"

"That is the risk," she admitted. "Do you still want to go—?"

"Wait a minute. I thought this was all theoretical—"

"Then you *don't* want to go?"

"I didn't say that, either. You've already got this approved, haven't you?"

She nodded. "We have conditional authorization, if we can find a suitable volunteer." She looked at me pointedly. "Someone who understands the real nature of the problem.

"Here's what we realized last night. The whole question of sentience is premature. We can't even consider it until we know if our two species are compatible. Can humans and bunnydogs even herd together? Forget communication until that question is answered."

"So, you were already planning a dance?" I said.

"None of this was in your briefing book because I wanted to talk to you about it privately. I know your sensitivity to the herd, James. This whole thing could be very dangerous to you personally."

"I came to you, remember?"

"James, I'm not trying to talk you out of it. I *want* you to go. I argued for this opportunity all last night. But it has to be *your* choice. Before I can authorize this, you have to know what all the risks are, so you can choose responsibly."

"I know the worst that can happen," I said. "The bunnydogs could be the worm predators. I could get eaten. But I have to deal with the possibility every day I get out of bed."

"The *worst* that can happen," Fletcher said, "is that we can lose you to the herd."

I stopped my reply before it fell out of my mouth and reconsidered what she'd just said. I looked at her thoughtfully. "You've put people in the herds before, haven't you?"

Fletcher nodded. "And we've lost some of them too."

"How long can a person stay in the herd before he's lost?"

"It varies. It happens fast. Four or five days is the maximum safe time. Even that's pushing the margin. The experience is too intense. It's a mindwipe."

"All right—so all I want is two days. A day and a half. I'll go in Monday morning, I'll spend a day getting acclimated, I'll spend one night, and I'll participate in the next day's gathering. You can pull me out at dinner time. That'll give me the rest of the week to debrief and assimilate the experience. Monday, I go back to work on the big mission."

She switched her clipboard off and put it back on her desk. "You're clear this is what you want to do?"

"I'm clear this is what I *have* to do."

"All right," she said, picking up her phone. "Jerry? It's a Go for tomorrow. Right. No, not at all. Thanks." She hung up and turned back to me. "Okay, we've got a lot of work to do this afternoon."

"Huh?"

"I'm going to train you."

"Train me? How do you train for a herd?"

"There are exercises we can do that will strengthen your sense of *self*. It might help."

"Meditation?"

"Mm, not really. Call it *soul-centering*. It's something from the Mode training."

"I thought you were down on the Mode Training."

She shook her head. "Nope. Only some of the people. I don't like what they're doing with it. But the training is one of the most valuable things I've ever done. It was the thing that kept me . . . rational . . . during the worst part of the plagues. I think it's what keeps me rational today. The truth is, I don't know if it will help or not. I just want to give you every advantage I can."

"I'll be fine," I said. "Really. I'm even seeing Dr. Davidson later today."

She didn't answer.

"What's the problem?" I asked.

"I know you're confident. I know you've thought this out carefully. So have we. But I'm still scared. I know how easy it is to miss something. And I would really hate to lose you *too*. . . ."

Q: What do Chtorrans call Carnegie Hall?
A: Tasteful.

48

Dr. Davidson

"I take it back. A full bladder is the world's second best alarm clock."
—SOLOMON SHORT

"You wanted to talk to me, Jim?"

"Yes, I did."

"Well . . . I'm here. I'm waiting. Now you have to do the talking. You've been sitting there in silence for almost ten minutes."

"I have—?"

"Yes, you have."

"I'm sorry, I—no, I promised I would stop apologizing for everything. It's just that—I don't know where to start. Am I crazy?"

"Everybody's crazy, Jim."

"Yeah, I've heard that one before too. It's my mantra. What I mean is . . . am I crazier than everybody else?"

Dr. Davidson didn't answer immediately. I was sitting alone in a comfortable chair in a big empty room. Dr. Davidson was somewhere in Atlanta. He had a very soothing voice.

"Jim," he said. He sounded very caring. "May I be impatient with you?"

"Huh? I don't understand—"

"You are impatient for a result. And at the same time, you are stuck. You want me to do something to make it better. Before I can do that, I have to have a contract with you. We have to make an agreement."

"Go on—" I said suspiciously.

"You have to agree to stay till the end of the session, even if you get angry. *Especially* if you get angry. And you have to promise to tell the truth."

"Sure. Okay. You're gonna tell me something that's gonna piss me off, right? Well, I can handle that. Do your worst."

"On the contrary. I shall do my *best*."

"Ha ha. So, okay—am I crazy or not?"

"You're putting your attention on the wrong thing. The question is irrelevant. It can't really be answered. There isn't any such thing as sanity. What there is, is the ability to be appropriate to your situation. It's your concept of sanity as a condition to be achieved that's driving you crazy; you think you're not there."

"Look," I said, interrupting him. "I put up with this bullshit for a reason. It's because I want to believe that you understand—because I want to believe that there's still someone in the world somewhere that I can talk to, because if I can talk to someone and have him understand me, then that means that I'm not so crazy that I can't start coming back. Please tell me that you understand."

"Jim, I understand—probably a lot better than you realize right now. Someday, perhaps, you'll see the joke. But let's take it one step at a time today. Let's start with a few simple definitions. Okay? Consider this for a moment. Sanity isn't something that you *are*. It's something that you *do*."

I considered it. "It's a performance, huh?"

"For some people, it is. So what?"

"You're saying, 'Fake it till you make it.' Right?"

"It can work that way, yes." Dr. Davidson sounded amused. I wished he'd share the joke with me, but I knew he wouldn't. It was another one of those things I'd have to figure out for myself someday—sort of like sex.

"So how does anyone know if they're sane or not?"

"Let me tell you what sanity *really* is, Jim. You'll probably be surprised."

"Hit me with it. I'm sitting down."

"Sanity is nothing more than a function of your language skills."

"Huh—?"

"You've been looking in the wrong place. You've been looking at people you think are sane and trying to figure out what they have. Try it the other way. Look at someone who *doesn't* have it and see what quality they're lacking. Look at the damaged people in the world, Jim. How do we know they're damaged? They can't communicate effectively. People who can communicate can succeed. People who can't interact with others appropriately don't succeed and are perceived as damaged."

"But they *are* damaged—!" I started to argue.

"Oh, yes. No question. The damage is real, and the causes are many. There are a lot of ways to damage a human being: drugs, sex, violence, lies, trauma, conditioning, abuse—and sometimes just plain orneriness. And most of these are self-inflected. Human beings are remarkably inventive in ways to avoid responsibility. Damaging yourself is one of the best. Have you ever noticed this about damaged people—the damage is never fatal? It's just enough so that somebody *else* has to take care of them."

"You make it sound like it's their fault—" I accused. "That's not very compassionate."

"You don't even know what compassion is, Jim. You think it's a hug and a warm tit. I promise you, it isn't. And I'm not talking about who's at fault, either. Fixing blame is a useless activity. What result does it produce? I'm talking about going after results. That's a whole different conversation.

"It doesn't really matter that much how a person gets damaged; what matters is the injury that's been inflicted. All those different ways to damage a person have one thing in common: the result is a human being whose effectiveness at communication has been significantly diminished, in some cases even destroyed."

I thought about that. "Okay. That's obvious."

"Too obvious, Jim. You're not seeing the rest of it. The damaged communication is the real problem. It isolates the being. There's no healing available if the pain can't be communicated. The person has to stay stuck in the injury. That's why we encourage people in your situation to participate in seminar groups: It's a place to practice your communication and become more accurate in your language skills."

"I don't need it," I said, a little too quickly.

"I didn't say you *needed* it. You're hearing your 'listening'— you're not hearing my 'speaking.' So let's try it again, and this time listen to the words I'm saying, not the meanings you think you're hearing behind them. You have invested a great deal of energy in your goals. You resent anything that keeps you from accomplishing your goals. You get frustrated and angry. I'm saying that a person like yourself needs to be able to bounce back quickly. You need to know how to heal yourself so you can get on with your job. Right now, I'll bet you feel like you're walking around with your belly ripped open and your guts hanging out.

That's why you came to see me after months of no communication at all. Am I right?"

I didn't answer immediately. Finally, I nodded.

"Your hesitancy speaks volumes, Jim. You're hurting and you're impatient, but you've learned not to let yourself be vulnerable—so you can't admit to anyone that you're hurting; so you can't heal and your impatience just aggravates the hurt.

"And the bad news is that you don't even know that you're not alone. You're just like the thousands of other people we talk to every week. And just like them, you're so arrogant, you think your particular hurt is so special that you have to hang onto it and nurture it for as long as you can. Can I ask you something?"

"What?" I said it angrily.

"What will you win?"

"Huh?"

"You get to keep your anger. So what? Sounds like the booby prize to me."

I started to say something; instead I shut up. He had me surrounded. It didn't matter what I said. I'd just be digging the hole deeper. And after a moment, I realized Dr. Davidson was right. "Okay—" I breathed out a sigh, almost of relief, but much more of resignation. "You caught me. So what?"

"You're in a hurry, Jim. I have to be rude just to get you to listen. But do you recognize that I am working toward a result?"

I shrugged. "Yeah, I guess so."

"*That's* compassion. This is what it looks like in action. I'm speaking to the person, not the symptoms."

"Oh," I said.

"You see, you don't have to be damaged to be inappropriate. We're all inappropriate to some degree or other. Usually it's because we don't have all the facts available to us. Sometimes we just haven't learned better. But most of the time, being appropriate is a function of listening to what's going on and responding to what you hear, not to what you *think* you hear. And that's how you *do* sanity."

"Oh," I said. I didn't know if I agreed with that or not.

"I know," said Dr. Davidson. "You don't know if you can accept that definition. That's the usual response—to argue with it, so you can be right about it. Don't be right, Jim. Just look and see how this applies to you and your own circumstances. All right?"

"All right," I said. "I can do that."

"Good. Thank you." Dr. Davidson sounded pleased, as if he'd accomplished something important. "All right, let me give you a couple last facts. Language is the stuff that thinking is made of, right?"

I nodded. "That's old news."

"Accuracy in thinking produces appropriate actions, right?"

"Right."

"Good. So any place that encourages you to practice your communication skills is also a place that will encourage your ability to heal yourself as quickly as you are demanding. This is a good place for you to be, for instance."

"I don't feel healed yet."

"I'm not through yet," Dr. Davidson said calmly. I could hear the smile.

I leaned back in the chair and unfolded my arms. I could play this game too. "Okay, but so far, all we've done is talk about talking. I guess that's some kind of an improvement. I mean, everywhere else in the world, everything feels like an argument."

"When you're there, yes, it does."

"Huh?"

"Have you ever noticed every argument you're involved in has one thing in common?"

"What?"

"*You're* there. You don't get along with anyone, do you?"

"That's not fair—"

"I never promised to be fair. But it's true, isn't it? What kind of payoff are you getting from all those arguments, Jim?"

"I don't understand—"

"You're getting a payoff. A communication channel has to produce a payoff; otherwise you stop investing in it. Why do you think a damaged person will invest so much energy in an inappropriate course of action? Because it produces the only payoff he recognizes. Even a bad payoff is preferable to no payoff at all. Haven't you ever played roulette? This is why damaged people are so annoying to the rest of us. Because they're incapable of going after the good payoffs, they don't recognize them; they insist on playing for the bad ones—and they'll manipulate everybody and everything around them to produce those bad payoffs.

"How *damaged* a person is, Jim, can only be measured by the appropriateness of the payoff he's playing for. *What in hell are you playing for?* That will tell you if you're crazy."

"Fuck you," I said.

"That's a truly appropriate response," Dr. Davidson said quietly.

"And the horse you rode in on."

"—But you still haven't answered the question. What are you playing for?"

"Goddammit! Who are you, anyway? Whyn't you come out from behind that curtain? Who died and appointed you God?"

"Sit down, Jim—"

"No!"

"Why are you so angry at your mother? What did she do to hurt you?"

"She didn't hurt me, dammit! She hurt my father! She punished him! She—didn't care about him! She doesn't care about him now! She—" I stopped. "You son of a bitch. That's none of your business."

"Yes, it is, Jim. You came here, looking for healing. I just showed you where the wound is. Now what are you going to do about it?"

"Nothing—"

"That's about as stupid a thing as you've ever said. Who're you punishing?"

"My relationship with my mother," I said coldly, "is *my* business."

"You don't have a relationship with your mother."

"Well, maybe that's the way I want it."

"I don't think so, Jim."

"Well, you don't get a vote! Thanks for nothing."

The trouble with sliding doors is this: You can't slam them.

I stomped out of the room. I crossed the compound to the pharmacy and paid a hundred dollars for a vial of dream dust.

I had a better idea. I'd put myself out for the rest of the weekend. I wouldn't have to wake up again until it was time to go into the herd.

Q: What do Chtorrans call a fat-farm?
A: An opportunity.

49

Mindwipe

"If you do something often enough, it becomes a habit."
—SOLOMON SHORT

"All right. I'm going to activate the collar," Fletcher said. She turned to the monitor in the back of the Jeep and typed something into the keyboard.

The collar around my neck beeped. Loudly.

"How's the signal?" I asked.

"It's good," she said. "So's your heartbeat and your respiration. All right, I'm going to lock it on." She stepped over to me and did something under my chin, I couldn't see what.

When she stepped back, I tugged at the collar experimentally. It was locked and operating. There was no way I could get it off or turn it off. Not until I was retrieved.

I had the feeling that there was something she wanted to tell me, but when I looked at her she glanced quickly at her watch. "I'm feeling fine," I said.

"I know," she said.

"I had an argument with Dr. Davidson. I spent the weekend high on pink."

"I know." She met my gaze calmly. "It doesn't make any difference."

"It doesn't?"

"Why should it? You're going into the herd. Is there an advantage in being rational?"

"From everything I've heard, it works better if you're crazy—" I stopped myself abruptly.

"Well, there you have it." Her tone was noncommittal.

"I see," I said. So that was the answer.

"You'd better get going," she said.

"Yeah." I took a breath. I began pulling off my shoes and socks. The herd was already starting to form in the plaza. It was going to be a warm day.

I was wearing shorts and a T-shirt. Was that too much? I wondered if I should take the T-shirt off. I glanced to the herd again. There were far more naked bodies than I remembered. I decided to take my cue from the group; I pulled my shirt off and wondered if I should abandon my shorts now too.

I glanced at Fletcher. She looked pensive. "You okay?" I asked.

"Uh-huh," she said.

"You don't look it."

She shrugged. "I was just thinking."

"About?"

"I wish we'd had more time."

I took her hands in mine. "I'll be all right," I said.

"I know you will. I guarantee it."

"No, I mean in here." I tapped my head with my forefinger. "I won't get lost. I promise."

She squeezed my hands and searched my face. "You'd better be right, because I'll break your leg if you're wrong."

"I'll remember that." I glanced over at the herd. Too much nudity. Modesty prevailed. I'd keep the shorts on. For now, anyway. "Well . . ." I said, "I guess I'd better . . ."

"Yeah," she agreed. Suddenly, she put her hands around my neck and pulled my face down to hers. Her lipstick tasted of roses and apricots and sunshine. I broke away, embarrassed. Her kiss had been a little too intense. I turned away quickly to face the herd. If I didn't do it now, I never would. The herd was a great milling mass of humanity.

They were so dirty, I could smell them from here.

I started walking. The dry grass was scratchy under my feet. The sun was hot on my back. My mouth was dry.

I stopped just before the fringes of the herd.

And studied.

I didn't know what I was looking for yet. Some clue. Some *cue*. Something that would tell me how to act.

A group of young bulls was posturing on the lawn. Two of them were casually wrestling. Some of them glanced over at me. There was a knot in my stomach.

I knew this feeling.

It was the first day of kindergarten all over again. The first time having to shower naked with the other boys. The first time with a girl. The first time I saw a worm.

It was the feeling of walking into a roomful of strangers and having them all look at you. Only, it was worse than that. I didn't know if these were animals or people.

They looked like people. They acted like animals.

Apes.

If I could act like an ape, the *right* kind of ape, they'd accept me.

So . . . now I had to figure out how to act like an ape.

"The problem is," I said quietly, "that nobody around here is giving ape lessons."

And then I realized the joke. Nobody ever taught me how to be a human either.

You just are.

I circled around the young bulls wrestling and headed toward a clear space in the center of the plaza. There was a long wide wading pool there. It was the water hole. Some of the children were playing and splashing in one end of the pool. I moved away from them. I found a place away from everybody else and dropped to my hands and knees. I looked to see how the other apes were drinking. Did they cup their hands or did they just lower their faces?

No. I had to find it out for myself.

I lowered my face to the water and drank. The water tasted horrible. Chlorine? And what else? I couldn't tell. I was glad I had my shots.

How do you act like an ape, anyway?

This was the same problem I *always* had with my own species. I never knew how to act.

Other people always seemed to know exactly who they were. I always knew that I was pretending to be who I was. I wanted to stop pretending. I wanted to just *be* a human being. Or an ape. Or whatever it was I had to be.

How did these apes feel about human beings, anyway? Did they resent us studying them? Watching them? Or did they tolerate us? Did they appreciate us feeding them? Or did they even make that connection?

Did they want us to join them? Or did they just allow us to join them because they had no way to keep us from joining them?

Or was it that there was nothing to join?

I started giggling. Wouldn't it be funny if everybody here was trying to act like an ape, just like me? Wouldn't it be funny if we were all pretending?

I wished I could stop thinking. My mind was chattering like a machine. "Chatter, chatter, chatter, chatter . . ." I said. "My mind chatters. Chatters. Chatters. Lumpty lumpty lump."

Nobody even looked at me. None of the apes noticed. Cared. The words were all meaningless. All words were meaningless.

And who made up the meanings for the words in the first place? I had. Who else? All the words and all the meanings in my head were connected with connections I had made. They could all be false. Or worse, just some of them might be false connections. But how could I tell which was which?

Where did it all start, anyway? "Ma, ma, ma, ma, ma . . ." I said. A baby makes noises and gets a warm tit shoved in its face. That's such a powerful lesson that we spend the rest of our lives trying to find the right noises to make so we can keep getting warm tits to suck on. We spend years shrieking and yammering at each other, looking for the right control phrases. Humans have more control phrases than robots. Say, "I love you," and you can get laid. Say, "Fuck you," and you can have a fight. It's as simple as any other machine—

—it clicked.

We treat each other like machines.

We manipulate.

When the apes gave up language, the control phrases didn't work any more. You could push the buttons all you wanted, but the machinery was broken. "Blabber . . . blabber . . . blabber . . ." I felt the grin spreading across my face. This was *very* interesting.

If you said a word over and over and over, and did it long enough, it lost all its meaning. But how do you lose a whole language? How do you detach all the meanings from all the words, the sounds, when you've spent a whole lifetime putting them together? How do you lose even the capacity for language?

"Blabber . . . blabber . . . blabber . . ."

I had the feeling I was doing it wrong.

I was sitting here trying to figure it out.

Maybe this wasn't something you figured out. You just . . . did it. That didn't make sense; but then, figuring it out wasn't making any sense either. I just didn't *know* enough. Maybe if I—

No. Stop figuring it out.

I was a part of the herd now.

Because I said so.

I was the part that was sitting here in red shorts trying to figure out how to be a part of the herd. I was the stupid part. I was trying to figure out how to be what I already was.

I could let go now. I was here.

A teenage boy squatted down in front of me. Uncomfortably close. He was dirty and naked. He had stringy black hair and a large narrow nose. His eyes were extraordinarily wide; they were a startling shade of liquid blue. He stared at me curiously.

"Hi," I said, and smiled. Almost immediately, I knew it was the wrong thing to do. There was too much meaning in the words, and not enough of that *other* quality.

The boy blinked and kept staring at me.

I felt as if I were being tested. As if the herd were some kind of macro-organism looking to see if I had been *assimilated* yet.

The boy scratched himself absentmindedly. His nails were long and dirty. Ape hands. That's what his hands reminded me of. He was skinny like an ape, too. He squatted on his haunches, studying me. I studied back. I stopped trying to figure him out and just focused on him like a camera, watching him. His eyes were remarkably interesting. Too blue to be real. He had thick dark lashes that shadowed his expression with mystery.

But why was he so interested in me? I couldn't tell what he was thinking by looking at his face. He was there—and he was unreadable. His soul was home, I could sense that—somehow—but there was nothing else going on. No . . . thoughts. No . . . identity. It was compelling, just to sit there and look at him looking at me. It wasn't a staring contest. It was a . . . a being with.

Fletcher had had me practice this. Being with. Intensely. I couldn't look away. I didn't want to look away. It was a strangely reassuring encounter.

I realized what it was about his eyes that disconcerted me. They were too *feminine*. If a woman had eyes like that, she would be a model or a movie star. On a boy . . . they were simply overwhelming.

There was a strange kind of peace here.

I could drown in it.

The boy reached out and touched my face. Like an ape, exploring a strange object. He touched my hair, patted it. His hand moved cautiously, drew back quickly. He smelled of dust.

And then he dropped his hand again. And waited.

I don't know how I knew what he was waiting for, but I knew that was an invitation.

I touched his face as he had touched mine. I touched his hair;

I let my fingers drift across his cheek. A smile spread across his face. He reached up and took my fingers in his hand and looked at them. I could see how clean my hand was in his. He sniffed my fingers. His pink tongue flicked out in a tentative, delicate movement and tasted my fingertips. He smiled at me again. He liked the way I tasted. He let go of my hand. And waited again.

Was I supposed to taste his fingers now?

I took his hand in mine. And sniffed it. And tasted. Dirt. I smiled at him.

He smiled back. It was good.

Complete.

The boy stood up then and walked away. Didn't look back to see if I was following. I didn't know why; I followed. Realized I wasn't used to going barefoot. The dry grass hurt my feet.

My body felt . . . held back. Not free. I knew what it was. I stopped and dropped my shorts, stepped out of them. Felt myself begin to disappear. Into the crowd. The herd. All bodies. Had to let go of bodies first. Be naked. Free. Vulnerable.

Accessible. Available.

Beginning to feel enveloped. Like sunshine. Bathe in it. Withhold nothing. Let it go. Giggling. Feeling. Silly.

Crazy. Mind-noise. Wondering what patterns. Meaning. Applying. Here. Confusing. Concepts. Silly. Feeling—

Shook my head. Puzzled.

Startled myself back to reality—

—turned around slowly in confusion.

Looking for?

I wandered in a daze, I wasn't sure how long. I remember stopping to drink at the wading pool again, and I remember emptying my bladder in a sodden ditch at the east end of the park.

I remember getting hungry and finding my way over to the trucks when they rolled into the park. I pulled off a piece of the loaf and found a place to sit and eat.

Blinking. What was—happened?

Moment after moment after moment, but none of them bound together—so none of them are remembered. All lost as soon as they occur. A roller coaster.

No control.

I'd thought I'd understood. I'd thought that I could get a sense of it. I was mistaken.

I had to get out.

I stood up and headed toward the Jeep. Toward where the jeep had been parked. And Fletcher. "I'm coming out," I said. I touched the collar. "This isn't going to work. Fletcher, are you listening? I'm coming out. This is Jim." I touched the collar like an icon. My life depended on it. "Fletcher?"

There was no reply.

Was the collar still working?

It didn't matter. I'd just go straight to the Jeep.

I realized I was naked. Some of them turned to look at me. Then they turned back to their own concerns. Their food. Their mates. Their games. Most of them were naked. Turning.

I didn't see my shorts. I gave up looking. There'd be a blanket at the jeep anyway, or a coat. I stopped and turned around slowly, scanning the edges of the plaza. Now, where—?

—am I?

No, don't panic. It's all right. She's probably monitoring from a distance. That's all. She said it herself, it wouldn't be a good idea for her to stay too close to the herd.

A note in the air. I turned to look.

Children, humming. A tuneless hum, but—

—and the females humming too. Chorusing. An odd atonal wail. All vowels.

Oh, no. No. That wasn't supposed to happen until tomorrow. Oh, God. The gathering. The tuning. It's accelerated again. Two days in a row now!

Others picking up the hum. Discordance. Babbling. Trying to find the note—

I have to get out of here. Now. I turned around in panic.

It was building rapidly. Much too fast. Remembered what happened to me last time. I have to get out of here while I still remember.

And now the males—the voices deep growling at the bottom end of the scale. And the females are unearthly, an almost heavenly chorus. The cubs' voices are high and sweet . . . and curiously musical.

And . . . I could hear what they were trying to do. All of them. It was a resonance in the air, and each one of us was trying to fit his or her own particular note into that resonance.

I turned around and around, looking for the way out, feeling like I was about to dissolve. Turning—

I could feel my own body vibrating in response. I wanted to add my own note. It was in my throat. It came welling up, rumbling like two heterodyning engines. Mmmmmhhhmmmmmhhhmm-mm . . ."

And I found it. It clicked into the chorus and I disappeared into

the sound. The sound was larger than the universe. There was no
me any more. Only the sound. The incredible sound. All the
voices. All together. And. All of us. Echoes of me. I put my note
out and it echoed in all those other throats, all those other bodies.
All the bodies, all the hands, all the bodies turning, not

not lost at all, not

and

turning

found

home

here

cry

happ

ing

Q: How can you tell a Chtorran was born in Vermont?
A: It puts maple syrup on the babies before it eats them.

50

The Black Lady

> *"God and I came to an agreement a long time ago. I don't ask Him to solve my problems, He doesn't ask me to solve His. This arrangement works just fine. God has more than enough to worry about already. So do I."*
> —SOLOMON SHORT

The fat black lady was naked.

She was sitting on an old toilet, laughing and rocking happily. She saw me and began to laugh even harder. Her eyes were twinkling.

I couldn't help myself. I moved closer.

Her breasts were large and voluminous. They shook like jelly with her every movement; when she laughed, they rippled with waves of hilarity. Her nipples were large and black against her chocolate skin.

Her arms were immense, thicker around than my legs. They shook too with great masses of flesh. I found myself grinning. Her thighs were massive. Her hands were balloons. I loved her. Who wouldn't?!

I could feel her joy. It poured from her like light. I wanted to bathe in the light.

She knew I was standing in front of her, watching her. She knew I was smiling with her, but she didn't do anything except watch me and rock and laugh.

I wanted to ask her who she was—except I already knew. She couldn't hide it.

She saw it in my eyes that I knew, and she laughed even harder. She laughed and laughed at the joke. Her joke. *Our* joke.

I laughed too. It was a terrific joke.

We looked at each other and we laughed like crazy. It was the craziest joke in the universe. There we were, the two of us, knowing what we knew about each other, each knowing how silly the other looked, each knowing how silly we looked to the other, each knowing how silly all of everything was—and we laughed and laughed, until we fell into each other's arms.

When the fat black lady hugged you, you stayed hugged.

I was happy in her arms. She loved me. She would hold me forever. I was happy here. She laughed and held me and rocked me and cooed at me.

I whispered, "I know who you are. . . ."

And she whispered back, "And I know who *you* are."

I glanced around at the others and giggled; I looked back to her and whispered again, "We're not supposed to be talking here, are we?"

She boomed with hearty guffaws then and hugged me to her massive breasts. "'S all right, hon-bun. None o' them can hear us. Not 'less we want 'em too." She stroked my hair.

Her nipple was near my mouth. I kissed it, and she laughed. I looked up at her sheepishly. She leaned down to me and whispered, "Don't you stop that, hon-bun. You know your mamma likes it." She lifted her breast toward my mouth and—

—for an instant, I was a baby again, safe and warm and rocking in my mother's arms, happily enraptured—

Mamma loved me. Everything was all right by Mamma. Mamma says yes. Come here and let your Mamma hug you, honey-bunny—

The tears were rolling down my cheeks again.

I looked up at Mamma and asked her, "Why—?"

Her face was kind, her eyes were deep. She brought her hand up to my cheeks and with her massive thumb, she gently wiped my tears away.

"Mamma," I repeated. "Why—why did you let this happen *here*?"

Mamma's face was sad. She whispered to me—something, but I couldn't understand the words—

"Say what, Mamma? I didn't understand—"

Her mouth was moving, but I couldn't—the sounds weren't turning into words—

"Mamma, please—Why?"

"Baba-baba-baba—" The black lady was babbling. She wasn't making sense.

"Mamma-Mamma—" I begged—

But she wasn't Mamma any more. She was just a fat black lady, dirty and smelly. Not laughing, not Mamma, not anyone I knew or wanted to know or—

I was crying again. Again and again for everything I'd lost— but especially for losing my mamma again.

Mamma, please don't leave me—Mamma—

Q: What do you do with a Chtorran who's just eaten 15 babies?
A: Burp it.

51

Globall

"Happiness is not a goal. It's a by-product."

—SOLOMON SHORT

When I was fifteen, I discovered chess.

We had at least thirty different chess-playing programs in the house, including a copy of Grandmaster Plus, the one that finally won the title and held onto it until they changed the rules to exclude artificial intelligence. Most of the programs were public domain, or review copies that had been sent to my dad.

One of the programs, *Harlie,* allowed you to redefine the pieces and the board, so that you could play "fairy" or nonstandard chess. I remembered, I'd never wanted to get involved with chess before, because it had seemed so rigid; but with *Harlie*, I could redefine the game the way I thought it *should* be played. In my own image.

I spent my fifteenth summer inventing new chess pieces and new playing fields.

One piece was the Time Traveler. It leapt forward in time, any number of moves—but they had to be specified at the beginning. If there was a piece on the square when the Time Traveler materialized, both were destroyed. That was how you destroyed a Time Traveler. You parked a pawn on his arrival point.

Another piece was the Gulliver. Gulliver was a giant. He stood on two squares at once, but they had to be the same color, so there was always another square between them. Because the Gulliver straddled, he could only move one leg at a time. You could only kill him by moving an enemy piece between his legs. Preferably the Time Bomb.

Two other pieces were the Magician and the Troll. The Magician moved like a Bishop, but couldn't capture. It moved into position so that another piece was attacking it. If a piece attacked the Magician, even inadvertently, it died. The Troll was the only piece that was safe from the Magician because it couldn't attack anything. It was just a big inert block that could only move one square at a time. It couldn't attack and it couldn't be attacked. It was useful for getting in the way.

I also invented Ghouls and Vampires and Zombies. Ghouls moved through tunnels under the board. Vampires attacked enemy pieces and turned them into Vampires too. Once you started a Zombie moving, you couldn't stop it. It just went on forever.

In order to play a game with all these new pieces, I had to redesign the chessboard. I invented a gigantic spherical playing field with the opposing armies starting the game at opposite poles. I found I had to put in oceans then, blank areas that no piece could move through to allow for edge strategies. Very quickly, I reached the point that the game could only be played on multiple high-resolution terminals. It was the only way to keep track of what was happening on all sides of the globe at once.

Then I added civilians, pieces whose loyalties were unknown until they enlisted on either one side or the other—or were drafted. Civilians always started out as pawns.

I also randomized the initial setups and board layouts to confuse opening-book strategies. It made the opening hundred moves far more tentative.

By the end of the summer, I'd written my own version. It was so big and complex that the strategy part of the program was taking almost five minutes to compute its options and report back its move. And I was running the program on Dad's desktop Cray-9000 with the 2-gigaherz, multiple-gate, 256-channel optical chip, with pseudo-infinite parallel processing. I was more proud than annoyed. I was the only person I'd ever heard of who'd produced a noticeable delay out of a Cray logic processor. But when I showed it to my dad, he pointed out that most of the delay was due to unnecessary branching. I was letting the program test every possible move, sometimes as many as ten moves ahead to see if there was an advantage, before it made its choice. That was when my dad taught me about orchards—in other words, how do you grow a self-pruning matrix of logic trees? He showed me how to implement the search for live and dead branches.

The rewritten version of my fairy-chess program was reporting back its moves even before I'd lifted my fingers from the keyboard. I was very annoyed at my dad for that. Sure, he was only trying to help, and yes, I appreciated the increased speed—but the total absoluteness of the machine's response was ultimately just too intimidating. It made me feel . . . stupid. As if the answer was so obvious, the machine didn't even have to consider it. I finally had to put in a random delay, but it wasn't the same. I still knew.

When I finally sat down to actually *play* the game, I realized that something very interesting had happened.

My perception of chess had shifted.

I no longer saw the game as a board with a set of pieces moving around on it. Rather, I saw it as a set of arrays and values and overlapping matrices of shifting dimensions—and the pieces merely represented the areas of influence and control. The game was not about tactics and strategy any more; it was about options and relationships.

I had a bizarre experience of looking at a chessboard and realizing that it and the pieces were actually unnecessary. They didn't need to exist at all. They were only place-holders in the physical universe, something with which to annotate the actual relationships which the game was truly about.

The pieces weren't the pieces any more—they were their move patterns. A King was a square block, three squares by three. A Queen was a star-shaped radius of power. A Rook was a sliding cross. A Bishop was an X-shape. And I didn't play chess by just studying the pieces any more. I looked instead at the overlapping relationships.

I rewrote my program one more time.

I added an option to display the relative strength of the opposing sides. The pieces were black and white, the areas they controlled were colored red and green. The more a square was under the black control, the redder the square was shown. The more a square was under white's influence, the greener it was displayed. Squares that were equally contested showed up yellow. It became possible to look at the sphere and see all the strong and weak points all at once.

The game was no longer chess. It had become something else. You didn't move your pieces to move pieces, but to change the coloring of the board—to control space. Controlling space was more important than capturing it. Capturing a piece tended to *decrease* the amount of area controlled. The game was won by juggling threats, not actions.

That realization transformed chess for me. The game took on a whole new dimension.

It became a game of balance more than one of action. There were very few actual battles in this game. Mostly it was minor skirmishes. When the end did come, it often came as capitulation before the inevitable. Or sometimes not. Sometimes, there was a flurry of battles that decimated *both* sides. That was usually quick and violent.

I remember, my dad was impressed. He spent more time play-testing the game than I did. Then he sent it out to a play-testing company for their evaluation. I'd almost forgotten about the game when he got their report back. I had already gone back to school, so Dad made a few minor modifications according to PlayCo's recommendations, named it Globall, and put it on the network. I made eighty thousand caseys the first year. Not too shabby. After that, it tapered off to less than a thousand caseys a month, which Dad insisted I put in a college trust.

The point is that there was a moment when chess stopped being chess for me and turned into something else: a perception of the relationships that chess was actually about. The pieces disappeared and all that was left were the patterns.

That's what happened to me in the herd.

I learned to see the patterns.

Q: What do Chtorrans call a swimming pool full of children?
A: Cold soup.

52

Quietude

"When you pass the buck, don't ask for change."

—SOLOMON SHORT

I kept fading in and out of consciousness.

My mind was like something else in my head. It was a voice that wasn't me. I had the weird sensation of not being my own mind any more. Instead, I was just a disembodied listener. All that babbling—it didn't have anything to do with me.

It was a network of connections. A computer made of meat. A reaction machine. Something with a hundred million years of history attached to it. A reptilian cortex. A monkey's reactions.

I remembered, I started laughing, "Help me! I'm trapped inside a human being." And then I cried because it was so sad. Why a human being? Why did God make us into these things? Why hairless apes!!

I could see the horror of it. I had a computer inside my head. A computer that I couldn't shut off. It was a vast, uncontrollable memory-storage-and-retrieval device. It kept bubbling up with thoughts and images and emotions—all those emotions—like bubbles in a tar pit. I felt as if I were drowning. I couldn't escape from it. I wanted to stop listening to it.

And then I did.

All that noise—that wasn't me.

It was as if I could see my own thoughts—so clearly—and how my body automatically followed each thought without question. The mind and body were one. The body was a robot, and I was just the soul trapped inside, watching and listening. I had no control at all. I never had. It was the machinery that ran—even the free-will machinery was automatic.

At first, I thought—

Thought. Hmp. That's funny. Thought. How can you think about thinking without thinking? Thinking is its own trap. But I wasn't thinking any more. I was just . . . looking. Looking to see what was happening.

It was very peaceful . . .

It was . . .

Like—

When I was sixteen, my dad took me to a programmers' convention in Hawaii. Globall paid for it. That was Dad's rule. You could do anything you want, if you could afford it.

The first night we were in Hawaii, we were taken out to dinner by three of the members of the convention committee. We went to one of those revolving restaurants that they always have on top of the tallest hotels. I remember, one of the ladies asked me what I thought of Honolulu, and I told her, I couldn't figure out what it was—but it was *different* somehow. But I couldn't figure out what the difference was.

She smiled and told me to look out the window. I did. I spent a long time studying the twilit streets of Honolulu below us. The cars were the same cars. The buses were the same buses. The street signs, the street lights, all looked the same as I was familiar with in California. Even the style of architecture was familiar. It could have been a suburb of Oakland or the San Fernando Valley.

"I'm sorry," I told her, "I can't tell what it is."

"No billboards," she said.

I turned back to the window and looked again. She was right. There was no outdoor advertising of any kind.

She told me that there was a state law prohibiting signs larger than a certain size. She said that was one of the reasons Hawaii always seemed so quiet to tourists. You walk down a city street anywhere else in the world and you're bombarded with advertising, so you learn to "tune it out." All that advertising is like a steady chattering noise in your ears. In order to function, we have to make ourselves deliberately blind and deaf to that part of our environment. The advertisers know that we do this, so they increase the size, the color, the intensity, and the repetitions of their ads. They give us more, better, and different ads. And we tune them out even harder.

But . . . when we get to a place where that channel of mind-noise is missing, the silence is suddenly deafening. She told

me that most people don't even notice that the signs are there, but
they notice that something is wrong when they're not. Like you
did, she said, they experience it as quietude.

"I like it," I said.

The herd is quietude.

Until you've experienced quiet, you can't know how loud the
noise is. It's all the mind-noise in the world that keeps us crazy.
All that constant mind-chatter is so distracting that it keeps us
from seeing the sky, the stars, and the souls of our lovers. It keeps
us from touching the face of God.

In the herd, you detach from all that noise—it floats apart from
you—and all that's left is a joyous feeling of emptiness and light.
It's so *peaceful*.

I think that's why people go to the herd. For the peace. That's
why I did. That's why I want to go back.

Q: What do Chtorrans call an obstetrician?
A: A caterer—he delivers.

53

A New Space

"Humanity persists in spite of itself."
—SOLOMON SHORT

I remember the screaming.

All that screaming. Everyone. And running too. I remember the running. All of us. Why? Melted canyons. Broken pavements. Scattering. Gunshots. Sirens. Roaring sounds. Purple sounds.

I remember hiding.

I remember a dirty place, bad-smelling. Brackish water, gathered in pools. I remember hunger. Wandering. Searching. Looking for the herd again.

I remember someone screaming at me. Making loud sounds in my ear. Slapping my face. Hurts! Piled-on hurts! Don't slap me!

I remember crying—

And slaps—more slaps—

Until finally, I screamed—"Goddammit! Stop that!"

"Oh, thank God! He's coming back."

I remember—

"Jim! Look at me!" Someone grabbed my chin, tilted my face up. A female. Dark hair. Grim face. "Jim! Say my name!"

"Wha—? Wha—?" Make sounds. "Wah—?"

Slap! Tears in my eyes.

"Wah—?" I try again. "Wah—?"

Another slap!

I remember screaming.

She holds my face and screams right back at me.

If I can only find the *right* scream—I had it once—"Goddammit, Fletcher! Stop it already! You're hurting me!"

"Who am I?"

"You're—Fletcher! Now leave me alone!" I want to climb back under and pull the covers over my head again.

"And who are you?"

"Uh—"

"Come on, James! Who are you?"

"I—I . . . name?"

"Come on, you're doing fine! Who are you?"

"I was . . . Jame—"

"Who?"

"Jame—no, James. Edward."

"James Edward who?"

"Who?"

"That's right. Who?"

"Who? Who?" It's soft and warm down here. "Who? Who. Whoo—"

Slap! My face rings, stings.

"Who are you?"

"James Edward McCarthy, Lieutenant United States Army, Special Forces Warrant Agency, on special assignment! Sir!" Maybe that will satisfy her. Maybe now she'll leave me alone.

"Good! Come on back, Jim. Keep coming back!"

"No, goddammit! I don't want to come back! I want to finish my dream!"

"It's over, Jim! You're awake! You can't go back to sleep!"

"Why—?"

"Because it's Saturday."

"Saturday?! You were supposed to pick me up on Thursday."

"We couldn't find you!"

"But the collar—?" I looked at her. Confused.

"Yes, the collar. Where is it, Jim? Do you remember?"

I reach for my neck. The collar is gone. I'm naked. Shivering. Cold. "Um—" More confused now.

Fletcher is wrapping a blanket around me. I'm starting to fade again. I have to say something, quickly. "I—uh—how did . . . you find me?"

"We've been watching the herd. We've been hoping you'd find your way back. Luckily, you did."

"Find . . . my way *back*?"

"Some yahoos from down the coast came in looking for some cheap and dirty sex. They ended up stampeding the whole herd. We've had deaths and injuries. It's the worst. Are you following this?"

"Yes!" I say quickly.

She lowers her hand. Lowered her hand. My time sense is—was coming back.

Somebody put a mug in my hand. It was hot. I drank automatically. Bitter. Coffee? No. I made a face. "What is this shit?"

"It's ersatz."

"Ersatz what?"

"Ersatz shit. We couldn't afford the real stuff."

"This is offal," I said. And grinned suddenly, "Hey—I'm alive again. I made a pun. This is offal. Get it? O-F-F-A-L?"

Somebody behind me groaned. Fletcher grinned. She said, "I never thought I'd be *happy* to hear someone make a pun that bad. It's a good sign. You're coming back into the language again."

I looked into Fletcher's eyes. As if I'd never seen her before. They were bright and deep. I spoke directly to her I said, "Fletch, I *understand* what's going on here. I don't know if you can understand it without experiencing it, but I know what it is now because I've been through it. It's terrifying—and it's wonderful—and I want to go back—and I want you to keep me from going back. It—" I pointed at the milling bodies behind us. "That—could be the end of the human race. That could get out of control. Very easily. It's got to be broken up, Fletcher. I don't know how, but it's got to be broken up."

"What is it? Can you explain it?"

I took a breath, I looked at the herd, then looked back to Fletcher. "No, I can't. I can make some guesses. I can describe what happened to me. But . . . any explanation would only be a tiny slice of the truth, not even a cross section of it. But . . . somehow, when you're in the herd, you know that words don't have any meaning any more. They're just sounds. All the meanings fall away. It gets detached. You can find the meanings if you have to, but—no—" I shook my head and waved my hand as if to erase everything I'd said. I took another drink of the terrible ersatz. "That's not right either."

I looked back up into her eyes. She was beautiful. I could mate with her. Now why did that thought come up? "It's—it's a kind of primal humanity, out there. Listen—there's a . . . space that's been created and defined over there. And in that space, you stop being a human being like we know human beings and start being a human being like *they* know human beings. Over there, the apes have the agreement.

"It's like . . . humanity has decided that thinking *doesn't* work and has abandoned it. To try something else instead. It's like a kind of telepathy, Fletcher; it envelops you. The closer you go, the easier it is to escape from the language. It's like letting go of a particular madness. Like language is a mental disease that we all agreed to share. Over there, they've created a new agreement—that they can be a species without thinking, without language, without concept. They exist totally in a moment-to-moment state. It's—I'm explaining it again, aren't I? We keep getting trapped in our explanations. That's our minds."

She stopped me with a finger on my lips. "Shh," she said. "Catch your breath. Take your time."

I ran a hand through my hair. It was matted. God knew what I looked like.

"What did it *feel* like, Jim?"

"It felt like . . . this is weird . . ." I looked at her and I could feel the tears coming to my eyes. "It felt like . . . freedom. As if my mind were a parasite in my body somehow. And for a while, I'd gotten free of it. And now that it's recaptured me, I have this . . . terrible *grief,* this . . . profound sadness." I looked back to the herd again. "They're so . . . happy over there." The tears burst from my eyes again.

She hugged me to her. I was oblivious to everything else except the warmth and the smell of her. She smelled like flowers. There were men standing around us. I didn't care. I let the tears flow. I buried my head against her breasts and sobbed. Why? Why the tears?

She stroked my hair. I could feel how greasy I was, but she didn't seem to mind. She said, "You want the official explanation?"

"What's the official explanation?" I asked.

She wrapped her arms around me and said, "The official explanation is that we haven't finished grieving for the world we've lost. The pre-plague years. How do you deal with the death of a whole planet?" She left the question echoing in the silence.

I found the mug again. The ersatz was cool enough to drink now, cool enough to taste. I could almost get used to the taste of it. In another hundred years or so. I pulled the blanket around me.

"How are you feeling now?" Fletcher asked.

"Fine," I said. "Really." I looked at the sky, I looked at the herd. They were starting to head into what was left of Brooks Hall, their stable for the night. "I should be going to bed too . . ." I looked to Fletcher, hopefully.

"Yes," she agreed. "But not with them. Not any more." She

nodded to someone and they helped me into the ambulance and we headed back to Oakland.

Q: What's the Chtorran national sport?
A: Hide and eat.

54

Coffee

"The nice thing about self-love is that it's hardly ever unrequited."

—SOLOMON SHORT

They kept me up the whole night, talking.

They filled me full of coffee—someone found some of the real stuff; I threatened to clam up if they handed me another cup of the ersatz—and they kept me talking.

I kept begging Fletcher to let me go to sleep, but she kept saying, "Not yet. Just a little while longer."

"Why? What are you waiting for?" I could hear the whining in my voice. I hadn't whined since I was five.

Finally, she admitted, "We want to make sure that you'll wake up human. We need to see that your brain is responding to language again. When you sleep, you let go of language. In the morning, we want to make sure you'll pick it up again."

"I'll be . . . all right," I said. "I think you can trust me now."

"Would you bet your life on it?"

"Huh?"

"If you don't wake up human tomorrow, can we kill you?"

"Say again?"

"I said, 'If you don't wake up human tomorrow, can we kill you?' Are you that certain?"

"Uh—" I held out my cup. "Can I have some more coffee?"

Fletcher grinned and took the cup from me. "You're fine." But she refilled the mug anyway. "We were thinking about leaving a radio on for you, low-level—but there're two schools of thought on that. One is that it will help keep you tuned to language. The other is that it will be just another babbling voice in the background and will encourage you to start tuning out again." She sighed. "Ultimately, it comes down to this: It's up to *you*. At some level, James, it's going to be your choice."

She turned my face to hers. "Do you understand? I know that you want to go back. You're going to have to resist the pull. Can you? Will you?"

I lowered my eyes. Her gaze was too intense to look at. I wanted to hide from it. "I think I can," I said. I looked back up at her. "I'll try."

"Don't try. Do it." She took my chin and turned my face to hers. "I am *not* going to lose you, do you understand?"

I nodded. All the words seemed so feeble somehow, but it was words she wanted most from me. I felt trapped.

"Do you want some help?" she asked.

"What kind?"

"Just a trick. Use your name as a mantra. Do it as you're falling asleep. Chant your name over and over again. I am James Edward McCarthy. I am James Edward McCarthy. And so on."

"Why? What will that do?"

"It'll set some instructions running that will help you tune back in tomorrow. Every day it'll get a little easier. Will you do it?"

"Yeah," I said. "I'll feel silly, but I'll do it."

"Good." She leaned over and kissed me on the forehead. "I'll let you sleep now."

As I drifted off, I found my body curling familiarly around a pillow. I wondered who I was missing. Who had curled up with me in the herd? I remembered the curve of a spine. The feel of skin. Liquid eyes. I missed—

I drifted back into wakefulness, missing my mate. Finding myself in a strange white place. Wearing a stiff white cloth. And—

"James Edward McCarthy!" I said. "My name is James Edward McCarthy!" And started laughing. It worked.

I found a jumpsuit in the closet. The ubiquitous army jumpsuit. And a pair of slip-ons. Good enough for what I had to do.

First thing, I had to let Fletcher know I was back.

Second. I had a dance to plan.

Q: What do Chtorrans call Amtrak?
A: Fast food.

55

The Asterisk

*"It is impossible to wean kittens. Wait till
their claws get sharp enough and the cat
will do the job herself."*

— SOLOMON SHORT

But before I could do anything, General Poole summoned me to
his office. I felt embarrassed wearing just the jumpsuit.

General Poole didn't get up from his desk; he just pointed to a
chair and asked, "Whose idea was it for you to go into the herd?"

"Mine," I said.

He shook his head. "In mah day, Lieutenant, that little stunt
would have bought you a Section Eight discharge. Ah expect
better behavior than that from mah officers."

"Yes, sir." I said. I resisted the temptation to tell him his day
was past.

"However," he continued, "this particular operation comes
from the Science Section, so perhaps you feel that the opinions of
your superior officers in the military aren't applicable. Is that
correct?"

"No, sir." I wondered what he was getting at. "It was my
understanding that I'd been authorized by the mission commander, Colonel Tirelli."

The general didn't respond to that. He adjusted his glasses on
his nose and peered at the file on the desk in front of him. "You
are a science officer, is that right?"

"Yes, sir."

"You have your degree?"

"No, sir. Not yet."

"Do you have a target date?"

"Three years, sir. I've been averaging one course every six to eight weeks. Three hours a day at a terminal, six days a week, I think I'm making pretty good progress. I'm a little behind right now, but I intend to get caught up right after this mission."

"Mm-hm. The mission." General Poole closed the folder and raised his face to mine again; his glasses made his eyes look small and mean. "Let me be candid, Lieutenant. Ah wouldn't start any trilogies if Ah were you."

"Sir?"

"This mission tomorrow—it looks like suicide on a shingle to me."

"With all due respect, sir, I don't agree."

"Of course not. But the fact remains, this mission is . . . of dubious military value. Do you understand what that means? That's why Ah let you volunteer."

"Huh?"

He tapped the folder with one forefinger. "You've got an asterisk."

"Yeah," I agreed. "I'm sitting on it." I regretted the pun instantly.

General Poole looked annoyed. "An asterisk is a little star-shaped mark. In this case, it means that you can be put in life-threatening situations."

"Terrific," I said. "How did I earn that?"

"Couple of ways." He ticked them off on his fingers. "One: You could be a telepath. Are you?"

"Not that I know of. Not unless someone snuck up behind me when my back was turned and gave me a secret implant."

"Hmp. Not bloody likely. Two: You got someone pissed off at you. Have you done that?"

"That I've done," I admitted.

"Or . . . three: You've demonstrated that you're a survivor. And that you can be trusted to produce results. Unfortunately, not all the asterisks are annotated. We'll have to find out which kind you are by sending you north."

"Yes, sir. Thank you, sir."

"Not so fast, Lieutenant. The purpose of this meetin' is a little old-fashioned fine tunin'. Call it an . . . attitude adjustment." The general picked up a pencil and held it delicately between his two hands.

"An . . . attitude adjustment?"

"That's right. How well do you think you can do your job if your loyalties are divided?"

"Sir? I'm afraid I don't understand."

General Poole looked across his desk at me. "Ah'll say it in English, son. I appreciate your scientific contributions, but—Ah want you to remember also that you are *still* a soldier in the army of the United States of America."

"I don't see the conflict, sir." I said hesitantly. "It seems to me that both the Science Section and the military are committed to the same thing—"

The general looked skeptical.

"—aren't they?"

"You tell me, Lieutenant. What's the purpose of this mission?"

I quoted from the briefing book: " ' . . . to establish a contact relationship with the bunnydogs and/or the gastropedes with the eventual goals of opening a channel for communication.' Sir." I added.

"Mm-hm," he said thoughtfully. "And what's the usual purpose of the military mission?"

"Uh—" I suddenly realized what he was getting at. "The destruction of the Chtorran ecology."

"That's right." He looked at me calmly. "Some people want to talk to these creatures—and some people want to kill them. Ah'd like to know, Lieutenant, what are your feelin's in the matter."

I was staring down the barrel of a 45-caliber loaded question. "I—I'm on the side of humanity, sir."

"And what does that mean? Are you committed to killin' worms or not?"

"It means, I want to do what will save the most lives."

"And you think that talkin' to the worms or the bunnies might do that?"

"I don't know. That's what we want to find out."

"But you do think there might be an alternative to killin' them? Isn't that so?"

I swallowed hard and met his gaze. "Yes, sir—I'm willing to try."

"Ah see. Well, let me tell you somethin', Lieutenant. The trouble with that kind of thinkin' is that it diverts precious resources of time and materiel. If we can just talk to the agency that's behind the Chtorran infestation, p'haps we can work out some kind of *negotiation.* I've even heard some people talkin' about *sharing* the planet with them."

"Sir— ?" I started to say.

"Share!" he continued over my protestations. "Why the hell should they? They're already winnin' the whole ball game! Why should they stop to negotiate a draw?"

"Maybe they don't know we're here!" I flustered. "Maybe they made a mistake. Maybe—"

"You don't kill five and a half billion human beings by mistake."

"We don't know that—"

The general looked astounded. "You don't think we're at war?"

"I know we're at war, sir! I just— "

"And you want to *talk* to the enemy?"

Was he deliberately baiting me? "Yes! I do! I want to find out who the enemy is! Maybe they're just as curious about us—"

"Y'know, that's the trouble with you—and with the rest of your so-called experts. You want to study everythin'. You want to question it. And you want to piss away our time! Sometimes Ah wonder just who's side you're really on—"

I stood up. "Goddammit! This may cost me my assignment—but if you're mad at someone, tell them! Not me! I just want to do the job I was trained for! The United States Army wants me to study the worms and the millipedes and the bunnydogs and all the other Chtorran creatures. Yeah, I'll admit it—I'm fascinated by them. These are the first extraterrestrial life-forms that humanity has ever encountered. But don't you go making assumptions about my loyalties, sir! That offends me. I want the Chtorrans off this planet just as much as you do, but I'm also realistic enough to recognize that might not be possible. If it isn't, I want to know how to survive among them. And if it *is* possible to neutralize the Chtorran infestation, you won't find anyone more dedicated than myself. I'll burn worms till you pry the torch out of my hands! You've got my record there on your desk—you look and see! But I can't stand people making up their minds about a subject before all the facts are in!" I added politely, "Sir!"

And sat down.

The general applauded. He grinned. "Not bad. You throw almost as good a tantrum as Ah do. You could use a little polishin'—but experience will take care of that."

Blink. "I beg your pardon, sir?"

"Son, sit down and listen for thirty seconds. It doesn't matter how Ah feel about this joyride. Nobody's listenin' to my opinion. Ah think you're a damn fool and Ah think this is a waste of valuable time. But the Science Section has given this a triple-A priority, so like Ah said, it doesn't matter what Ah think.

"But—" he continued, "you are still under my command—and Ah am responsible for your life. So, if nothin' else, Ah want to know that you're sure about what you're doin'. Ah don't have to be sure, but you do. Ah've found that a little bit of certainty makes a lot of difference in the results you produce."

"Yes, sir."

"It looks to me like you're actually willin' to put your life *and your career* on the line. Ah'm impressed, Lieutenant. With that kind of intention, you just might have a chance of comin' back. But—" he added, "Ah still wouldn't start any trilogies."

"Yes, sir. Thank you, sir." I felt like I should be looking for the Dormouse and the March Hare. "Uh—would you like to hear about my plan? I'm very well prepared."

He shook his head. "No. Ah'm going to trust you."

"But I really think you should."

"Lieutenant, don't press your luck. It might be a very stupid plan. And then Ah'd have to reconsider my decision. No, Ah think Ah'll bet on your certainty more than your intelligence. And Ah will trust Colonel Tirelli's faith in you. Have a nice trip."

He stood up and reached across the desk to shake my hand. I had to stand up again to grab it. "Uh, thank you, sir."

"Oh, one more thing. It might be some small comfort to know, if you get killed, you'll be automatically promoted one rank. It'll be a consolation for your family."

"Uh, thanks. What about if I live?"

"We'll talk about it when you get back. Now, get the hell out of here. Ah have some real work to do." He sat down again and I left, shaking my head and marveling.

Q: Why did the Chtorran eat Mt. Everest?
A: Because it was there.

56

How To Be a Monkey

> *"This neurotic pursuit of sanity is driving
> us all crazy."*
>
> — SOLOMON SHORT

Fletcher spent most of a week training me.

On the morning of the first day, she showed me how to listen.

"It's about listening with your whole soul—" she began.

"You have to listen so completely," I said, "—that you become the person you're listening to."

She looked at me surprised. "Who told you that?"

"A telepath."

"Well, he/she was right."

On the afternoon of the first day, she defined *bullshit:*

"You use that word all the time, James—but you don't even know what it means. 'Bullshit' is a colloquialism. We use it to say that something is *inaccurate*. A lie is bullshit. An excuse is bullshit. A justification, a rationalization, a reason, an explanation. All bullshit. Anything you use to excuse yourself from being responsible.

"From this moment on, any time you are inaccurate, any time you let bullshit fall from your mouth, I will bust your chops. You got that?"

On the morning of the second day, she showed me how to listen even more deeply than before.

"Close your eyes and actually *look* at how you're feeling. Look at your emotions. Look at what your body is doing. Look at the memories that come floating up to the top. Pick an incident from your memory, or make one up. Look at the incident—and notice what your machinery is doing. Notice how you feel. Notice what your body is doing. Notice what memories are connected—"

We did that all morning.

On the afternoon of the second day, we talked about righteousness:

"Do you know that most people, when they tell you something, they're really just second-guessing? They're trying to figure it out afterward, explain it or justify it—and, ultimately, prove themselves *right*. Listen, that kind of *right* is the enemy. When you try to be right like that, you add inaccuracy. The specific word is righteousness.

"You can't make yourself right without making the other person wrong—that automatically makes him your enemy. It doesn't give him room to do anything else. You can't go out into that circle being right about being human. You can't take your pain and grief and rage into that circle. The bunnies want to *communicate*, not have a shrieking match with the monkeys at the waterhole.

"You cannot have enemies in that circle, James—only partners."

On the morning of the third day, she showed me how to center my sense of my*self*.

"Did your telepathic friend tell you about identity?"

I nodded.

"Then you know that you are not what you *think*. You are the person who hears the thoughts. The question is whether or not you're really listening.

"Do you know there are three levels of listening? First, you hear the sound. Second, you hear the meaning. And third, you hear the meaning under the meaning. You can't be 'centered' unless you're listening on all three levels—"

"This is starting to get confusing—"

"I know. A lot of it comes from the telepathy training, and more of it comes from the Mode Training. I know it's a break in your reality—the reality that you've made up for yourself. You can't get out of that reality, James; all you can do is learn how it works. That's the point here. All of this information comes from looking at how people experience things and how they react·to them. Call it the technology of living. You've been running your machinery without an instruction book—"

On the afternoon of the third day, we talked about concepts:

"Your *name* for this object is 'chair.' This is not a chair. This is a collection of molecules, a focus for your attention. This is a *thing* that you use for the purpose of *chair,* but the chair*ness* of it exists only in your mind. It's a concept.

"This object is a chair only to the extent that it matches that concept. If you were cold enough, this would not be a chair any more. It would be firewood—well, not *this* chair, but you know what I mean. Do you follow this? See, you think the connections you've made between your concepts and the physical universe have meaning. They don't—only in your head. If you believe the world is flat, does that make it flat? No, of course not.

"Now I'll ask a hard question. If you believe the world is round, does that make it round? Take your time. Right—what you believe is irrelevant. The Earth is an oblate spheroid; and it doesn't care what you believe. You don't get a vote on the physical universe. It is what it is, regardless of your opinion about how it should or shouldn't be. The only thing you have any control over is what *you're* going to do about it—"

On the morning of the fourth day, we talked about *creation:*

"Creation is *not* making something up out of nothing. You can't create in the physical universe—the best you can do is reorganize its molecules. No, *real* creation happens in here—" She reached over and tapped my head.

"Creation is the act of discrimination. You separate this from that and you have created a space between them. Creation is also the act of connection. You connect this *to* that and you have created a new entity or a new relationship. Creation is the act of drawing a line. Nothing more. You use the line to connect or separate or enclose; but you're the one who drew the line in the first place.

"The question is, what do you want to create? What kind of line do you want to draw? Do you want to draw a circle around humans and bunnydogs? Do you want to draw a line between humans and worms? How are you going to make it up? You need to be clear about the circle you're creating before you walk into it."

And in the afternoon of the fourth day, we *created.*

"Are you ready for the last lesson, James?"

"Yes."

"It's bad news."

"I can handle it."

"All right. This is it. You're a monkey."

"Huh?"

"I'll get you a mirror. Your umpty-great-grandmomma and umpty-great-grandpoppa swung naked in the trees and lived on bananas and coconuts. You're their umpty-great-grandson. You live in a house, but you still like bananas and coconuts. And if we took away your clothes, you could climb back into the trees and nobody would ever know the difference. Are you getting this?"

"I'm not sure. What's the point?"

"The point is, you're a monkey. You are—or at least, you think you are—the dominant species on this planet. That may be a conceit. It's ultimately irrelevant. You can't go out there thinking that. You can't go out there being anything but a monkey, because that's all you are. A monkey. You are not a representative of all humankind. Most humanity doesn't even know you exist, and if it did know, it probably wouldn't want you as its representative."

"You have a great way of pumping me up."

"Listen, you have to operate in the real world. Out there it will be a circle and some bunnydogs. And you are a monkey. A naked monkey. You have to go out there and be a monkey meeting a bunnydog. That's all you can be. You can't speak for any other monkey on this planet. Are you getting this?"

"Yes, I think so."

"Good." She looked at me. "So what are you?"

"A monkey." I scratched myself in a monkey gesture and made an "eee-eee" sound.

She grinned. "Mates and bananas, James. That's the bottom line. Remember that. There's not a lot else for monkeys."

"So, do I eat the bunnydogs or screw them?"

"That's up to you," she said. "Now—look, you need to be clear about what monkeys do. What happens when a monkey comes up against something new, something outside of its experience? What's the very first thing that happens?"

"Um . . . it shrieks. I shriek."

"Yeah—startlement. That's where the human race has been with the infestation. We're still running around startled. What comes after startlement?"

"Fear. Obviously."

"Mm-hm. Good. You did your reading. A monkey has only two responses, James. Yipe and Goody. There aren't any others. Everything is variations on that. There isn't an animal on this planet that doesn't have that basic mechanism hard-wired into its cerebral cortex. That's your machinery. You can't *not* react with yipe or goody. And most of the time, just to be on the safe side, you react with yipe. So you spend ninety-nine percent of your life running your yipe machine. And it doesn't matter how much intelligence you've superimposed on it, James. The intelligence doesn't control the machine, it serves the machine. The intelligence only expresses the yipe on a higher level."

She pointed forward. "Those creatures out there—those bunnydogs—no matter what kind of animals they are, no matter what kind of culture they operate in, no matter who they pretend to be—they have the same machinery. Or equivalent machinery. Or they wouldn't be there. I'm talking about basic survival machinery. If you don't have a yipe machine you don't survive. Evolution automatically produces a yipe machine. So, what you need to know is that those creatures out there are as scared of you as you are of them."

I nodded my agreement.

She continued, "What comes after fear?"

I thought about it. "Running?"

"No—let's say you can't run from the thing you're afraid of. What do you do next?"

"Um . . . I get angry?"

"Are you asking me or telling me? What happens when someone threatens you and threatens you and threatens you?"

"I get angry."

"Right. Anger. After fear comes anger. How do you act out anger?"

I bared my teeth at her. I growled.

She grinned. "Right. You counterattack. You start by baring your teeth and growling and making terrible faces. If that doesn't work, you start screaming and shrieking. And if that doesn't work, you start throwing coconuts. In other words, you put on a performance of rage. All monkeys do. You do it when your survival is threatened—or the survival of anything you identify with, anything you consider as part of your identity.

"It's all part of the automatic machinery. If you scare away the thing that you're angry at, then the machinery worked; you survived. At the very worst, you might have to fight, but most of the time a good performance of anger is all that's necessary to *prevent* a fight. There. I've just told you everything you need to know to understand international politics."

She let me appreciate the truth of that joke for a moment, then she continued, "That may be fine for monkeys, James. It may even be fine for human beings, though I doubt it. It is definitely *not* fine for dealing with worms. That's what you need to know.

"Some of us are moving through fear and are starting to move into anger toward the Chtorrans. It could be a fatal mistake. Running doesn't help. And there are no goodies. So, the next step is rage."

"I know—I've seen it—"

"Go on. Tell me, what's rage?"

"Rage is the fighting machine gearing up."

"Right," she said. "And we know we can't fight the worms, can we? They've already demonstrated that we can't outfight them. So, what comes next, James?"

"Uh—"

"What comes after rage, James?"

"I don't know—"

"Come on, what happens after you've been arguing the same argument for a week?"

"I don't know about you, but I get bored."

"Right. Boredom." She nodded with satisfaction. "After you've raged and raged and raged and used up all your energy and frustration, suppose the thing you're frightened of, angry at, raging at, is still sitting there picking its teeth and grinning at you. That's when you get tired of being angry. We call that boredom. Or annoyance. But now that you've given up being angry, there's room for you to actually become *interested* in that thing—whatever it is—that scared you in the first place. That's how the machinery works. It isn't until you let go of the yipe that you have room for the goody, right?"

"Right."

"That's the machinery, James. That's what you're operating on top of. You can't stop it from running. You never could. Now, why do you think I'm telling you all this?"

"So, I can—uh . . . well, the object of this is to establish communication, so this is about not letting the monkey machinery get in the way of the communication. Right?" I grinned; I knew it was.

"Right." She grinned right back. "I want you to finish being afraid and angry and bored in here. Don't take that into the circle or that's what the circle will be about. When you give up all that stuff—what can you do?"

I shrugged. "Nothing, I think."

"Don't be flip. What can you do after you give up all those monkey-machine reactions?"

I shrugged again. "Have a party?"

"That's exactly right. After all that other stuff is taken care of, there's nothing left to do but play together. You make up a game—call it business or marriage or United States Congress—but it's still only a very fancy game played by very fancy monkeys. So . . . do you know what you have to do in that circle?"

"Make up a game for monkeys and bunnies."

"You got it. That's all you have to do. If you're fun to play with, the communication will take care of itself."

"Yes, I see—I really do." I was marveling at the simplicity of it. "I have to leave my rifle behind. I have to leave my military mind-set behind. I have to even leave my scientist act behind. I have to just—I see it!—I have to just go in there as a monkey who wants to play, don't I?"

"Congratulations." She beamed at me and shook my hand. "As Chief Medical Officer of this operation, I hereby pronounce you fit for duty. You are the *best* chimpanzee in the United States Army." She handed me a banana.

"Only a banana?" I asked. "Don't I get a mate?"

"That, James, is part of the graduate course."

Q: What's the Chtorran word for Jacuzzi?
A: Cup O'Soup.

57

Lizard

"Every time you fall in love, it's the first time."

—SOLOMON SHORT

The final meeting of the presentation team took place at eighteen hundred hours.

Colonel Tirelli, Dr. Fletcher, Dr. Larson, three staff members I didn't recognize, the two women on the audio-video team, five observers, three mission specialists, six pilots, two programmers, two spider handlers, and the weapons team. I almost felt crowded.

There wasn't a lot of business that needed to be handled. Even Dr. Fletcher admitted that. We checked the weather forecasts, narrowed our choice of target sites—we'd make the final selection tomorrow morning—and then opened it up for questions. There weren't a lot.

Colonel Tirelli took over then and asked if anyone wanted to reconsider their decision to participate. This was a strictly volunteer operation and if anybody present wanted to drop out, they could do so now—or they could see her privately if they preferred. "You have until—" she looked at her watch, considered, and said, "twenty-one hundred hours. There are backup people available, I assure you—so don't feel that you *have* to do this. The operation is dangerous, so do consider your participation carefully. If I don't hear from you by twenty-one hundred hours, I will assume that you have made a complete and total commitment. Did everyone understand that?"

Affirmative nods.

"Well, then—that seems to be it. Does anyone here have anything else to add?"

No. No one.

"Good. Thank you—and good night! Get yourself a good dinner, get to bed early, and get a good night's sleep!"

Most of the team headed for the doors. I headed for the front of the room. Colonel Tirelli was conferring softly with two of her pilots, so I waited politely to one side. When she finished, she looked up and saw me. "Yes, McCarthy?"

"May I talk to you privately?"

Her eyes shaded. "You want to drop out?"

"No! It's just—"

"If it's not about the mission tomorrow—"

"It's something that could *affect* the mission tomorrow." I said it as pointedly as I could.

"Mm-hm. Wait a minute—" She handed her clipboard to one of her aides and then took me out into the hall, around the corner, and into a deserted office. She closed the door behind us and leaned back against a desk, leaving an uncomfortable distance between herself and me. "What is it?" she said. Her expression was polite, curious—and very, very cold.

I felt myself flushing. "I—I guess this is a personal thing," I started. "But it's really getting to me. I mean, what's going on?"

She blinked as if she didn't know what I was talking about. "I don't understand."

"We had a date planned, remember? You and I and the biggest lobster on the West Coast, remember? I mean, you said some things in the chopper—and I don't know if that was for serious, or if it was just . . . well, you know, real casual, or what?"

Lizard noticed an ink smudge on her palm. She rubbed at it with her thumb. She wasn't looking at me as she remarked, "That's what I like, a question with a lot of certainty in it." She shoved her hands into her pockets and looked up at me. "Listen, McCarthy. Everything I said to you in the chopper was true. You're cute. You're probably fun in bed. And you're also a lieutenant. One thing I know about lieutenants is that they have permanent erections. It's convenient at times. Most of the time it's not. Your problem is that you're trying to think with your erection. Please don't. It wasn't designed for that."

I stared at her. I wanted to ask, "Who are you really and what have you done with Lizard Tirelli?" Instead, I merely opened my mouth and said, "Is that it—?"

"For now." She looked at her watch. "Don't you have one more meeting tonight?"

"I have some kind of counseling session, yeah—"

"Well, I suggest you get to it." Her expression was impassive.

I could see that even being confused would be a waste of time here. I shook my head and stepped past her to the door. Halfway through it, I turned back to her. "This does not make sense to me. And it sure doesn't make me confident about tomorrow."

"I'm sorry, McCarthy—but that's the way it has to be."

"Yeah, sure." I closed the door behind me. Colonels! I'd never understand them.

I found Fletcher back in the meeting room. "Listen, about this counseling session—"

She shook her head. "I'm not your counselor, James. I have nothing to do with that."

"Well . . . listen, I just want to skip it. I don't feel—"

Fletcher's face hardened. "You do and you don't go tomorrow. You get your ass downstairs, right now!" She turned to one of her assistants. "Jerry, will you escort Lieutenant McCarthy down to the basement? Make sure he gets there."

I remembered Jerry Larson from Denver. He'd lost some weight and cut his hair; it made him look more intelligent than I remembered.

He led me down three flights of stairs (it was faster than the elevator), past the holding tanks (four worms), through the uncatalogued specimen section, and into the greenhouse.

The air smelled overpoweringly sweet. On either side, behind thick glass walls, I could see banks of purple and red plants.

"See that one?" Larson pointed to a shapeless black bush as tall as a man. Its leaves were ragged and shaggy. Whatever form or structure the plant had was impossible to see; it looked like a big pile of dirty laundry. "That one walks. Very slowly. We call it a shambler. It feeds on carrion. It's probably a scavenger. I don't think it kills—but we've got it isolated just in case."

"What're these?" I pointed to the opposite side. The plants there were more colorful. Banks of red and yellow blossoms cascaded across the tables.

"Oh—" said Larson. "We call those mandala vines. You have to look at them close up. You see those blossoms? Each one is made up of hundreds, perhaps thousands, of miniature blossoms all clustering together."

"They're gorgeous—" Even from this side of the glass, I was dazzled. The blossoms were pink and scarlet and purple; but they were also speckled with yellow and orange and white.

"Here—you can see this one a little better." Larson pointed to one of the smaller vines, hanging against the glass.

The tiny blooms huddled in groups to form flower-sized clusters. Each little cluster had its own bright pattern of colors, lightest at the center, brightest and gaudiest at the edges.

Lower down on the vine, I could see how all the clusters expanded and gathered around a larger central one. "I see where it gets its name," I said, grinning. The vines were beautiful; the clusters of clusters formed a dazzling mandala. There was even a sense of a pattern. "How big does it get?"

Larson shrugged. "We don't know. We haven't got the room to let it grow. I'll tell you this—it drives the bees crazy."

"Is that its danger?"

"We don't know. It's here. We're observing it. It's pretty, isn't it?"

"Yeah, it really is."

"You should smell its perfume. It smells like all the good things in the world all rolled together. Honeysuckle, fresh bread, the inside of a new car, you name it; it smells different to everybody."

I followed Larson through two sets of double doors, out of botany and into biology. We moved through a vast white warehouse full of cages and terrariums. The air was full of dark animal smells. I couldn't identify any of them.

"We discovered something very interesting about the meeps," he said.

"Meeps—those are the weasely looking red-brown things, aren't they?"

"No, you're thinking of eggworms. A meep is a mousy pink furball. Here—these are eggworms."

I looked into a large glass enclosure. The eggworm looked like a small polite Chtorran, except it had no eyes, no arms, and only the finest coat of downy orange fur. It was about the size of a mole or a badger. There were four of them in the terrarium.

"They burrow," said Larson. "They eat small rodents: rats, mice, chipmunks, bunnies, and meeps. Here—up here. These are meeps." He pointed at a row of cages.

"Oh, right. We saw some of those on the chopper windshield. Kinda cute. What about 'em? I bet they breed like crazy, right?"

Larson shrugged. "We don't know yet. This is what I wanted you to see. We put three of 'em into a cage with a mamma rabbit and her litter. Mamma rabbit rejected her own babies to nurse the meeps instead."

"You're kidding!"

"Nope. The same behavior has been repeated with a dozen

other rabbits. If the babies are small enough, the meeps will eat them, but they prefer to nurse on Mamma."

"Yick. I wish you hadn't told me that."

"Oh, you haven't heard the worst of it. The meeps will nurse a mamma rabbit to death." He added somberly, "And she doesn't appear to object, either. She dies happy."

We passed out of the specimen section into a storage area; we walked past bags and bags of various animal feeds. The air was fresher here.

"Listen." I stopped him. "I want to apologize for shooting down your plan. I guess I came on a little strong—"

"You want to hear my theory about the bunnydogs?" Larson asked. He looked me straight in the eye. "I think they're like the meeps—only for humans. The bunnydogs are so cute, they're irresistible. The first time people see those videos, they all go, 'Awwwww.' Especially women. They all want to pick the bunnies up and cuddle them. I'll bet a woman would put her own baby down to cuddle a bunnydog. I'll bet tomorrow you'll find out how friendly the bunnydogs *really* are—"

"Thanks. I think I can find the rest of the way myself." I interrupted him deliberately.

"It's just down there." Larson pointed. "Past those steel doors. Follow the red stripe to the security section."

"Security?"

"It's an isolated block. It sits on springs. It's earthquake-proof and self-contained. That's where we control the whole operation. All our files are stored there. It can be locked down tighter than Iron Mountain. It's got an independent air supply, power supply, and a six-month supply of food. It's safe against the entire electromagnetic spectrum, including lasers, masers, xasers, all kinds of radiation, magnetism, and television reruns. It's blanketed by scrambler fields. *Nothing* goes in or out without permission. Oh—and you'll have to decontaminate too."

I looked at Larson. "Isn't this a little extreme for just a counseling session?"

He shrugged. "It's the best place in the world for privacy." He turned and headed back the way we'd come.

I followed Larson's directions: through the steel doors, past a security scan, detoxification, through a security tube—through a triple airlock—then through another security tube and a final scanning station.

The robot at the desk directed me down a hall to a corridor of personal apartments. "Room fourteen, please."

I knocked on the door politely.

A woman's voice. "Door's open. Come on in."

I pushed it open. The first thing that struck me was the smell of lilac perfume.

And then, Colonel Lizard Tirelli came out of the kitchen wearing an apron and an embarrassed smile. "Come on in, Jim."

Q: What's the difference between a Chtorran and Viet Nam?

A: The Chtorran burps.

58

Enthusiasm

"If we are all part of the image of God, then each of us is closest to God when we are held in the arms of another human being."

—SOLOMON SHORT

"I guess I owe you an explanation—and an apology," she began.

"I should think so." I was still standing in the doorway.

"Come in, Jim, and close the door behind you." When I didn't move, she stepped past me and pushed the door shut herself; then she took me by the hand and led me into the room. "Lieutenants," she muttered. She pointed at the couch. "Sit down and listen."

I sat. She pulled up a chair and sat down opposite me.

"Do you want something to drink?" she asked.

I shook my head. The apartment was furnished very comfortably. There was nothing at all to indicate that it was thirty meters underground.

Lizard began softly. "I treated you abominably, I know. Believe me, I feel terrible about it, but there's a very good reason why it had to be this way."

"A good reason? Yeah?" I waited.

"The problem is . . ." she continued, "I can't tell you what that reason is. All I can do is ask you to forgive me." She searched my face expectantly. "Jim?"

This did not make sense.

I shook my head. "I don't know. I'm confused." I rubbed my forehead, my face. I looked back at her. I couldn't think of words to say. "I—just—You're crazy! You know that?"

She sighed and nodded her agreement. "Very probably, I am. But this is the only way I could make it work."

"Make *what* work?"

She looked unhappy. "My promise—to you."

"Your promise—?" I crossed to her and pulled her to her feet. I held her arms and demanded, "Just what the hell is going on?"

She went rigid in my grasp, but her expression wasn't angry—it was *frightened*. Of me? Abruptly, she burst out in frustration: "I'm being monitored! You're being monitored! By the military! This is the only place where we're guaranteed any privacy. I think."

I let go of her in surprise. I could still smell her perfume. "Monitored—? Why?"

She shrugged helplessly. "Why not?"

I stared at her. My mind was whirling. "So that little performance upstairs—that wasn't for me? Was it?"

"I am so sorry about that . . ." she said.

"You did that to me without—?" I could feel the fury rising into my face. "I don't understand. I've been monitored before. Everybody on the goddamn base knew about the time Ted got me drunk. They're already gossiping about you and me. So what does it matter if somebody sees us or looks at a tape or something—?"

"You don't know. It matters to me!" she said.

"Why didn't you tell me?"

"I *couldn't*!"

"Why? What am I—some kind of a cretin, or a thing?—that you'll only be my friend if you can keep it a secret from me?"

"Y'know, it isn't easy being your friend!" she snapped back. "Sometimes you *are* a jerk."

"And you're a stuck-up, fat-assed, iron-clad, dragon-faced, red-headed gorgon who can't even keep a plastic eggbeater in the sky! But you're the one who wants to go to bed with me!"

"My ass is not fat! And I thought it was mutual—"

"It was!" I shouted back.

"Well, then—" And suddenly she was flustering close to tears. Lizard? "—Can't you just accept it? Jim, please?"

"And wake up tomorrow and find you've turned back into Medusa? Dammit! That *hurt*!"

"Jim—" She took my hands in hers. Her eyes were incredibly blue. "I am so terribly sorry and unhappy to have hurt you. You are an extraordinarily precious human being. Please believe me, if there had been any other way . . . but this was the only way I could manage it."

"I want to believe you," I said. "I really do . . ." I kept on holding her hands in mine. They were very warm. "But I—I just don't know—"

"I wanted to be with you tonight," she said. "That was the whole purpose of this—"

"I want to be with you too!" I felt my throat tightening. "I just want to know that you *care*."

"I do care." Her voice was very soft. "Believe me. I really do."

I couldn't deny it. She was telling the truth.

And I wanted her so badly—

I leaned forward and touched my lips to hers. She tasted sweet. After several eternities, we broke apart and looked at each other. We were both relieved—and embarrassed.

"So you'll stay for dinner?" she asked.

"Well . . . maybe. What are you making?"

"P-rations and bottled water."

"You promised me a lobster."

"Listen, it was hard enough to reserve the apartment—"

"I'm sorry, it's lobster or nothing."

"Well . . . all right." She led me into the dining room.

The lobster on the table was large enough to have been a threat to dogs, cats, and small children when it was alive. There was a bottle of wine chilling in the bucket.

"Pretty sure of yourself, aren't you?"

She shrugged. "When the day comes that I can't outthink a lieutenant—"

I pulled away from her. "Hold it! Before we go any further—no more military stuff, okay?"

Colonel Lizard Tirelli of the United States Army, Special Forces Warrant Agency, nodded her head in agreement. She unpinned her long red hair and let it cascade down to her shoulders. "Deal," she said.

Dinner passed like a dream.

She was too beautiful. I couldn't stop watching her. We traded a lot of embarrassed smiles and kept our conversation deliberately casual.

"I have to admit something," I said.

"What's that?"

"I—was jealous of you. I thought that you and Danny Anderson were—you know—lovers."

"Really?" She laughed. "Don't be silly. Danny's gay."

"Huh? You're kidding! I'll be damned. Is that why Duke—?" I shut my mouth.

"Probably."

"Well. Gosh." I shook my head unbelievingly. I couldn't imagine Danny—

"I have to admit something too."

"What?"

"I was jealous that you were spending too much time with Lois Fletcher."

"No!"

"Yes."

"But she's—" I shrugged. "I just never thought of her that way."

"I'm glad."

Eventually we moved to the bedroom and I started to tense up again. I didn't know why.

While I waited for her, I busied myself with bridegroom things. I turned the lights and the music low. I turned back the bed. Finally, I pulled off my clothes and slipped between the sheets to wait.

After all this time. . . .

She came out of the bathroom wearing a nightgown so sheer two silkworms couldn't have spent more than an afternoon on it. She got into bed next to me and I wondered if I should reach for her. I wanted to.

I looked over at her.

She looked back at me expectantly. "Are you going to make the first move?" she asked. "Or should I?"

"Uh—" I said. This wasn't going to be as easy as I thought. "You are so beautiful. . . ."

She stroked my cheek. "You don't need the compliments any more, Jim. We're beyond that." She added gently, "Now we're at foreplay."

I said, "I—I know this is going to sound stupid, but you're *too* beautiful. I don't know if I can make love to a woman as beautiful as you."

She looked like she was about to laugh—then smothered it quickly, compassionately. "I'll let you in on a secret," she said. "I'm really very plain. I walked into that bathroom and looked at myself in the mirror and said, 'Ick. What a mess.' Really. But then I said, 'But Jim deserves the best, so I'm going to pretend to be gorgeous just for him,' And see, you believed it."

"I think you *overdid* it," I said. "I hate to admit this—but I'm scared as hell!"

"You're kidding." She said it straight out.

"I am twenty-four years old," I said. "I lost my virginity when I was nineteen. I have been with three different girls in my life—four, if you count Ted. That's it, the sum total of my experience. I have never been with a woman as *intensely beautiful* as you are. And—" I added, "I have *never* been with anyone I cared about as much as you."

She was studying me thoughtfully. "You *are* scared, aren't you?"

"I'm terrified . . . that I won't be good enough . . ."

"Thank you," she said. "For being so *honest*." She reached over and put her hand on my chest. It felt like fire—like electricity. For a moment, all I could feel was that hand, those delicate fingers, the fingernail tracing a circle in the little patch of hair over my breastbone. After a moment, she said softly, "Listen, sweetheart. This isn't an audition. You're not being graded. Let me play Mommy for about two seconds here and I'll tell you something. The only thing that you need to do a good job is *enthusiasm*. You got that?"

"I've got *lots* of enthusiasm," I said. "So much I'm afraid I'm going to burst a blood vessel."

"Good," she said. She shifted her position so we were lying side by side. "There is no right way to do this, Jim—so you can't possibly screw it up. And if you do anyway, I forgive you in advance."

I moved my hand to her breast. She was warm. My hand was cold. I was afraid to move it. I said, "I, uh—I can't help it. I feel like I should ask permission."

She didn't laugh at me. She took my hand in hers and held it. She kissed my fingers. She took a breath and whispered, "Sweetheart, you are so caring, but you have to stop thinking of sex as something you do to another person, and start thinking of it as something that two people share together."

"I'd really like that—" I said. "But I've never experienced it that way."

Lizard's expression remained open. She wasn't judging me. She was just hearing what I had to say. She squeezed my hand again. "Listen to me, stupid—" The way she said it, it was a term of endearment. "I'm going to tell you everything you need to know about sex."

"I don't think we have that much time," I admitted.

"It's all right. There isn't that much you *need* to know. It'll only take a minute."

She lifted herself up on one elbow and put her finger on my lips. Her fingers were exquisite. I kissed them.

"The only thing in the world that you *really* own," she began, "is the body that you live in. So that's the only thing you really have to share."

"I never thought of it that way," I said.

"Hush, child—I'm not through. Have you ever noticed that you never go to bed with anyone unless you're interested in their body?"

I nodded.

"Well, nobody ever goes to bed with you either without being interested in *your* body. Sex is about bodies. Either you like bodies, my dear, or you don't have sex."

"I like bodies," I said. "I like yours." I put out a tentative hand and let my fingers touch her arm.

"I like yours." She smiled back at me.

"See—" I said, "that's the part I have trouble with. I never knew that."

"I know," she said. "That's why you're such an asshole. Cute, but still an asshole. Why do you have such a low opinion of yourself? Do you know that's an insult to the people you go to bed with? It means you don't think much of their taste either. It also means that you have to con people into your bed, and when you get them there, the best you can do is use them. Here's what I'm trying to tell you, my sweet lover: You can't have good sex with anyone else until you let yourself experience your own wonderfulness."

"My own wonderfulness . . . ?" I squeaked. I cleared my throat. "I, uh—always thought that a person should be . . . um, modest."

"Hmp," she said. "Modesty is the most arrogant form of conceit. Modesty is an excuse to hide yourself, and that rips people off. If you're wonderful—and you are—then, share it. Don't you think people like being around wonderful people? Don't you?"

"Sure. But I'm not—what you said—wonderful."

She sat up and stared at me. "Who made up that shit?"

"Huh?"

"I said, 'who made up that shit?' That you're not wonderful? Trust me, sweetheart—you are positively terrific."

"No, I'm not."

"Yes, you are."

"This is making me very uncomfortable—" I said. "Couldn't we just get on with what we set out to do . . . ?"

"No, we can't. Not until you let it in. I think you're wonderful."

I looked away. She was too beautiful.

She put a hand on my chin and turned my face back to hers. "It's all right for you to think I'm gorgeous, huh? But not for me to think you're terrific?"

"But, I'm not—"

"I. Say. You. Are." Her tone of voice left no room for argument.

"I hear you—" I managed to say.

"Do you? Do you really? You need to let this in, stupid. I don't go to bed with losers. I *chose* you. Did you ever stop to think *why*?"

"Bad eyesight?" I joked.

She slapped my face. Hard.

When my vision cleared, I was lying on my back and she was on top of me, glaring down at me. "Now that I have your attention," she said, "don't ever do that again!"

"Do what?"

"Insult my taste in lovers. You're so busy denying your own sexiness you can't even see how horny I am for you. Will you let it in?" Her face was very close to mine. Her eyes were almost too close to focus on. I felt like I was staring into an abyss that I wanted to jump into.

I wanted to tell her something, but I didn't have the words for it. I wanted to ask for help, but I didn't think she could help me. I felt her fingers on my shoulders. I felt her weight on my chest, her legs around mine. I felt myself stiffening with desire—and I was terrified.

She must have seen it in my eyes. She raised herself up and looked down at me.

"Something's the matter, isn't it? There's something deeper, isn't there?"

"I don't deserve you," I said.

"Oh course you don't," she agreed. "I'm a gift, not a payment." And then she stopped in mid-thought and studied me. "But you don't know how to *enjoy* sex, do you?"

I didn't answer. She was right. I'd seen other couples laughing and playing together. I'd always wondered how they managed it. I always felt . . . left out.

"All right—I give up," she said. "We'll do it your way." Abruptly, she rolled off me and out of bed.

"Where are you going?"

"I'll be right back—"

She padded back in carrying an American flag. Fifty-two stars, thirteen stripes. I remembered there had been a small meeting room next door.

She climbed back into bed and began settling herself with exaggerated care. "I'll tell you what," she said seriously. "I'm going to put this flag over my face—" she pulled it up over her head like a sheet, "—and you can do it for love of country." And then she lay there and was very, very still.

"What—?"

She didn't answer.

I pulled the flag down off her face. She was grinning up at me. "I don't know what else to do," she said, and pulled the flag back up.

"You come out of there!"

"What's the matter!" Her voice came up through the stars and stripes. "Aren't you patriotic?" She cradled her breasts. "Here—pretend that this is the bosom of liberty!" And then she jiggled her tits.

"Lizard—!"

She jiggled her tits again—harder this time.

"This is not funny!" I said.

The flag started shaking. "Then why am I laughing so hard?" she asked. She was making little squeaking noises in her throat. Her chest shook.

I reached to pull the flag away. She grabbed it and held on. I poked her in the ribs instead. She shrieked and jerked her hands down to her stomach. I reached for the flag—she grabbed it again. I gave her another poke in the ribs—and another—"Here! You want patriotism? It's Pearl Harbor Day!" I made explosion noises to punctuate each poke. She yelped each time, but she wouldn't stop giggling. She pulled her knees up to her chest. I hollered, *"Banzaiii!"* and smacked her on the bottom!

"Oh, you're gonna get it now—" she started.

"Yeah! You and what army?" I pulled the flag away and poked her again; she doubled up on her side, giggling too hard to resist. I grabbed her and rolled her over on her back. "Bosom of liberty, huh? It looks more like the two-party system to me. First I'm going to party here—"

"Jim!" she shrieked in surprise.

"—and then I'm going to party over here! And what's this? A cleavage in the body politic?" I put my face between her breasts and made a big wet razzberry sound. She was laughing like crazy now. She pulled her legs up to kick me away, but I pinned her knees under my chest and held her shoulders down with my hands. I was laughing as hard as she was. "And what's this down here—? The crack of doom?" Her eyes met mine.

And in that moment—I knew. And grinned. I could feel my face splitting in joy. I could see the laughter reflected back in her eyes.

I couldn't catch my breath. I was giggling too hard. And so was she.

We giggled and laughed together and in the middle of it, I bent my face down to hers. Her knees parted, her legs opened beneath me, and I lowered myself onto her and into her. She wrapped her arms and legs around me and held on tight. We both did. I gave myself to her, and she to me—and we were joyous.

She was right. I was wonderful.

Q: What's the difference between a Chtorran and a volcano?
A: The volcano has better manners.

59

Flag Day

*"Sex is better than chess, because sex has
two winners."*

—SOLOMON SHORT

Satellite Recon gave us the morning pictures: three primary targets
and seven backups.

I voted for the one closest to our original crash site. Both
Colonel Tirelli and Dr. Fletcher agreed and that settled that.

We reconfirmed our choice a half-hour before liftoff, and then
we were on our way. Three huge choppers clattered into the air
like malevolent insects and turned north across the bay. I
remembered this view from before.

I glanced around the chopper. Dr. Fletcher was conferring with
Jerry Larson about the layout of monitor probes and sample traps.
The crew in the back were sleeping. It was a good idea. We'd been
up since before dawn. I made myself comfortable—

—and was awakened by the beeping of the autopilot. The
chopper was dropping. "We're there," called Lizard. I straightened up and looked out the window.

We were falling toward a wide grassy pasture. It was overgrown
with tall blue-green grass. I could see it waving in the wind. I
glanced backward. The follow-choppers were still in formation,
coming down with us.

The three ships settled down into the soft ground right in the
center. There was at least a kilometer of clear space on every side
of us. Good. Nothing would approach us undetected.

"All right," growled Lizard, "everybody stay in your seats until
the ground crew declares the area secure."

I peered out the window. A security team, armed with torches, caustic sprays, and rocket-launchers, was just fanning out. I envied them. At least they knew what they were doing.

As soon as security declared the area yellow, the science team hit the ground running. Their job was to put out probes and sensors. I saw several small mobile units rolling out through the grass, including two walkers and a spider.

My orders were to stay inside until we went to condition green. I climbed forward and parked myself in the copilot's seat again. Directly ahead, the walkers were beginning the process of clearing a wide circular area. A gathering circle. A friendly sign for the bunnydogs. An invitation.

I thought about a beer. I opened a Coke instead.

The afternoon got suddenly dark. The camouflage dome was being pulled into place over the chopper. Soon it would be inflated and sprayed. The whole process would take less than an hour. The theory was that the choppers would have negative associations for the worms and bunnies. So we'd hide them. If we needed to scramble, the camouflage domes could be blown away in seconds.

Somebody switched the cabin lights on. I glanced back. Colonel Tirelli was just climbing forward. She dropped into the pilot's seat.

We were alone in the chopper.

I turned to look out the opposite window. I made sure she saw that my studied nonchalance was deliberate.

She ignored me. She clicked her controls this way and that and looked very busy. I wondered if she had anything to say to me.

Either she didn't—or she wasn't ready to say it yet. The silence stretched on.

Maybe I should say something. I turned to her—

—and noticed a tiny American flag pin on her lapel. I nearly cracked up laughing. I had to bite my tongue to keep control.

Lizard looked at me curiously. "Are you all right, Lieutenant?"

"I am fine," I said, grinning. "Just fine!"

Q: What does hair on a Chtorran mean?
A: It masticates.

60

The Meadow

"Reality can be useful."
—SOLOMON SHORT

The two robots had stamped out and cleared a wide, mathematically precise arena. A perfect circle.

I stripped down to my shorts and sat in the center and . . . imagined. I closed my eyes and imagined what it would be like to be surrounded by bunnydogs. And worms.

I tried to imagine sitting naked before a curious worm.

I shuddered. And not because the wind was cold.

I tried to imagine the smell of the animal. The look of it. The feel of its fur. I had touched the fur of living worms. It *tingled*.

I tried to imagine what it would feel like to stand naked before a worm. I couldn't imagine myself feeling anything but terrified.

No bunnydogs showed up the first day.

Or the second.

We kept close to the chopper domes and worried.

Fletcher and I practiced. We did communication exercises, clearing exercises, confrontation exercises—things that seemed to make no sense at all, and yet . . . I began to feel as if I were the center of the world here. I began to feel . . . *focused*. There was a clarity of purpose developing here.

Every moment was preparation. Every moment was a drill.

Fletcher would ask me, "What are you doing now?"

And I would reply, "I'm eating."

She'd ask, "And *why* are you eating?"

"Because I'm hungry."

"What's your purpose in eating?"

"Taking care of my body, so I can do the job." It felt like a catechism, but . . . I could feel the meanings under the words. It was true.

"And what job is that?"

"Creating a relationship with the bunnydogs, a space in which communication can occur."

"Good. Do you have any other purposes?"

"I did want to . . . have a relationship with Lizard—but I've let go of that now."

"Good, James. Anything else?"

"No."

I felt myself entering a *different* state of consciousness. The difference was *profound*.

I felt in control.

As if I were creating it.

All of it. The forest. The meadow. The domes. The quiet, distant faces.

Especially the faces; they were all so *detached* from me. They were my herd. And I was—the leader? Not . . . quite. I was the . . . magician.

The feeling was curious.

I told Fletcher I wanted to walk in the forest.

She shook her head no.

I insisted. I said it was necessary—for me to be clear.

She said all right, but only if she could send a security team with me.

I told her I needed to be alone. I needed to feel *ownership* of the land—especially if I was going to invite a bunnydog family to *share* it.

I insisted.

She gave in. She let me walk.

I knew the team was following me at a discreet distance. I didn't mind. As long as I wasn't tripping over them.

The forest was a cathedral, green and gold.

Its ceiling was so high it was invisible, a canopy of lofty branches and dark broad leaves. God's light slanted down through the pine and the redwoods, turning the tree trunks ruddy. The beams were so solid you could feel them with your fingers. They struck sparks of golden dust in the air.

High above, a cold wind played across the roof, letting the bright blue sky peek through in tiny patches here and there. The breeze rustled the leaves like an organ and dappled the light. My footsteps fell lightly on a carpet of fresh green pine needles. The earth was soft and brown.

I breathed deeply, and the air smelled of heaven: pine and honeysuckle and cascades of beautiful growing *green* things. There was no pink left anywhere.

I could have stayed here forever.

Somewhere ahead, I heard water—a stream. I followed the sound and—

The forest opened out onto a meadow.

A riot of color, gaudy brilliance, dazzling to the eye!

But such a meadow! Nothing like this had ever been seen on the Earth before!

I stepped forward hesitantly.

Purple ivy, streaked with lavender and white, curled away from me. Black shambler bushes struck silver sparks in the air. Slender red growths rose like fountains, exploding into feathery black and pink fronds.

And over everything—mandala vines.

They captured the eye, they overwhelmed the senses. They were a carpet, they rolled away in endless waves. The mandala flowers piled themselves high; they dripped from stumps of rotted trees; they hung from branches in a riotous celebration of color, a royal display.

I stood and gaped in awe and wonder. Silver and crimson, orange and indigo so dark it was black, magenta, yellow and blue, cascades of hue and shade beyond the eye's ability to differentiate.

And, oh—the smells!

Waves of scent swept over me—fresh-baked bread, strawberry jam, thick fresh cream, apple cobbler, peaches—and scents for which I had no name at all. Dark purply scents laced with scarlet overtones: sweet chords of gold and opium perfume. Heady aromas of magic, sparkling spells; doorways into crystal heavens and beautiful trips through Hell.

The forest behind me was forgotten.

Dammit! Why did the invasion have to be *beautiful,* too?

On the morning of the third day, the sensors picked up a worm on the east edge of the meadow.

A quiet voice on the radio said, "I think I've got something."

We crowded around the monitors. The big display showed a smallish looking worm poised on the high end of the slope. It seemed *confused*. Its eye-stalks swiveled back and forth as it studied the three mottled domes in the middle of the pasture below it. It flowed a few meters forward—

—stopped. Hesitated. Swiveled its eyes. Backward. Forward.

We went to full magnification. The eyes irised shut and open again. *Sput-phwut*.

The worm half turned and looked behind itself. Then it swiveled its eyes toward us again.

I felt as if I could read its mind. It was a five-year-old child, seeing something very interesting, but not knowing if it should investigate by itself—or go tell Mommy first.

It made up its mind. This was a well-trained five-year-old. It completed its turn and headed off to the east as fast as it could go.

Nothing else happened for the rest of the day.

During the night, the sensors picked up movement on the ridge, but it could have been deer or coyotes.

Q: How does a Chtorran have an abortion?
A: It eats the eggs.

61

Return of the Bunnydogs

"Beware of geeks bearing gifts."
—SOLOMON SHORT

Lizard woke me up. "Jim—"

"Huh? What?" Everything was dark. "What time is it?"

"Shh. Be quiet. It's almost dawn. I want you to come forward."

I rubbed my eyes and fell out of my bunk—

"I said, be quiet!" she whispered again.

I followed her forward. "What do you want?"

"Look—" She pointed.

I looked to the monitor screen on the console. I looked out the window. Through the netting, I could see—

There were three bunnydogs sitting on the opposite side of the circle.

"This is it," I said. I looked at her. "Isn't it?"

She nodded.

I started unbuttoning my shirt. "We should get started."

She put her hand on my shoulder. "There's time. We'll do it by the mission book."

"But they could leave."

"I doubt it," she said. There was certainty in her voice.

I turned to her. "How long have they been there?"

"For an hour."

"And you didn't wake me?"

"As mission commander, I felt you needed your sleep. If they're here to communicate, Jim, then they'll wait. And if they're not, then it's a mistake to rush into anything. We'll follow the checklist. I'm calling condition yellow. I have to open two separate channels to Oakland, satellite and direct. I have to wake the observation team and the defense team; I have to activate the high-level monitors. You might as well have breakfast and go through your exercises with Fletcher again. It'll be at least ninety minutes before I'll go to condition green. Probably longer. Until then, my *friend,* you're still under my command. Got that?"

"Yes, ma'am."

"First thing, I want you to put on a medical harness. I want you to stabilize your heart and respiration before you go out there."

"Is it that obvious how excited I am?"

"Just do it," she said, hooking a thumb over her shoulder. "I've got work to do."

I moved. I went and woke up Fletcher, showed her our guests, and then the two of us fell into the familiar routine of preparation and clearing. The excitement was growing in me like a bomb. This was worse than Christmas.

Fletcher took me to the back of the chopper and began talking to me low and quietly. At first, I couldn't hear a word she said. All I could think of was the bunnydogs.

"Jim!" Her tone was urgent. "Pay attention."

"Yes, ma'am."

"What are you here for?"

"The bunnydogs. Um, creating a relationship with a bunnydogs so communication can occur." The words fell out like a recorded phrase.

"Sorry, I don't get it. Where are you, James?—because you're sure not here with me."

"I'm sorry. I guess I'm just excited."

"I know. All right, strip down and put on the harness. Let's see what's going on."

The decision had been made that the contact—me—should be naked. Or as close to naked as possible. To allow the bunnydogs to experience the *animalness* of the individual first. The physical beingness. I'd voted in favor of shorts. We'd compromised on a loincloth.

As soon as I'd stripped, Fletcher had me slip into the medical harness. She studied her console and frowned. "Is there any part of you that *isn't* elevated?" she asked.

"Well, there is one," I said, glancing down. "But, if you want—"

"Knock that off." She was all business. "Close your eyes, James. Good. All right. Here's the exercise. Thirty deep breaths. Like I taught you. See how long you can take."

I closed my eyes and concentrated on my breathing. Breath

number one. Breathe for your toes. This oxygen is for your toes. Take in as much as you can. Take care of your toes. Hold it as long as you can. Now, let it out. Breath number two. Breathe for your left foot. This oxygen is for your left foot. Take in as much as you can.

I could hear Fletcher and Colonel Tirelli conferring softly in the front of the chopper. I couldn't hear what they were saying, but I knew it was about me. I could sense the concern in their voices.

This breath is for your right knee. Take in as much as you can. I was going to go through my whole body this way. I was going to be thoroughly oxygenated. I knew I was letting myself be distracted.

The sounds from the front of the chopper were too negative. If I wasn't ready, they weren't going to let me go. That's what they were discussing. If I was too *excited*, I wouldn't be able to hold my focus.

Breathe for your stomach. This oxygen if for your stomach. Breathe for your chest.

They stopped talking then and the only sound in the ship was the sound of my own breath.

Breathe for your brain. Take in as much as you can. Hold it for as long as you can.

When I opened my eyes again, Fletcher was sitting opposite me.

"How are you feeling now, James?"

"Better." I added, "But I'm still not ready. I can feel it. I'm too giddy."

"You're doing fine," she said. "It's just that you think this is important. It's not. It's only an oddball little experiment that no one is taking seriously. So there's nothing at stake here. You got that?"

"Yes."

"Good. So that means you're off the hook, Jim. No matter what happens out there, you can't screw up. Whatever happens, we still learn something. The experiment is already a success. All that's left is to find out the results."

"I wish I could believe that."

She shrugged. "It doesn't matter if you believe it or not. It's still true. Listen," she added, "that circle that we cleared out there is an invitation to a party. It's the same invitation that they offered you and Duke and Colonel Tirelli three weeks ago, only you couldn't recognize it for what it was. Now that we know what it is, we can return the invitation. And they want to accept it.

They're waiting for us. The *hard* part is over." She studied me intensely. "So, now what's the next move?"

"I go out there."

"And . . . ?"

"And—" I stopped. "Uh . . . I know the answer, Fletch—but knowing the answer doesn't change anything. I'm still running the monkey program. I'm excited—and I'm *scared*." I looked at her, frustrated. "How do I let go?"

"Right. That's why you can't go out there, James. Not yet. You're still not ready to just *be* with them and play with them. You're still too busy being with your own feeling." Without missing a beat, she said, "Tell me a dirty joke."

"Huh?"

"Tell me a dirty joke. Any joke. Make one up."

"Why?"

"No reason at all. Tell me a joke!"

"Um—okay. What do you call a Chtorran who eats his own children?"

"Well adjusted. Tell me one I haven't heard."

"What do you say to the Chtorran who's eating a Revelationist?"

"I give up, what?"

"Eat faster!"

She smiled. "Okay, my turn. What's the Chtorran word for midget?"

"What?"

"Hors d'oeuvre. What does a Chtorran call a jogger?"

"Fast food. I've heard that one."

"All right. One more. What do you get when you cross a Chtorran with a gizzly bear?"

"What?"

"A very cross grizzly bear." She glanced at her console.

"How'm I doing?" I asked.

"Better." She grinned at me. "We may make it after all."

I felt myself surging with excitement. And immediately tried to suppress it.

"No, it's all right," she said. "You're excited. Let yourself be excited. If you try to stop being excited, it'll just keep building. Just let it run itself out." She pushed the console aside and turned to me. "Okay, here's what I want you to do:

"I want you to go up front, sit in the copilot's seat, and study the bunnies. Just watch them. Watch them until you are tired of watching them. Until you are bored silly with watching them.

Watch them until there is nothing left to do but watch them. Remember your herd experience. There's a point at which you will feel a shift in your experience of the bunnydogs. I can't explain what it will feel like, but you'll know when it happens.

"I don't want you to move until you know that you're absolutely ready. When you are, get up quietly, take off the medical harness, and go out and do whatever is appropriate. You'll know what that is too. Have you got all that?"

I nodded.

"Good." She pointed me toward the front of the chopper.

I slipped into the copilot's seat and stared out at the bunnydogs. There were still only three of them. Papa, Mama, and baby? Maybe.

I remembered what Tanjy had said. Listen with your whole soul.

The bunnydogs were sitting patiently on the far side of the circle. Occasionally one or the other would scratch itself behind one ear. The littlest one had curled up and gone to sleep. It looked like a little pink pillow. That was interesting. The bunnydogs were naturally pink, even without the dust.

I remembered what Fletcher had taught me. Look beyond what you're seeing. Look at the surface. Look beyond the surface. And look inside yourself to see how *you're* seeing.

I was beginning to get a sense of the bunnydogs' patience. It wasn't their circle. It was *ours*. They were waiting to see what kind of a game we were inviting them to play.

And . . . we were too scared to play.

We couldn't even offer an invitation without hiding guns behind it.

The invitation lay empty.

The game hadn't been created yet.

Once you step into the circle, the game begins. So, the question was, what kind of a game did I want to create with the bunnies?

No.

The question was, what kind of a game could all of us create together?

I looked across at the rabbity little puppies and wondered: Could these creatures play the game of *sentience*?

It was time to find out.

I levered myself out of my seat.

There was no one else in the chopper. They had left me alone. They were probably sitting in Colonel Anderson's command ship, watching the monitors.

The door was open. I stopped and removed the medical harness. I was wearing only a loincloth and a neck chain with a small three-way transceiver hanging on it.

I stepped down out of the gunship.

I crossed to the wall of the camouflage dome and stepped through the netting.

Q: What do you say to a Chtorran who's eating the president?
A: Bon appetit.

Q: What do you do when it's finished?
A: Bring it the check.

62

Invitation to the Dance

"Most people live their lives as if they think God isn't paying any attention to them."

—SOLOMON SHORT

The bunnydogs sat up straighter as I approached.

I stepped to the edge of the circle opposite the bunnies and sat down cross-legged. They needed the chance to study a human.

The two larger bunnies began to chirp and gobble at each other. The littlest bunny sat up, yawned, stretched, and scratched himself. He looked around and saw me—and jumped nearly a meter in the air in startlement. His eyes went impossibly round. He was probably only a child. He edged sideways until he was hidden behind the largest bunnydog. Then he peered around curiously and blinked at me.

I waved at him.

He pulled his head back quickly, disappearing again behind his—what, his papa? No, that was a human assumption. Maybe the females of this species were the larger.

The two adult bunnies ceased gobbling and reduced their conversation to a series of coos and chirps.

They reminded me of something I'd seen in the herd. There were two young women who liked to sit opposite each other, cooing and gobbling nonsense syllables. If you didn't know the language—or the lack of it—you could almost think that they were really talking. It looked like they were totally engaged in some happy casual chatter—and in one sense, they were. But there were no agreed-upon symbols, and there was no transmission of any experience at all beyond the shared one of sitting and gobbling.

If an alien didn't know human language, would it assume that they were communicating?

And then, having made that assumption, if it had turned and looked to the observers of the herd, Dr. Fletcher and myself, and studied our quiet sidewise exchanges, could that same alien have perceived a difference? If anything, the two gobbling women would have looked *more* in communication than Fletcher and myself. At least it was obvious that they were acting in relationship.

This was the real question.

If two creatures are sitting and gobbling at each other, how do you tell if they're talking—or just gobbling? Were these bunnydogs actually using a language? Or were they simply making noises at each other?

It sounded like a language. But then, so did the herd noises.

Two more bunnydogs were hopping down the slope to join the three sitting opposite me. They bumped noses with Mama, Papa, and baby bunnydog. They patted each other's fur. A greeting ritual?

The two newcomers looked older and more cautious than Mama, Papa, and baby. But they took up their places at the edge of the circle and waited also.

I felt a little like a guru. Naked. Patient. Mysterious.

A sixth bunnydog joined the vigil.

There were other bunnydogs hopping and waddling toward the circle.

There were more up on the hill. Some were just sitting and watching. A few were advancing.

I waited until the gathering was complete. They gobbled and greeted each new arrival; there was much exchanging of nuzzlings and nose bumps, even a few pats and hugs, before settling down—and then I stood up.

The bunnydogs sat up alert.

I stepped to the exact center of the circle.

I could feel their eyes. This was the center of the world.

Every bunnydog was watching me; so was every human. Everything I did was being monitored from the choppers hidden in the domes. Recorded. Photographed. Analyzed.

I stopped and waited. I let myself feel the wind on my body. I let myself smell the grass and the scent of pine in the cool afternoon air. There was another scent on top of the pine, a sweet peppermint smell. The scent of the bunnies? It would be appropriate.

The bunnies were watching me attentively, but none of them had entered the circle yet.

They were waiting for me to do something.

I remembered what the bunnies had done before.

They had danced.

I touched the transceiver at my neck and said, very softly, "I have a problem. I don't know how to dance."

Fletcher's voice, just as softly, replied, "They don't know that. They've never seen a monkey dance before. Whatever you do is the right way."

"Oh, yeah. Thanks for reminding me."

I took a breath.

I started dancing.

I capered, I bounced, I shouted. I made Indian whooping noises with my hand over my mouth. I did a jig, a Charleston, a freddy, and a break. I jumped and hollered and shook.

The bunnydogs looked at each other curiously.

"Well, come on!" I shouted. "Don't you want to dance?"

Several of the bunnies took a hop backward. Oh, shit. I was going to lose them.

I dropped forward in a somersault, came up on my knees, hooked my fingers in my mouth, crossed my eyes, stuck out my tongue, and said, "Boola-boola-boola! Labber-labber-labber—"

Two of the bunnies started giggling. The littlest bunny came charging into the circle then. He stopped in front of me and shook his head rapidly back and forth. He let his floppy lips and tongue shake like an ape. "Lubber-lubber-lubber," he said in a high squeaky voice.

In seconds, I was surrounded by bunnies, all of them making incomprehensible gobbling sounds. They were bouncing and hopping all around me, somersaulting and turning upside down, shrieking, bubbling, and shouting. They danced and jerked like little spastic puppets. I looked up the hill and it was covered with fluffy pink bodies bouncing down toward the circle. They were coming to join the party too. We had won!

A bright red worm came over the crest of the slope. Two more followed after it. And then two more. And another—I didn't care. The bunnies saw and began cheering and shouting. It was beginning to sound more and more like a language.

"I think we've done it!" I laughed. "We've done it! I don't know what we've done, but we've done it!"

The bunnies were all around me now, patting me and touching

me affectionately. Their fingers were soft and furry. And they tickled.

I dropped to my knees. The bunnies came up close to inspect my face. Their tiny hands touched my cheeks, my nose, my skin. They were fascinated by the hairlessness of my body. They stroked me curiously. Their eyes were huge and round. They looked like little toy animals, pink and cuddly. But when they yipped, I could see that they had sharp white teeth. But then, so did puppies.

One of the bunnies took my hand and began licking my fingers. He put my middle finger in his mouth and sucked on it thoughtfully. Then he let go and looked at me and . . . giggled. I reached over and tugged his ear gently and we both knew it was all right.

The new arrivals plunged into the circle and joined the curious crowd. All of them wanted to get as close as possible. I reached out and touched as many of them as I could reach. I began to tickle them and poke them affectionately. I patted their heads and skritched their ears. They really loved that. I even picked up the baby bunnydogs and gave them little hugs and kisses. They shrieked and giggled with delight.

My transceiver started beeping. The bunnydogs cocked their heads at it curiously. I held it up for them to see—a tiny little button on the chain around my neck. I said, "See, it's nothing. It just makes noises. Make a noise, button."

The button said, "Oh, great and powerful god of small pink things, look around you now."

The bunnies were fascinated. One of the babies sniffed the button. Another tried to put it into his mouth. I had to take it away from him.

I looked up, beyond the small pink bodies.

There were worms here.

I was surrounded by worms.

Nine. Ten. Eleven worms.

All sizes. From the smallest I 'd ever seen—about the size of a St. Bernard—to three huge monsters the size of Greyhound buses.

"Well, hi guys. . . ." I said. I stood up and looked at the worms. The last worm was just being herded into place by three energetic little bunnies. Again I thought of a jumbo jet being directed to dock by the ground crew.

All right—assume that the bunnies control the worms. The question was why? What did the bunnies use the worms for?

We were about to find out.

Q: What did the Chtorran get when it ate Mary Poppins?
A: Diabetes.

Q: What would a Chtorran get if it ate the Supreme Court?
A: Food poisoning.

63

Going Home

*"If Helen Keller falls down in the forest,
does she make a noise?"*

—SOLOMON SHORT

Some of the worms swiveled their eyes to study me. Some of them closed their eyes and looked like they were dozing.

And that was it.

They stayed outside the circle. Why? Did that mean something? Or not—?

Most of the bunnydogs were ignoring the worms. They were here to party. The worms were just . . . wallpaper. Or protection. Or . . . what? I couldn't even guess.

Several of the bunnies were tugging at me. I allowed myself to be turned away from the worms. They wanted to play some more. I let myself be pulled into a cluster of them. I grinned. I giggled. I laughed out loud.

Then, one of the worms *chirruped.*

Several of the bunnydogs looked over at it. So did I. It was one of the bigger worms, red fur rippling brightly across purple skin. It—he? she?—had soft pink stripes along its sides, shading almost to white. Three small Chtorrans with similar markings waited a respectful distance behind it.

Was this the head honcho? The senior Chtorran? The daddy? The camp counselor? The den mother? What?

Some of the bunnydogs started moving out of the circle, started moving over to the Chtorrans.

They began climbing up onto the big red beasts, patting them and making reassuring clucking noises, grooming them and nuzzling them. Even the largest of the worms was covered with little pink shapes, patting and stroking at its dark purple fur. The fur seemed to shimmer with color as I watched. The stripes of the worm rippled and flowed along its sides. The movement was clear and distinct.

I realized I was being left alone in the circle. Were the bunnydogs abandoning me?

No—one of the bunnydogs had grabbed my hand and was stamping its feet impatiently. It tugged at my arm, and looked at me with its large cookie-button eyes. Its expression was *expectant*.

"I think they want to introduce me to the worms," I said.

"Go on," said the button.

I let myself be tugged toward the edge of the circle.

I looked to the worms. Most of them were preoccupied with their attendants. Were the bunnydogs grooming the worms? Or were the worms *mothering* the bunnydogs?

What was happening here? Had the bunnydogs rode in on their worms like cowboys riding to a square dance? Or had the worms brought their bunnies out to play, like nannies in Central Park?

The bunnydogs pulled me toward the largest Chtorran. It swiveled its eyes around to study me. I gulped. I could feel the panic response starting to come up.

"Easy, Jim," I said. Or someone said it into my ear. Voices. I was getting blurry. It was that feeling again. Like I was sitting on top of a tree. Right. I'm a monkey.

The bunnydogs just wanted to show me off. They wanted me to meet the—the (?)—I knew the concept, I didn't have the word for it. Something about a father-mind-fragment? No—

Sput-phwut.

The big worm slowly blinked its eyes. The others swiveled their eyestalks around to study me. All the worms, all around the circle, were looking. I craned my head around to look at them. I couldn't tell what they were thinking. They seemed placid as elephants—except two of them were absentmindedly clacking their mandibles. Ugh.

The Chtorran studied me without emotion, goggling its eyes from one position to the next so it could see me from several different perspectives, as if it couldn't quite figure me out. It was curious, but it was a detached curiosity without any deep feeling attached. The creature didn't react; it didn't show any kind of response at all. Eventually the bunnydogs got bored and wandered away. A couple other bunnydogs came up and sniffed my fingers or my toes or my crotch. One of them reached up and fingered my loincloth, fondled my genitals curiously through the cloth—I yowped in surprise, then laughed and pushed it away. It wandered off. The Chtorran eyed me.

I looked around the circle. What were the bunnies doing? Some of them were staring into the worms' great eyes. One of them tapped a worm on the side and it lowered a hand and lifted the bunny up before its face.

Was it that simple? Eye contact?

I looked back to my worm. *My* worm?

It goggled its eyes sideways, one above the other—the ultimate expression of Chtorran curiosity. Those huge orbs must have been a third of a meter across. They were hypnotic.

I took a step toward the worm. And another.

The worm straightened its gaze. It studied me head-on. It shifted its arms on its back.

I gathered my courage and closed the remaining distance between myself and the Chtorran. I stood before it and looked deeply into its eyes.

The creature was fantastic.

For just a moment, I felt as if I could hear its thoughts. It blinked. *Sput-phwut.*

How odd. I felt perfectly safe looking into its gaze like this.

I lifted my arms and spread my hands out before me.

The worm unfolded its arms. They were jointed like wings and attached to the sides of the bony brain case behind the eyes. The arms came over the creature's eyes and then downward. I was reminded of a scorpion's tail.

The worm opened its hands toward me. It was echoing my gesture.

"It's intelligent," I said. "I don't know how I know, but I know. It's intelligent. Too intelligent to be just a domestic creature. . . ."

I took a step forward, my hands still out.

The worm hunched toward me.

Our fingers touched. The worm took my hand in its claw and turned it this way and that, studying it curiously. It dipped its eyes close, refocusing as it did. It saw me studying the way its eyestalks moved and peered into my face. Then it turned its attention back to my hand.

When it finished, it let go of me, but it held out its own claw in front of me. It was offering itself for mutual inspection. I took the claw in my hands and lifted it up to my face. I turned it over, back and forth, and studied it as the worm had studied mine. There were three digits, all opposed. There were three joints to each digit. I moved the fingers around. The worm could use any of its digits as a thumb opposed to the other two. Convenient.

I let go of the worm's hand. I met its eyes again and said, "Thank you."

The worm dipped its eyes—that gesture, it was an acknowledgment of some kind—and made a burping sound. *"Ctrlp?"*

"You're welcome."

The worm extended both its hands now and touched my shoulders. I flinched at the contact—but I looked into the creature's eyes again. "It's all right. Go ahead."

The worm began patting me, stroking me, and touching me as the bunnydogs had done. It was as fascinated with my body as the bunnydogs had been.

The worm's fingers touched my transceiver curiously. It lifted the chain, then let it drop. It looked at me as if wondering why I was wearing such an obvious piece of *technology*. It lowered its fingers to my loincloth and tugged at that. I wondered if I should take it off—but the worm was already ahead of me. It snapped the cord with its claw and dropped the loincloth carelessly to the ground. It blinked curiously at my genitals. It extended one finger toward my penis, tracing the length of it with a gentle claw. It blinked curiously, then lost interest and turned me around to examine my back.

I saw that the other worms were watching. Their interest seemed *more* than casual. Were they waiting for something? What? The bunnydogs were so engrossed in grooming the worms they had forgotten about me. Was that a good sign—that they were taking my presence for granted? I just didn't know. The bunnydogs seemed fascinated by the worms and each other in a way that went beyond mere curiosity. Their activity was almost *sexual*. Several of the bunnies even appeared to be . . . copulating? No. I must be misreading the behavior.

The air was cold on my body. I could feel the worm poking at my buttocks. I said, "It feels like a medical inspection."

And then another thought occurred to me. "It feels like a meat inspection. My uncle used to be in livestock and—"

Fletcher's voice on the button, very calmly, but very firmly: "Jim, don't bring *that* into the circle."

Abruptly the worm grabbed one of my feet and yanked, lifting me upside down. I managed to holler, "Hey—!" Then the worm goggled its eyes sideways at me as if to ask, "Yes?" And then it resumed studying my foot with its giant eyes. It poked and stroked and once even drew one dark finger across the soft flesh of my arch. I couldn't help it, I started giggling.

The worm grabbed one of my hands and lifted it up beside my foot. It was comparing.

"It's intelligent! It has to be!" I was still hanging upside down. "Do you see what it's doing?"

Abruptly, the worm let go of me. I tumbled back to the grass. I climbed back to my feet, grinning. "You ought to ask first," I said to the worm.

Did it expect me to do something? I wondered if it would be all right for me to touch it like the bunnydogs did?

It blinked at me.

I had to try.

I walked around to its side and . . . reached out and touched it. It crooked its eyes backward to watch me. The fur *tingled*.

I leaned into the creature. It *tingled* my whole body. I could feel the creature's—*not a heartbeat*— rhythm. A rumble, not a throb. It felt like there was a great and powerful engine, somewhere deep inside this creature; it was a low-pitched sensation, a continuing vibration, like the resonance of a great internal roaring furnace; it echoed throughout the giant creature's substance as if from a deep dark distance.

I tapped the creature's shoulder like I'd seen one of the bunnydogs do.

It lowered its arm to boost me up.

I—gulped—and put my foot into the creature's hand and it *lifted* me up and onto its back. I lay there naked on its fur, letting the tingling sensation wash back and forth across my skin, letting the rumbling sensation permeate my flesh and vibrate my bones. This was more than *sensual*—it was *sexual*. If you could build a machine to give you this sensation—

I sat up on the Chtorran's back like a cowboy. It swiveled its eyes backward to look at me curiously.

"Giddyap?" I suggested. That was a stupid thing to say.

Or maybe not.

The creature *moved*.

It turned and flowed up the hill toward the three smaller worms with similar markings. I could feel its flesh rippling beneath my legs. I yowped in surprise. I had this nightmare vision of not being able to get off the worm until it delivered me to its larder.

But it stopped to let its—*partners?*—have a look at me.

I slid down off the worm quickly. It didn't seem to mind. If I was going anywhere, I wanted it to be my choice. For a moment, I was surrounded by all four of them, all of them goggling at me curiously. Uh—perhaps getting down off the worm hadn't been such a good idea. . . .

The big one grunted. Or belched. It was a soft sound and it could have been anything. Or nothing. It was just the first sound it had made yet. But the other three in its family looked up expectantly.

The Chtorran made another sound. This one was a deliberate burping noise. It added a quick chirpling trill, rippled throughout its entire length, and then turned and slid off up the hill. Had it forgotten me or did it just not care? The other three worms followed easily in its wake. Two of them had several bunnydogs riding on their backs. Other bunnydogs scampered after. A couple of them grabbed at me in passing.

"They want you to go with—" said the voice in my ear.

"I can see that."

"Keep the button aimed at the good stuff, Jim."

"Yeah."

The bunnydogs bounced and skipped over the top of the hill after the worms. I hurried to follow after. I wondered where we were going, and I knew without being told. There was a nest nearby and we were going home to wait out the hottest part of the day.

"Still with me?"

"Be a monkey, Jimbo."

"Ted? Tanjy? Is that you?"

"Shut up."

"Yeek yeek," I monkeyed.

And then we were under the trees—the worms, the bunnies and me. These weren't Earth trees; they were tall and red and thick-stemmed. They looked like banyans. Or red ficus. I remembered these trees. I remembered sitting on top of one. There were thick ropy vines winding their way up and down the trunks, across the branches and disappearing high above our heads. They were the scarlet plumbing of a bright new future; there were vines of other colors too, darker and moodier. They crept low across the ground, winding and twisting and finally disappearing into the thick red vegetation that clustered around the sprawling roots of the trees. Those roots were thick, they curved in and out of the ground like the toes of a dragon.

Above us, the leaves of these giants were huge fluttery things like elephant ears; some of them were big enough to be used as bedsheets. The canopy of vegetation was so thick the sky was totally blotted out. It seemed as if we were in the deep gloomy twilight of a gigantic cavern. Even the bunnydogs fell silent as we left the ochre sunlight behind.

We moved across a soft carpet of blue tuft-grass. There were clumps of black ivy everywhere, outlining the gloom with tiny pipes of red neon. Tiny things filled the air; I didn't know what they were.

The forest smelled like honeysuckle and sweet apricots and dark red things rotting. It wasn't pleasant. It wasn't unpleasant. It was *different*.

The worms didn't seem to care that I had joined the scampering bunnydogs and was following them back to their nest. Had they adopted me? Was I a guest? Or did it just not matter to them who lived in their ecology?

The Chtorrans moved slowly through the woods—slow enough for the bunnies and me to keep up. Was that a courtesy? Or was it that the Chtorrans only moved fast in battle? Mostly, I'd only seen them in battle. This had to be their *normal* speed.

I thought about that. A creature that size had to generate a lot of heat when it worked—and it had much too low a surface-to-volume ratio to radiate that heat quickly. The Chtorrans probably had to watch their internal temperatures and pace themselves accordingly. Maybe that was part of the reason why the creatures rippled their fur—to fan themselves.

I wondered if the big Chtorran would have let me ride it all this way. Probably. The other worms weren't objecting to their passenger load.

But . . . I wasn't ready for that yet.

The ground slanted downward suddenly. I nearly tripped. I skidded down the hill after the worms and bunnies, and I would not have been surprised to discover that we had passed underground into a whole new world; but no—suddenly we came out into sunlight again. A rolling red and pink meadow, little more than a clearing, really—just an opening in the gloom; but in the middle of it there were totem poles, a cluster of melted-looking things. They had holes in them—big holes, little holes, holes edged with serrations. One of the Chtorrans went up to one of the totem poles and began chewing on it. I wanted to stop and watch. I was beginning to suspect—

"Big hole, three smaller ones," I said abruptly. "That's the motif. Big worm, three smaller ones. That's what the holes mean. All the smaller holes are—" The mind clicked over into a different mode. "—I got it! It's a picture of the worms' perceptual space, their relationships as seen from the inside. All the other holes all around represent the other things they deal with, the bunnydogs, the other families— "

"*Jimbo, shut up.* You're trying to analyze. Stop it. Just be a monkey right now. Listen with your whole soul."

"Yeek yeek."

"Good boy."

We passed the cluster of totem poles; I thought we were heading back into the forest, but no—the clearing was longer than I had realized. At the far end of it was a nest, a cluster of nests—a *mandala* of nests. Six nests, spaced evenly around a larger one in the center. And corrals too.

"The spacing! It's mathematically precise. They grow into it. The corrals will fit exactly into the next ring of expansion domes," I realized and shut up. "Yeek yeek—*yeek*." Good monkey, I reassured myself. There's a banana in it for you, if you're good.

Most of the Chtorrans had lost interest in me and had wandered off. Most of the bunnydogs had scampered away too. But the few who had taken custody of me were following the big Chtorran who had first—what?—*claimed* me? I followed after. Into the nest.

Turned into the left side tunnel and spiraled down to the right, down and down and down. The walls were blue and furry here—and slightly phosphorescent. They smelled good too. Abruptly I realized how bare the walls of all the nests we had seen before really were. This nest was *furnished*. There were fat little red creatures on the walls, bladderbugs the size of golf balls and water balloons. Some of them were glowing softly, casting a soft red light across the tunnels. I saw pink pipe-cleaner bugs, fat furry meeps, and dark brooding nightwalkers. I saw a millipede skulking behind a cable—no, a vine. They looked like cables, only thicker.

The vines ran along the floors, they also wrapped themselves up and down the walls like arteries and veins. I felt like I was inside a living creature. These vines were thicker than the ones crawling up the trees, but they were the same strident colors—red, purple, black, dark ochre, umber, and sienna. They sprawled everywhere like cables in a TV studio, up the walls, across the ceilings—but only rarely across the center of the corridors, and where they did, they flattened out into wide flat bands. Interesting. Obviously, those little tiny feet of the Chtorrans needed a relatively smooth surface to walk upon.

The Chtorrans had disappeared into the shadowy gloom ahead.

I kept following the bunnydogs down and around. We peeled off into a leftward-turning ramp, the valve-door popped open to let us in, and we kept on heading down and down—

Someone was coming up the other way.

At first I thought it was a dog. Then an ape. Or a headless chicken the size of a child. Then my mind stopped trying to make sense of it. This wasn't anything I recognized.

It was chest high and it shambled slothfully up the ramp. It was studying the floor in front of itself. It didn't have a head. It was yellowish-red, smooth-skinned, and oily; it looked like a slug on two legs. Half its body was tail, the other half was neck. It didn't have a head. At the end of its neck was—a mouth. A nozzle. A collar of tiny eyestalks ringed the place where the neck narrowed.

The headless mouth was snuffling like an animated vacuum cleaner, moving back and forth across the floor and the walls. It was eating, but very selectively.

It snuffled up to me, snuffled up one leg, across my crotch, and down the other leg; then it moved on.

It found a bladderbug, inhaled it off the wall, and began to chew. I could see the bulge of the bug sliding to a point halfway down the length of the creature's neck. Then it hesitated while somewhere inside that neck, the thing bit and chewed, crunching the bug softly. Some of the juices dribbled thickly out of the mouth the next time the thing snuffled the floor. The mouth snuffled over the juices, inhaled them again, and moved on.

"The cleaning thing—?" I asked.

The bunnydogs were already moving on. One of them was looking back at me and tapping one foot impatiently. It looked like Thumper.

I took one last look at the snuffler—it was the weirdest thing I'd ever seen—then followed the bunnydogs forward and down.

I wondered how deep we were going—and if we were even still on Earth.

Q: Why did the Chtorran eat only one of the Vice-President's legs?

A: It didn't want to leave him without a leg to stand on.

64

"Hi, Dave!"

"Cream isn't all that floats to the top."
—SOLOMON SHORT

This was the most furnished Chtorran nest we'd ever seen. It was the most *lived-in*. This was the most fleshed-out cross section of the Chtorran eco-culture we'd yet discovered.

And I didn't have the slightest idea what any of it meant.

There were clusters of purple plum-like things on the wall. They smelled rich and soupy. Were they food? Or did they have some other function? How could I tell? There were patches of wormberry plant. Why? There was a thing hanging like a net across the ceiling. Was it alive?

But, hell, what would a Chtorran make of my mother's silk curtains? Besides lunch, that is.

I held the button in my hand and pointed it at everything I saw. This would keep Dr. Zymph and her Ecology Section busy for years—except we didn't have years. I wondered . . . if I could move in here, if I could live here, if I could become part of this nest—that's what we really needed. Someone to live with the Chtorrans.

It had to be possible. After all, I hadn't been eaten yet, had I?

It was the *yet* that worried me.

"Chrple?"

A small Chtorran came rippling up the ramp. I stepped aside, out of its way. It was a very small one, only dog-sized, but its manner was eager and curious. It peeped at me and swiveled and cocked its eyes as it passed. It peered backward at me over its own rump, staring at me until it curved up and around and out of sight. Apparently it was on an errand for Daddy. Or Mommy? Or who?

Damn. There was so much we didn't know.

And somewhere along the way, I had forgotten how to be a monkey. I didn't know what I was any more.

One of the bunnies grabbed my hand and pulled at me. I let myself be tugged. We had wound down and around, peeling off first one way and then the other, but always winding down and around until I was totally lost. Under those seven surface domes was a great network of caverns and tunnels. Who—or *what*—had dug them? How had all this been accomplished?

"Oh, little button, are you getting all this?"

"Just fine. Shh."

Somewhere below—*just how deep was this complex?*—I could hear wormsong. Deep. Rhythmic. Satisfying. Ethereal. Otherworldly. It resonated throughout the tunnel.

How many Chtorrans were there here? Did they sing four at a time or *more* at a time? Lord, it was beautiful. I'd never heard anything so compelling in my life. Now, I pulled forward ahead of the bunnies. I didn't need them to lead me anymore.

I wanted to follow the sound to its heart. I wanted to see who was singing. I wanted to *be* who was singing. I wanted to feel the sound with my whole soul again. I wanted to hug into it again—

Like the herdsong.

Like—

And then the bunnies pulled me into a tunnel that peeled away from the sound and up and around a corner and into a dimly lit room and there were little bunnies hopping all around. It was the bunnydog nest. They gabbled and squeaked and bounced and tumbled and—

They weren't all bunnies.

Some of them were children.

A four-year-old, a toddler, waddled forward with a happy smile on his dirty face. He had blond hair, he was naked and dirty, but he looked well-fed and healthy. "Hi, Dave!" he called at me. "Hi, Dave!"

There were other children here; they were naked too. They stayed back, behind the bunnydogs: a baby, too young to walk, barely able to crawl; a little girl, maybe seven; and a cowering boy, maybe nine or ten. He was curled up in a fetal position, sucking his thumb and lost inside himself. He didn't even know I was here. The girl stared at me, wide-eyed and distrustful. The baby didn't care. He just cooed happily to himself.

"Oh, shit—" I said. And, "Oh, God. Oh, no." And, "Oh, shit," again.

Dilemma.

Continue with the mission? Find out what's in this nest? Or save the children?

What's more important?

I hesitated.

I felt so—torn.

The wormsong. The children. The button. The job. The questions. Everything all at once.

The pressure built up in my chest like a fire.

"McCarthy, what's the matter?"

"I can't leave them here."

"The mission—"

"Screw the mission. We didn't figure on this."

Silence.

Then: "McCarthy, listen to me. This is about communication with the Chtorrans. Nothing else. Don't blow this!"

"If I leave them here, you know what's going to happen to them."

"*You don't know that.*"

"Yes, I do."

"This is *different.*"

"—And you don't *know* that."

Silence.

Then: "McCarthy?"

"Fuck you. Shut up."

The button shut up.

The button was right of course.

But—being right only gets you the booby prize. The bunnydogs were gobbling curiously around me, trying to pull me this way and that. I didn't know what they wanted any more.

Dammit! I'm the one who has to live inside this soul!

"Hi, Dave!"

Hell, I knew what I was going to do. Why was I dithering? I scooped up the little boy and hugged him tight and nuzzled his neck and kissed him and said, "Hiya, stinker." I tousled his hair and he giggled. He did stink—but so did I. We all did. We all stank of worms and rotting red things and despair and wormsong.

I stepped through the gobbling bunnydogs to the girl. I squatted down to look her straight in the face. "Hi, my name's Jim. I'm here to take you home! Are you ready to go home?"

"Where's my Momma?"

"Do you want to go home?" I repeated.

"My Momma's dead. I can't go home," she said.

"Will you come with me?"

"Where's my Momma?"

Stupid me. *Wake up, Jim! She can't hear you.*

I turned and picked up the infant and put him in the girl's arms. "You carry the baby, okay?" I said it firmly. It was an order. *"You carry the baby."*

She nodded.

Good. Maybe we had a chance.

What would the Chtorrans think of this—me taking the children out of the nest? I didn't care. It had to be done. But just how did they regard these four? As a different kind of bunnydog? Or just a different kind of snack in the cupboard? For that matter, maybe the bunnydogs were nothing more than snacks too? Purina Chtorran chow—a free kid in every bag. Ugh.

I put the toddler down—at least he could walk—and turned to the ten-year-old in the fetal position. I unbent his limbs; he didn't resist. He might as well have been unconscious. Maybe he was. Maybe I should leave him. Sure. And maybe I should stop respecting myself too. I scooped the boy up and draped him over my shoulders in a fireman's carry. I grabbed the girl's hand. The toddler took her other hand and we started walking out the tunnel. The bunnies didn't try to stop us. We started up.

And up.

The tunnels looked different when they were all uphill. They were harder to climb. And I wasn't sure of the way out, either. But I figured if I just kept going up—

I could feel the song again. I had to resist it.

I made a wrong turn and we found ourselves in the wrong room. The biggest room of all. It was filled with worms.

No. It was filled with *worm.*

Singular, not plural.

The light was dim and the wormsong was suddenly overwhelming, but I could see—

There were Daddy worms here—Alphas, we called them—but only three of them. The rest of the chamber was one gigantic Chtorran. It looked like a big red blimp. *Like the big red blimp in the sky that all the worms had tried so desperately to reach.*

It was the size of a truck. A twenty-six-wheeler. Or bigger. It was too big to move. It was just this big red thing. A hairy red pudding. Its eyes were each a meter across. They turned slowly to look at us. At us. They blinked. The room echoed with the sound: *SSSPPPUUUTTTT-PPPHHHWWWUUUUTTTT.*

The worm was rumbling. It sounded like an earthquake purring. It was humming. The sound went through my bones. It was singing—the chords pierced through my head.

What was this *thing*?!

The Daddy worms—the Alphas—were lost against its bulk, but they were singing too. They were writhing against it, chirruping and burping and—

I'd seen this before.

A thousand years ago.

I'd walked into a nest and I'd seen a family of worms writhing together and singing. And I'd touched them. I'd hugged them.

This was the same thing. Only magnified—

The Alphas were the lesser worms here. They were the family of this gigantic king-worm.

"My God." Was this the intelligence we were looking for?

Oh, no. It couldn't be.

This was some bizarre practical joke that the universe was playing on the human race. This bloated thing was a travesty, a diseased cancerous mistake.

It made a sound. "*Blurph!*" The chamber echoed.

Beside me, the girl whimpered.

"It's okay, honey," I said.

And then I did the bravest thing of my life. I began stepping away. We backed slowly out of the room. Into the tunnel. "That way." I pointed with my chin. "Just keep going up, okay? Don't stop. Carry the baby. Come on, let's go home now. Maybe there will be some nice big strong men waiting for us at the top. Wouldn't that be nice? Are you listening, button?"

No answer.

Shit.

I kept talking to the kids. This was no place for monkeys any more. I had to keep them human. I had to keep them moving up and out. Something rumbled in the tunnel above us. It sounded purple, so I backed the kids into a side passage. The valve-door popped open and we hid inside the tunnel while we watched two, three, four big Chtorrans go sliding and rippling down the passage. They were murmuring to themselves as they went. I didn't think they were Alphas, but they were big enough to be.

"Everybody fine? Everybody ready? Okay, let's keep going—" It was getting rougher now. The kid on my shoulders was growing heavier every second, but I couldn't leave him here. My heart was pounding in my chest. We staggered upward. "Good girl, don't let go."

"How much farther is it?"

"Just a little bit more. You'll see—oops."

We stepped aside to let a snuffler pass us. It had diamond patterns of red and black markings across its ochre back. I wished I had the time to stop and study that thing. I rearranged the weight on my shoulders and we pressed on. Up and around, up and around—

There was something in the tunnel ahead of us. Something angry.

It looked like a bunnydog—but it was bigger than any bunnydog we'd seen yet. Thinner, leaner, sharper-boned, and naked-looking; we couldn't see it clearly, but it was hissing at us. A warning? An order?

I had no weapon. Nothing.

"Don't move—" I lowered the unconscious boy to the floor, leaning him up against one wall. I pulled the little girl and the toddler over, turned them to look at me. "Don't move. Don't do anything. Stay right here."

And then I turned back to the bunnydog thing.

It was angry monkey time.

I curled my lip into a vicious snarl. I jutted my jaw forward, I thrust my head forward. I hunkered, I squatted, I pulled my arms up like a gallows, clutched my hands like claws. I squatted low and stomped my feet hard. I growled in my throat. I let it build, let it gather and come roaring up and out of my throat in a scream of rage. I *threatened* the little bastard as ferociously as I could.

It worked.

Whatever the bunnydog-thing was, it *flinched*. It yelped and skittered backward, making *ki-yi-yi-yi-yipe* noises all the way up the tunnel.

It was cold in this tunnel, but the sweat dripped off of me in rivulets. I wanted nothing more than to get out of here as fast as possible.

I turned back to the kids.

"Hi, Dave!"

I didn't know who Dave was, but he was literally a life-saver.

Q: What would a Chtorran get if it ate a tank?

A: Its minimum daily requirement of iron.

Q: What would a Chtorran get if it ate a Revelationist?

A: An American flag pin.

Q: What would a Chtorran get if it ate Congress?
A: The President's personal thanks.

65

To Coda and Fugue

*"The last two words of the Star-Spangled
Banner are not 'Play Ball!'"*
—SOLOMON SHORT

Somehow, we got out of the nest.

I don't know how I did it. I picked up the boy again and put him over my right shoulder. He was as limp as if he were dead—and maybe he *was* dying, but just the same, no human being should ever have to die alone. I grabbed the toddler's hand and started upward again. The little girl carried the baby and followed me because I told her to, but she kept asking for her mommy the whole time.

I followed the ramps upward. Every time we came to a valve-door or a branching or a room, I looked for the next upward-sloping ramp. Sooner or later, we had to reach the top. Somewhere, there had to be an exit.

I talked the whole way. I talked to all four of the kids. "We're going to go home now. We're going to have hamburgers and french fries and Cokes and ice cream. We're going to watch our favorite TV shows and we're going to go to the movies and the beach and—and we'll see all of our friends again and we're going to scrub up in the tub with lots of bubble bath and toy boats and rubber duckies and we're going to have clean pajamas and nighties and we're all going to have nice warm beds to sleep in and we're each going to have someone wonderful come and kiss us good-night. And we're going to find our daddies and our mommies—"

I choked on that one. I didn't have a mommy any more. She'd divorced me.

Well—shit.

"—And we're all going to be *human* again. No more monkey business. Not ever again."

I started talking to the boy on my shoulder. "Listen, you—don't you dare die on me. I didn't come all this way to rescue a corpse. I came a long way for you . You can hear me, I know you can. My name is Jim. Jim McCarthy. And I know you want to come out and play with me and be my friend. I know you're scared and I know you've been through some pretty frightening stuff and it's all right to be scared, but now it's time to start coming out. It's time to start coming home. We're going to start making it better now, okay?" I readjusted his weight on my shoulder. "Okay?"

"Okay," he said softly. I almost didn't hear it. I was three more meters up the tunnel before I realized he'd answered me and then fallen silent again.

But he was still limp on my shoulder. Had he become conscious for just a second? Or had he been unconsciously echoing me? Or had I actually *touched* him?

I knew what I wanted to believe. So I believed it.

"Good," I said. "That's the way. Just keep listening. And when you're ready to talk, someone will be there to listen. I'll listen to you. Any time, okay? *Okay?*

"Okay," he murmured again.

God, he was heavy. I wished I could get him to walk, but this was faster.

And then, suddenly, we were blinking in the pink sunlight and there were bunnydogs scampering around us curiously, but I ignored them and pushed out of the dome .

It wasn't the same dome I'd entered by; that one was on the opposite side of the cluster. We wound our way around through the domes heading toward the meadow, the slope, the forest—the circle and the camouflaged gunships. We were going home. Three of the bunnydogs followed.

It was such a long way, I didn't know if I could make it carrying the boy on my shoulders. My whole back was starting to ache. I was going to have to pace myself—and the kids too. Maybe we could rest under the trees for a minute. . . .

"Hang in there, Jim. You're doing just fine."

The voice was comforting, but I was running out of strength.

"You're out of the nest. It's all downhill from here, Jim."

"Something wrong with your screens?" I growled. "I know an uphill when I'm climbing one."

"Trust me, Jim. It's *down*hill."

"*Sure* it is—" I started to say, then stopped myself.

The voice was right. I hadn't been paying attention. While I'd been so busy complaining, I'd topped the slope of the hill and it was all downhill toward the forest now.

"You can make it to the trees, Jim."

The boy felt lighter on my shoulder now. The aching eased in my back, and for a moment, I felt almost jaunty. We were going to make it.

And then—we were in the shadows, and I very nearly tripped over a root. I lowered the boy down carefully to the ground. I took the baby from the serious little girl and rocked him in my arms. "Sit down for a minute," I said. "We gotta catch our breath before we go on."

They sat. The three bunnydogs sat.

"Who are you talking to?" the little girl asked. "Are you talking to my mommy?"

"No, not yet. I'm talking to the nice man who's waiting for us just on the other side of these trees. Okay?"

"Okay," echoed the unconscious boy.

"Hi, Dave!"

"Hi," I answered the toddler.

The baby gurgled. I tickled its tummy. "Hiya, Max," I said. "Will you grow up to be a big strong soldier for me?" I was falling in love with all four of them. Naked, dirty—all of them probably traumatized beyond belief—but they were human and they needed loving, and I couldn't help myself. I wanted to see them safe and happy and taken care of. They deserved it. We *all* deserved it. But if I couldn't have it, then I wanted *somebody* to have it. These four were a place to start.

The three bunnydogs that had followed us started gobbling among themselves. Language? I doubted it. Maybe they had some kind of gobbling game—maybe that was how they interacted. The meaning wasn't in the words but in the process of gobbling.

Who cared?

Something had shifted for me.

This morning I had wanted to talk to the worms. I had wanted to meet them on their own ground and see if possibly humans and Chtorrans—*whoever the real Chtorrans were*—could somehow *negotiate*.

That was who I was this morning.

And then I had found four children in a worm nest.

Now I knew different. What I thought I wanted wasn't what I *really* wanted.

What I wanted was the chance to simply be *human*.

Whatever it meant to be human.

I wanted the chance to find out.

And I wanted my children to have the chance too.

Maybe we could talk to the worms or the bunnydogs—or whatever else the scarlet ecology would throw at us—but if it meant giving up our humanity, then the price was too high.

And that's who I was this afternoon.

I wondered if I would feel the same way tonight.

I hoped so.

Damn. I had to laugh. I was turning into Duke.

And then, abruptly, there were hands pulling me to my feet—"Are you okay, Jim?"

I blinked in confusion. I hadn't even seen them come up—or heard them. There were four of them, big and brawny and stripped to their shorts; they were wearing camouflage paint all over their bodies.

"Come on, we gotta get going."

"Huh?"

"You win. We gotta save the kids."

I recognized them now. They were from the squad of Air Marines backing up the mission. Mostly they'd kept apart from the Science Section. They were huge.

Each of them scooped up one of the children and started dog-trotting back into the thick red forest. The one with the toddler—"Hi, Dave!"—grabbed my arm. "McCarthy, you okay? Can you make it?"

"Huh? Sure. You just caught me by surprise. That's all." I followed after, running hard to keep up with them.

The bunnydogs tweeped and dweebled, then came hopping and chittering after us.

Q: What would a Chtorran get if it ate the President?
A: Heartburn.

Q: What would a Chtorran get if it ate the Vice-President?
A: Our deepest sympathies.

66

Sput-Phwut

"Understanding the laws of nature does not mean that we are immune to their operations."

—SOLOMON SHORT

We came out of the forest and over the hill and down the slope, toward the empty circle and the camouflaged gunships waiting for us. There were naked people standing near the circle. And there were bunnydogs too—the people were playing with them.

There was even a worm, sitting and watching everything.

Obviously, the mission team had been making overtures of their own. They turned to look at us as we came bounding down the hill. Several of the bunnydogs started bouncing up toward us—and some of the people too. I recognized Jerry Larson and Roy Barnes, and two of the observation team, though I didn't know their names. And Fletcher. All had stripped to their underwear, or less.

Just a little bit farther—

Fletcher met me halfway up the hill. She was naked. I hardly noticed that she had terrific tits. She caught me by the arms. "Stay cool, Jim. Be a monkey again." She stopped me from following after the Marines. "It's okay. You did good. You did right. Now, come back to us."

I didn't take my eyes off the children. The four Marines just loped on down the hill with them and around to the back side of the camouflage tent where they disappeared inside the netting.

"It's all right, Jim. The kids were more important. Everybody here was cheering for you. Mission control was *wrong*."

"So was I," I said. "So is this whole mission."

"No, Jim. The mission isn't over!" She turned me sideways to look at her. "We need you."

I shook my head. "I'm no good for this. I don't follow orders. And I don't know if I want to talk to the worms. Not after what I saw inside that nest."

There were two more Marines coming up the hill toward us. "You need help, Ma'am?"

"No," she said sharply. "Let me handle this." They moved off, but not too far.

"Jim—we've established some kind of contact here. It's a necessary start. This could be the breakthrough! We need you."

"I don't understand why."

"Because you're the contact point. For some reason, the bunnies like *you* the best."

"I speak their language—gibberish," I said. But I let myself be led down the hill toward the circle. Some of the bunnies came hop-skipping toward us.

Something made me look around—a flick of Fletcher's eyes perhaps as she saw something up the hill. I turned and saw more bunnydogs hopping over the crest, followed by two Chtorrans and some of the taller, naked-looking bunnydog-*things*. They looked more like rats than bunnies, and they looked naked because they had hardly any fur at all, only a few patches of red stubble here and there on their bodies. Great. Just what we needed now. Giant naked rats with mange.

And more worms. Five, six, eight more worms came flowing and rippling over the hill.

"Dance—" I said to Fletcher and pushed her toward the circle. "Huh?"

"Dance!" I shouted at the two Marines too. "Come on, let's go dance. We've got company again—let's show them a good time!" *Because you don't want to know what the alternative is.*

I didn't know how I knew that, but I knew it.

If we were going to survive this, we had to dance naked with a big pink worm.

The bunnydogs bounced and squeaked, squealed and laughed. It was so obvious now. These were the children. The *other* things, the naked-rat things—they were the adult form.

No wonder these creatures were so damned playful. No wonder the worms were so interested.

In their own way, *the worms were children too.* The adult worms were all like the big fat blimp thing I'd seen in the nest!

No wonder the worms were so crazy.

All of them were orphans!

Hatched from eggs or whatever or however they got here—there weren't any adults until the first of the orphans grew up.

My God.

No wonder they freaked when they saw the blimp in the sky. It wasn't an angel to them. It was *mommy!*

Oh, shit.

How many more mistakes had we made?

I bounced into the circle. I danced. I hopped. I freddied around like a big goofy jumping jack, turning and grinning and tumbling—anything to make the bunnies join us. *Anything* to keep them laughing.

Until I figured out how to get out of here.

We were in trouble.

Or—wait a minute—maybe we weren't.

"Everbody keep dancing! Keep the bunnies laughing!"

This was no place to try to think things out, but it was the only place I had. The idea was inescapable. *What if we could make friends with the bunnies and the worms while they were children?* What kind of adults would they turn into? But if this *wasn't* the place to consider that question, then where *was?*

I glanced up the hill. Nineteen. Twenty. Twenty-three worms.

Oh, shit.

Maybe my first impulse was right. This wasn't the place to worry about *that* question. The worms came rippling and slithering down the hill, moving right up to the circle.

Why did the worms like to watch the bunnies dance, anyway? What was *that* all about? We still didn't know what their relationship was. And how did the bunnydog-*things*, the naked rats, fit into the picture?

I put on my plastic grin, grabbed a bunny, and tumbled him ass-over-teakettle, enthusiastically tickling him all the way—him? Uh, yes. *Him.* The little bastard was getting an erection. Was this bunny-sex?

I rolled into a whole crowd of bunnies, sending them scampering and laughing every which way.

They bubbled and bounced and fell all over me, screaming and giggling just like the children they were. They seemed to be asking for something. The bunnies tugged at me and made little begging noises. "Hi, Dave!" "Where's my Mommy?" No wonder the worms were so attracted to Earth children—they looked like bunnydogs to them.

I chucked a bunny under a chin. We giggled together and made funny growling noises. I batted him gently, and he rolled and somersaulted backward like a happy little croquet ball. He scampered back for more.

I started working my way around the group, gently urging people, "Start moving toward the nets. Keep smiling. Keep dancing. Strategic withdrawal."

The bunnydogs were touching us all curiously now. I had started it with my tickling; now they were tickling back. One of them tugged at Larson's shorts, sniffing and even biting. Another reached up and poked at Fletcher's breast with a stubby finger. She laughed and squatted down so the creature could examine her close up. She examined it right back. There was no modesty here.

I called across to her, "They must be mammals."

She grinned and called back, "Don't bet on anything yet."

"I bet we should start withdrawing," I said carefully.

She looked around, concerned. So did I.

The bunnies circled around all of us, clustering and gobbling and petting and touching. I looked to the worms; they looked bored. The problem was, we knew how to start a dance, but we didn't know how to end one. Just what was a bunnydance a prelude to? Maybe, if we could just establish that it was all right for all of our species to dance together, then maybe we could begin to build a relationship on that.

Maybe we could even—*train*?—the worms and the bunnydogs somehow. . . .

"Jim?" That was Fletcher. "The bunnies." She turned around slowly looking at them.

I saw what she meant immediately. The bunnies were calming now. They were turning around to notice the worms.

And then the bunnies began to *sing*.

It was an eerie sound, but high-pitched and sweet. No two of the little creatures were singing the same note, nor were they warbling in anything approaching unison, but the impact of the whole crowd of them cooing and tweebling all at once like that was incredible. It was the sound of a fairy chorus. Their voices blurred in a way that was distinctly otherworldly and oddly pleasant.

I looked to Larson, to Fletcher, and to the others. Their eyes were bright with wonder. They were as enchanted as I was by this little miracle.

"It's just like the herd!" I called.

Fletcher laughed back, "I know—I can feel it!"

"They're singing to the worms!" It was wonderful. Maybe I'd been wrong again. Maybe there was a chance . . . Damn. I didn't know anything any more. God, I wanted to believe in these creatures!

Now, the bunnies began turning back and forth in little quick hops. They bleated as they bounced. They chirped and bubbled and sang arias at each other. It was a conversation of song sweeping around and around, twirling like a laughing elephantine ballerina in a great gaudy silly extravaganza of drunken clowns.

I turned with the sound, around and around in the middle of it all, turning to get a sense of the entire group, turning like a bunny myself. The other bunnies were turning—the other humans, too. The motion was picked up and reflected around and around. Other monkeys, other bunnies, were turning around us, turning, all smiles and delight. The sound grew rounder. The monkeys were singing now. And all the bunnies were turning now. I was turning. All of us turning were a reflection of my turning and I was a reflection of all of us in me. This was what the herd was trying to be. A little piece of God. We were wheels and gears in a grand machine of wheels and gears. A mandala of God.

I added my note to the bunnysong—just like in the herd. My note was deep, deeper than I thought I was capable of. It resonated throughout my body. The monkeys grinned as the note carried across the circle—and joined in too. It was monkeysong, bunnysong, wormsong, Godsong. It was all the songs at once. The bunnies laughed. And kept on singing. The note was infectious, intoxicating—like a zillion souls all humming *Oooommmmmm* at once.

We turned together. Individuals circled to me, then swirled away. There was no pattern at all to anyone's movements, but all was harmony and wholeness in this gathering. I could feel it enveloping me like a big warm fizzy bubble bath.

It felt like *home*.

One of the worms, one of the bigger ones, flowed slowly into the circle then. Was it the same worm I'd met before? I couldn't tell. It looked like it. Two of the other large worms followed it.

I said, "I know this doesn't make sense, I know I'm contradicting myself—or maybe it's just the effect of the bunnysong—but I'm actually beginning to feel . . . friendly . . . toward these creatures."

I had to know. I approached the big one.

The worm lifted its arm high then. A stretch? Its mouth opened in front of me. I squatted to my knees and peered in. Huge. Dark. And it smelled awful.

But I was grinning. I was the first human being on the planet to look into a worm's mouth without being pushed. I was actually feeling cocky—

—that's what saved my life.

I was turning around to look back toward the domes, I was about to say something stupid, when one of the bunnydogs let out a yelp—a yelp cut suddenly short—

I turned and saw—

One of the worms just crunching a bunny into its mouth.

I turned back toward the worm I'd been with. It was just rising up into an attack position—

I stabbed a finger at it and commanded, "No!" I didn't know what I was doing, I just bellowed, "That's very bad manners!"

The worm hesitated.

"Down!" I shouted. And pointed. "Down!"

The worm came down.

It looked confused.

I started backing away. "Get ready to scramble!" I said quietly. I glanced behind me. Barnes had dropped into a karate position—a cat stance. The others were backing away slowly. Fletcher's eyes were wide. She looked ready to bolt. "Slowly . . . !" I commanded. "Don't break . . . !"

The worm started to follow me. It started to flow after me,

I pointed at it and said, "No! Stay!"

It worked

And then—

—another bunnydog yelped. Another worm was feeding.

And then another, and another—the air was suddenly filled with yelping!

The worm moved—

I broke sideways—I ran for Fletcher, leaping and knocking her flat on the grass—

Something purple chirruped behind us. Something roared close over our heads and exploded! The blast blew us sideways; we bounced against a furry wall. Fletcher gasped and started screaming. I rolled her over on her belly, rolled on top of her—

More explosions—the blast slamming into us—a wall of heat—

Larson was screaming—Barnes was shrieking—"Oh, Momma, Momma!" There were flames—

—and pulled Fletcher to her feet and ran, scrambling toward the chopper. A worm was burning. Something small and pink and flaming rocketed past us. Another worm was skidding, turning toward us—

The dome was already exploding off the chopper—the door was open—a man was on the ground before it, firing past us! I saw the streaking of incendiary bullets.

The door was open. We pounded up into it, past the man with the rifle. He gasped as something grabbed him—and then we were airborne. The open door looked down on Hell—

Q: Where does a 500-lb. Chtorran eat?

A: Anywhere it wants.

67

Chtorr Whorrs

"Life never gets so bad that it can't get worse."

—SOLOMON SHORT

We watched from the air.

It was horrible.

There was nothing we could do but watch and photograph and be horrified.

If it had been a feeding frenzy, it would have made sense. It would have been understandable. It would have been a shark pack out of control.

But this wasn't out of control.

It was calm and deliberate.

The bunnies were unafraid. They continued about their business, grooming and patting the worms, and even attempting to copulate with the giant creatures. One of the little pink bunnies was even sprawled on a worm's great flank, humping at it while the worm was stuffing a baby bunnydog into its mouth. The baby did not struggle.

"They look like they're doped," said Fletcher.

"They're *not* doped," I said. I *knew*.

Lizard was arming her weapons. "I'm going to burn them," she said.

"No, don't—" I grabbed her arm.

She shook my hand off, but she stopped what she was doing. She spoke into her headset for a moment. The other two choppers peeled off, leaving only our machine circling over the nightmare below.

"All right, Jim. What is it?" she asked. She must have heard it in my voice.

"We were *wrong*," I said. "Terribly, terribly wrong." Fletcher turned to stare at me. She looked ashen.

I nodded and continued, "We're so trapped inside our terrestrial thinking that even when we attempt to create a new domain of perceptions—I'm sorry, Fletch—it didn't work. We were wrong in trying to think there's anything more to these creatures than we've seen. There *isn't*. This is what they are." I looked away from the carnage below. I couldn't take it any more.

"But—all the contact procedures *worked*," she insisted. "You *danced* with them." Poor Fletcher; she didn't see it yet.

"No, they didn't work. I wish they had." I shook my head. The proof was dying below. "The worms *don't care*. The bunnydogs don't care. We're just *furniture*."

"And the singing—?" Lizard asked.

"That's the worst part of all. The singing—it's a . . ." I didn't have the language for it. "It's how the *food* announces it's ready to be eaten."

"Oh, my God," said Fletcher. "The herds—"

"Uh-huh. The herds." I felt sick with the knowledge. "Whatever it is that's happening to the human race, the herds are one of our possible futures. We're being *trained* or *mutated* or *transformed* into . . . lunch that doesn't fight back." I could hardly get the words out. "And in return, the worms will guarantee that our species will survive. *That's* the relationship they have with the bunnydogs. It's the same arrangement we have with cattle and chickens and sheep."

"Fuck that shit," said Lizard. "I'll never be sheep." Her hands moved instinctively back to her weapons board. I couldn't blame her.

Below, the worms continued to feed. Despite myself, I couldn't help watching. Each of the larger worms had eaten several of the bunnydogs. The smallest worms ate only one or two. Rank? Or appetite? There was so much we didn't know.

The bunnies were moving away from the worms now, sorting themselves out and shaking themselves awake. They looked . . . happy.

"No," said Fletcher. "You're guessing."

"You want to go back down there and argue with them?"

"You don't know that, Jim. This is just a—a feeding frenzy, that's all—" But her protest was only halfhearted.

"Yes, it *is* a feeding frenzy," I said. "Only it's the food that's frenzied. The bunnies have whipped themselves up into some kind of religious worship of the worms. It's an honor to be eaten. They love the worms."

Lizard looked up from her controls and glanced back at me sharply. "How do you know that, Jim?"

I shrugged helplessly. "I don't know how I know it. I just do. I . . . I *feel* it."

"Look," said Fletcher.

The worms were clustering into groups, three or four to a group. They moved together, circling around and around, and then tumbled into a writhing mass, three or four at a time. *We'd seen this before*, Lizard and I. A moment more and all the worms were writhing and rolling together.

"My God," said Fletcher. "Just like Lucky—and Tiny."

"You don't see it yet, do you?" I said very quietly. Either she didn't hear me or she didn't want to. She didn't respond.

The worms were slowing now. They held their positions for a moment, then shifted again, finding new partners and sliding together.

"It looks like a snake pit," said Lizard. "What are they doing?"

"It's called *communion*," I said. "And that's how they communicate with each other."

"No," said Fletcher. "It's just a meeting dance. It's something they do when they—"

"No! It's something they do when they *talk*!" I nearly shouted at her. "I don't know the mechanics of it—and I know that the Science Section says it's impossible—but that's what they're doing, somehow, in some way that we still don't understand."

Fletcher glared at me—but she stared out the window again, looking for proof that I was wrong. Or right.

"It looks like they're copulating," said Lizard.

"Copulating is a kind of communication," I said without thinking.

And then it hit me.

Communication. It was *all* about communication.

Only, we'd been looking at it from the *concept* of communication instead of from the *experience*. Fletcher was right and wrong at the same time—and I was an even *bigger* fool. I'd stumbled into that circle believing that a few yeek-yeeks and a belief in bananas were all I needed to start communicating with these monsters!

I said abruptly, "I know what's happening here. And I know why we failed. We were on the wrong wavelength."

"Huh?" said Fletcher, looking around at me.

I said, "We could never determine enough of a pattern in the Chtorran shrieks and trills to determine any words. That's because their language isn't a verbal one. Or, it's only partially verbal—it's half words and half sign language. We've been trying to figure out their language from the vowels, but we've been deaf to the consonants." I pointed below. "*That's* their language. We *can't* communicate with them. *Not ever*. Communicate? With that?! How?!"

Lizard was circling the writhing worms as low as she could. The chopper swayed unevenly and my stomach complained. I realized that Fletcher and I were both still naked. It didn't matter. Nothing mattered.

Below, the worms ignored us. They were lost in each other. The bunnies were tending them again or munching at the flowers or curling up and going to sleep. The worms kept rippling and sliding around and around in a complex dance of interwoven circles.

My mind was racing now. The ideas were tumbling out one after another. "Consider this: We're verbal creatures. Except for our genitals, the most sensitive parts of our bodies are our mouths. That's where we do our most intimate experiencing. So that's how we do our communicating too. But the worms wear their nerves on the outside. They experience *everything* at once. How do you think they experience themselves? Or their place in the universe?" I answered my own question. "I'll bet they perceive themselves to be much more connected to their environment and to each other. We chatter at each other like food. They *make love*."

Lizard cut me off impatiently. "Save it, Jim, for the postmortem. You just told me what I wanted to know. You just told all of us." She reached forward and armed her weapons board again.

"The only good worm is a—"

The chopper's guns roared, drowning out her last two words.

Q: What does a Chtorran call a grenade?
A: A jaw-breaker.

68

The Grenade

"*Morality and practicality should be congruent. If they're not, then there's something wrong with either one or the other.*"

—SOLOMON SHORT

I went to see Duke.

He looked better. And he looked worse. The bitterness was obvious now. When I sat down next to his bed, he turned his head away from me.

I said, "I won't stay long. I came to deliver something."

He still didn't look at me.

I waited till the nurse was out of the room. I said, "I don't know how you're going to hide it, Duke, or where, but . . . well, *here*." I slipped the grenade into his hand. His one remaining hand. The grenade was small but lethal. It would do the job.

Duke didn't move. The grenade sat in his hand like a rock.

Had I made a mistake? Had I reminded him again of his own fear?

Perhaps I should just go.

Duke turned his head.

The hand with the grenade lifted up as if it had a life of its own. It carried the grenade painfully upward to where Duke's eyes could focus on it. They blinked and cleared and looked at the grenade dispassionately. The hand turned the grenade over and over. The thumb found the safety catch.

Duke's mouth opened. The hand brought the grenade forward so he could grab the ring with his teeth. Was he going to detonate it now?!

No. He wasn't. He let go of the ring. He was just testing the feel of it. He looked at the grenade again, and there was just the slightest hint of a smile on his face.

And then the hand holding the grenade disappeared beneath the covers.

Duke still hadn't looked at me. Still hadn't met my eyes.

I waited, but he turned his head away again, toward the wall. Not even a thank-you.

After a while, I got up and left.

That was the last time that I saw Duke.

ABOUT THE AUTHOR

David Gerrold made his television writing debut with the now-classic "The Trouble With Tribbles" episode of the original *Star Trek®* series. Since 1967 he has story-edited three TV series, edited five anthologies, and written two nonfiction books about television production (both of which have been used as textbooks) and over a dozen novels, three of which have been nominated for the prestigious Hugo and Nebula awards.

His television credits include multiple episodes of *Star Trek*, *Tales From the Darkside*, *Twilight Zone*, *The Real Ghostbusters*, *Logan's Run*, and *Land of the Lost*.

His novels include *When H.A.R.L.I.E. Was One*, *The Man Who Folded Himself*, and *A Day for Damnation*. His short stories have appeared in most of the major science fiction magazines, including *Galaxy*, *If*, *Amazing*, and *Twilight Zone*.

Gerrold has also published columns and articles in *Starlog*, *Profiles*, *Infoworld*, *Creative Computing*, *Galileo*, *A-Plus*, and other science fiction and computing periodicals. He averages over two dozen lecture appearances a year and also teaches screenwriting at Pepperdine University.

David Gerrold has completed working on the staff of *Star Trek: The Next Generation* and is now preparing a new SF TV series for the Arthur Company and Universal Television.

A Special Preview
of the long-awaited
Book 3 in
**The War Against the Chtorr,
A RAGE FOR REVENGE**
by David Gerrold

David Gerrold's fans of **The War Against the Chtorr** have been looking for the third volume for years. They've hounded every publisher in town hoping someone would say, "Yes, it'll be coming out next month." They've found Gerrold on computer billboards and offered to trade software for a look at the manuscript. Well, it's finally happened. Bantam Spectra will be publishing the next book. *A Rage for Revenge* will be on sale in April 1989, but here's a little something to whet the appetite.

The battle against the invading Chtorr has taken its toll on many of Earth's defenders. After long months of fighting the aliens, Lieutenant James McCarthy finds himself in a place of refuge. But, as we see in the following scene, the soldiers in this war can never truly rest.

Day of Blood

"Violence is the last word of the illiterate. Also the first."

—SOLOMON SHORT

I strode up the street. Some of the kids were playing a game, the object of which seemed to be to see how much noise you could make while moving a soccer ball up and down the road. I crossed to the park to get out of their way. I could smell honeysuckle and pine and roses.

Maybe I should trust B-Jay—I didn't want to leave here. I liked it here.

But it was a trap. There was no place to run to. If someone was determined enough to come over the hiking ridge, they could surprise the whole village. A pride of Chtorrans could sweep the length of the peninsula in minutes.

What would it take to make this place safe?

We could mine the hiking ridge, we could bury booby-traps the whole length of it. But that still wouldn't be sufficient. Nothing short of blowing up the isthmus would work. And we couldn't do that, because all of the service cables for phones ran through the isthmus—as well as the power cables that fed electricity to Santa Cruz. Somewhere out there were five great turbines, churning silently in the ocean current.

What else could we do?

We could evacuate?

Betty-John wouldn't even consider it.

And she was right. Where else in the world could she find facilities like this?

No, the only alternative was to move everyone to the south end of the island and establish very tight security, constant patrols and hold regular classes and drills for every person on the island. We should start teaching the teenagers how to use grenade launchers and torches.

But B-Jay didn't want the kids growing up in a police state. "That kind of stuff creates an atmosphere of fear and paranoia."

Behind me, I could still hear the children screaming and hollering. They sounded happy. B-Jay was right—they didn't need fear and paranoia.

But was I wrong? They did need to be *safe!* That was where the argument had started. Dammit. I couldn't get it out of my head. The sentences replayed themselves in endless loops.

And all I wanted was for us to be safe!

I knew what was happening inside my head.

It was that survival mind. The mind is a computer. It wants to survive. It will do whatever it perceives as necessary to survive. There are no limits to what it will ask for. The more you think you have to protect, the more vigorously you will try to defend it.

It's neither good nor bad, it's just the way the mind works.

And I wanted to protect my kids.

I realized I was walking down to the hiking ridge again. I wanted to see if any more of the worm lines had been disturbed. I wanted to see what else I could do. Every problem has a solution. There had to be one here.

Behind me, the screaming grew louder. And suddenly took on a shrill sound. I whirled around to look.

The children were shrieking and scattering in all directions.

I heard it before I saw it. *"Chtorrrr! Chtorrrrr!"*

Three Chtorrans broke out of the park, a squad of men and women running with them!

Huh—?

And even before I asked, I knew what had happened.

They'd come over the ridge and gone straight into the park. Not down the street—they'd have been seen immediately. They used the park as cover.

The Chtorrans plowed into the children like bulldozers. I yelled. I started running toward them—

—then zigged into the park and started heading for home. And the jeep.

The alarm went off as I was running. It was a flat double-note wail, quick-rising and falling. I hurtled down a grassy slope, over the little Japanese bridge that crossed the brook, and up the opposite side. There were children standing confused, trying to figure out what the siren meant.

I pointed ahead. "Run for home! Get out of the park! Get out of the streets! Do it as fast as you can!" Where were my kids?!!

As I came charging out of the park, I saw Holly standing in front of the house staring down the street. There were sounds of rifle fire coming from the village. Dammit.

I scooped her up in my arms and went charging through the front door.

"You have to hide, sweetheart. This isn't a game anymore!"

"No, Daddy! No!"

I went down on one knee and grabbed her by the shoulders. "Listen to me, I love you! And you have to hide!" God forgive me. I shoved her into the closet and locked the door. I grabbed my torch and ran.

The Jeep whirred to life and leapt forward. I swung it around in a tight turn, going up over the curb and ripping out a bush as I headed south. I would meet the Chtorrans at the plaza. The rifle fire had stopped now. But I could still hear that dreadful purple screaming.

As I headed toward the south curve, one of the Chtorrans came flowing around to meet me. It stopped in amazement. It hadn't expected to see a Jeep coming barrelling down toward it. I stood on the brakes and came screeching to a halt a hundred meters away from it.

"Come on, you big red slug! Come to Poppa!" I was standing on the seat now, just pulling the torch tanks onto one shoulder. I unlocked the safeties and double-checked the charge.

The worm cocked its eyes at me, one high, one low. It chirruped a question. It hesitated. It probably wanted to back up, but it didn't dare. It had been sent this way as a scout.

Its behavior was atypical. This was no ordinary worm. The wild worms would have screamed and charged. This one could recognize the threat I represented to it. This one wanted to survive. The question came up in the back of my head—did Chtorrans have minds, too? Or was it only the tame ones?

"Come on!" I challenged it again. It was still out of range. I couldn't drive and fire the torch at the same time. The worm couldn't attack. It was a standoff.

It couldn't last. Sooner or later, the others would come around that curve. I didn't think I could burn three worms at once.

I heard footsteps behind me. Before I could turn and look, Little Ivy was sliding into the driver's seat of the Jeep. "Move over," she said.

I grabbed hold of the top of the windshield and braced myself. "Go slow," I said.

She eased the Jeep forward. The Chtorran began backing up. She increased our speed. I steadied myself and braced the torch. I would only get one shot here.

The worm reared up abruptly, issuing its challenge. *"Chtorrrrr! Chtorrr!"* Then, it came down flowing—

I burned it before it hit the ground. The jet licked out and touched the purple and red horror. The flames exploded around its body. The creature raised up again, whirled in the air and came down writhing and twisting across the road. Its screams were horrible. I'd never seen a worm die like that before! It was like watching a man die!

And then it wasn't alive any more—just a burning thing, greasy and rubbery and sending huge clouds of black smoke into the air.

"All right—let's go!" I pointed to the road beyond the worm. Little Ivy backed up so she could go around it—and saved our lives. The grenade carved a hole in the street where the Jeep had been. I saw the flash—was slammed down in my seat by the concussion—felt the Jeep lift off the ground, then drop back—felt the gravel and pieces of road spatter us from the sky.

Four men and three women were just running around the curve. Two Chtorrans were moving with them. They were a perfect skirmish line. For a moment I could only admire the military beauty of the operation. Humans and Chtorrans together—the effect was devastating.

Then—moving automatically, I was standing again with the torch—I was still too dazed from the grenade to be conscious. They saw me and scattered sideways.

Another Chtorran came around the curve then, and four more humans I recognized the Chtorran. I don't know how I knew—whether it was his shape or his coloring or the way he moved—but it was Orrie. And the humans. I recognized Marcie. And Delandro.

Marcie was carrying a bazooka. She went down on one knee—

Little Ivy was already backing the Jeep. She swerved and the burning Chtorran was between us. Our view was obscured by the cloud of greasy smoke.

Ivy put the Jeep into forward and pointed it into the park. She stood on the pedal and we leapt over the curb and down the slope. Something exploded behind us. I had a glimpse of trees splintering and flying through the air. I hung on for my life. We bounced and skidded across the grass and into the stream, then up the opposite side. I looked back—I couldn't see them any more.

I pointed ahead. "Head for the road. We'll come around behind them—" I scrambled around to try to reach the grenade launcher in the back of the Jeep.

We bounced up onto the pavement again. There were bodies lying in the street. There was red blood flowing in the gutters, pooling into dark puddles. There were children standing, dazed or crying. There were people running—we skidded around them and kept going—

—around the south loop, around the curve, past the burning Chtorran again—

They were heading northward—up toward my house—where Holly was locked in a closet. I fired the first grenade at the fat Chtorran in the rear. The explosion sent it flying, tumbling, rolling across the lawns. The explosion scattered the humans. Two went down. The others broke for the trees and the park.

They were met by a hail of gunfire. I saw Jack and Dove step from the trees, each carrying an AM-280. The laser beams stabbed and pointed. The guns burped molten fire and carved holes in the men and Chtorrans they touched. Two more renegades fell.

And then Orrie was upon them. He fell across Jack and leapt for Dove. I didn't see what happened next. The renegades charged into the trees after Orrie.

The last huge Chtorran was just whirling around to charge toward me. He raised up for a challenge. I fired the second grenade—but the shot was low, the explosion went off in the street. The concussion hurled the Chtorran backwards, slamming it into a house. My house. Windows shattered.

The first Chtorran was getting up now. Black blood was flowing from its wounds. It was limping across the street toward the safety of the park. I fired the third grenade—it imbedded itself into the Chtorran flesh and there was a muffled thump. For just a second, the Chtorran seemed to puff out—then it disappeared in a ball of flame.

There was one more grenade. I sighted on the last Chtorran again. It was peeling itself off the wall—the Jeep hit a blast hole in the road and the grenade went wild, exploding the roof off the rear of the house. The Chtorran charged for the trees and was gone.

"Go after them!" I pointed. Little Ivy said something I didn't catch. I looked at her. Blood was dripping down her face and shirt. When had that happened? "Go on!" I screamed at her.

She gulped and drove. We bounced up and over the curb and down into the park again. We slid and skidded down the slope, carving up the grass and trees. Two robot gardeners were trying to mow across a path of chewed up ground— where an injured Chtorran had dragged part of itself. We careened into one of the robots and sent it spinning across the grass and into the stream.

We slid to a halt—

"Which way?"

I pointed ahead—

The Jeep lurched and slid. I saw something purple. I fired

a grenade—the explosion was a ball of orange that toppled trees and left a smoking crater that we had to swerve around—I'd missed the worm.

They plunged down the slope ahead of us—Oh, God—there were children still at the swimming hole. They were clustered together, naked, by the big rock—all huddled and scared-looking.

Orrie hit them like a torpedo. The bodies went under him like kindling wood. Their screams were horrible. I held my fire. The humans went charging after Orrie, leaping over small bloody bodies. Little Ivy was swearing next to me, a stream of invective that would shatter glass. Still I held my fire. The second Chtorran disappeared over the rocks after its companion—

Little Ivy let the Jeep slide to a halt above the carnage. She leapt out and ran to the children. Shit. Just when we had them. I slid over into the driver's seat and stood on the pedal. The Jeep skidded out and I went around the big rocks. Something exploded behind me. I came around the rock to see Marcie just standing up, the smoking bazooka in her hands.

I aimed the Jeep directly at her. She leapt sideways—the bazooka went spinning. The Jeep plunged into the water. I put it into reverse and tried to back up. A spume of water sprayed out from the wheels. I had to ease it out. I started swearing. Marcie was getting away. "Come on, Jeep!" I banged the dashboard. It leapt backward. "Thank you!"

But the renegades were gone. The Chtorrans were gone. They'd disappeared into the thickest part of the park, where the Jeep couldn't follow.

No problem. There was only one way out. And I was going to be waiting for them. I backed up, turned the Jeep around and headed for the street. I wasn't through. Not yet.

The Jeep banged out of the park and skidded and swerved across the road. I pointed it north. There were people running toward me and pointing behind them. I couldn't hear what they were saying. I must have been deafened in one of the explosions. I recognized Birdie. There was blood streaming down her face. I waved her out of the way. I moved the Jeep ahead.

There were more bodies here. My God—what had they done? This was the worst thing I'd ever seen.

North—to the north end of the loop. They had to come out of the park there. And I'd be waiting for them. I couldn't hear the siren any more. Was it still going?

I switched on the Jeep siren. There were more people heading south toward me on the road. I didn't want to slow down—I swerved to the right and headed past them on the sidewalk! Then back down on the street and around the curve.

—and there they were just disappearing over the crest of the hiking ridge! I hadn't been fast enough.

I fired the grenades anyway. I blew the top of that hill away. I didn't know if I hit anything.

And then there was silence.

It was over.

The War Against the Chtorr *chronicles humanity's last great struggle for survival on a near-future Earth ravaged by plagues and invaded by man-eating aliens. At last, the saga begun in* A Matter for Men *and* A Day for Damnation *continues in* A Rage for Revenge. *Here is the gripping story of Jim McCarthy's capture by Renegades—who cooperate with the Chtorr and brainwash their "guests"—and his solitary battle to beat them at their own game.*

Read A Rage for Revenge, *Book 3 in* **The War Against the Chtorr**, *on sale April 1989 wherever Bantam Spectra Books are sold.*